Cathy Williams can rememb[er] books as a teenager, and now she remains an avid fan. For her, there is nothing like creating romantic stories and engaging plots, and each and every book is a new adventure. Cathy lives in London. Her three daughters—Charlotte, Olivia and Emma—have always been, and continue to be, the greatest inspirations in her life.

USA TODAY bestselling author **Trish Morey** just loves happy endings. Now that her four heroines-in-training have grown up and flown the nest, Trish is enjoying her own happy ending—the one where you downsize, end up living in an idyllic coastal region with the guy you married and, better still, realise you still love each other. There's a happy-ever-after right there. Or a happy new beginning! Trish loves to hear from her readers—you can email her at trish@trishmorey.com.

TRAPPED
WITH TEMPTATION

CATHY WILLIAMS

TRISH MOREY

MILLS & BOON

First published in Great Britain 2026
by Mills & Boon, an imprint of HarperCollins*Publishers* Ltd,
1 London Bridge Street, London, SE1 9GF

www.harpercollins.co.uk

HarperCollins*Publishers*, Macken House, 39/40 Mayor Street Upper, Dublin 1, D01 C9W8, Ireland

Trapped with Temptation © 2026 Harlequin Enterprises ULC

Maid for the Italian © 2026 Cathy Williams

Greek's Royal Runaway © 2026 Trish Morey

ISBN: 978-0-263-41766-1

01/26

This book contains FSC™ certified paper and other controlled sources to ensure responsible forest management.

For more information visit www.harpercollins.co.uk/green.

Printed and Bound in the UK using 100% Renewable Electricity at CPI Group (UK) Ltd, Croydon, CR0 4YY

MAID FOR
THE ITALIAN

CATHY WILLIAMS

MILLS & BOON

CHAPTER ONE

THIS WAS SHEER, unadulterated luxury.

Of course, Georgie *knew* that the chalet, nestled in the mountainside of Whistler, was sheer, unadulterated luxury. She should do. She cleaned it on a weekly basis, banishing non-existent dust from the pristine surfaces, checking to make sure no errant spiders had found any cosy corners to have a nap, turning taps on and off just in case, on the off chance, the plumbing had decided to go on strike.

Her duties were confined to her weekly cleaning routine when the place was unoccupied. She had an elaborate schedule, which the agency updated on a fortnightly basis so that she knew exactly when guests were arriving. She would be advised of numbers and dietary requirements and would then have to make sure that suitable basics were in before the professionals stepped in and took over. This was a rare occurrence.

The staff of five, which included a personal chef, a sous chef and various other people, were there to make sure everything ran smoothly as and when the place was occupied. They were, as she liked to think, *front of house* whereas she was definitely *strictly background, to be neither seen nor heard.*

As soon as the last guest left, back in she came to clear up behind them and her weekly duties were resumed. Who owned the place? She had no idea but had long assumed it to be some arrogant businessman with more money than sense and a wife who thought diamonds were trinkets. Georgie didn't care. She did her weekly job and for this she was paid a small fortune.

What was there to complain about?

And now, especially, there was absolutely nothing whatsoever to complain about because the next lot of guests weren't due for another seven weeks, which was plenty enough time for her to spend a week *at most* in the chalet while Alison one of the two girls she shared a house with in the bustling ski resort a mile away, got on with the business of dealing with her chickenpox.

Georgie had never had chickenpox in her life before. Her mother had confirmed that when Georgie had asked her a few days ago and her sisters had both issued stark warnings about avoiding it at all costs as an adult because if she caught it, she would end up disfigured for life.

So while the third housemate had been fine to stay put with Alison, immune from lifelong disfigurement because she'd already had it, she, Georgie, had tactfully and handily removed herself to this…she closed her eyes and sank a little lower into the bathwater…this *haven of sheer, unadulterated luxury*.

She practically purred with contentment when she eventually stepped out of the bath, pausing to appreciate, yet again, through the sprawling floor-to-ceiling panes of glass, the unstoppable panorama of white outside, which was cleverly brought into sharp focus by outdoor lighting designed to beam towards the snow-capped slopes. The things a clever designer didn't think of when money was no object!

It was a little after six in the evening, a bitingly cold February evening. It was a Monday, her day off, and she had done nothing but bask in the glory of being a sneaky lodger in the chalet she cleaned for her princely sum.

Was it actually *a crime*? Georgie didn't think so. How could she be breaking and entering when she actually had a key to the place? Besides, it was just for a handful of days and she would leave the place looking even more immaculate than when she'd arrived. Linen would be laundered and every surface would be cleaned. There would be absolutely no trace of her left behind when she returned to her shared house.

She hummed to herself and cast an appreciative last glance over her shoulder to the wondrous bathroom.

Heated floors? Tick! Oversized, freestanding tub? Tick! Rainfall shower with lots of glass and stone? Tick! Not to mention the fabulous dressing area with all sorts of backlit mirrors and custom-built cabinetry.

Not a stitch of clothing to be seen in any of the guest bedrooms, but why would there be any when it was used so rarely? The main suite was kept locked so whoever owned the place probably had valuables stashed there. Diamonds and pearls for the lady and whatever expensive toys her rich husband might be interested in. Watches, probably. She'd wondered over the past few months, when she'd come to clean, whether the *front of house* staff were responsible for making sure everything was in order behind that locked door.

Who cared?

Georgie looked at her reflection in the full-length mirror in the dressing room with a critical eye.

Five four, long, curly blonde hair that was in need of a cut, brown eyes and a slim figure. She had no illusions about her looks. She was, as her sisters were fond of telling her, *cute as a button*.

They were both older than her, taller than her, and far more striking than her in the looks department, with stunning, curvy figures, long, long legs and breasts that had no idea what a padded bra was all about.

Sometimes, Georgie wondered whether being called cute from an early age had somehow directed her towards choices that were cute, as if she'd been somehow set on a path fashioned from her family's opinions of her and then fulfilled her expected destiny by following it.

She had favoured football over violin, climbing trees over putting on nail polish and hanging with the boys instead of flirting with them.

She was the tomboy. Where she had watched her sisters weave their magic with the opposite sex, she had enjoyed being *one of the lads*. Until, of course, being one of the lads had left her with the broken heart that had mended only when she'd come here, to Whistler, so far away from everything she'd known.

Her sisters had gone on to respectively become professionals in the fields of medicine and law. She, on the other hand, was, at the age of twenty-six, only now working out what she wanted to do with her life. Better late than never was how she chose to look at it.

She'd left school at eighteen, had half-heartedly done a foundation year in graphic art and then promptly absconded for a year and a half to France, where she'd turned one of her favourite sports into a paying proposition by becoming a ski instructor. She'd loved every second of it.

After vaguely wondering where her passion was hiding, she had finally discovered what she really loved. Teaching kids. She loved the outdoors, was great at everything to do with sport and she loved kids.

Academia had been out of the question anyway because of her dyslexia, diagnosed later than it should have been when she'd been struggling so badly in secondary school.

She had returned to Surrey, where she still lived with her parents, and for a year and a half she'd diligently worked to achieve her certification in sports education.

And as soon as she'd finished…she'd gone back to Val d'Isère, back to Hans and the gang.

But no, she wasn't going to let her mind go there. She was here, and she couldn't be happier.

She coached kids on the slopes in winter and in summer, when the resort was put to different use, she taught tennis and football to the under tens and even a little art, calling on her foundation-year skills in graphic art.

She hummed to herself as she got dressed.

Jogging bottoms and a warm, baggy grey jumper and bedroom slippers because, although it was toasty warm inside the chalet it was freezing outside. In the world of the mega rich, she had discovered, heating costs never registered because it was imperative everything was in tip-top, ready-for-anyone-to-descend condition all year round. Both pools, indoor and outdoor, were meticulously maintained for the same reason.

The sprawling chalet was contained on three floors and every single room on all three floors afforded a view of the spectacular scenery outside.

Downstairs, huge double doors opened into a massive foyer with heated stone flooring. What else? There was just enough wood panelling on the walls to look elegant instead of tacky and an enormous mudroom was custom-built for skis and gear.

There was a fully equipped bar and a games room and then all the usual suspects…dining area, gourmet kitchen, living room with soaring vaulted ceilings and exposed timber beams and two huge stone fireplaces. There was even an outdoor fireplace for anyone hardy enough to want to sit outside in winter and absorb the magnificent scenery. And, of course, the pools.

One floor up was the main suite, hidden behind three doors, which said a lot about just how big it was, along with another informal sitting area, a fantastic snooker room with a bar and three further bedrooms, all en suite.

And then the top floor, where she had taken up residence…equally luxurious and definitely with the best views as far as she was concerned. Gazing out at the infinite stretches of white was something she could have just sat and done for hours, without moving a muscle.

Right now, though…dinner beckoned.

Conscious of her status at the chalet, which was *shouldn't really be there at all*, Georgie was careful to leave no sign of her presence behind her, *just in case*. No mess anywhere and the few bits and pieces in the fridge were neatly on one shelf and there wasn't an errant dish to be seen anywhere.

She knew with her head that there would be no *just-in-case* scenario, but she was very much aware that this job and the pay cheque that went with it were invaluable.

For the first time, she was actually managing to put money aside for when she returned to England.

She was twenty-six and the thought of living with her parents with no end in sight didn't bear thinking about and a teacher's salary would never have stretched to a flat in London, which was where she wanted to live.

She grimaced and switched off annoying thoughts about living arrangements because what was the point of planning how to cross bridges that weren't even on the horizon yet? She commanded Alexa to play her favourite rock tracks instead, then she turned up the volume and began tidying away the tiny amount of mess she had made in the bedroom.

Just in case…

* * *

'What is that noise? I'm hearing something. What am I hearing, Alessandro? Miguel? Henry? All of you! *Can you hear something?*'

'I don't hear anything, Sophia.'

Alessandro suppressed a sigh of utter impatience. They'd been in the villa for five minutes, barely time to remove the coats, scarves and gloves, and already he knew that this was not going to be smooth sailing.

But then had he expected anything less from his ex-wife? If she could make life as difficult as possible for him, then it was an opportunity she would never bypass.

This time though?

No more playing Mr Nice Guy. He'd been playing Mr Nice Guy for the past two and a half years and if the only way to end it was this way, then so be it.

He looked around his chalet. He hadn't actually been here for over eight months. Various of his employees had used it as reward for certain special projects that had required extra hours or effort beyond the call of duty. Occasionally, his mother and a couple of her friends might venture here during the summer months but never in winter because she'd never skied.

But for him? Yes, downtime when he took to the slopes for a few snatched days of pitting himself against the most challenging runs, but his life rarely allowed for that indulgence.

He'd thought about selling it, but then why bother? He could easily afford to keep it just for those occasional times when he chose to make use of it. It was cleaned, aired, kept heated with geothermal energy-efficient heating that cost a fortune but was environmentally kind, and generally maintained to a pristine standard for those times when it was put to use.

Right now, Alessandro was extremely grateful to have it at his disposal because there was nowhere else on earth where they could have been assured of the privacy he needed for this meeting with his ex and their respective lawyers.

Some subterfuge had been required but all was fair in love and war.

They were here and he wasn't about to let his plans for this agenda be derailed by his ex-wife trying to go off-piste with lame diversionary tactics.

'Sophia,' he said coldly, 'I've asked you to come here, with lawyers in tow, so that we can put differences behind us and regulate the situation that's been getting out of hand and we both know what I'm talking about.'

'There was no need to come out here, in the middle of nowhere, Alessandro! We could have discussed this like two civilised adults. Have you chosen to forget that we were once married?'

'Call me cynical but I've given up on the civilised adult route. You have a nasty habit of briefing paparazzi whenever there's any hint of a showdown between us. You enjoy playing the victim and you like having the back-up of an audience.' He looked at his ex-wife with cool indifference.

She was a stunningly beautiful woman with curves in all the right places and the sort of dramatic dark looks that made men walk into lamp posts. Those looks had stopped working for him a long time ago.

'You're here because signatures are going to be put on documents that will be binding, Sophia. No more trusting you to play by the rules out of respect for a past relationship. No more playing fast and loose with our informal custody arrangements. What happens now isn't going to be about you and the fragile mental state you keep telling me about. It's going to be about me and my right to see Flora on a regular basis without having to endure insufferable last-minute cancellations for spurious reasons.'

'I have been in and out of therapy for four years! Did I ask for a divorce? No! That was *your* decision! You have left me suffering and it is *not my fault* that I am now battling with my mental health!'

Alessandro suppressed yet another sigh of impatience because this was well-trodden ground and he was sick of it.

Their window of marital bliss had been lamentably short. They had met seven years ago and what, he later thought, should have come to a natural end had, instead, been propelled into a walk down the aisle because Sophia had fallen pregnant.

In fairness, he hadn't been dismayed. True, it hadn't been in his timeline of what the road ahead looked like, but Sophia, as a girlfriend, had been all smiles and eager to please, if a little on the unchallenging side. Yes, she could be vain and demanding, but who was he to point fingers when he had such impossibly high standards himself? There was no such thing as perfection. Having a baby and getting married wasn't going to be the end of the world and, in fact, he had found himself growing more and more excited as the pregnancy progressed.

But then… Flora had come along and how things had changed. Still working his way up the ladder, determined as he had been from the age of ten to shed the chains of his working-class background and grasp the only things that could ever buy him freedom, which were money, status and power, Alessandro had found leisure time in short supply.

He'd done his best. However, having completed his MBA at Harvard on a fiercely fought-for scholarship, he had been working long hours at a top investment bank with little time to spare.

What time he did have, he'd wanted to spend with Flora and gradually Sophia had succumbed to a mixture of boredom and resentment.

Her affair had been predictable but had still come as a nasty shock to Alessandro.

Divorce had been inevitable. It had not been in his nature to forgive infidelity, especially when he'd found out that the last had not been her first. The very fact that he'd been relieved to have found a reason to walk away from a marriage that had been a terrible idea had shown him just how little he had ever loved the woman he had married.

His lips thinned as he looked at her now, playing yet again to an audience of two lawyers, hoping to sway things in her favour.

'You're going to sign formal joint custody papers, Sophia, and you're going to do that right now, witnessed by both our lawyers. In addition, you will sign an NDA. Leak anything to the press and I won't hesitate to take you to court and wash whatever dirty linen is out there in public. I don't want to fight you for fair access to my daughter, but fight you I will if you decide to stand in my way. I've reached the end of the line.'

'I haven't had time to consider any of this, Alessandro. I need your trust, not warfare!' She cast a pitiful eye at the two lawyers, who were sitting in silence to the side, ready to spring into action but, in the meantime, diplomatic enough to know not to intrude. Or, worse, take sides.

'Trust will be resumed when papers are signed.'

'You do not make a good role model for our daughter,' Sophia said bluntly, tossing her head, expression going from pleading to crafty. 'Women on your arm all the time…the press taking pictures of you *cavorting* with a different glamour model every week! You think I rest easy in bed knowing that that is the example our beloved Flora will be exposed to?'

Alessandro stiffened because this was the crux of the matter. Affair or not and whatever men his ex-wife chose to entertain couldn't stem her bitterness at having to accept that he was now indifferent to her.

Alessandro knew the vital importance of a mother in his child's life, but time was slowly altering that opinion. He had forced himself to empathise with the body blow of her realising that she meant nothing to him. She was a vain woman and that would have stung.

But now her games had gone too far. It had been four months since he had seen his daughter and his patience had come to an end.

He opened his mouth to pursue the conversation to its inexorable end when, this time, he heard it.

Not just a sound but *music*.

Coming from...*somewhere in the house* and yet how was that possible? Had one of the staff who looked after the place left some sort of alarm on, which had now activated into life?

He looked towards the direction of the music. They all did, not that they could really see anything at all. They had come straight in and headed to the sitting room towards the side of the house. Sophia had thought that they would be meeting for a mediation opportunity and certainly not for an ultimatum and he had allowed the misconception. They had converged at a five-star hotel in Whistler, had a bite at the bistro there and then onwards to his chalet, with food out of the way and ultimatums waiting to be delivered.

He had been charming, attentive and conciliatory towards his ex but as soon as they'd reached the chalet, he had led them through to where they all were now, hearing *music*.

'What is going on here, Alessandro? I want to go. Right now. I thought we would be talking about perhaps getting back together! You said that we would be meeting to find new, mutually caring ways forward! I was under the impression that we would have mediation specialists here, not two men with pens and papers to sign! Now I am here and you want to upset me and, on top of everything else, someone is in the house and I have no intention of staying here to find out who. One of your women, I expect!'

She moved to reach for her thick fur coat on the chair behind her, with both lawyers following suit in alarm along with Alessandro, who distractedly took a step towards the open door.

They all spotted her at the same time. A slight figure with tumbling blonde hair who was lustily singing as she made her way past the door, a fleeting figure not glancing in their direction because the room was slightly set to the side. She was clearly expecting no one to be there and so no one was there.

Alessandro felt the taste of pure, electric shock and complete bewilderment.

But he was the first to break the stunned silence and before his brain could totally engage, it could already smell the danger.

He exited the sitting room at lightning speed, catching up with the mystery singing woman as she headed off in the direction of the kitchen.

He could see the little buds in her ears. She was in a world of her own. Music blaring from upstairs while she sang along to whatever she was listening to on her headphones. Had his house suddenly turned into a club? Would he head upstairs to find a rave going on while whoever this was strolled around, doing her own thing, for all the world as though his house belonged to her?

She was about to be brutally wrenched from whatever world she was in, Alessandro thought grimly.

He had no idea who the woman was, but he was very keenly aware of the trio of onlookers now poised by the door with avid interest and he had lots of ideas on how a random woman making herself at home in his chalet was going to go down. Leading the pack on the accusation front would be his ex-wife, but the lawyers, always so impassive as they were paid to be, were there as well, drawing conclusions they couldn't afford to draw. Could things be worse?

Alessandro reached out.

She was wearing loose clothes that looked enormous on her slender frame. A soft jumper that stopped at the waist and some very baggy jogging bottoms with the elasticated waistband rolled so that a slither of skin was visible.

He could feel the slimness of her body as he tugged her towards him. He made sure to provide a barrier between himself and his audience of three and he was glad he had because the look of utter astonishment on her face as she took him in was priceless.

Her eyes opened wide, her mouth parted and she inhaled sharply while fumbling to yank the little buds out of her ears.

'Don't say anything,' Alessandro said in a low, commanding voice. 'Tell me your name.'

Up close and personal, there was something about her that made him feel a little unbalanced and he put that down to the shock of finding her in his house in the first place. Her hair was very fair, vanilla blonde, and very long and very unruly. Her eyes were huge, almond-shaped and brown, the same chocolate brown as her eyebrows and her long, curling eyelashes, and her mouth was soft and perfectly defined.

She smelled of something clean and floral and, with absolutely not a scrap of make-up, her skin was satin smooth.

He scowled at an unwanted physical reaction, which was so out of character for him.

'You tell me yours first,' she hissed right back at him, trying her best to peer round his shoulders.

He was having none of that and fortunately he was broad enough to block her from the inquisitive eyes behind them, but time wasn't on his side.

'All you need to know is that I own the villa in which you're trespassing.'

'You do?'

'Name. Now. What is it?'

In return the fiery blonde shot him a simmering, hostile look under her lashes but there was enough sudden wariness there to alert him to the fact that he had the upper hand and thank God for that. He shuddered to think what a field day his ex was going to have with this situation. She would grasp whatever ammunition she could and wield it against him like a claw hammer and Flora would be caught in the middle.

He was going to have to wing it.

Trespassing.

Georgie quailed inside. Of course, she couldn't possibly know for sure whether this *complete stranger* was telling the truth or not, but she was getting the distinct impression that this was a guy who didn't do a lot of larking around.

His deep, dark eyes were coldly intent as they roved over her face. Her heart was slamming against her ribcage, a combination of intense apprehension, nerves and...

An awareness that was darkly, shockingly sexual.

He was the most beautiful man she had ever seen in her entire life. Tall, dark and handsome *on steroids* didn't begin to sum it up.

His features were perfectly chiselled, his raven-black hair was cropped short and he had a mouth that could drive any woman to distraction.

She had to peel her eyes away from that way too sexy mouth, away from *him*, as she frantically tried to gather herself and rescue some semblance of self-control. As much as a trespasser could have, was what she thought faintly.

But his hand was burning with the force of a branding iron through her jumper and she was finding it hard to get any words out as their eyes continued to tangle in electrifying silence.

Eventually, she managed to croak her name.

'Listen to me carefully,' he said, leaning towards her so that she could feel his breath against her face. 'You're going to follow my lead. Understood?'

'Or else what?' Georgie did her best to maintain a robust veneer, very much aware that she was half this guy's size, although what could he do to her? There were other people around. She'd just about managed to glimpse them although he was so broad that there was no chance of her seeing who those people actually were.

'Or else you'll discover that trespassing on a billionaire's property carries some hefty penalties. Let's talk jail.'

'Are you trying to scare me?' Georgie gasped.

'I already admire the way you can read a situation. Are you going to do as I say? No questions asked?'

'Do I have a choice?'

But instead of feeling intimidated or scared, she was curious and breathless.

Something about this guy was crazily thrilling even though in a situation like this, with anyone else, she would have been livid, whether she was trespassing or not.

She very much had never been in favour of the macho types and this guy was Mr Macho personified.

'Wait. What's *your* name?'

'Alessandro. Alessandro Barbieri.'

Before she could pepper him with any more questions, he was turning around although, instead of letting her go, his hand loosened on her arm and drifted to her waist.

A light, semi-possessive hold that made her blood fizz in her veins.

And now she could see exactly who was there with him. Three people, although her eyes were immediately drawn to the striking woman poised in the hall, hand on hip, beautiful face puckered in a mixture of rage and confusion.

She was dressed for winter on the slopes in just the sort of outfit Georgie recommended her pupils never, ever wear.

Soft cream cashmere rollneck, skintight leggings and leather boots. Her dark hair was tailored into a sharp, shoulder-length bob and her sultry sexiness was emphasised by a liberal dose of make-up. From ruby-red lipstick to grey eye shadow and the most perfectly manicured nails imaginable, she was the essence of physical perfection.

Perfection or not, if this was a skiing holiday, then Georgie hoped she'd brought some more sensible kit with her.

The two guys hovering slightly behind couldn't have been more ordinary compared to the man with his hand on her waist and the woman who was presumably his other half.

In which case, *why was his hand still on her waist*?

Suddenly mortified, Georgie shifted a little, which resulted in his hand tightening.

'This is Georgie…'

Georgie smiled stiffly, bewildered.

'Georgie, this is Sophia, my ex-wife.'

The pressure on her waist tightened. Georgie had no idea what was happening but, alert to her status of *trespasser who could get in a whole heap of trouble*, she kept smiling politely and hoping that things would get clearer than mud.

'What is a woman doing here?'

'She's surprised me with a visit.'

He looked down at her and Georgie, in turn, looked up and up and up at him.

His dark eyes were pseudo tender, not fooling her for a second that his thoughts were anything like tender because the tacit warning in their dark depths was unmissable. At least to her.

'Haven't you, my darling? Surprised me with a visit and what a glorious surprise.'

Georgie could have got lost in the sexy, husky timbre of his voice.

'She has a key to the chalet? Since when do you give women keys to your houses?'

We're supposed to be an item... For whatever mysterious reason, Georgie knew that she had been suddenly thrust into some kind of role that she was expected to play. She also knew that the deck wasn't stacked in her favour when it came to having a choice in the matter.

He'd mentioned *jail*.

She watched the way he half turned towards the shrill voice before resting his eyes on her and, in that instant, Georgie read something, *felt* something. Resignation...was that it? Or maybe the patience of a long-suffering man who had reached a point of desperate measures.

She couldn't put her finger on any of the feelings that raced through her, but she did know, with some weird but very definite sixth sense, that he was a fair guy even though he'd had no trouble in blackmailing her into doing what he wanted.

She wondered how that made sense.

'Since when does he give a woman keys to his chalet? Since now!' Georgie trilled, sidestepping Alessandro as she reached into her pocket to dangle the house keys in front of her.

The expression on the other woman's face was priceless. A combination of utter astonishment and utter rage.

If they were no longer involved with one another, then why was she livid at the thought of another woman having the keys to a chalet?

Her busy speculation had managed to banish every shred of nerves or anxious foreboding of where, exactly, she would be left after this little charade. She wasn't expecting what came next.

She should have been.

She should have felt the slide of his hand on her waist, been aware of the way he lowered himself towards her and then the low whisper when he thanked her.

Maybe deep down she knew that he was going to kiss her but there was no way that she had prepared herself for the shock of it.

His cool lips touching hers, a kiss that was feathery light and yet felt impossibly intimate. Caught up in the moment, she felt every rational thought leave her head in a whoosh and she leaned into him, reaching up on tiptoe to curve into his body and feeling the hard muscularity of it with devastating sensual awareness.

She could have stayed there for ever, oblivious to an audience of three, but common sense and a gut realisation that she needed to protect herself from this sort of crazy, visceral reaction to a complete stranger made her tug back, horrified at herself and her weakness.

How could she? Hadn't she learned anything at all? Didn't she know how important it was to protect herself and her vulnerable heart? How vital to actually count to ten before you flung yourself into situations that weren't based on reality? Had she completely lost her senses?

He released her just like that.

'We can continue this conversation in a while, Sophia,' he threw over his shoulder as he began guiding her away from his ex-wife, hand still on her, making sure, she thought, that she didn't bolt. 'I hadn't expected Georgie to have come here to surprise me. For the first time and hopefully not the last.' He turned to Georgie with a sexy, wolfish smile. 'Don't think this surprise visit hasn't made my day. It has.'

Georgie thought that lying had never sounded so seductive.

'So,' he continued to his ex and her companions, 'you'll understand if I excuse myself for an hour or so just to play catch-up? It's been the better part of a very long fortnight without one another. Henry… Miguel…can I trust you to get through some of the preliminaries before I head back down? Ensure that Sophia fully understands everything that will be signed and the ramifications if they aren't.' He looked once again at Georgie. 'Can I leave you for a short while this evening, my darling? To wrap up a few thorny and much overdue issues? Trust me, I'll be sure to make it up to you later.'

'Er…'

The smile he flashed her was wicked, sexy, devastating and left no room for debate because he began urging her up the very staircase she had earlier descended without a care in the world.

The further up the stairs they climbed, the more his hand on her waist lost that loving touch and by the time they hit the top of the impressive staircase and were out of earshot, it had dropped abruptly to his side.

'Right,' he grated, stepping back and looking at her with forbidding cool, 'what the hell are you doing in my house?'

CHAPTER TWO

GEORGIE SPRANG BACK on wobbly legs.

'I wasn't expecting anyone to be here!'

'That doesn't answer my question. Follow me. I'm not having this conversation here. Walls have ears.'

He spun round on his heels and began striding down the wooden-floored corridor towards the sprawling, seldom-used office at the end of the landing. Georgie knew precisely where he was going because she wafted a feather duster through the room on a weekly basis.

Massive space…the same floor-to-ceiling windows that characterised the rest of the chalet…polished hardwood flooring and a custom-built desk made of reclaimed, burnished timber that was as big as a single bed. There were chairs, a sofa and bookshelves with books left behind by guests and heavy, dense financial tomes.

He shut the door behind her just as soon as they had entered, at which point the nervous fluttering in her stomach ratcheted up several notches.

'Sit!'

Georgie sat, rigid as a plank of wood as he circled her like a predator trying to make sense of some unusual prey.

'You're making me nervous.'

'Good. You should be.'

'If you give me five minutes, I can explain why I'm here. I suppose I should ask you for some sort of identification…?'

'You really shouldn't. You can trust me when I tell you that I own this chalet and identification isn't something I'm obliged to provide.'

He eventually pulled up a chair and sat facing her, which didn't do a thing to calm her racing nerves.

Even sitting, he still managed to radiate a mesmerising combination of power, threat and sinful sexiness.

'So…' Georgie cleared her throat. 'As you may have noticed, I happen to have keys to…er…your chalet…'

He tilted his head to one side and didn't say a thing.

'I clean here once a week.'

'You're a cleaner.'

'Amongst other things.'

'Why is the cleaner roaming through my chalet in my absence? Wearing casual clothing and singing songs, for all the world as though she lives here?'

'I don't make a habit of *roaming through your chalet in your absence*. As it happens, I temporarily found myself… er…with nowhere to live for a few days so…'

'I have an hour to spend here with you before I need to go and take care of important business downstairs. You have fifteen minutes to tell me exactly what's going on here, after which I will present you with a number of options, all of which I intend to suggest you grab with both hands. What I'm saying is I don't have limitless time to listen while you stammer through whatever garbled, fantastical story you're now trying to think up.'

'I don't make things up, Mr Barbieri!'

'Get to the point and explain yourself.'

'I live in the ski resort.' Georgie tried not to bristle at his imperiousness. 'I share a tiny house with two friends, Claire and Alison. You might be wondering at my English accent and what I'm doing in this part of the world.'

'I'm not. I have zero interest in where you come from.'

Georgie gritted her teeth and balled her hands into fists. Naturally she could storm out in protest at the man's high-handed behaviour. That said, she would be walking away from, basically, the nest egg she was steadily collecting from her cleaning duties, vital money to go towards a deposit on a flat when she returned to the UK. More worryingly, how far was his reach? An angry billionaire could end her time here and she would be heartbroken.

She wasn't ready to return to the Home Counties with her tail between her legs and her independence compromised. Her parents were perfect until you happened to be living under their roof, at which point they reverted to treating her like the kid she no longer was.

She *needed* to be here, needed this time out to fully recover from the shambles at Val d'Isère. Her heart was so nearly patched up. Would it start unravelling if she had to deal with the stress of going back to Surrey? Back to the claustrophobia of living with her parents, which would give her too much time to start rehashing everything that had happened between her and Hans? Start thinking how Hans had ended up being just the icing on the cake of guys who had never taken her seriously? Never seen the hesitant, hopeful, longing girl wanting to be desired instead of the tomboy, affectionately expected to be one of the lads? No way. She didn't need to go down that painful road.

And then, of course, there was the jail remark.

'One of my housemates has chickenpox.' Georgie cut to the chase and pushed uncomfortable thoughts away. 'She caught it on holiday and told us that she was going to return to the house to recuperate because her parents have house guests so there's no room for her to stay with them. Anyway, they live in Hawaii and I'm not sure she was keen on incurring the added expense of travelling there. So it was okay for Claire, my other housemate, to stay put because she's immune, but I couldn't afford to catch it. So…'

'Are you telling me the truth?'

'I never lie.'

'You realise I could check this story with a single phone call and if I discover that you're lying, you'll not only be out of a job with me but the authorities would have to get involved.'

Georgie paled. 'I'm telling the truth! You can make whatever phone call you want to make to the agency you use to service the chalet about my job here! And I'm happy to give you the name of the instructor I work for! He can confirm that Alison's bedridden for the next few days.'

'So let me get this straight. You decided to make yourself at home in my chalet, without my permission, because…'

'Because I needed a few days somewhere till the worst was over with Alison's chickenpox. I mean, this place is empty most of the time and I honestly had no idea you would be returning because the agency always gives advance notice as to when it's going to be occupied. I didn't think that you were going to show up out of the blue or else I would never have come here.' Georgie hesitated, then looked at him from under her lashes. 'I don't get what's going on. Why were you pretending that you knew me?'

Alessandro paused.

He hadn't banked on any of this but now that the situation had presented itself, he recognised that he was in a bind.

The slip of a thing perched with barely concealed defiance opposite him was sharp, despite the tangle of long blonde hair and the big brown eyes and the heart-shaped face that emanated an air of sexy, foxy innocence.

Much as he was loath to admit it, he found himself, for the first time, on the back foot.

Unwittingly, she had become a participant in a charade and now what was he going to do about that?

How much was he willing to tell her? He was a billionaire. One phone call would confirm whether the woman genuinely cleaned for him, but, presuming that she did, then how fast was she going to recognise the weakness of his position and demand money in exchange for her complicity?

It was an unforeseen messy situation but, for the life of him, he could think of no way round it with Sophia there, ready to do her worst.

Of course, he could go downstairs and launch into the perfectly truthful explanation of why the woman was where she was, but he knew his ex-wife and knew that there was not a single thing she would believe about the story and, even if she believed all of it, there was no way she wouldn't wilfully misinterpret the situation to her advantage.

There was nothing worse than a woman scorned and he'd been paying for that ever since their divorce.

'I ask the questions here.' He paused. 'Your unauthorised presence here has complicated things.'

'I'm really sorry.'

'I involved you in a situation on the spur of the moment and believe me when I tell you that I am not a man who does anything on the spur of the moment.'

'What's the situation? The one that you involved me in? I mean, why didn't you just say that you had no idea who I was?'

'Like I said, it's complicated and any information I choose to tell you will be strictly on a need-to-know basis. Right now, you have no need to know.'

'You can't involve me in whatever you have going on

with your ex-wife and expect me to go along with it without question.'

'You're a trespasser on private property. Right now, your right to ask questions is limited.'

'Technically I'm not *a trespasser*.'

'Technically, if you want to push that point, we can leave it up to a judge to decide. If I were you, I wouldn't start putting bets on you winning the case.'

He was staring at her with a thoughtful frown, leaving Georgie ample time to consider her lack of options.

'Okay,' he eventually said with unconcealed reluctance. 'I suppose you might deserve some sort of explanation, which isn't an invitation to ask questions. My ex-wife is a suspicious woman and it would have…complicated my life had she thought that you were…' He shook his head and raked his fingers through his hair.

'Some floozy you happened to have staying in your chalet?'

'That's a crude way of putting it, but yes.'

'Why would she care, if you're divorced? Unless she wants to get back together with you?'

'That question comes under the category of ones there's no point asking because you won't be getting an answer. First things first though—however foolhardy it may have been on my part to drag you into a temporary charade, I want to make it perfectly clear that this does not give you…'

He allowed the silence to thicken between them and, in that silence, Georgie could read the direction of his thoughts as clearly as if they had been written on his forehead in neon lettering.

He was rich, he was powerful and he was, at this precise moment, vulnerable because he had been forced into putting on a show in front of his ex-wife for reasons she couldn't fathom and knew didn't concern her.

He was a man who never acted on impulse but he had been forced into doing so. Did he think that she would now somehow use the situation to blackmail him? All the cards were in his favour because if he decided to launch some sort of lawsuit against her, then he'd win, hands down. It wouldn't just be a case of her getting the sack and losing her cleaning job.

Her lips thinned as she fought to contain her temper.

'Give me what? The right to try and get money out of you? Even though you already made sure to tell me that I'd be in trouble if I didn't go along with your make-believe scenario that we knew one another? That you would be willing to involve the authorities? Honestly? I don't think trying to get money out of you would be worth a stint in prison.'

'Why *are* you here?'

'I *told* you. My housemate has chickenpox and I had nowhere else to go. Well, I suppose I could have shelled out for a room in one of the hotels but I haven't got money to burn. That's why...'

'That's why what?'

'That's why this cleaning job means a lot to me. You don't have to worry about me blabbing. I won't breathe a word to my housemates or to *anyone*. I would just be grateful to hang onto this job. I'm good at it and I enjoy it. It's peaceful cleaning this house and the pay is amazing. I know I should have asked the agency whether I could make use of the house while Alison got over the chickenpox but...'

'Naturally they would have said no. I meant, why are you here? In Whistler? When you're English.'

'I thought you weren't interested.'

'If my ex-wife asks one or two obvious questions, then

it would be convenient if I had the truth to hand. I doubt that will happen but preparation is the master of success.'

'So you're not *actually* interested...'

'No.'

'It's personal.'

'It wasn't personal five minutes ago when you began volunteering the information. Talk fast, Georgie. Time's moving along. I need to get things sorted.'

'Well... I was working in Val d'Isère and...' Suddenly it did feel very personal, if she were really to tell him what had happened. Suddenly it felt like *yesterday*. Hans...the hurt... her wounded pride...the humiliation she'd done well to hide.

'And I fancied a change,' she said, lowering her eyes. 'It gets claustrophobic after a while, hanging out with the same people. It's a tiny crowd. I wanted a change and Alison, who'd worked the slopes with me there for a year, had returned here to Whistler to pick up where she left off. She knew I needed a...*wanted* a change and she pulled some strings and here I am now.'

Her voice petered off into silence and, for a few seconds, it felt as though his dark eyes could get to the very depths of her and pull out truths she hadn't told.

'So,' she said lamely.

'It was quick thinking to pull those keys out.' He changed the conversation with a slow, amused smile that made her go a little weak at the knees.

Why was she having this reaction to him? She hated it. She had sworn off men. One day she would find herself walking back to them, looking for a partner, but right now? Right now, she couldn't be less interested.

She ignored the smile and the warm, fuzzy feeling his half-baked compliment had given her.

'I don't have any intention of asking you for anything, Mr Barbieri.'

'You can call me Alessandro.'

'I wouldn't feel comfortable doing that. I don't like being on a first-name basis with someone who's just threatened to set the police on me.'

'I didn't think I'd progressed to threats and I'm afraid you'll have to try because my ex-wife will be here this evening and will be spending the night before leaving first thing tomorrow. Between now and then I expect you'll meet her again, if only briefly, and, considering she thinks we're an item, calling me *Mr Barbieri* might not be appropriate and, yes, if you don't go along with that then there might very well be consequences.'

'Why is it so important? That I… I…' Her voice trailed off.

'I get your curiosity, Georgie, but the *why* doesn't matter here. I appreciate you're confused but that doesn't negate the fact that you're in my chalet without my permission and what's at stake here is important enough for me to tell you that your best option is to fall in line with what I say. No further explanations will be forthcoming. Tomorrow I'll be leaving and your life can carry on as though this interlude had never happened.' He paused. 'In fact, I'll make sure you get a generous pay rise.'

'No need,' Georgie said quickly. 'I'm already paid more than enough.'

'I doubt you mean that.'

'Of course I do! I don't suppose,' she said slowly, 'that you know how much you actually pay me, do you? Because it's all through an agency, but trust me when I tell you that it's a huge amount for cleaning an empty house once a week.'

Alessandro stared at her, head tilted to the side, allowing

the silence to build, then he stood up and continued looking down at her.

'I will tell you how things are going to move forward at this point,' he said slowly. 'I'm going to go downstairs and finalise what requires finalising. You are going to remain right here, safely tucked away under my watchful eye. You're going to go and fetch your possessions, whatever you've brought. here, and transfer them to my bedroom, which we will be sharing tonight. It's the one with the locked doors. You'll find the key...' he nodded in the direction of a cupboard to the right of him '...in the safe there. Combination 1884.'

'I'm not sharing a bedroom with you!'

'I'm afraid you don't have a choice in the matter.'

'I do!'

'Tell me what your choice is. I'm curious.'

Georgie looked at him with a downturned mouth. Did she have a choice? No. Not really. Of course, she could lose her job and that would be unfortunate but bearable. She could, however, lose everything here and, worse than that, he could summon in the police and rightfully accuse her of breaking and entering, key or no key.

She paled at the vision of herself malingering in a cell somewhere, with only a handful of rats for company. Hadn't there been a film about that?

'Good. We're in agreement. Normally, as you might have guessed,' he mused, 'I would be concerned that you might be tempted to trade a juicy story for money, whatever you have to say about being as quiet as the grave, but you're smart enough to realise that to do so would bring the full force of my displeasure down on you.'

Alessandro allowed that to sink in. Should he consider getting her to sign an NDA? It would mean involving a lawyer and he didn't want that. Besides, gut feeling told him that any threat of getting the police involved was enough to guarantee her co-operation.

'This evening, you can stay put.' He frowned. 'Have you eaten anything?'

'I was on my way to get myself some dinner when I was hijacked.'

'Hijacked. Provocative word. I can't remember any woman accusing me of hijack before. In fact, I'd say that there were quite a few times when it felt enjoyably the other way around. Okay. I can bring something up for you. I'm assuming that, as you've set up camp here, the fridge is nicely stocked?'

Georgie was torn between thinking about him being hijacked by a woman, *'enjoyably hijacked', whatever that meant*, and the food she had bought and nonchalantly left in the fridge when she'd been busy treating the mansion like her own private playground.

'I only planned on staying a few days, like I told you,' she mumbled, 'so, no, there isn't heaps of food and there's no need to bring me anything. I find that I've completely lost my appetite.'

Alessandro shrugged and stood up.

'Suit yourself. I'm going to head downstairs now and I'll see you later, nicely settled in my bedroom where I can keep an eye on you. And don't worry, there won't be any bed sharing. You can make yourself at home on the sofa in the sitting room in my suite.'

'The sofa?'

'That's right. You don't think that I'm about to give up my bed for someone who shouldn't be in my house in the first place, do you?' He looked at her incredulously. 'At any rate, you will probably cross paths with Sophia tomorrow morning for five minutes and, once she's gone, you'll be free to return to the slopes and carry on doing whatever you've been doing there. I'm assuming you do do something for the remainder of the week when you're not cleaning my house?'

'Is this another question you're asking even though you're not that interested in the answer?'

'Correct. I was ending things on a polite note.' He glanced at his watch then stared at her for a couple of seconds. 'I'm not sure what time I'll be back in the room. No need to wait up.'

With that he was gone and Georgie sprang into action.

She raced upstairs and gathered the scant belongings she had brought with her, making sure to leave the bedroom as neatly tidied as if no one had stepped foot inside.

Her head was all over the place. What was going on? In a weird way, she was lucky that whatever was going on between him and his ex-wife had meant that he had had to involve her in a conspiracy. If he'd just rocked up to find her in his house, she had no idea how he would have reacted. She would probably have been promptly marched down to the nearest police station and tossed into a cell.

She thought about all the valuable artifacts dotted around the chalet and shuddered at the thought of him jumping to conclusions that she might have been after them.

As soon as she was in the master bedroom, she did a quick check on her computer and confirmed that he was, indeed, who he said he was.

Already panicked and in a rush, *just in case another just-in-case moment happened and he came in just as she was reading all about him, not that anyone could blame her,* Georgie merely glanced at the highlights, which seemed to be scores of pictures of him with a varying line-up of sexy women clinging to him like limpets.

Then she slammed shut her laptop and took a few moments to look around her.

The space eclipsed everything she had seen in the chalet. Same floor-to-ceiling windows but with a massive ubermodern fireplace that anchored the room. The bed was enormous, with a plush headboard and linen that was, as she swept her hand over it, soft and silky. Definitely eight-million thread count. There was a dressing room and then the bathroom, which she ignored because she wasn't going to be using it. She'd already spotted separate facilities off the sitting area in which she would be sleeping. The sitting area itself was large enough for a huge cream sectional sofa and oversized armchairs, which framed yet another fireplace with a flat-screen TV to the side.

There was even an outside terrace with private access to a hot tub. Very swish, considering it would be used only once in a blue moon.

Georgie knew where everything was in the chalet. She fetched bed linen and made up the sectional sofa quickly and efficiently, but could she relax and actually get to sleep? No.

She wondered what he would have told his ex about her absence from the scene. In his high-octane world, women were probably there to be seen and not heard. As an ex-wife, she was probably used to that, poor woman. Maybe she had once been fiery and independent but had ended up squashed and subdued. Maybe that was why she remained so bitter and angry.

From the little she had seen, Alessandro Barbieri was forceful, arrogant and commanding. She thought that he was probably very good at making women angry.

He was also stupendously good-looking, a little voice reminded her. She killed that thought by fetching her book and reading, but her head refused to allow her to concentrate and even after she'd slipped into her pyjamas, she still couldn't find sleep.

It was after eleven by the time her eyes began to feel heavy. She had long ago switched off the little light on the table by the sofa. On the verge of finally nodding off, she heard the door open and there he was, a tall, dark, muscular silhouette with the light from the corridor behind him.

Georgie's breath hitched. She kept as still as possible, huddled under the duvet she had fetched, and watched as he strolled through the door, spun round to lock it behind him and then absently began unbuttoning his shirt.

He'd cast a quick glance at her and hadn't turned on any lights, but every room in the chalet was designed to let the outside in and, right now, outside, a full moon was lovingly outlining a fabulous body.

He didn't take the shirt off once all the buttons were undone and she could see the movement of his muscled body where the shirt no longer covered his torso. He strolled towards the small space where a coffee machine was housed, along with a cream retro-styled fridge and a bar area with glasses.

When he stopped to drink from the bottled water he had removed from the fridge, Georgie forgot how to breathe.

She resented that.

Why weren't her memories protecting her from staring at Alessandro Barbieri? How could she have sidestepped the lessons she had learnt after Hans?

The slopes of Val d'Isère and the camaraderie of all the ski instructors out here felt like a dream now. All of them, the instructors and the girls who worked in the chalets and the young people working through gap years at the hotels and resorts...they'd all come from different parts of the world, but they'd bonded through their shared love of skiing. Georgie had loved it. Boys and girls and having fun when they weren't working. And Hans had been part of that group, tall, blond, beautiful Hans. They'd started going out in a loose kind of way, sometimes on their own, often part of the group and then more seriously. Very quickly, Georgie had fallen hook, line and sinker for his ready smile and his charm and the way his blue eyes crinkled when he laughed.

For the first time in her life, she'd actually felt as though she was no longer *one of the lads*. She'd felt special and sexy and feminine and in love. She'd forgotten the adolescent heartache of fancying a boy, really wanting him to notice her, catching his smiles and passing affectionate-slap-on-the-shoulder compliments like precious gems and hugging them to herself only to realise that, to him, she was just a good mate.

Hans had felt different, had made *her* feel different.

So much in love that her thoughts had turned to a future together. He planned on becoming a lawyer. He hadn't scoffed when she'd teased him about moving to London instead of remaining in Holland. She'd pictured him fitting right in with her family. She'd been overwhelmed by the urge to follow in her sisters' footsteps and settle down.

Georgie remembered what it had felt like at that big Christmas party, everyone dancing and drinking and laughing. She'd gone to get them a drink and then she'd spotted him, dangling a stupid bit of mistletoe over his head and kissing a cute redhead who'd joined the team a couple of weeks back.

She'd frozen on the spot, then their eyes had met and, in that instant, she had seen just how wrong she'd been about them as a couple. He'd pulled back and winked at her and she'd *known* that he had never thought of them as an exclusive couple.

That had been the worst bit. She'd been nothing to him but a bit of fun and if he could have fun with her, he could have fun with other girls.

She'd laughed and pretended that it was all just fine because she was as much of a free spirit as he was, but she'd been breaking inside.

She'd told only Alison. Only Alison had known how hurt she'd been and how fragile everything had become after that. Hans had still been the same old Hans and nothing had been said, but they'd mutually drifted away from one another and then Alison had left, back to Whistler, and, just when Georgie had been on the verge of packing it all in and heading back to England, that call from her had come. A job where she worked in Whistler. Would she take it? Georgie hadn't thought twice.

And everything had been fine until now, until this man had appeared and thrown everything into tumultuous confusion by making her think about herself, once again, as a young girl with needs and urges and not the ice maiden she'd tried to become.

She hated how a stranger, an arrogant, *blackmailing* stranger, could make her feel against all her better judgement, how he could make her forget that she had to be careful with her emotions. She wasn't going to let him see that he affected her. She would be herself. She would say exactly what she thought. She wasn't going to be awed by him. Treat him just like anyone else and he wasn't going to be a threat to her peace of mind.

Right now, he was walking towards her, checking to see whether she was asleep, and she duly shut her eyes, forced herself to breathe in a convincingly steady rhythm and then released one long breath when she heard his bedroom door shut behind him.

* * *

'What are you doing?'

Standing by the sectional sofa and scanning her phone for emails or messages, Georgie started at the sound of Alessandro's voice behind her.

She spun round to find him lounging against the doorframe in a pair of black trousers and a long-sleeved black tee shirt that defined his lean, muscled torso in a way that sent her imagination off on a crazy, magical mystery tour.

'What do you mean?' She dragged her eyes away from him and glanced around her. 'I've made sure to tidy everything and I've stashed the linen in the cupboard.'

'What are you wearing?'

'I'm wearing...' Georgie frowned, confused '...clothes?'

'You're wearing ski gear.'

'I'm back to work today. You asked last night what else I did apart from cleaning your chalet once a week, just before you told me that you weren't interested anyway, but now that you ask? Answer... I coach kids on the slopes.'

Georgie reached for her backpack and began checking through it and when she looked up it was to find Alessandro towering over her.

'How does your *going into work* begin to make sense? Sophia thinks we're a loving couple. Oddly she doesn't think that you're a ski instructor at a resort a mile away. You won't be going into work until she disappears, which won't be for another couple of hours.'

'But it's nearly eight and I have to head over to get things going—'

'Remember what I said about playing along with this because, honestly, it's by far the better option?'

Georgie gritted her teeth. 'How could I forget?' she muttered in a driven undertone and when she slid her eyes to his face it was to see him smiling coolly at her. 'Are you going to remind me again that I'm an intruder and you'll have me sent to prison if I don't comply with what you want?'

'No, we can move past that. What else do you have to wear in your bag of tricks? If you let me have your phone, I'll call your boss and inform him or her that you won't be in until later.'

'I can do that myself,' Georgie said, mentally resigned. He'd folded his arms and she caught herself staring at the bulge of rippling muscle, taut under the tight long-sleeved tee shirt. She tore her eyes away. 'I'll put my joggers back on.'

'No, no, no,' Alessandro tut-tutted. 'The joggers were a little teasing welcome outfit. This morning...something else will have to make an appearance.'

Georgie stared at him. 'Something else *like what*?'

'Hmmm...now let me have a think.' Alessandro lowered his eyes. He realised that he was enjoying their sparky conversation. Actually, he was enjoying looking at her as well. She was in a maroon thermal bodysuit with a half-zip up the front and the thermal leggings showed off legs that hadn't been on show earlier when she'd swept past the sitting room in a world of her own.

Shapely legs. Slender. Slender legs, slender waist, all that long, tangly blonde hair and those big brown eyes.

His eyes dipped to her breasts and he flushed, surprised at his lapse in self-control.

'I guess you're looking for the sort of sexy outfit a woman might wear to impress you?'

'Not necessarily...'

'I googled images of you. I saw the sort of women you go out with. I'm afraid I don't have any skimpy clothes to hand. Miniskirts and skintight Lycra dresses are impractical for coaching kids on the ski slopes.'

Alessandro grinned, suddenly amused despite the stress of the situation.

'Okay. I'll leave it up to you. Sophia will be on her way out, not that that will stop her noting every inch of your appearance.'

'Did you…manage to sort out whatever it was that needed sorting out?'

For a second, Georgie thought that he wasn't going to answer and who could blame him, considering it was none of her business, but eventually his eyes cooled and he shot her a thin, humourless smile.

'I expect to get what I'm after.'

'Oh, good.' That smile said it all about a man who always got what he wanted. She wished she'd read a bit more about him, although, from the little she'd glimpsed and aside from the images, the information seemed to be largely a boring chronological, detailed account of business deals and company takeovers.

'I'll leave you and your imagination to come up with an outfit that's a little less casual than jogging bottoms, shall I?'

He moved towards the door and threw over his shoulder, in a dry postscript, 'We'll be in the kitchen and I'm guessing there's no need for me to tell you where that is.'

Georgie flushed. 'I'll head down as soon as I've changed into suitable clothing from the little supply I brought with me.'

'Fifteen minutes. And as before, Georgie? Leave the talking to me.'

CHAPTER THREE

GEORGIE KNEW EXACTLY what Alessandro had meant when he'd told her that trackpants and an oversized jumper weren't going to do as a counterpoint to ski gear.

He was probably the sort who liked assets to be on display or else what was the point of them? Perhaps he hadn't noticed that her assets weren't exactly noteworthy.

How on earth he expected his sultry, sexy ex-wife to believe that they were actually a couple was a mystery.

But she didn't have much time to dwell on that.

She left on the tight thermal leggings because they were a nuisance to pull on and off but she replaced the utilitarian ski top with a black cropped vest and a black cropped cashmere cardigan with little pearl buttons down the front. The cardigan was a present from one of her sisters, who had decided three years ago that she needed *feminising*. Georgie had laughed out loud at the time but in actual fact had ended up wearing it non-stop. She swept her hair up in a ponytail.

The only shoes she had brought with her were trainers, ski boots and bedroom slippers, so trainers it had to be, and she was sprinting down the stairs to the kitchen in under fifteen minutes.

Voices reached her before she hit the kitchen door. Stilted conversation between the men. No breathless girlish laughter. No woman's voice at all, so either Sophia wasn't there or else whatever had been sorted between her and Alessandro had left her literally speechless.

The door was ajar and Georgie automatically raised her hand to knock before remembering that she was supposed to be having some sort of relationship with Alessandro and so would hardly be announcing her arrival with a polite knock on the door.

She quickly took in the scene. A matter of seconds to get the picture. What was the opposite of light-hearted? *Borderline murderous maybe?* Coffee had been made and poured and although there was, actually and thanks to her, food available for a breakfast, there was nothing on the table. Alessandro was standing, perched against the granite kitchen counter, sipping coffee. The other three were at the table and while the men were doing their best with some conversation, hence the voices she had heard before entering, Alessandro's ex-wife was most definitely not participating.

Georgie glanced at her. She'd changed overnight into a pair of skintight leopard-skin-patterned jeggings and a long sleeved very tight tee shirt that emphasised her abundant breasts and cleavage. She was wearing high-heeled, knee-high leather boots and her make-up was immaculate. Their eyes met and the brunette looked at her with loathing.

If looks could kill, Georgie thought, walking towards Alessandro while wondering what was going to happen next in this scenario.

From his vantage point, leaning against the counter by the window, Alessandro watched her approach.

Her bag of tricks had not yielded anything along the lines of designer or fancy, yet he was finding it hard to peel his eyes away from her slight frame as she strolled towards him with the sort of insouciant smile that barely concealed her nerves.

He'd been tough on her but needs must. The stakes were high and there had been no question that he'd done exactly what he'd needed to do. Still. She'd been unwittingly caught in the crossfire so it was no surprise that she looked nervous.

But sexy.

In the same thermal leggings but a restrained little cardigan and a small matching vest underneath it, and trainers. Grey and pink trainers.

His dark eyes flashed to Sophia, who was glowering at the kitchen table.

She'd brought an outfit she'd hoped would send his pulses racing. Instead, the leopard-skin print and the high heels and the long red nails looked tacky and distasteful.

'Georgie…'

He reached towards her and lovingly tugged her to him and then dropped a light kiss on top of her head. No overt display of anything but enough to make him a little giddy, genuinely giddy, and when his eyes met Sophia's he could see that his ex-wife had registered that tiny, involuntary response.

Time to hustle this along, was what he thought, and so for the next ten minutes, he did the talking. He talked a little business, talked a little weather, kept it light, glanced pointedly at his watch a couple of times.

He kept Georgie right there by him, offered her coffee and couldn't have wished for a more credible display of their relationship when she accepted a cup and then asked whether anyone wanted anything to eat.

'There are croissants! I just have to bake them! Honestly as good as fresh!' She broke free of him and moved towards the fridge. 'Also eggs…some bacon and lots of cheese…'

'How long have you been in my ex-husband's chalet?' Sophia queried icily.

'Oh, a few days.'

Georgie pulled out croissants from the fridge and made a deal of reading the baking instructions on the packaging before reluctantly returning her gaze to the other woman.

'And how long have you two been seeing one another?'

'Not your business, Sophia,' Alessandro interrupted.

'It is,' the other woman said acidly, 'when your latest conquest is going to be—'

'Drop it.'

Going to be what? Georgie wondered. She realised that her presence had been temporarily forgotten in the war of words.

'You may have got me to sign your papers, Alessandro, but we both know that you are not a man who holds down relationships. Where do you think this is going… Miss… whatever your name is? Do you think that you are the first to become besotted with my husband, only to find yourself discarded on the usual heap by the side of the road? You will soon be joining a queue, my dear. I speak from experience.'

'And on that note, I think transport awaits you, Sophia. Miguel… Henry…is there anything else we need to do or has everything been completed to your satisfaction?'

'I can have everything sent to you by email no later than tomorrow evening, Signor Barbieri.'

Georgie took a back seat as the dregs of coffee were drunk and the two older men stood up, getting ready to go.

Outside, there was no falling snow but the winter wonderland of white seemed to announce too beautiful a day for the unpleasant atmosphere inside the chalet.

Bags were already by the door. She expected that Alessandro would have had a driver at the ready to come and fetch the party of three. She had no idea how they had arrived at the chalet but she didn't notice any cars outside.

She was startled when she heard the whirring of something overhead and she followed in awed silence as they all turned in the direction of the sound, with Alessandro being the first to lead the way out of the kitchen, grabbing a jacket from the console by the front door while the others slipped on coats.

He pulled open the door to the sight of a helicopter hovering in the clear, cold turquoise sky over a cleared patch, a helipad, which Georgie had never really noticed because, even in summer, her duties did not involve her doing anything outside the chalet.

As it came closer, the noise of the blades became louder and louder until, at last, when they whirred to a stop, the sound of silence was almost as deafening.

Georgie had never seen anything like it. Surely she would have heard if they'd arrived in a helicopter? Perhaps they had been driven to the chalet and now this was just the most expedient way of dispatching them.

She watched, her mouth agape, as someone hopped out and then there was a flurry of activity as Sophia's Louis Vuitton holdall was gathered up, along with the two duffel bags belonging to the guys.

'So, Alessandro…'

'Please, Sophia. Not now. Everything is settled and I will be in touch with you tomorrow about a schedule of ongoing arrangements. I hope I've made it perfectly clear that change of plans at the last minute will carry consequences?'

Georgie began sidling into the background. Soon, she too would be dispatched in the most expedient way possible. Not a helicopter…more a few curt words, a warning or two and then a door slammed in her face once she'd called a taxi to collect her.

'Wait here for me.' Alessandro briefly looked at Georgie.

'Should I do anything?'

'Anything like what?'

'Say a few goodbyes,' Georgie suggested vaguely. 'I don't want to appear rude.'

'Why not? You won't be seeing any of them again, least of all my ex, and the less interaction from you, the better. Sophia will look for any excuse to cause trouble so the less ammunition she has, the better off we'll all be.'

'Okay. I'll head inside and start cleaning up.'

'There's no need.'

'Who else is going to do it?' she asked wryly. 'It's what I'm paid to do, after all.'

He looked as though he was about to say something but then, instead, spun round on his heels, headed out towards the helicopter where the men were already climbing up the stunted steps. He had his hand on the small of Sophia's back, urging her along to follow suit. She was having none of it. She was glaring at Alessandro and engaging him in urgent conversation about who knew what.

Now what? Georgie thought.

For a start, she was back to having nowhere to stay for the next few days, which was something she hadn't even thought about earlier when she'd dressed for work.

She'd still been too caught up in whatever drama she'd found herself in.

But now...?

She saw Sophia look daggers in her direction, smile and then she disappeared into the helicopter, but not before slapping away Alessandro's offer to help her up.

At that point, Georgie turned back into the chalet and

headed to the kitchen. She swept up the coffee cups and was busily washing them when the kitchen door was pushed open and there he was, face like thunder.

'Okay…' She smiled what she hoped was a soothing smile as he strode in her direction to help himself to some more coffee, only to growl under his breath when he realised that it had gone cold. 'Why don't you sit at the table and I'll bring you another cup of coffee? There are also the croissants still waiting to be baked.' She looked at him warily. 'Not to mention those eggs. I could rustle something up. I guess it's been a stressful…er…time…'

'We need to talk.'

Georgie took a deep breath and went for it. Now that the act had dropped, she could see just how angry he was that she was under his roof. 'I know you want me out of your house as soon as possible but I can't return to my place yet because Alison's still contagious.' Deep breath. 'Would it be okay if I…have a couple of hours to find some alternative accommodation at the resort? It's very busy at the moment but I know lots of people who work at some of the hotels and lodges and I might just be able to—'

'I thought you couldn't afford that option?'

'I'll have to dive into my savings.' Georgie licked her lips and mentally braced herself for imminent sacking. 'It would be a shame,' she pleaded to a better nature, 'because I've been doing my *utmost* to save for a deposit for somewhere small when I return to England but… Look, please. If you're going to fire me, then could you get it over and done with quickly? At least then I can start thinking about my future.'

'I'm not sacking you.'

'You're not?' She beamed. 'That's *such a relief.* I can't tell you how much this cleaning job means to me and I absolutely *swear* that you won't regret that decision.' She made a zipping gesture across her mouth. 'Also, I *won't breathe a word* about what happened here.' She sucked in a deep breath. 'So shall I head up and start clearing my stuff out? I don't mind forking out for somewhere cheap to stay for a few days now that I know I'll still have my job here.'

'No need.'

'Really? No need? Are you sure?' She handed him some fresh coffee without realising that she'd actually made some.

'Sit.'

She didn't. 'If you're sure I can stay for a couple more days, then I should really be heading off to work now. Pierre was a little put out when I told him that I might not make it in. He's already having to deal with Alison out of action.'

'You seem to think that I care about Pierre and his work schedules. I don't.'

'Well, actually, *I* do, considering it's my pay cheque at the end of the month and, like I said, I really need the money so that I can carry on saving… Signor Barbieri. Sir.'

'We've gone past the *sir* stage. Whatever you're being paid there, I'll triple it because you're going to be taking a little more time off than you probably expect.'

'I'm not following you.'

'Maybe those croissants might be a good idea. And more coffee. Whisky would definitely work better than both but is probably not wise at this hour in the day.'

'I want to know what's going on, Signor Barbieri.'

'Not *sir* and not *Signor Barbieri* either. Alessandro.'

'We don't have to be pally now that we're no longer pretending to be some kind of item.'

'Sit down and listen to me without interrupting. When I'm finished talking, you can ask questions.'

Georgie opened her mouth to tell him that he couldn't order her around but then stopped because, right at this very moment, he actually could. She was in his house and, whether she liked it or not, she was indebted to him for not chucking her out when she had nowhere to go while Alison was still contagious. Also, for allowing her to hang onto her cleaning job.

'Shall I get the croissants first? Or does the sitting still and listening come first?'

'I need to make a call. I'll be back in twenty minutes and I'll…do my best to explain what's going on when I get back. You can do whatever you need to do to the croissants in my absence.'

Georgie didn't have time to answer because he stood up without glancing in her direction and stalked out of the kitchen, leaving her more confused than she had been before.

She chucked the croissants into the oven, grabbed crockery and cutlery, and retrieved some jam from the fridge.

Why had he said that some whisky would work better than coffee?

How could she possibly be involved in whatever was going on with Alessandro and his ex-wife when she'd never met either of them in her life before?

Pondering this conundrum, she only snapped out of her thoughts when the door was pushed open and she looked up to see him standing in the doorway, a vision of crazy sexiness in his black, long-sleeved tee shirt and black jeans. Her heart picked up speed.

The fact that they were now alone in his splendid chalet suddenly made her redden with a rush of illicit thoughts.

'Is everything okay? Hang on, I'll get the croissants from the oven. They'll be ready.'

'I'll get the croissants. You may clean my house but you don't have to serve me.'

'Are you sure? I do realise that I'm probably not your favourite person at the moment and I want to thank you again for—'

'Remember what I said about keeping quiet while I do the talking? Question-and-answer session to follow? Let's say the silence begins right about now.'

Alessandro looked at her while grappling with how to expand on his explanation of why she had been roped into playing a part she hadn't anticipated playing.

He hadn't given her much of an explanation in the first place because he hadn't seen the need. But now?

He hadn't predicted this. A simple charade would be over and done with in a matter of hours and then he and Georgie would go their separate ways. *That* was what he had predicted.

Now, however, Sophia had done her worst and put him in a bind. She knew that he had never, not once, introduced any woman to Flora. On principle, he abhorred the idea of his daughter becoming fond of any woman who was not going to be on the scene for longer than five minutes. That was something he had always made clear, to allay any fears of the very thing Sophia had now decided to use against him.

His relationship with Flora was sacrosanct and that was how he liked it. No threat of any woman thinking that there was a *wife and mother substitute* vacancy in need of being filled and no potential for Flora to get too attached to anyone.

As far as Alessandro was concerned, one failed marriage was enough to put him off the institution for the rest of his life.

Sophia was well aware of that and would have known that, key to chalet or no key to chalet, he would have stuck to the playbook and not introduced Georgie to Flora.

But circumstances had conspired to rouse her jealousy and malice.

She had misjudged his intentions badly, only realising what was afoot when it was too late for her to catch a flight back to New York. She had found herself with an ex-husband who was no longer prepared to indulge her because she was the mother of his child and she hadn't liked that. Nor was he interested in rekindling anything at all with her. She hadn't liked that either. Sign the papers or stringent controls would be placed on her extravagant spending. In return, she had been forced to allow him, in writing, unfettered access to his daughter with a schedule decided in advance rather than occasional access depending on her variable moods.

And then to have met Georgie…unexpected and upsetting the apple cart when it came to all the relationships he had had since their divorce. Georgie with the keys to his chalet, Georgie who had stocked the fridge with food, Georgie who was so physically different from all those women he'd dated in the past.

Sophia had reacted accordingly and now…

Alessandro brought the croissants to the table and sat facing Georgie, who tactfully said nothing.

'You've been caught up in something,' he began, 'that has nothing to do with you. It was just a case of being in the wrong place at the wrong time.'

'I think I got that.'

'You're wondering what's going on.'

'I am, although, of course, if you don't want to say anything then that's fine. Perhaps it's a case of the less I know, the safer I am?'

'This isn't a movie about the Mafia, Georgie.' His eyebrows shot up and he shote her a sudden amused smile. 'I hadn't expected to find anyone here.' Alessandro stated the obvious and raked his fingers through his hair.

'Yes, I know.'

'Least of all a woman.'

He broke the tension with the shadow of a smile.

'My divorce hasn't been the most…agreeable. A short marriage followed by a bitter divorce. Sophia was pregnant when we married. We were both young and, if I'm honest, we would never have married if she hadn't been pregnant, but there's no point arguing with the past. Lately, things have become complicated and, essentially, I came out here with Sophia and two lawyers in tow so that certain…difficulties could be put to bed.'

'You mean the documents that needed signing?'

'I mean the documents that needed signing,' Alessandro agreed. There was no way that he could avoid a complete explanation of a very personal situation and it occurred to him that this was a place he had never visited. He had never discussed his private life with any of the women he had dated in the past and many of them had tried hard to entice him into sharing confidences.

But his past…if the bare bones were there somewhere on the Internet, then the flesh on those bones remained locked behind closed doors.

He looked at Georgie, young, fresh faced and curious, and he suddenly felt a thousand years old. He seldom delved back into the past but now he thought about the poverty in which he'd been brought up, abandoned by his father before he could walk and raised single-handedly by his mother, who had broken her back making sure that he got out of the impoverished Italian quarter near the Bronx where he had been brought up.

She'd drummed into him the importance of education because without it he would be stuck where he was for good, going down the same road as many of his friends would.

It had been a life of struggle with eyes to the bigger prize. Brains, drive and ruthless determination had given him the wings to fly and to get what he wanted, but along the way he'd lost the very thing he was looking at now. Curiosity, openness, a fundamental faith that life would be kind. He was thirty-two but every second of the hard road he had travelled was embedded inside his soul like a prong of steel.

'I have a child,' he said bluntly and watched as she stared at him with wide-eyed shock. 'You look surprised. People do. It's not that uncommon.'

'Yes… I kind of thought…from what you said just then and no, of course people have kids, I realise it's not some big surprise…but…'

'But what?'

'But you don't *look* like a dad.'

'Should I take that as a compliment?'

'Maybe not,' Georgie blurted with unflattering honesty. She thought of her own dad. Bespectacled, clever, genial. Always ready to listen to whichever of his daughters had something to moan about. He mowed the lawn, took the bins out on a Monday, allowed her mum to chivvy him into wearing clothes he didn't want to wear because they weren't comfy enough.

On no level did this sexy guy staring at her now fit into that category.

The way he was looking at her, with humour in his dark gaze, a smile tugging the corners of his mouth…

Her heart picked up speed and she found herself leaning forward, hanging onto the conversation.

'So,' she said breathlessly, 'you were telling me that you have a child. A boy? Girl? How old?'

'Six and a girl. Flora is her name.'

The harsh lines of his face softened when he said that.

'So what does this…? I mean, I'm still confused, if I'm honest. Why am I involved in this at all?' She tilted her head to one side and nodded. 'Is it to do with custody?'

'Very good. How did you guess?'

Georgie thought back to the scenario into which she had inadvertently found herself.

The awkwardness…an ex-wife who had looked at her with open hatred…the lawyers, there to do a job whatever the atmosphere. Alessandro, hard as nails and cold as ice, a man on a mission.

'She still fancies you, I guess.'

'You're jumping to all sorts of conclusions.'

Georgie noted his dark flush and shrugged. 'None of my business, I know. I'm just saying what I felt and saw when it came to body language. Maybe she still thinks she has a chance with you and using your daughter as a pawn is something she does to keep you dangling on the end of a hook. Maybe she hasn't really wanted to let go.' She paused. 'Actually, I had a friend whose mum was a bit like that. Gail. She was always caught in a tug of war. Her mother was always fighting for more money, always cancelling visits with her dad without warning. Twice, she showed up at school when she wasn't meant to be there and caused an almighty scene, saying that Gail couldn't spend the weekend with her dad because of plans her mum said she'd forgotten about. It happens.'

'Duly noted.'

'But I still don't get what the whole charade was all about when you found me here. You didn't want to make your ex jealous, so…'

'You're right. Sophia has been playing fast and loose with my visiting rights, which, until now, have been informally agreed at her request. You're also right, there have been attempts to—how shall I put it?—engineer a reconciliation of sorts. Attempts that I have ignored. With each woman I've dated, Sophia has become more and more vocal that I'm not the sort of guy who is responsible enough to see my own daughter. I work too much; I play too hard. Several times, she's contrived to inform the paparazzi of her thoughts on the matter, which, naturally, has resulted in them snapping me on a more and more consistent basis. I brought her out here, far from all reporters, so that I could pin her down into signing everything I should have made her sign years ago but didn't.'

'I see...'

'The minute she saw you, I knew what she would have been thinking. She would have jumped to the conclusion that you were yet another one of my women, that I was again proving myself to be the sort of philanderer who could never be seen as a role model for a young child. Having her lawyer there would have led to a major headache for me.'

'Yes.' Georgie winced. 'I'm sorry. Again.'

'Hence the charade. I thought it was going to be something temporary, just until she returned to New York on the helicopter, but unfortunately...'

There was a long silence during which Georgie tried and failed to work out where that enigmatic statement was going.

Judging from the angry thinning of his lips, she had a feeling that she wasn't going to like the direction of travel.

'Unfortunately?' she prompted uneasily.

'Sophia has been making noises for some time about a holiday with Flora. Various very expensive places have been suggested, most of which would have held little or no interest for a six-year-old child. The only reason she's run any of the options past me is because she wants an extraordinary injection of extra cash to cover all sorts of ridiculous costs and because she wants to rub home that she's willing to put the time in taking Flora on holiday while I either work too much or play too hard.'

'Ridiculous costs?'

'Private island, fully crewed yacht, sufficient bedrooms to accommodate at least a dozen adults and perhaps a child or two—chefs on tap. I wouldn't give a damn about any of that if I knew that it wasn't motivated by spite.'

'You don't need all of that to have a wonderful holiday. I remember my family holidays—little rentals on the coast and board games. I always lost, now I think back to it.'

'Your family holidays couldn't have been further from mine.' He frowned, impatient with himself for going off-piste.

'I guess, with money to burn, board games and rentals by the coast weren't your thing.'

'I wasn't born a billionaire, Georgie. I had to fight tooth and nail to make it to the top.'

He remembered his childhood holidays, the cheap annual one-week breaks during summer when he and his mother would visit the seaside, explore the boardwalks, enjoy the ocean—only able to afford the places that were a bus ride away. Money set aside every week for that small break.

Now he could afford to buy all the boardwalks, but the quality of the holidays hadn't improved because of it.

He couldn't remember the last time he'd had any genuine downtime.

'How did you do it? How did you make so much money?' She laughed. 'I obviously need some lessons from you and then I might not have to rely on cleaning houses and teaching kids to save for a deposit on a flat that'll be the size of a shoebox.'

Alessandro was startled to find himself laughing along with her.

For a second, he really got it why his mother told him on a loop that he worked too hard, to which he would wryly respond that he was simply obeying what she'd taught him.

Flavia Barbieri spent most of her time in Italy now and he didn't see her nearly as often as he knew he should. He brought her over twice a year so that she could see her granddaughter and, more often than not, he only occasionally participated in all the stuff they did together. Time was scarce and work commitments had no respect for leisure activities.

He felt a pile-up of guilt wash over him.

'That's beside the point,' he said flatly. 'The fact is that Sophia has thrown a curveball. She's informed me that the only place Flora is interested in going is Disney World.'

'Nice.'

'Next week. Ten days in Disney World. Staying at a dedicated hotel in the park.'

'Sounds terrific for a six-year-old.'

'She expects you to accompany me on the trip.'

'Any little girl's dream holiday.'

'Did you hear what I just said, Georgie? You're expected to come with me.'

'*What?* Why on earth would she expect something like that?'

'Believe me, I don't want this any more than you do.'

'You'll just have to tell her that it's not possible for me to take time off for any kind of holiday, anywhere!'

'Easier said than done.'

'I have work! I have commitments here. I also don't know you and I've never met your daughter!'

'Like I said, Sophia has found the best place to put the spoke in the wheel and she's grabbed the chance. She's enraged that I've finally pinned her down to a timetable of visiting rights, that she won't like the consequences if she fails to comply. She also loathes the possibility that this so-called relationship of ours might be more serious than anything I've had in the past, as evidenced by the fact that you were here, in the chalet, when we arrived, key in hand and clearly knowing the lay of the land.'

'Women you date never have keys to your house? Flat? Penthouse apartment? Wherever it is you live?'

'Never.'

'Okay…and they also don't have a clue where to locate a fridge?'

'I don't believe in encouraging any woman to get too comfortable in my territory.'

'What a catch you are,' Georgie said with thick sarcasm. 'Women so love a guy who doesn't want them to feel they can get comfortable in their territory. Do you think that if you let them through the front door and they manage to locate a bottle of water from your fridge they're going to start putting down roots?'

'I tried the permanent situation once. It didn't work. I'll never go there again. But, moving on from that, here we are and I wouldn't ask what I'm asking now but, if you don't come, it'll be a door opened to my ex snooping around my private life, pushing paparazzi in my direction. Squeezing information out of Flora, who doesn't deserve to be caught up in an ugly tug of war.'

'But it's not as though this is a relationship. I'm not going to be sticking around.'

'No, but if Florida happens, then there's a chance Sophia will accept that this relationship really might be serious and, when we break up, she'll also accept that I'm never going back to her, that I'm in the right place for serious involvement with a woman I want permanently in my life. On top of all the legal requirements that are now in place, she will finally concede defeat sooner rather than later and life will return to where it should be. If the happiness and stability of my daughter weren't an issue here, then there's no way I would ever consider asking this from you. Trust me, I don't take any of this lightly.'

'And if I refuse? Because, actually, I do have a job here and I do have commitments. For all you know, I might have a partner who would go nuts if I decided to take you up on your offer.'

'Have you?'

'Er…'

'Because I'm thinking that if you do, you might have taken refuge in his place instead of letting yourself in here and risking prosecution were you to be discovered.'

'Is that your way of reminding me that you can blackmail me into doing what you want?'

'Blackmail is a strong word and it's not in my nature to go down that road, whatever impression I chose to give you. I'll pay you.'

'You'll *pay* me? Not everyone can be bought!'

'I beg to differ. You're holding down two jobs to afford a deposit on a shoebox.' He tapped into his phone and pushed it over to her and Georgie's eyes widened as she read the sum he had typed in.

'Enough for you to visit your family whenever you choose

or else put in the piggy bank. I'll also guarantee this job and make sure your pay is doubled while you remain here. And naturally I'll clear the ten days with the resort.'

'I couldn't possibly.'

'What are your objections? You won't risk losing your job at the resort, you'll have ample time to make sure your housemate is over her illness before you return and you'll get a nice injection of cash.'

'It's not all about the money.'

'No, it's not,' he said quietly. 'My daughter comes before everything. Continuing this charade for a little bit longer would mean a lot to me. I'm asking a lot but in exchange you can view it as an all-expenses-paid holiday. I'll make sure that whatever hotel suite I get will be more than big enough for you and my daughter and, because this is just a matter of…necessity, you can spend your time as you wish. There'll be no need for you to play a part when we're over there. There'll be the occasional photo that Flora can send back to Sophia but all Sophia will need is to know that you were present, confirming all her worst suspicions.'

'I can do my own thing?'

'The less contact with my daughter, the better. Flora isn't old enough to register that you're not around very much.'

'I don't feel comfortable with this sort of deceit…'

'You felt very comfortable letting yourself into my house and squatting indefinitely, so spare me the sudden conscience.'

'That's not fair!' But ten days in Disney World… Alton Towers was the only theme park she had ever been to. Plus, she would be able to do her own thing. And most of all, she would be helping out in a situation where there was a kid at the centre and she worked with children and loved them and understood how awful it would be for his daughter to be bounced back and forth between two parents at war with one another. He'd been patient for years and now he'd been trapped and she might be the way out.

'I'm going to work for two hours and then I'll be leaving for New York so that I can get things in order for this unexpected interruption to my schedule.' He paused. 'Before I leave, I'll want your answer. Whatever you decide,' he added heavily, 'it's fair to say that you can stay here until your housemate is over the worst. Obviously no money will change hands. That, I'm afraid, will be a perk of the job.'

'I've already decided,' Georgie told him. 'I'll do it. I'll come.'

CHAPTER FOUR

TWO DAYS LATER, Georgie was at Vancouver airport where she was due to meet Alessandro before they both flew to Orlando.

Everything had gone like clockwork from the second she'd agreed to go with him. Money had been deposited into her bank account, more than she'd expected, with an accompanying text saying that she was to buy herself suitable casual wear, and she had been informed that a driver would collect her from his house in Whistler and deliver her to Vancouver airport. Just as she was leaving the house her phone had pinged with another message from him.

Meet me in the first-class lounge. I will be there with my daughter. You're a big girl. You don't need me next to you to check in.

How rude, she'd absently thought when she'd read his message.

She had done her fair share of Internet sleuthing, not that it could be called sleuthing because you didn't have to be a PI to find out about him. The man was everywhere on the World Wide Web. He was the real deal in the world of business. Mostly she'd devoured the spread of images of him with various women in tow. Most of them had been gazing at him with proprietorial adoration. He came with bags of money, killer looks and obviously oodles of charm, but none of that charm had been wasted on her in the very brief messages he had sent her.

As a byline, she had skimmed over his meteoric rise to success with a lot of attention paid to his seemingly other-worldly talent at spotting trends in developing technology and his ability to make sharp decisions about dubious companies that always ended up turning to gold at his touch.

He'd told her, in passing, that he hadn't been born rich, that he'd had to fight to get where he had, but there was very little about his background at all. Only mention of his scholarship to Yale and his sporting prowess, which was as impressive as his intellect.

No wonder he thought he could rule the world, she'd concluded. From rags to riches would do that to a person.

The driver had instructions to deliver her to the check-in desk but as he swung towards the airport, Georgie told him very firmly that he could do away with that task. Maybe Alessandro thought that she needed delivery to door in case she got cold feet at the last minute.

She was braced for what lay ahead. No cold feet and complete discretion.

Alessandro was trusting her on that front and it was very easy to remember that lazy suggestion of power he emanated, the sort of power that could grant wishes just as fast as it could punish in equal measure.

The truth was, though, that Georgie knew that discretion was something she could handle. She was talented when it came to keeping things to herself.

Underneath the perky, cheerful façade, she'd learnt to hide the hurt she'd felt, growing up, as she'd watched her older sisters and her friends get the Valentine's Day cards and the eager phone calls from boys while she got the invites to play tag rugby with them on a Sunday morning.

She'd joined in with her friends in the jumbled years of adolescence but could never get serious enough about make-up and flirting and so had awkwardly hovered in the background in her jeans and sweatshirts, content to hear their tales of boyfriends and broken hearts, having her crushes and quietly putting them away every time they came to nothing.

How she'd hidden her unhappiness when boys had confided in her, never really seeing her as a blossoming woman. If she'd been starring in a movie, she would have been the bridesmaid but never the bride.

Then that miserable Hans episode. Putting it in perspective, she knew it hadn't really been true love and her broken heart might mostly have been wounded pride, but it had still hurt and she had continued to put a smile on her face and carry on regardless.

So keeping stuff to herself? Definitely within her remit.

Events might have hurtled towards her with the suddenness of a sinkhole but there was a spring in her step as she made her way to the first-class check-in.

She checked in at the speed of light.

It was only when she was heading to the first-class lounge that she felt the first twinge of nerves.

Her phone pinged. Alessandro.

'Checked in yet?'

The deep timbre of his voice made her heart skip a beat and she pulled over to the side and leaned against the wall by one of the coffee shops.

'I'm just making my way to the first-class lounge.'

'Good. Flora and I are here but before you meet my daughter there are a couple of things I need to discuss with you first. If you go past the reception area you'll see a bank of sofas to the right. I'll be waiting there.'

'With Flora?'

'I can leave her to amuse herself for fifteen minutes. I'll make sure I can see her from where we're sitting. She's good at occupying herself.'

'What else do we need to talk about? I haven't breathed a word of anything to anyone, if that's what you want to quiz me about.'

'It's not. I trust you not to have said anything to anyone. I'll see you in twenty minutes. That should be plenty of time to wend your way there. Coffee, how do you take it? Or would you rather something else?'

'Er...'

'The flight leaves in an hour and a half so let's move along, Georgie.'

'Coffee. White. One sugar. Thank you.' She could picture him impatiently looking at his watch.

'No dawdling, please. I'll see you in fifteen.'

Before she could launch into something sarcastic about *dawdling being the furthest thing from her mind*, he'd hung up and she sprinted with her pull-along, following signs to the lounge and getting there with barely any time to spare.

She spotted him as soon as she had managed to get past the three women guarding the lounge like gatekeepers on a mission to make sure no riff-raff managed to con their way into the sanctuary where only the wealthy were allowed.

Incipient nerves had disappeared in her haste to get to the meeting point but now they returned with a vengeance.

She felt instantly out of place.

She'd dressed for comfort and the cold, even though they would be heading to warmer temperatures because Florida would be basking in the twenties.

Her trousers were black, loose and fleece-lined and she had layered up so that she could strip off as necessary. Vest, tee shirt, long-sleeved tee shirt and a cosy waterproof jacket because she would be returning to deep winter and would need it when she got back. She doubted she would have the luxury of a chauffeur-driven car once her role was over.

When she looked at the tribe of smartly dressed, self-assured men and women in the lounge with their shiny patina of people living jet-setting, busy, expensive lives, she couldn't help feeling just a tiny bit like a bag lady.

Alessandro was where he'd said he would be.

He had his computer in front of him and was frowning as he scrolled on it.

It gave her a couple of seconds to take him in and to realise that his masculine beauty hadn't conveniently dimmed since she had last seen him.

He was dressed casually in dark grey trousers and a white shirt cuffed to the elbows and even among the wealthy, glamorous people around him, he managed to stand out.

It wasn't just his beauty, although he truly was spectacular with his dark hair, his rich, burnished skin and the autocratic set of his features.

Something about him was compelling, which was why she was still staring like a star-struck teenager when he suddenly looked up and their eyes collided.

She reddened and walked quickly over to where he was sitting.

With every step she felt more like a fish out of water.

'You made it,' was the first thing he said when she was standing in front of him.

He closed his computer, glanced past her and then returned his dark eyes to her face.

She certainly hadn't dressed to impress, he thought, taking in every inch of what she was wearing without seeming to notice at all.

He'd transferred her a generous amount of cash so that she could invest in the usual designer gear but if she had, then she had forgone that option for travelling.

Well, that was a first.

He was so accustomed to women dressing to impress that he almost did a double take now.

'I know what you're going to say.'

'Why don't you sit? I've ordered coffee.' He signalled to someone behind her.

'You're going to tell me that I haven't dressed appropriately.'

'Was I? Thank you for reading my mind.'

'Where is Flora?'

She twisted this way and that, gripped with curiosity, and then sat back as a pot of coffee and china cups were placed on the table in front of them, along with a little plate of interesting-looking savouries.

'You'll meet her soon enough but, as I said to you, there are a couple of things I feel we ought to get clear from the start.'

He poured her coffee, added milk and pushed it over to her.

'Firstly, I touched on the fact that the less close you get to my daughter, the better.'

'Yes, although I'm going to have to talk to her now and again or else she's going to start getting suspicious if we don't seem to know one another. People who are supposed to be going out usually spend a tiny amount of time in each other's company.'

'She's six.'

'I teach kids. You'd be surprised how quick they are at catching on at what's happening around them.'

'Naturally, yes, we'll do one or two things together, but I've always made a point of not allowing any of the women I date to have any participation in that side of my life. Unfortunately, I'm stuck with this situation but my ground rules remain roughly the same. I will not allow my daughter to get close to anyone who will be vanishing from the scene. In your case, vanishing from the scene in a matter of ten days.'

He suddenly coughed, apologised and scowled.

'Message received loud and clear.'

'Next on the agenda, I want to remind you that this situation isn't real.'

'You don't have to remind me. I've never been in a less real situation in my entire life. I spent most of the journey to the airport pinching myself and wondering whether I was due to wake up any minute.'

'Good. Glad we're on the same page because this isn't a relationship. This is an inconvenience that's been foisted onto me and you've been sucked into the drama through no fault of your own. But sucked into it you have been.'

He paused, giving her time to reach the obvious conclusions, but she was staring at him with clear brown eyes, her expression polite and questioning.

Alessandro suppressed a sigh but it was vital he spelt these things out so that misunderstandings didn't arise.

'What I'm saying is that it's important you don't get tempted into thinking that this necessary charade will ever develop into anything.'

'Develop into anything?'

'I don't think I need to spell it out, do I?'

'You think I'm suddenly going to start getting it into my head that I'm in love with you?'

'In love might be over-egging the pudding.'

He flushed, coughed again and wondered what the hell was the matter with him. Was he coming down with something? Or was he just discomfited by the whole situation, which felt more perilous than it should have?

He could feel the nag of an impending headache.

'You don't have to worry that I'm going to *get any ideas*,' Georgie said flatly, eyes narrowed. 'This is going to sound weird, but I can't see myself falling for a guy who threatened to hand me over to the authorities for breaking and entering before coercing me into pretending to be his fake girlfriend because his ex-wife was being difficult.'

Their eyes tangled and he burst out laughing before succumbing to a coughing fit.

'By the way,' Georgie added coldly, 'you don't look great.'

'Never felt better.'

'Is that what you had to tell me? Or is there more?'

'We've pretty much covered it.' The coughing had gone but he was smiling, a genuine, amused smile, and Georgie knew that she was blushing as they briefly looked at one another before he stood up. 'Time for the fireworks to begin. I'll take you to meet my daughter and remember...'

'I haven't forgotten. Business arrangement. Money has changed hands. Stick to the brief or else. Prison may or may not still await.'

He chuckled and it was a disarming, youthful sound that made the hairs on the back of her neck stand on end. She slid a surreptitious glance across at him and shivered at the thought of being in the same suite of rooms as him, business arrangement or no business arrangement.

Flora was sitting quietly in a circular arrangement of

soft chairs with a round table between them on which was a pull-along emblazoned with Disney characters.

She was colouring and she looked up as soon as they approached, pushing away her book and sitting back and staring with her head tilted to one side.

Children were open with their curiosity but that didn't faze Georgie because she was used to it. She smiled and remembered that talking would have to be kept to the minimum.

'Is that your girlfriend?' Flora asked in a soft, slightly breathless voice.

'A friend,' Alessandro corrected smoothly, taking it down a notch. 'Georgie is a friend, who, yes, happens to be a girl. But mainly, a friend. Georgie, this is my daughter.'

He casually rested his hand on the small of her back in a gesture that was affectionate without being intimate, the sort of gesture that felt like a reminder of what he had just said.

'Hi, Flora! Wow, what are you colouring? That's amazing.' The first thing that struck Georgie was just how beautiful the child was.

Long dark hair hung over one shoulder in a braid and the eyes that looked up at her were huge...dark...and serious.

Flora looked at Alessandro quickly and half smiled just as she stood up to politely reach out her hand in greeting.

'Oh!' Georgie grinned. 'You're a hand-shaker! Very pleased to meet you, Flora. I've heard a lot about you.' She briefly held the tiny hand in hers.

'From my dad?'

'Er...yes?'

The dark eyes shifted to Alessandro, who was smiling down at her.

'You must be *so* excited about going to Disney World.'

The serious eyes lit up and she clasped her hands together

as if standing to attention. 'I've seen all the Disney films.' She reached for the colouring book and handed it to Georgie.

'I'm seriously impressed.' Georgie's voice was warm. Was this too much chat? Just the right amount? She didn't know how she could avoid talking without seeming rude.

'I teach kids and some of them are your age and I've never known any of them to colour as neatly as this.'

'Really?'

'Really. I'm a pretty good artist. Maybe I could teach you how to draw one of your favourite Disney characters.' She felt the hand on her back deliver a tiny prod. 'Time permitting. You'll probably be all wrapped up going on rides with…er…your dad.'

'With us both,' Alessandro's voice said smoothly from behind her. 'Flora, why don't you carry on with what you're doing? We haven't got long before the flight's called. You can finish up colouring…'

'Elsa from *Frozen*.'

'Quite.'

She sat down and reached for one of the felt tips that she had arranged neatly in a row of ten on the table.

Georgie had no idea what to make of their brief conversation. For a minute she looked at the little girl as she took her time with the lines, shaking her head now and again when a colour strayed over the edge.

Next to her, Alessandro had flipped open his laptop and was scrolling through it, losing himself in work, occasionally glancing at Flora but, basically, he had returned to business.

He adored her. That was obvious in the unguarded expression on his face when he looked across at her. Now and again, he murmured something encouraging under his breath and Flora's eyes would light up.

That said, they were so formal with one another!

Was that because he had been messed around with custody? Because the times when he had seen his daughter had been inconsistent?

If Flora had been caught in the middle of a vengeful mother and a father who had ended up finding himself sidelined, then, yes, that would explain the hesitancy between them.

She'd seen that before on the slopes.

One thing she'd clocked from all her time working with kids was that it was usually the very obedient, quiet ones who came from difficult situations and were hesitant when it came to being too loud.

Or complaining too much.

They had learnt that to be quiet was the safest way to deal with inconsistent parenting.

She felt a tug on her heart watching their interaction.

When she looked at Alessandro, slanting, concealed glances when he wasn't looking, she didn't see the open, joyful, delighted expression her father wore whenever he was with her and her sisters. There was a restraint that made her heart constrict, although she knew that that was none of her concern and certainly nothing she should ever think of voicing.

And Flora?

So beautiful and quiet, engrossed in her colouring, barely glancing around her. There wasn't a single six-year-old she knew who wouldn't be making a complete nuisance of him or herself in this first-class lounge.

Or maybe she was thinking about her and her sisters, who would have raided that buffet bar several times over and would now be nagging their parents about something or other. They would have been too excited to keep still.

'What are you smiling at?' Alessandro murmured, snapping her out of her thoughts.

She turned to look at him. 'I was wondering whether I should help myself to something from that buffet bar. Looks pretty amazing.'

'Be my guest.'

'I have to admit—' she lowered her voice from low to practically inaudible and shot a few glances around her '—I've never travelled like this in my life before.'

'And *I* have to admit—' he lowered his voice with similar drama '—that I never had myself until I did.'

'It must have been incredible...you...er...okay, I think I might be about to overstep the brief.'

'Really? Then take a step back.'

'I read up on you. I just think it must have been incredible as you climbed the ladder until you got to a place where you could afford private jets and houses here, there and everywhere.'

Alessandro knew what he should say at this point.

He should add a third clause to the two he had already detailed. Clause one—don't start building bonds with his daughter.

Clause two—don't start getting ideas that he might be up for grabs, because he wasn't.

And now clause three—don't even begin to think about looking for a backstory and plumbing any depths.

Her brown eyes were calm and interested.

'How old are you?' he asked.

'Sorry?'

'Mid-twenties?'

'I'm twenty-six. Why do you ask?'

'You look younger or maybe...' he thought back to that

jaded feeling he'd had '…maybe you just make me feel a hell of a lot older.'

'Older than what?'

'Thirty-two. I feel a hell of a lot older because I've probably been through a hell of a lot more than you have. What's it like where you grew up?'

'Where I grew up…nice. Lots of countryside. I say nice… when you get to a certain age, it can be downright boring. But yes, growing up there was a lot of space. Cows and trees and stuff like that.'

'Cows and trees and stuff like that.'

'No cows or trees where you grew up?'

'Alcohol, drugs and making sure to look over your shoulder when you walked the streets after dark. Not a cow in sight and trees were few and far between. Course, it's a lot more gentrified now but, yes, that was where I grew up so I suppose it was incredible climbing the ladder and making it to the top.'

Alessandro felt the throb in his temples, the steady progress of a headache he hadn't had when he'd headed to the airport earlier on.

He felt exhausted.

Exhausted and a little spaced out. Overtired? He'd been up until one in the morning working on emails.

He heard himself say, in a low, pensive voice, 'Although it has to be said that the higher up the ladder you climb, the more you forget how strong the desire was to have all those incredible things within reach. The houses and yachts and jets lose their allure.'

'I imagine so,' Georgie murmured.

'Right.' He belatedly remembered the number three clause, which he had temporarily and inexplicably put to the back of his mind. 'That's our flight.' He tapped Flora on her shoulder. 'Time to board, my little flower.'

The six-year-old looked up at him and beamed at the endearment.

I will not get involved with this family, was what Georgie was thinking as they began bustling to go. *I will not stick my oar into things so that I can be rebuffed yet again. I will definitely not speculate about father and daughter and those spaces between them, or anything else for that matter. Not my business.*

Even though, she admitted to herself, she'd already started speculating, and those things he had said…

Well, curiosity, which had been muted before, had crept through the crack in the door that had opened between them and was coursing through her.

She wasn't going to feed it by asking any more questions, she decided.

Anyway, she was certain that he would shut her down if she tried to carry on the conversation. She could tell in the sudden stiffness of his stance as he reached down to hold Flora's hand and began heading back towards the reception.

She busied herself with thinking about what the next ten days would look like.

At least she knew about the sleeping arrangements. She'd googled the details. She and Alessandro might be sharing a suite but it was vast enough for them to have separate bedrooms and sitting areas. Flora would be in a mini suite of her own, linked to theirs via an adjoining door. Georgie figured it was the sort of arrangement suitable for a couple who couldn't stand one another but were having a holiday for the sake of their kid.

He'd texted her the link, probably to put her mind at rest

or maybe to remind her that this was a business arrangement lest she forget, and she'd checked out every small detail of where they'd be staying.

Would Flora be hurtling in and out through that adjoining door?

Unlikely. She didn't seem the sort of child who did a great deal of hurtling.

Georgie glanced across at her and stifled another thorny surge of curiosity to find out more about her, about why she was so quiet, about the things that interested her, made her laugh.

Would she notice that her dad and his girlfriend weren't sharing a bedroom? Probably not and if she did, Georgie doubted it would register as anything suspicious. Even if Flora had not been so incredibly subdued by nature, six-year-olds weren't given to the sort of speculation an adult would have shown at something like sleeping arrangements.

The email Alessandro had sent her had listed a military-style approach to the theme park. Rides and lunch, but then downtime because he had to work.

He had suggested that if she was around for some of the morning activities, then she could do whatever she wanted during that downtime.

Flora, he had informed her, was good at entertaining herself, which was something she was now appreciating.

Georgie had wondered whether that had been a not-so-subtle reminder about the non-involvement clause with his daughter in their deal.

Dinner would be an early affair and then he would return to work.

At the end of the ten days, he would fly back to New York with Flora to be collected by Sophia and Georgie would return to her duties on the slopes.

She hadn't asked him how their so-called relationship was going to taper off and he hadn't volunteered the information.

That was added to the list of things she wasn't going to be curious about.

There was so much she was under instructions to *not be curious about* and so many *Keep Out* signposts to be obeyed that she wondered whether she had the navigational skills to deal with it all.

She wanted to shamelessly wallow in the luxury of first class but as she watched father and daughter slip into their ridiculously comfortable seats, blasé and indifferent to their uniquely privileged position, all she could focus on was her chattering mind and her desperate attempt to shut it down.

CHAPTER FIVE

FLORA WAS EXHAUSTED by the time they made it to the theme park. She was yawning and as they checked in, Alessandro scooped her up and draped her over his shoulder so that she could nod off.

Georgie, on the other hand, was wide awake and more than making up for Flora's sleepiness with high levels of excitement.

The hotel was busy but she imagined less so because of the time of year and because it was evening and rides would be winding down. She hung back, gaping while Alessandro did the checking in.

She could see the black still water of a lagoon outside and, in the distance, a stunning view of a turreted Cinderella castle, which was lit up like a Christmas tree.

Kids in the grand foyer were being entertained by Disney characters, from Minnie Mouse to Rapunzel.

Music to one of the Disney films was playing in the background and all in all it was magical.

'Ready?'

Georgie blinked at the sound of Alessandro's voice because she'd forgotten that he was there.

'You've checked in already?'

'The bags are being taken upstairs and I think I'll have to get Flora off to sleep. Too much excitement.'

'She'll be fresh for tomorrow.'

'Are you hungry? It's after eight and it's probably been a long day for you.'

He was walking and talking at the same time, heading for one of the lifts while a porter scuttled along in front of him, eager to please, until Alessandro told him that he could make his own way to the suite while fishing in his pocket and handing over some notes that made the guy's eyes light up.

'Well?' he prompted, once in the lift. 'Hungry? If you are you can order up whatever you like or you can explore if you want to and eat wherever you want. It will all be covered by me. I'll give you one of my credit cards and the pin. Use it as you want.'

'That's very generous,' Georgie said politely. 'What will you do? I mean once you settle Flora?' She hesitated. 'Am I supposed to do something here? Help settle her? I can get her ready for bed or is that overstepping my duties?'

'Just sort yourself out, Georgie, and leave my daughter to me.'

'Okay.'

Stung, Georgie turned away and stared at the elevator door. Burnished matte silver. She could see her reflection in it as well as his.

He looked irritable and she wondered what she had done to provoke that.

It shouldn't matter.

Georgie knew that. She also knew that she sometimes took passing comments to heart.

She knew where that stemmed from, knew that her reactions were sometimes overblown and irrational, but, at moments like this, her instinct was to retreat into herself and fall silent.

Growing up with her dyslexia, which had fostered such a confusing feeling of disadvantage before she could understand that there was even something wrong with her, had made her wary and always on the lookout for any kind of takedown.

And with the opposite sex? She knew when to back off, when to protect herself. Only with Hans had she forgotten to obey that basic instinct. However attractive this man was, she would have to remember that instinct.

The lift doors opened and they were disgorged onto a very large landing adorned with chairs and a sideboard on which stood the largest vase of fresh flowers she had ever seen.

She wanted to reach out and touch one of them, but she just followed Alessandro to an imposing door, which he opened with a key card.

The silence felt suffocating.

She was as excited as a kid, eager to find out what was on the theme park.

Instead, all she could think was that now that they were here, now that he was facing the prospect of being stuck with her for ten days, he was waking up to the fact that she irritated him.

Insecurities that she was so adept at hiding, that barely troubled her at all, began to creep in.

Was he embarrassed by her?

Here in this uber-expensive hotel where even the kids running around were decked out in designer clothes? She was sure she spotted a baby in a pushchair wearing Gucci.

She sneaked a glance at herself.

She'd layered up and as soon as they'd got off the plane, had begun de-layering.

She'd tied her jumper round her waist, stripped down to

the tee shirt and stuffed the coat into her carry-on so that it bulged as though on the point of explosion.

Which it probably was.

She'd worn trainers because they were comfy, and had plaited her hair.

One long plait that had made it its mission to unravel pretty much as soon as she'd left Alessandro's house on the way to the airport.

Mortification tore into her and she did her best to fight it, using every mantra available.

'Choose whichever room you want,' he said, interrupting her introspection.

When she looked at him, it was to see him disappearing towards the open adjoining door.

Flora was in a deep sleep. Through the door, Georgie could glimpse a suitcase in Flora's suite, along with the garish Disney pull-along she had had at the airport.

Instinct would have propelled her to follow him, to make herself useful, because she was so accustomed to dealing with children. The ski resort ran a kids-only camp for a month over the summer holidays.

She knew all about tucking kids into bed, making sure they had their showers, often reading them stories even though the kids who stayed there for maybe a week at a time would have been older than Flora.

Kids were kids and who didn't like a good story read to them?

He half shut the door behind him and Georgie gazed around her, her light dimmed.

It was beyond luxurious.

For the guy who had come from nothing, this was the top of the ladder he had climbed when it came to hotel suites. She didn't think anything could surpass it.

It was simply enormous.

The living area, in which she now stood, was a canvas of soft pastel tones and the walls were adorned with large, framed Disney posters from way back when. The atmosphere, drenched in the whimsy of the age-old cartoon characters, was still sophisticated, elegant and tasteful.

Off to one side, there was a separate, spacious area, a TV zone with plush seating and a sideboard, which she guessed would always be laden with snacks.

She could have carried on staring but, instead, she took her case, which had been brought up and spent a couple of minutes shamelessly gaping.

The entire area was larger than most people's apartments. Georgie didn't know that a hotel suite could actually have such an enormous footprint.

If she'd had any apprehension about sharing space with him, then that would have been instantly dispelled.

Her quarters included a sitting area as well as a massive bathroom and a walk-in dressing room in which she had precious little to put.

There were also facilities for making hot drinks and baskets of fruit.

She would have to have something to eat but, first, she would have to at least say goodnight to Alessandro and find out what their plans would be for the following day.

She emerged from her rooms to find him prowling through the living area, still frowning.

The second she walked in, he looked at her but before he could say anything, she rushed into nervous chatter.

'Is Flora asleep?'

'She barely opened her eyes when I settled her into bed.'

'Poor thing. Long day for a small child and when you add the excitement in…' Georgie laughed a nervous laugh. 'This is an amazing place, by the way!' She made a wide gesture with her arms. 'A person could get lost in here! And you're not going to believe the size of the bedrooms!'

She didn't want to dwell on how she looked because that would have returned her to the place of thinking that he was embarrassed to be seen with her.

She didn't want her insecurities to stamp all over common sense.

They weren't going to be here for very long and she mustn't forget, she told herself, that *she* was doing *him* a favour. In a manner of speaking.

But she couldn't help but register that, even after an equally long and tiring trip, he still managed to look cool and elegant and sophisticated.

Her eyes were compulsively drawn to the way the dark hairs on his wrist slightly curled round the matte gold of his watch strap.

The breadth of his shoulders pushing at the shirt and the length of his muscular legs.

'I… I just came to say goodnight.' She plunged into a bit more nervous chatter and dragged her eyes away from him. 'I think I'll order some food to eat in my room and…and… you can tell me what time you'd like me to join you tomorrow morning. I know you sent that email with everything laid out but it'll save time if you just tell me when I should surface.'

'You must be tired. Join me in a drink before you order your food.'

'Er…'

'Wine? Gin and tonic? Water?'

He moved towards a mini-sized open-plan kitchen area and threw over his shoulder, 'The bar will be fully stocked with whatever you want. If you want something different, they'll bring it up to you.'

'Amazing.'

'You pay for what you get. What do you want to drink?'

'I guess I'll have a glass of wine. Thank you.'

She hovered, watching him, looking out for more signs of irritation.

When he reached to hand her a glass of wine, she could barely control the slight tremor in her hand.

'I'm not going to bite, Georgie, so you don't have to look so nervous.'

'I'm sorry.'

'What are you apologising for?'

'I… I know you're irritated with me but it's not my fault that you're here with me!'

She hadn't meant to say anything because maintaining a dignified silence would have been so much better, but she hadn't been able to help herself and now that she had said what she had, she looked at him with simmering defiance.

'I'm not irritated with you.'

'Is it because…? No, forget it.'

She went to sit on one of the comfortable sofas, although she would rather have skulked off to her bedroom. She'd initiated a conversation and now she wished she hadn't. He'd told her that she made him feel old. She could have said that he made her feel way too young and green around the ears for her liking.

She sipped her wine and stared at the ground, but she could feel his dark eyes on her as he strolled to sit on the very same sofa next to her.

'What am I forgetting and is it because *what*? Georgie, I apologise if I was a little short. The truth is I'm exhausted.'

Georgie slanted a glance across to him. He was rubbing his eyes then he sat back on the sofa and briefly closed them.

He looked beyond exhausted.

She was staring at him when he opened his eyes and looked at her and, for a few seconds, the atmosphere was very still as the silence continued for a fraction longer than it should have.

Her heart began to thud.

Sexual awareness zipped through her. She wasn't just admiring a good-looking guy. This wasn't a detached appreciation of someone who stood out from the crowd and this didn't feel at all like the harmless crushes she had had on guys in the past.

What she felt now was potent and overwhelming, an electric awareness of him that made her dampen and made her nipples tingle at the thought of being touched.

By him. By those long brown fingers at which she now seemed to be staring.

Her mouth went dry and she fought to try and get her scattered thoughts in order.

'Well?' he prompted.

'I thought that perhaps you were embarrassed by me,' she said in a rush, and just as quickly she finished the rest of her wine and covered the empty glass with her hand because no way was she going to have any more.

'Embarrassed? Why would I be embarrassed by you?'

Georgie shrugged. 'Doesn't matter. What are the plans for tomorrow? Like I said, I know you sent me that email but I wasn't sure whether we would be sticking to it rigidly. Is there anything you want me to book? I could do that.'

'You don't have to book anything. You're not here in the capacity of my secretary. Why would I be embarrassed by you? And, yes, it matters. We're going to be here for ten days. It matters if you've somehow got it into your head that...that what? Exactly?'

Georgie took a deep breath.

'I'm quite a down-to-earth person,' she said. 'I don't do designer clothes. I work with kids and when I'm not teaching them how to ski, I'm teaching them how to play sports. My entire wardrobe is comprised of comfy clothes.'

'I'm not following you.'

'I thought you'd woken up to the fact that your companion isn't going to be decked out in expensive casual wear, with diamonds on my fingers and Gucci loafers on my feet. I've seen the crowd here. The clothes some of them are wearing could kit out the matchbox in London I haven't even bought yet.'

'Why are you so insecure? Trust me, nothing could have been further from my mind.' He smiled and yawned.

'Okay.'

'I can tell you're going to get along with Flora and, whatever I've said about not getting close to her, it's a relief that there won't be any tension between you.'

'She's a great kid.'

'Back to what you said, though. Tell me where that came from.'

'What?'

'The fact that you felt insecure about not being decked out in the usual expensive nonsense that most women feel the need to wear.'

'Remember I've seen all those pictures of you online. The women you go out with don't seem to hang around in jeans and old tee shirts.'

'We're not going out, though. You're not one of my women. You can wear what you want to wear, but I thought that you might like to treat yourself to all the things you might not usually buy for yourself. And you're right, of course. The crowd here are the usual moneyed lot. If you feel more comfortable blending in, then that's fine. If not,

wear what you want, like I said. The thick clothes you travelled in might be a little inappropriate, though. At least, if
you want to avoid heatstroke. There's no need for you to
feel insecure about your looks.'

Georgie reddened but his smile was warmly genuine and
he looked as though he was enjoying the conversation, enjoying being in her company.

She felt a swoop of pleasure.

'I guess I grew up comparing myself to my sisters. We're
only separated by a few years and they're both older than
me and more successful than me. Well, I say successful,
they've become professionals. Katherine's a lawyer and Emily's a doctor.'

'Go on. I'm listening.'

'They were bright and popular with boys and I suppose
that as I was the youngest and maybe because I wasn't as
academic as they were I veered off in the opposite direction. I decided I'd be the one who didn't do *girly* and then
I found my passion, teaching kids, and there was no need
to ever do *girly*. So coming here…' she rolled her eyes and
smiled, relaxed in a way that was surprising, given her reaction to him '… I feel out of my depth.'

'You're insecure.'

'No, of course I'm not!' But then she thought of Hans
and the pain of feeling like an idiot when she'd caught him
kissing that girl and then winking at her, pulling her into a
conspiracy of agreeing with him that what they'd had had
meant nothing, had all been a bit of a laugh.

She thought of the countless times she had laughed with
the lads, played football with them, listened to their tales
of woe with girlfriends and felt small inside because she
would have so wanted to join in with the cool gang of girls

with their flirty smiles and giggling gossip but had just not known how.

She'd boxed herself in, had been the tomboy in the family and after a while she hadn't known how to *unbox* herself.

'I'm boring you.'

'I agree you don't give off the impression of being insecure,' he mused thoughtfully, ignoring her interruption.

'Because I know how to dig my heels in and stick up for myself.'

'Don't knock it.'

'What do you mean?'

'It's a refreshing change from a lot of the women I've known in the past who make it their mission to never stick up for themselves just in case it offends me.'

Alessandro frowned because he had no idea how the conversation between them had meandered into the place it was now. There was work to do. He had a ton of emails to get through and various reports to look at.

He opened his mouth to rein it in but then looked at her and shifted.

She'd tugged her long plait over her shoulder and was idly playing with the end of it, twirling it between her fingers with a small frown on her face, as though her thoughts were a million miles away.

It was easy to feel insecure if you compared yourself to other people.

He had never suffered from that problem, even though he had grown up in lack.

From the minute he could understand the world around him, he'd set his eyes on the prize and gone for it with the energy of someone who fully believed in himself.

The goal at the end would be freedom, because that was the one and only thing money really bought.

Freedom from having anyone call the shots.

Everything else had been blocked out until Flora had come on the scene. Before her arrival, he had had no faith in relationships. Why would he? He had been abandoned by his father and had grown up in a world where things around him were transitory.

People came and went. In the case of his adolescent contemporaries, many in the direction of a jail.

His mother had been a constant, but he'd known from an early age that his father's abandonment of them had broken her somewhere deep inside. She, too, had learnt the pain of loving and having that love rejected. With him, the pain of the child not comprehending the callousness of the parent and with his mother...the pain of the wife whose love had nowhere to go, abandoned by the man she'd set her heart on with a child by her side to take care of.

The one constant?

The acquisition of power and wealth that would protect him from the frailty of human nature all around him. Love was loss and loss was pain. His daughter was the only one who held the key to his heart.

Unaccustomed to introspection, Alessandro dragged his eyes away from Georgie even though some wilful part of him wanted to remain with the conversation for a bit longer.

'Moving on,' he said, and she blinked and focused on him.

He looked at her with lowered eyes. She really was very pretty in an ultra-feminine way. Big brown eyes...that unruly tumble of hair...her slightly parted lips as though always on the verge of saying something. Her dewy-eyed innocence was captivating.

Finding himself staring, he frowned and cleared his throat.

The headache was back and worse.

'Flora will probably be up early so maybe we should aim to start the day by eight-thirty. Breakfast downstairs. I'll get someone at Reception to improve on the schedule I emailed you and we follow it.'

'I'm not sure six-year-old kids adhere to that kind of military approach when it comes to having fun.'

'No option. I don't want to spend my time wandering around aimlessly because I want to be back at the hotel by one so that I can catch up on work.'

'Okay.'

'You can do whatever you want between one and six.'

'Sure.'

'Flora will be happy to watch television and, at four, I'll do something with her, let her lead the way.'

'She'll love that,' Georgie said warmly.

'At six, we can go to the restaurant and she can have her dinner. Once she's asleep, you can do as you wish because I'll grab something and catch up on work.'

'Do you ever stop working?'

'Here. I'll barely be working while I'm here.'

'But what about all that *catching up on stuff*?'

'My normal day stretches to a great deal more than catching up on stuff,' he said wryly. 'Do you have any questions about the timetable?'

'Er…'

'You have the email I sent you?'

'Of course.'

'You can look at it for guidance. It details all the suitable rides and my PA has helpfully calculated timings getting between them, allowing for occasional pit stops.'

'That's very efficient. Wow.'

'Now, your clothes.'

'Yes? My clothes?'

'Have you managed to buy more suitable gear for the weather? It's not going to be scorching hot but you won't feel comfortable in thick joggers or sweatshirts. It doesn't have to be designer if that doesn't take your fancy.'

'I've bought suitable clothing, yes, and thank you for sending me money to cover the expenditure.'

After that rush of personal information exchanged between them, Georgie felt as though she had been brought back down to earth with an almighty bump.

He'd made it very clear that she wasn't to infringe the boundaries he had in place.

Yet, somehow, she had ended up confiding in him in a way she never did and certainly never with a guy.

Even when it had come to Hans, theirs had been a relationship built on outdoor activities and having fun.

He'd told her about what he wanted to do as a career. She'd told him about her love for teaching kids.

But she had never felt tempted to share anything really personal with him. No wonder he hadn't taken her seriously.

There had been laughter and fun and hanging out, but the element of seriousness had been missing. She could appreciate that, now that she was staring at Alessandro and wondering how he had managed to draw so much information out of her.

Who could blame him if he was pulling back at speed?

Did he think that this was the first step to her thinking that there was something more to this than an arrangement she had been forced into?

One minute she'd read the message and got the memo.

The next minute she'd flung both in the bin and was trying to infiltrate her way in via confidences?

'I should think about getting something to eat,' she mumbled.

'Out of interest, what did you tell your friends about the sudden holiday here?'

'I didn't say anything about going on a holiday.' Georgie was caught off balance by the sudden change in subject.

Maybe this was all about fact-checking. Getting stories straight. She couldn't see the relevance. Hadn't she been under orders to breathe nothing?

'Naturally, I didn't breathe a word about you.'

'That's a given.'

'Then I don't know why it matters what I said,' Georgie told him honestly.

'It doesn't. I was curious.'

'I said something about a family emergency. Not one that involved me travelling all the way back to England, of course. I told them a distant relative was having a few problems.'

'What sort of problems?'

'I kept it vague. Why are you so interested?'

Alessandro flushed at her openly puzzled expression. He could hardly blame her.

Why wasn't he sticking to the programme? Was it because he felt zoned out? Overtired?

'I suppose because I've never met anyone quite like you before,' he confessed.

'Oh. Okay. That makes sense. You wouldn't, moving in the circles that you would move in. I've never met anyone like you before either. I don't get to meet too many billionaires.' She paused. 'I said something about trouble with one of their kids and that I would take the holiday time out to go visit because it would solve the problem of where to live while Alison recovers from her chickenpox.'

'They didn't know you'd decided to squat in my house?'

'I mentioned that I had second thoughts because I felt uncomfortable doing that. I don't like the word *squat*. I wasn't *squatting*.'

'It's good to have a bit of background information about you, Georgie.'

He stood up and then looked down at her.

'We're going to be sharing space and, if for no other reason, it makes things a little less stilted between us for the duration of the time we're here together.'

So that's what all that was about! No need to start getting all hot under the collar by his show of interest.

'Yes, it does.'

'Comfortable with the sleeping arrangements?'

'Very comfortable. Thank you.'

'And won't you go out for something to eat? Like I said, feel free to eat wherever you choose and whatever you want. I will ensure that your account is suitably topped up and to-morrow I'll let you have one of my cards. There's no limit to what you can spend.'

'That's very trusting of you.'

'Believe me, it's not. I will keep an eye on all expenditure. Trust isn't something I have much time for when it comes to money. I'm going to head in now.'

He pressed his thumbs on his eyes and she was struck again by just how tired he looked.

'Anything else you want to know?'

'Do you want me to check in on Flora during the night? Kids can sometimes wake up and feel a little spooked if they're in a strange environment.'

'Not your job.'

The irritation was back in his voice. Georgie heard it and her lips thinned but now, as she looked at him, she could see that all he wanted to do was get rid of her post haste.

Was he going to work?

Probably.

He was a workaholic.

'You don't look great,' she said on impulse, springing to her feet and resting her hand on his forearm. 'You should get some sleep and not do any work.'

'You sound like my mother.'

But his voice was mild and, when their eyes met, he briefly smiled at her before staring at her hand on his forearm until she hurriedly yanked it off.

She stepped back and only realised how tense she was when he'd disappeared with the door of his rooms firmly shut behind him.

CHAPTER SIX

THERE WAS NO sign of Alessandro when Georgie woke up at a little after seven and peered outside her door.

She'd set her alarm. If they'd planned on heading off at eight-thirty, then she wasn't going to cut it fine.

His door was ajar and she paused in front of it then hurried through the adjoining door to find that Flora was up, although still in bed and drawing.

The bed drowned her and her long dark hair spilled around her small face. She looked like a tiny angel and that was even more evident when she glanced up and smiled at Georgie.

'Have you been up long?'

Flora shook her head and Georgie strolled over to see what she was drawing, to find that it was an eerily accurate depiction of a cartoon character she was copying from a book.

Listening out for the sound of footsteps, she perched up on the mattress and then her natural instincts took over.

She remembered how satisfying it had felt when she had begun as a ski instructor, the kids all trusting her expertise, eager to learn and quick to pick things up.

She remembered that wonderful feeling of finding her place, a place where she felt comfortable, where she no longer anxiously wondered whether she would ever settle into anything. Comparing herself to her clever, talented sisters had become so ingrained that, despite the fact that she adored both of them, their easy successes had always cast long shadows over her and the choices she had made in life.

Her dyslexia had made her early years academically challenging. Until she was diagnosed, she had learnt to hang back as a means of self-defence against being laughed at in class and had nurtured a lack of self-confidence that had ended up bleeding into her emotional life. As a tomboy, there had been no need to prove herself successful with the opposite sex, but she had been unprepared for her headlong rush into crazy infatuation with Hans, the first guy she had ever felt truly fancied her, until she'd seen him with that other girl and realised that camaraderie had been more powerful than lust.

She looked at Flora's dark-haired beauty, such a replica of her handsome father, and mentally told herself that the hurt she'd felt with Hans would be a pointless experience if she didn't learn from it and snuff out her inappropriate interest in a guy who had no interest in her whatsoever.

She heard herself chatting now as she reached for a piece of paper and began to draw freehand.

'I used to draw all the time as a kid,' she confided. 'It was the one thing I was really good at.'

'What about Maths and English?'

'I got by. When I started secondary school, I got diagnosed with dyslexia. That's when things are jumbled up in your head and it's hard to make sense of words and, in my case, also numbers. I don't tell anyone that, so you're very special. But what I'd do was I would draw, just like you.'

'I draw because when I'm home, Mum doesn't like me waking her up. Sometimes the nannies come but I prefer to stay in my room and draw or colour.'

'Why doesn't she like you waking her up?'

'She puts on an eye mask and says she needs to sleep or else she'll get wrinkles. I'm not allowed to disturb her. The nanny drops me off to school. My friend's brother has what you have.'

'Hmmm…yeah…?' Georgie was busy mulling over the picture taking shape of Flora wandering through an empty mansion, surrounded by nannies and all the stuff that money could buy while her mother dropped in now and again to touch base.

She looked at her phone, which she'd brought in with her, and saw that it was nearly eight and, with no sign of Alessandro, she suddenly felt a spurt of panic.

'Okay, Flora. You wait right here and I'll go check on your dad. I'll switch the telly on. You can have a look at all the stuff there is to do here. Would you like that?'

She didn't wait for an answer. She switched it on anyway but kept the volume low.

At the door, she turned around and said, 'Shall I get some clothes out for you?'

'I always pick my own clothes.' Flora looked at her and smiled a shy, angelic smile. 'And shoes. I've picked my own clothes and shoes since I was three.'

Georgie smiled. She'd read somewhere that the younger a child was when she picked what she wanted to wear, the more it indicated a measure of self-assertion and independence. Those were things that would get Flora far, even though the image Georgie had of her was of a trapped little bird in a golden cage.

She understood in a whoosh why Alessandro had done what he had, why he had coerced her with veiled threats to come on this trip.

He would surely be aware that his ex-wife might not be

the most devoted of parents. From what she had picked up, Sophia was materialistic and manipulative and happy to use their daughter to further her own ends.

But he hadn't played hardball until he'd reached a point of having no choice.

Why was that?

She thought back to those confidences when he had told her about his background and she could understand that he would have had an inherent deep respect for the mother figure in a child's life and so had allowed his ex more leeway than he should have.

Before she'd met Flora, it had been easy to feel manoeuvred and resentful.

Now, though, she was glad that she was here if the sham drove his ex to a place where relations between them changed into something healthier.

If Sophia accepted that her ex was really and truly no longer within her orbit but had embarked on something serious with another woman, then surely she would accept defeat and move on with her own life and that could only be good for her and Flora alike.

It was easy to get stuck in one place and then moving on became impossible.

When other people got dragged into that dynamic, as in the case of a six-year-old kid, then it could be a disaster.

The door was still ajar and there was still no sign of Alessandro when Georgie returned to their shared living area.

She wondered whether he had taken himself off somewhere to work or else had maybe got wrapped up in something and had lost track of time.

She knocked.

No answer plus the lights weren't on. At least not in

the outside sitting area off which his bedroom, like hers, would be.

She walked through into darkness, switched on the light and then tentatively headed towards the bedroom.

As with the outside sitting area, the door was ajar.

And likewise, it was dark inside. She pushed the door and whispered his name.

If Flora made a surprise appearance now, then heaven only knew what would go through her mind.

She was supposed to be her dad's girlfriend. Girlfriends didn't do a lot of tiptoeing and anxious whispering. Even a child of six might find that odd.

When she eventually got up the courage to fully open the door it was to find Alessandro sprawled on the bed and for a few heart-thumping seconds, as her eyes adjusted to the darkness, she could feel her mouth go completely dry.

Was he…*naked*?

Beads of perspiration formed on her forehead and she loudly cleared her throat and took a couple of steps into the bedroom.

The room equalled hers in size but the figure on the bed gave it an intensely masculine feel that hers lacked.

The covers were twisted around him and he was lying on his back, one arm flung to the side, the other resting on his torso, most of which she could see because he had obviously thrashed around during the night.

He had a beautiful body.

Burnished brown against the white covers.

One leg was fully exposed, long and muscular. The other was half concealed by the rumpled bed linen.

She shouldn't have to be doing this!

Since when was it part of her remit to wake a slumbering Sleeping Beauty because he had overslept?

She spun round on her heels and banged on the top light and then instantly turned it to dim because it revealed just a little too much heart-stopping reality for her liking.

'Alessandro!'

From the dim recesses of sleep, Alessandro heard his name being called and he half moved under the covers and opened his eyes without sitting up.

He grunted.

Georgie was standing by the bed with her arms folded glaring at him.

'Why are you still in bed? We're supposed to be leaving in half an hour!'

Alessandro reached out and fumbled on the bedside table for his phone and began shrugging off the covers.

'No!'

'No?'

'Are you *wearing anything*?'

'I can't believe how late it is.'

'You look awful, Alessandro.'

Her voice had gone from sharp to hesitant and she took a careful step forward and felt his forehead and then sprang back.

'You're burning up!'

'That's impossible.' He began to push back the covers, registering another horrified squeal from her, and immediately fell back onto the mattress.

'You're ill.'

'I'm never ill.' He looked at her balefully.

She was dressed and raring to go in something that was, thankfully, a little more suited to the weather and the occasion. Some pale jeans, a cute orange and green tee shirt that clung to her slender body like some very fetching cling film, and plimsoles.

She looked fresh and young and sexy.

Alessandro recognised that he was lodging all these details in his head even though he felt like crap and yes, like it or not, he was burning up.

'I'm never ill,' he repeated in a futile attempt to deny the obvious.

'Wait a minute while I check on Flora. In the meantime, I'll bring you some tablets. I always carry a first-aid kit with me. Habit. You're to take the tablets and then wait till I decide what to do with you.'

'Are you giving *me* orders?'

'Yes!'

She turned away but, before she left the room, she said over her shoulder in a voice that brooked no argument, 'And keep yourself suitably covered! I'll be back in a minute.'

She ran in to check on Flora, told her that her dad wasn't well but maybe best not to go in just yet, wait till he was feeling a little better, and that she could go check the fridge and help herself to some juice.

'By the way,' she added, before disappearing, 'I love the choice of outfit!'

'You do?'

Flora beamed, although her little face was anxious about Alessandro. She'd packed her mini backpack and Georgie didn't have much trouble guessing what would be in there. Activities and maybe a favourite toy.

She was a quiet, serious, methodical little kid and Georgie wondered whether that was her way of dealing with a chaotic background with a mother willing to play tug of war with her and a dad who had been denied access for many months and before then? Who knew?

Alessandro was a workaholic. He adored his daughter

but did he let his hair down when he was with her? Laugh and fling her in the air and play ball and try and braid her hair when there was no one else around to do it?

Or were those activities reserved for the nannies?

Having told herself that she wasn't going to be drawn into the family drama because it was one she would be leaving behind in a matter of days, she was now being drawn in.

She shook her head with frustration, ran to fetch some water and two minutes later she was back in Alessandro's room to find him sitting up and looking like death warmed up.

'Okay. I give in. You're right. I'm not well. This has never happened to me before. Where is Flora?'

'I've told her to give you a little time to get back on your feet. Also, it would be awful if she caught anything. It would ruin her time here and she's so excited.'

'You might be the one to catch whatever I have.'

'I'm probably more robust than you.' Georgie smirked. 'That's the joy of living an outdoor life. Take the tablets.'

'I abhor taking tablets.'

'I don't care. Take them. You need to be up and running as fast as you can. Flora's brimming over with excitement and it'll be nice for you to spend the time with her.'

She remembered her thoughts about how he might spend his time with his daughter. Money might be able to buy a lot, but no amount of money could buy quality time and, for a workaholic, quality time could be in thin supply.

Or maybe, in the grip of never-ending ambition, he had forgotten how to take time out and do nothing, which was often what a kid needed from a parent.

But that was just speculation.

'Perhaps you could run me a bath,' he said, lying back on the pillows and closing his eyes.

Georgie sighed. He looked vulnerable, which she knew was dangerous because she could already feel herself softening when she was determined to remain detached.

With his eyes closed and without the guarded, cool self-assurance she had become accustomed to, he looked boyish and much younger.

'I'll… I'll get Flora some breakfast and, okay, I'll run you a bath.'

'I'm glad you're here,' Alessandro mumbled in such a low voice that she had to lean towards him to hear him clearly.

'I beg your pardon?'

His eyes flicked open, catching her unawares and holding her startled gaze for a few silent seconds.

'Glad you're here. I can't remember a time… I don't do this but…doesn't feel awful…you being here…'

'You're not making any sense.' She felt his forehead again with the back of her hand. 'You're clammy. Your fever's doing the talking. You should try and get some sleep once you've had a bath.'

'I've never been in this situation before.' He clasped her hand with his and carried on looking at her. 'Never been ill. Can't even remember being ill when I was a kid. Never known what it's felt like for someone to bring me tablets with water with no agenda. Feels okay.'

Georgie reddened. She felt heat course through her because there was a sudden searing intimacy between them that locked her in place.

Did he feel it as well?

Or was he babbling because he had a high fever and that was what you did when you had a high fever? You babbled without thinking.

Her eyes slipped down to the primly covered body and

she had a vivid image of what that primly covered body might look like, naked and beautiful and tempting.

She felt faint.

'I'd do this for anyone,' she said roughly, pulling back and fiddling with the packet of tablets she had brought in with her. 'I'll be back in a minute to run the bath. Do you want anything to eat? I could order room service.'

'Not that hungry.'

'You should eat. Feed a cold, starve a fever and all that.'

'You're bossy. I like that.'

His voice was drowsy and she felt dangerously close to really liking all the stuff he was saying. She had to remind herself sternly that none of it counted because he wasn't well.

In a fluster she gave Flora some biscuits to tide her over, told her she could have a chat with her dad but stay by the bedroom door.

'Germs have a habit of leaping about,' she cautioned, making leaping motions with her fingers and feeling gratified when Flora burst out laughing.

'But you're looking after him.'

'That's what partners do,' Georgie said, thinking on the spot. '*Loving* partners and, besides, I have a separate bedroom so those leaping germs won't get to me.'

Too much information? It was an impulse statement just in case reports filtered back to a prying ex.

She heard Flora chatting to her dad as she phoned through for room service, which was speedy thanks to the fact that they had their own personal concierge.

She and Flora would have breakfast downstairs in the restaurant.

'Right, miss, I'm going to run a bath for your dad so why don't you listen out for someone bringing up some food?

You can let them in and supervise while they set the table in the kitchenette? Think you're responsible enough for that super important job?'

And then it was rush, rush, rush as she headed straight to Alessandro's en suite to run a bath.

Her nerves were all over the place when she returned, bath run, to find him still under the covers.

'You'll have to help me to the bath.'

'No way.'

'Okay.' He began edging himself from under the covers and just when she thought her heart was going to slam out of her ribcage, she realised that he was wearing boxers.

She stared with bold fascination and he slowly levered himself into an upright position.

He was magnificent. She couldn't breathe and only reached to half support him when she saw that he looked a little dizzy at the effort.

The heat from his body slammed into her and she felt the weight of his arm draped over her shoulders as hot and heavy as a branding iron.

'I'll bring your food in and leave it on a tray by the side of your bed…' She began backing out of the bathroom. 'Are you okay to…er…?'

'I'm already feeling better.'

'I'll be back…'

'This isn't what I had planned.'

'I get that.'

He hesitated and then flushed.

'I'll be back on my feet by this evening. I don't do ill health.'

'Ill health might disagree with you.'

He looked at her and smiled. His dark hair was tousled

and he had a six o'clock shadow on his chin because he hadn't shaved.

Arousal almost made her pass out.

'I like your chirpy pep talk and your bossiness. I shouldn't but I do.'

For a second, he looked as though he needed to sit down and take the weight off and she almost wanted to wait till he'd made his way into the bath but the very thought made her feel even more like passing out, so she smiled back at him.

'Well… I'll take care of Flora for the day. In fact, don't worry about her. I'll make sure she enjoys being here and when you're better you can take over.'

She turned away but then he said, which made her pause with her hand on the doorknob, 'Georgie? Thanks.'

The day had come and gone. Where? How? It had just disappeared by the time Alessandro heard Georgie opening the door outside. He was still too knocked out to do much but half sit up and listen to Flora's excited chatter and then the lower, laughing voice as Georgie replied to whatever was being said.

For the first time in his adult life, he hadn't worked. No emails, no conference calls, no reports read or data analysed or remote meetings held.

He'd had a bath, eaten some of the breakfast Georgie had ordered for him and then spent the entire day in bed, drifting in and out of sleep, unaware of the minutes and hours passing by.

In a weird way it had been pleasurable. Now, as he heard their voices outside the room, he felt a deep sense of contentment.

His bedroom door was half open and he was looking at it when Georgie pushed it open.

'You've been out all day.' He looked at his watch and was startled at the time. 'It's nearly six-thirty!'

'Dad!' Flora ran up behind Georgie, squeezed past her and came to a screeching stop as she remembered the mantra that she should keep a bit of distance or risk getting ill on her holiday.

'Good day, little flower?'

He smiled and listened as Flora embarked on an excited description of everything they had done. The breakfast they had eaten.

'Elsa from *Frozen* was there!'

The rides they had been on. 'Magic Kingdom's *amazing*, Dad! We took a boat and saw so much stuff! And…and… and…tell Dad about that ride, Georgie! The one where you said you were scared!'

Flora's cheeks were flushed, her normally neat hair was dishevelled and she was wearing a motley assortment of colourful patterned clothes, bright cartoon-character top with flowered leggings and sparkly trainers, which was unlike the more formal designer clothing she usually wore whenever he came to collect her for days out.

This wasn't the serious little girl he would take to expensive restaurants or on expensive shopping trips.

For the first time, she could have been any other six-year-old, overexcited, hopping from foot to foot, waving her hands in a flurry of childish pleasure at the day she'd had.

And looking up to Georgie just enough for Alessandro to sense a bond being formed.

A bond he had specifically not wanted to encourage.

'Have you eaten?' he asked, and was bombarded by details of the burger she'd had in the restaurant. *I had waffles for dessert, Dad, and they were shaped like Mickey Mouse!*

'How are you feeling, Alessandro?'

Alessandro looked at Georgie and shrugged. His eyes dipped to register how comfortably Flora was holding her hand.

'I haven't moved from bed except to eat the breakfast you ordered and have that bath.'

Was he feeling sorry for himself? Surely not!

He scowled. 'Flora, darling, you must be exhausted after your long day. I expected that you would be back after lunch in accordance—' he looked at Georgie, smiling and affectionate although the affectionate smile was pointed '—with the routine we previously discussed.'

'I know.' Her voice was rueful and sympathetic. 'But sometimes routines get tossed out of the window when circumstances change. Have you taken some more tablets? What time?'

'Of course I've taken more tablets,' Alessandro said irritably. 'Time? No idea.'

He looked at her from under his lashes. If Flora was pink-cheeked and dishevelled, then so was Georgie.

They both looked overexcited.

Had he ever seen Flora like that? Certainly never when she'd been with him and no one could say that he didn't treat her to the best that money could buy, including a day out at a toy store with the promise that she could have anything she wanted.

'I'll settle Flora,' Georgie was saying now although she'd stiffened, reading his expression and correctly interpreting it. 'I can order up some more stuff for you to eat if you let me know what you'd like.'

He nodded curtly but was now wide awake and alert to her returning to his room.

He felt strangely out of sorts, as though he'd lost control of the reins of his life.

Was it because he still felt ill? Because germs that he had successfully managed to keep at bay for thirty-odd years, bar one or two childhood infections, had decided to make up for lost time?

She was forty-five minutes and by the time she pushed open the bedroom door, she'd showered and changed into some loose grey culottes that fell softly to her calves and a white vest that showed off her slim arms and small breasts.

He allowed the silence to swirl around them for a few minutes as he stared at her, eyes narrowed, restless and edgy and not knowing how to tackle those unusual feelings. Eventually he asked whether Flora was asleep.

'Out like a light. It was a big day for her. Shall I get you something from room service? Have you thought about what you'd like to eat? I might…venture down and have something in the restaurant…'

'Why are you hovering by the door? Come in. You can close it. Not fully, but I don't want Flora to wake up.'

Georgie hesitated.

She sensed the atmosphere and she knew why it was there, but was it her fault that she'd had Flora for the day? Was it her fault that she'd completely stampeded through *Rule Number One…make sure you keep a distance from my daughter*?

She took a step into the bedroom and shut the door behind her.

'I know exactly what's going through your head, Alessandro!'

'Do you? Isn't that the second time you've said something like that to me? You must have been a mind-reader in another life.'

She was relieved that he was wearing a tee shirt and that

the covers were pulled up to his waist, nicely concealing anything that might get her blood pressure soaring, but it was still suffocatingly intimate in his bedroom. This even though he'd opened the windows and pulled back the curtains so that a nice cool breeze blew through the room.

Self-righteous anger built the closer she got to the bed and she was fuming by the time she'd pulled a chair over so that she was sitting next to him.

'It's not my fault that I spent the day with Flora. I know what you said about making sure I kept my distance and, believe me, I understand completely why you said that, but what was I supposed to do? You were bedridden and you still are! Whatever bug you've picked up is probably going to take days to clear. These things can linger and if you try and get out there too soon, they just come back with a vengeance! So go right ahead and start preaching to me about those ground rules of yours, but I *still* won't have a choice because Flora's having a ball and I don't see why she should pay the price of having her fun curtailed because you don't want me taking her out!'

She looked at him with narrow-eyed, thin-lipped defiance.

Alessandro had never seen any sight so riveting. Her hair was all over the place, long and blonde and unruly, and her face was scrubbed clean of all make-up.

He had a fierce desire to reach out and touch and kiss the stubborn, pouting mouth.

What the heck was happening to him?

He ran a distracted hand over his forehead and then felt her own small hand push his away so that she could feel him.

'You still have that fever and I'm worried now. I think I'll call Reception and ask them to send up a doctor.'

'Don't be ridiculous.' He missed the feel of her cool hand when she removed it.

'I'm not being ridiculous, Alessandro! You're still in bed and I'm betting that's a one-off for you and you're not bothering to look after yourself. You can't even tell me when you last took any medication!'

'I'm not sure I took any after you left.'

'And you want to get better?' She clicked her tongue and softened. 'You're worse than some of the kids I look after when they get ill.'

She popped two tabs from the packet and handed them to him with the glass of water by the bed and watched with a bemused expression while he swallowed them.

He appeared so strong, so powerful, so *invincible* that it was disorienting to see him like this and she liked it. Why? That made no sense. But…

It was *endearing*, which wasn't something she'd thought she'd ever associate with him.

Her thoughts blurred over and she blinked away a crazy weakness to run the back of her hand across his cheek, to caress him.

'What do you want me to do tomorrow if you still can't make it out?' she asked gruffly.

'Of course I want you to take my daughter out. I…when you got back here, I could see that she'd had…a wonderful time…'

'It was an amazing day and it wasn't just Flora who had a great time. I did as well. I'm afraid I ignored your schedule of events. We just went where the urge took us. Honestly, Alessandro, you wouldn't believe what you were missing. The rides! Of course, we just went on the small ones suitable for Flora, but she's tall enough to go on bigger ones so we'll see what happens tomorrow. If, that is, you're still bedridden.'

'Have dinner with me.'

'Sorry?'

He nodded to the circular table by the window. 'I had breakfast there. Comfortable. Nice views out. We can have dinner together. You can tell me all about what you and Flora did.' He shot her a crooked smile. 'Whatever it is I have, you've either caught it already or else it's going to pass you by so sitting opposite me to eat won't alter that.'

'I'm robust. Don't you remember? The healthy outdoor life? Not cooped up behind a big, dusty ledger making lots of money?' Georgie smiled and felt something warm inside her, a feeling of kinship. 'Okay. I'll bring the menu in and we can decide.'

She walked out into the sitting room, went to check on Flora to find that she was sound asleep and, walking past the floor-to-ceiling mirror by the door that led to the wide landing outside, she paused and looked at her reflection.

She'd dressed in a hurry, had thrown on one of the outfits she had bought when he had stuck money into her account with instructions to buy suitable clothing.

At the time, she had thought about the sort of suitable clothing he had meant, going on what she had seen of the women he dated, but hadn't been able to bring herself to buy anything involving sequins, leather or prints mimicking animal skins. Too short was also out and too revealing.

Which had left her with just a few more expensive versions of the sort of stuff she usually wore.

She wasn't going to let her own insecurities worm their way into her head.

This wasn't some kind of date. In a way, you could almost say that it was a meeting of sorts, an opportunity to debrief on her day with his daughter.

Shame she didn't have a nice *debriefing outfit* like a suit. She would have felt a lot more comfortable. But she was wearing what she was wearing and it wasn't as though he was interested in her that way at all, anyway.

CHAPTER SEVEN

THEY ORDERED LOBSTER SALADS. Fresh bread. Various cheeses and biscuits and wine, although she told him firmly that alcohol of any kind wasn't recommended to someone with a cold.

'More than a cold, I think.'

'Okay, then, flu if you'd rather.'

'You need to work on your Florence Nightingale persona.' But he was smiling when he said that and, as their eyes met, Georgie felt a little ripple of awareness shimmer through her, light and feathery and reaching deep into all parts of her.

To distract herself, she glanced through the window. From where she was sitting at the little circular table, she could see the sky in all its radiant, dusky colours of pinks and purples and indigo blues reflecting on the calm waters of the lagoon.

The suite, the most expensive in the hotel, was on the very top floor of the main building and the panoramic view was extensive. Breathtaking.

When you were out and about, mingling with the crowds, the sights were almost too big to fully appreciate.

From here, the Cinderella castle was a distant silhouette, coming awake as it was lit up, and the monorail that she and Flora had ridden earlier in the day glided soundlessly by in the distance, ferrying guests through the various resorts.

She tore her gaze away and looked at Alessandro, who was reclining on the sofa, having made it out of the bed.

While she'd been checking on Flora and ordering food, he'd changed into some comfortable tracksuit bottoms and a black polo shirt and he looked stupidly handsome and not at all ill.

'Did you work at all today?' she asked curiously, swivelling the chair so that she was looking directly at him.

'No. Not at all.' He grimaced. 'I can't remember the last time I took a full day off work. I thought about opening the computer but I fell back asleep before I could do anything with that thought.'

Georgie hesitated.

'If you want me to stop asking personal questions, then tell me, but right now...'

'Look, this is a very different situation for me,' Alessandro said heavily. He looked at her with a thoughtful, assessing expression until she reddened. 'I... I'm not in the habit of discussing anything personal with women, but this isn't a relationship and never will be, so do I object to you asking me personal questions? Oddly, not as much as I would normally.'

'What do you talk about when you're with...er...those women you date? If you never discuss anything personal? How far can you go chatting about the weather and world news?'

'Am I picking up a certain amount of disapproval in your voice?' His eyebrows shot up and she reddened a shade more.

'Of course not.'

'There's a lot more to a relationship than talking,' he murmured. 'In fact, I find that the non-verbal part of a relationship is always a lot more satisfying.'

'Um!' Her mind filled up with images of Alessandro enjoying that non-verbal side of a relationship and threatened to implode from the hot, graphic nature of what she was thinking.

'Have I embarrassed you?'

'Of course not!' She laughed dismissively. 'Do I strike you as the sort who embarrasses easily?'

'Yes.'

'That shows how little you know me,' Georgie said gently. 'Which is understandable. Like you said, this *isn't a relationship* so you're really not going to know the first thing about me. Truth is, I get along really well with guys. Always have done, which is why I don't embarrass easily. You wouldn't believe the stuff they've confided in me over the years.'

'Is that so?'

'Yes!'

'What sort of things?'

'Oh…problems with girls…disappointment with being dropped from sports teams…hassle with friends…' She rolled her eyes.

'And that's a good thing? Playing agony aunt to angst-ridden immature boys? Are you agony aunt to the grown-up versions of them as well?'

'I never said they were angst-ridden or immature, and yes. It's…yes, of course it's *a good thing*. Why wouldn't it be? It's very rewarding to be empathetic. Actually, I'm not sure why we're having this conversation. Didn't you want to have dinner with me so that you could find out what Flora and I did today?'

'I'm finding this topic of conversation more interesting at the moment. Can't say I've ever met a woman who's found fulfilment in playing agony aunt to men. I, personally, can't think of anything more repulsive than pouring my heart out to a DIY agony aunt in the hope that she might come up with some hocus-pocus solution to my problems.'

Georgie's mouth tightened.

In one fell swoop he'd managed to somehow put his finger on the swirling insecurities that were embedded in her dealings with the opposite sex.

'That's not what empathy is all about,' she muttered with a surge of sour resentment. 'Listening and being sympathetic is all it takes to make someone feel better about themselves and their situation.'

'And what about the power of attraction?'

'I beg your pardon?'

'Sex. What about that?'

'I have no idea what you're talking about. I mean, *obviously*, I know what the power of attraction is all about! I'm just not sure where you're going with that…er…observation…'

'Where does animal attraction fit in with all these men you counsel? Doesn't that reduce your relationships to platonic ones? You surely can't find any man attractive when you're done mopping up his tears and giving him a pep talk about squaring up to the playground bullies?'

He grinned and Georgie wanted to smack him because he was just so damned self-assured.

Self-assured and just so *sexy*. Hair tousled, dark stubble, dark eyes glittering with amusement. Stupidly, unfairly *sexy* and the conversation, instead of turning her off, had sparked something inside her that had ratcheted up every nerve in her body.

'I like to think of myself as a nuanced person,' she told him coolly and his grin widened.

'What does that mean?'

'It means that maybe we can decide on what we're going

to eat because it's been a long day for me and I'd like to get to bed.'

'Sure.'

He shrugged but he was still grinning.

'I haven't asked...how are you feeling?'

'Decidedly better now that the tablets have kicked in and I'm having some human interaction.'

And a bit of fun, was what Georgie thought. He was a man who was accustomed to filling every second of every minute of every day with action.

He worked hard and he played hard and in between there was precious little downtime.

But, right now, ill health was in charge and he'd been forced into having some downtime and he was bored.

Hence, he was having a little fun at her expense because the devil played on idle hands.

'Food should be here in a minute,' she told him politely. 'Do you good to eat.'

'Yes, I think I've had your bracing advice about keeping my strength up by eating.'

'It's actually not my job to give you bracing advice about anything and I honestly don't care whether you eat or don't eat, but I do care that Flora would like to have your company and the longer you're cooped up in here, the less time she's going to have to spend with you.'

In receipt of this flatly delivered snub, Alessandro looked at her with a guarded expression.

He should have been turned off. Actually, he should have been livid. He was neither. He was intrigued.

Was that because this relationship was very different from anything he'd ever had with a woman before? Not exactly an employee but definitely not a love interest.

Was it the utter novelty aspect of her that made him want to get under her skin? Was she someone who had come along without warning, like a creature from another planet, managing to rouse the curiosity of his jaded palate because she was everything he wasn't used to?

He could appreciate her without feeling the threat of someone who might want more than he was prepared to give. He could talk to her without thinking that any confidence shared would be stored and used against him at a later date.

He enjoyed the thought of getting inside her head, finding out a bit more about her for the duration of their time here.

He liked the way she blushed and looked discomfited by the tiniest foray into her personal life when, compared to him, she was as pure as the driven snow and as transparent as an open book.

Everything about her intrigued him and if he felt a feathery whisper of alarm at this, he swept it aside before it could even begin to register. He was the master of self-control and he was unshaken in his belief that no one could get past his defences if he didn't allow them to.

There was a buzz at the door and he watched as she scuttled off to open it. She was so much at pains *not* to look at him as the food was brought in and the table laid with so much pomp and ceremony that he wanted to burst out laughing.

'Shall I tell you what Flora and I got up to today?'

Georgie finally looked at him as they both sat at the table, which had been set to Michelin standards.

'I would very much like to hear.'

She told him. In detail. It was called time filling and a welcome distraction from his amused, scorching dark gaze on her.

She ate and got lost in the retelling of the day.

'Hence why I'm so tired,' she finished, after her barely interrupted monologue.

'Sounds like you both had a lot of fun.'

'What do you do with her when you…take her out? Can I ask?'

'What do we do?'

'Where do you go? I guess you have houses all over the place? Do you do lots of travelling between them with her? I mean, during the school holidays.'

'I…' Alessandro frowned. 'It's been haphazard. And time isn't always my friend when it comes to completely relaxing.'

'I have no idea what that means.'

He pushed his plate to one side. He'd eaten but not much. Now he stared at her, giving her question consideration.

'It means it's been a game of chance trying to pin my ex-wife down to honouring dates that have been set in advance and when I have had Flora…no… I haven't travelled with her.'

'That's a shame. Does she get to see your mother often? My parents can't wait to be grandparents. If my mum could knit, she would have already started. She's shameless.'

'I don't…no… I don't see my mother as much as I'd like. She lives in Italy now. First thing I did after I made my first million was to set her up close to family there. I try and get her across at least twice a year but it's always a matter of fitting it in. Time has a habit of taking over and suddenly you find you're in deficit.'

'I'm not making you uncomfortable, am I?' she queried innocently. 'With all my personal questions?'

'I'm a big boy. I can take it in my stride. You're a big girl. You can take it in your stride when I ask you a few of my own. Can't you? You don't feel uncomfortable, do you?' His lips twitched with sudden amusement.

Georgie ignored that. 'If you really want to do something,

you make the time. It's easy to just put stuff off and then say, afterwards, that you were too busy. That's just lame.'

For a second, Alessandro felt his hackles rise and then wryly realised that he had become so accustomed to other people never disagreeing with him that he wasn't exactly sure how to react to her honesty.

The taboo thrill of the unknown was nudging something in him he hadn't felt in a very long time.

Ever since his hungry days, when life had still held risk and adventure and the possibility of failure.

'Lame? Tell me you're not calling me *lame*...' But his eyes roved over her face, lowered to gauge the small, delicate bump of her breasts, and he wondered what they would feel like in the palm of his hands, wondered what her nipples would taste like and how she'd respond. 'Let's retreat to the sofa, Georgie. I'm finished with this food. Are you?'

'Such a shame that there's food going to waste but I'm stuffed. Alessandro... I should really be hitting the sack now.'

'Why?'

'Because...'

'Not enjoying our conversation?' The murmured question hung in the air between them and he could see, in that fraction of a hesitating second, that, like him, she was conscious of that *sizzle of something electrifying and inexplicable that neither of them could put a finger on.*

'Have a coffee with me,' he urged, standing up and moving towards the sofa. 'Make a feeble, lame old man happy.'

Was he flirting with her?

Georgie's pulses began to race. He couldn't be. Could he?

He shot her a look over his shoulder and half smiled and her mouth went dry.

'I suppose…there's no harm…'

'But only if you promise not to play the agony aunt.'

'Are you sure you shouldn't be retiring to bed, Alessandro?'

'I feel passable now that the tablets have kicked in. Once they start wearing off, I'll be a good patient and tuck myself under the covers and try and get some sleep.'

'Okay…' She hovered. This was certainly not like being *one of the lads*. But then what was it? He wasn't interested in her as a woman. He'd made a point of telling her that she shouldn't start thinking that what they had was real, because it wasn't.

So, what was he doing?

Was she imagining something exciting and sexual and unspoken going on between them? Maybe her lack of experience with the opposite sex had made her gullible when it came to reading signals that weren't there.

She remembered the thought that had occurred to her earlier.

Sexy guy…nothing to do…bored and not averse to a little fun…and here she was, the perfect naïve target, nothing like those experienced glamour pusses he dated who would have known just how to handle the situation.

'I take my coffee black.' He jolted her out of her frantic reverie and she blinked and focused. 'No sugar.'

'Okay.'

'And then you can do the talking.' He patted the space next to him on the sofa. 'I have a sore throat.'

'You should really see a doctor, Alessandro.'

'My masculine pride couldn't handle it.'

But he was smiling with his eyes half closed, sprawled on the sofa, his long legs extended and lightly crossed at the ankles, his fingers linked loosely together on his stomach.

A big, powerful predator temporarily at rest was what she was thinking as she made them both a cup of coffee and then, as an afterthought and because she hated waste, a plate with some cheese and biscuits on it.

He smiled when he saw that.

'I can't bear to think of these lovely home-made biscuits being chucked out.' She flushed and sat where he had patted, except not quite as close as he'd indicated. She stuck the plate with the cheese and biscuits between them like a physical barrier.

'You're so different, Georgie. Tell me why you are the way you are.'

'Again, you're talking in riddles.'

'You don't seem to have a lot of guile. I know that you're still young but you seem so innocent. I like that.'

'You like it because it's different,' Georgie pointed out with prosaic honesty. 'If you were surrounded with lots of women like me, you'd soon be bored and desperate to meet someone like your...er...'

'Like my ex-wife?'

'I don't know what she's like so I can't say anything about her and, anyway, I'm not interested.'

'Not curious at all?'

'No.' She gulped a mouthful of hot coffee and swallowed it down.

'I don't believe you, because I'm curious about you.'

'And because you're curious about me, you think that it's inevitable that I'm likewise curious about you?'

'You're good at getting to the heart of the matter.'

'Well, that's very egotistical. Besides... I thought...that wasn't allowed,' Georgie said breathlessly. 'Curiosity...'

'I know. It wasn't but I didn't expect to find myself bedridden on day one.'

'I don't know what that has to do with anything.'

'I'm usually always in control, but this time I don't have control over whatever germs are having fun inside me so maybe I'm not thinking as logically as I normally would be. Hence, I'm curious and you're curious too. Tell me why you were never tempted to follow the sister who went into medicine. Isn't that along the same lines as teaching? Both in the caring profession but with one being a little more up close and personal with the human body?'

Georgie blushed.

Dyslexia was the thing she rarely discussed even though, logically, she knew that that was silly because it was so widely recognised as a diagnosed disability.

If she had to declare it, as had been the case during her work career, then she did, but it was mostly something she kept to herself.

Was it because, for those years before she was diagnosed, she had become accustomed to feeling a little second best?

Had a certain amount of insecurity around it become in-grained in her psyche? Making her think that to admit to it would be opening herself up to pity?

If that was the case, then it defied logic because no one in her family had ever made her feel inferior in any way, but then emotions sometimes bypassed logic.

'I've always been more of an outdoorsy type,' she said vaguely. 'As a kid I couldn't sit still long enough to do well enough to get all the exam results that would have qualified me to do something serious with my life. I found my level. It may not be as important as what my sisters do but—'

'Don't say that,' Alessandro interrupted sharply.

'What? Don't say what?'

'What you do is incredibly important and incredibly serious. I've never seen Flora so engaged as when she got back here with you, so what you do? Incredibly important.'

'Oh. Okay. Well. Thanks.' She went bright red.

'And…you shouldn't put yourself down.'

'I didn't think that was what I was doing. Anyway, it's okay for you to preach about that. I bet you were born knowing you could conquer the world. I bet your first words were "I'm going to be a billionaire".'

Alessandro looked at her in silence for a few seconds. She was tentatively sipping her coffee and looking at him over the rim of her cup, her huge brown eyes mildly inquisitive, mildly teasing.

It felt good being here, having this conversation. He realised just how little he confided in anyone. His mother, perhaps, was the only person in whom he trusted that whatever he said would remain private.

Climbing ladders and reaching the pinnacle of success brought a lot of things but it also took away a lot of things.

Trust was the first thing to go, although in fairness he'd probably dumped that when he was old enough to realise how dangerous it was.

If you couldn't trust your own flesh and blood not to walk away from you when you were a baby, then who could you ever really trust without the promise of pain just round the corner?

Confiding in someone…also a thing of the past if it had ever been there.

He hadn't even done that with his ex-wife.

He could buy whatever he wanted but right here, right now…this *moment in time* felt priceless.

'Yes, you read me so well. Those were my first words.' He grinned. 'Seriously, though,' he mused, 'if you don't have utter confidence in yourself, chances are you'll never fulfil your potential and believe me when I tell you, I was always going to make sure that I fulfilled mine. Settling for mediocrity was never on the cards.'

'Very driven.'

'A lot of women find that sexy…'

He shot her a slow smile and kept his eyes fixed on her reddening face.

'Not me,' Georgie said unsteadily.

Alessandro lowered his eyes. He didn't understand where that provocative remark had come from but there had been something in the atmosphere, something in their loose, semi-intimate conversation that had stirred his libido, had made him think of sex. *And not for the first time…definitely not because he was bored because he had felt it, an odd pull of attraction, the minute he'd set eyes on her. So perplexing when she was nothing like the women he dated, when she was so careless with his boundaries, so comfortable telling him exactly what she thought, whether he wanted to hear it or not.*

And her quick denial?

Very telling because he hadn't believed a word of it.

He wasn't interested in making a complicated situation even more complicated. He would follow her lead and relegate that brief, disturbing frisson between them to the bin.

Made sense.

He gritted his teeth as he battled with his suddenly lively libido and took a few deep breaths.

She wasn't even his type! He'd never gone for slender girls who asked too many questions and ignored his *keep out* signs.

Weird how sexy Georgie was…no make-up…hair everywhere…boyish figure when he usually went for the voluptuous ones…

She beamed at him and Alessandro instantly had to steady himself because it lit up all of her face and knocked him for six.

'I... I should get to bed now, Alessandro.' Georgie stood up and, as she did so, he reached out to circle her slim wrist with his hand.

'Don't think I don't appreciate you being here,' he said with rough sincerity. 'I do.'

Georgie stared at him, mouth parted. She registered his eyes as they dropped to her mouth and lingered there for a few heart-stopping seconds.

The atmosphere thickened and she drew in a sharp breath as he rose to his feet to tower over her.

'Well, thank you very much.' She half laughed but her skin was burning where his fingers touched it. 'A prison sentence is a surefire way of getting a girl to do what you want...'

'You were never facing a prison sentence.'

This was a dangerous place. The ground was giving way under her feet and the curiosity she had backed away from had morphed into something darker and more powerful, a mad, incomprehensible hunger to touch that wasn't like anything she'd ever felt before.

Her eyes widened when he released her but only to stroke her cheek with the back of his hand.

'Alessandro...'

Just for a few electric seconds, she felt that he was going to kiss her and she wanted that so badly that it was terrifying.

He stepped back abruptly and dropped his hand.

'Georgie...' He raked his fingers through his hair and seemed as shocked as she was by what was happening, *had just happened*. 'Think it might be time to reclaim the bed.'

'Yes! You *should get some rest*! You've already been up for way too long! Wouldn't want to set back the healing process! I'll get rid of this stuff! Stick it outside the door so that it can be collected in the morning!' She sounded hysterical.

'Good idea.'

He remained where he was, looking down at her, and she could feel his eyes boring through her as she began stacking stuff.

Her cheeks were burning and she didn't glance his way as she began ferrying the dishes from the table to the trolley, which the waiter had wheeled outside.

'Right!'

Job done, she finally looked at him, making sure to keep some healthy distance between them.

Alessandro tilted his head to one side and debated saying something.

He'd touched her. He'd touched in a way that was clearly sexual and nothing to do with a gesture of thanks for the day she'd spent with his daughter.

He'd brushed her cheek with his hand, which was the least physical thing he could have done and yet it had felt impossibly erotic and very intimate and now she was flustered and could barely look him in the face.

'Tomorrow,' was all he could say.

'Yes! Tomorrow!'

'Hopefully I'll be back on my feet.'

'That would be good!'

'But should I wake up feeling the way I did this morning...'

'Understood!'

'What are you understanding?'

'That I'll repeat the routine tomorrow. Flora and I will

have our little adventures and then get back here in time for her to fall into bed. That's fine. I'm enjoying it!'

Somewhere, in the dim recesses where a bit of common sense still held sway, something clicked and he said, perfunctorily, 'Just so long as you're not enjoying it too much.'

'Don't worry.' Georgie got the message immediately. 'I'm not.'

'Good. And about what just happened between us.'

'Nothing happened between us.'

'Actually—'

'I don't want to talk about it. Nothing happened.'

'I touched you in a way that was unacceptable and for that you have my apologies.'

'Why do you think it was unacceptable?'

It was out.

Georgie was so appalled that she covered her mouth with her hand and her eyes widened as the implications of what she had said settled between them in the thick silence.

'What I'm *saying*…' she continued into the lengthening silence, 'is that I know the rules so you don't need to remind me by harping on about what…actually *didn't happen*, just then.'

'Right.'

'Actually, you have nothing to fear from me. I had a very bad experience with a guy at my last posting at Val d'Isère. Enough to have warned me off a certain type of man.'

'And I belong in that category?'

She heard outrage in his voice. For the guy who'd hauled himself up the ladder, starting from nothing, the thought of being lumped in a category with other mere mortals was obviously not to his liking.

'I'm afraid so.'

'What did the guy do to you?'

'He didn't have the sort of moral compass I'm interested in seeing in a guy.'

'You caught him cheating.'

Georgie shrugged.

'I can assure you that I have never cheated on any woman in my life before,' Alessandro said coldly.

'I don't know how we got to this point and I'm not saying that you're anything like Hans. I suppose…' Honesty drove her to qualify what she had said even though it felt as if the hole she was digging was getting deeper with every passing word.

'I'm listening.'

'I could never be tempted by any guy who wasn't serious when it comes to relationships.' She thought back to Hans and realised that the most hurtful thing about that kiss under the mistletoe she'd seen was the fact that he'd found it a bit of a laugh.

'What about fun?'

'Fun, for me, is serious. Serious fun. Anyway. You should get some sleep. Should I wake you in the morning or will you come out if you're up to it? Flora would be thrilled if you could make it out.'

'I'll see.'

His dark eyes were still on her flushed face but then he lowered them, which was the signal for her to go.

Everything she'd said to him made perfect sense and yet something about the man drew her like a magnet.

Which meant that she had to be careful around him. He made her want to swoon, but swooning was out. Lustful thoughts were out. Encouraging heart-to-hearts also out.

He would be back on his feet in no time at all and she would keep her distance by reminding herself and him why they were there, and it wasn't about them, it was about his daughter. Involve him in everything...force him to throw himself into the thick of it and she would be able to take a step back and put things into perspective.

She would keep it light and stick to the brief.

It would do her good, anyway, to see him shorn of all that crazy self-confidence that was so sexy. Great big guys sitting on a mechanical horse on a merry-go-round could never be sexy.

Plus, once he was up and running, she would make sure that he spent every available minute with Flora, which would give her plenty of opportunities to sneak off on her own.

Downtime away from the man would also put things in perspective.

'Serious fun,' he murmured with amusement and Georgie made sure to keep her voice polite and her eyes safely focused on the picture hanging on the wall behind him. Amused dark eyes could do a lot to her nervous system, too much. 'I don't think I've ever come across that concept.'

'That's right. Serious fun. Romance. Love. Courtship and a marriage proposal followed by children in very quick succession. After Hans, that's all that could ever work for me.'

She folded her arms and raised her eyebrows, challenging him to continue the conversation. She had plenty more descriptions up her sleeve when it came to her perfect guy and she was pretty sure they would all be anathema to the commitment-phobe staring at her with that annoying half-smile still on his face.

'On that note,' he said with a grin, utterly unfazed, 'I'll go get some beauty sleep.'

And with a brief nod and a mocking little salute, off he disappeared into his bedroom, shutting the door firmly behind him.

CHAPTER EIGHT

'DAD! DAD! Look at this! Look!'

Alessandro looked. Flora had run off to a touch-sensitive screen and was *pretend wiping away* golden, dripping honey on the screen to reveal characters from *Winnie the Pooh*.

It was hot. The queue snaked pleasantly through an attractively designed wooded area with rustic wooden fences and storybook signposts and lots of honeypots and barrels everywhere.

'Don't fast-track to the rides even though you can,' Georgie had warned him two days previously, when he'd surfaced from whatever bug had kept him bedbound for two days. 'The best bit is walking in the sun enjoying the sights.'

He'd acquiesced with good humour.

Things had changed between them. She was determined not to confront that fact and the more she'd stuck out her chin, daring him to push past her barriers, the more temptation had beckoned.

The temptation to knock down every single barrier and do what he'd wanted to do, do what *she* wanted to do as well, if she could allow herself to relax and accept that.

She would.

If the sexual tension between them was getting to him, then it was getting to her. Alessandro knew women. He might not have delved deep into their psyches in an attempt to analyse what they thought, but he knew their sexual responses to him with instinct born from experience.

She might *say* that what she wanted was her *serious fun, whatever the hell that was* but her sidelong glances and the tremble of her body when he was near her told a different story.

'Magical, Flora.' He went to stoop next to her and obligingly swiped the screen.

'I know! Shall we go and see Rabbit's Garden?' She was hopping from one foot to the other, pointing to a patch of giant vegetables.

There were kids everywhere. Ice creams were being eaten, babies were dozing in pushchairs and parents were laughing. Alessandro laughed.

'I think we should stick to the queue,' he advised gravely. 'We don't want to lose our place.'

'No.' Flora looked wistfully at a batch of oversized fake carrots. 'Dad.' She slipped her hand into his and looked at him seriously. 'Can we live here?'

Alessandro stifled a laugh. 'I don't think that would work out.'

'Okay, but then can we stay longer? *Please? Please, please, please?*'

Alessandro met his daughter's dark eyes and his heart flipped over. She'd been like a normal little six-year-old girl for the past few days and now he could see how much of a contrast that habitual seriousness he had got accustomed to really was.

For a second now, the worry was back as she chewed her lip and gazed at him with huge, imploring eyes.

The line was moving but they weren't in it.

Georgie would be moving with the line. They'd find their place but for the minute…

'That's not going to be possible,' he said quietly. 'But, Flora, things have changed. Daddy's going to be seeing you regularly now and you'll get to do whatever you want when we're together. Have fun. Who knows? We may even come back here.'

'But can I come and live with you? Mummy's no fun.'

'I'm going to make sure that she's a lot more fun now, darling. You wait and see.' He stood up and swept her into his arms and held her still for a few seconds before depositing her on the ground and then leading her to where Georgie had made progress in the queue.

Bitterness and regret left a sour taste in his mouth.

He'd placed so much emphasis on the importance of a mother figure, because his own mother was so important to him, that for too long he'd chosen to overlook the very simple fact that his daughter had not been having a good time with Sophia.

She'd been left too much with nannies. She hadn't been *mistreated* in any way. She'd just been left to her own devices and that had shaped her personality, had made her cautious and self-contained. Sophia, self-absorbed, vengeful and narcissistic, had been an inconsistent and indifferent parent. Nothing at all like his own mother.

He'd been a damn fool.

Things would change and not a minute too soon.

He looked at Georgie, who had spotted them and was smiling, and he felt such a powerful tug of intense attraction that he sucked in a sharp breath.

He watched the way Flora detached from him and skipped over to her, slipping her hand into Georgie's as though that was its natural default position, turning to look up at her as she laughed and chatted about something or other.

'Ready for this ride?' Georgie smiled as soon as he was

standing by her. 'We'll be in a honeypot. Have you ridden in any of those before? Might not be the same as your private jet. Think you can handle it?'

Alessandro met her eyes.

She was cheerful and friendly when Flora was around, but the minute there wasn't a six-year-old chaperone, her guard was back in place, keeping him at a distance.

He didn't want to be kept at a distance any longer.

They had a few days left here and he knew, *with complete certainty*, that if they walked away from one another without acknowledging this powerful sexual connection between them then he would regret it and so would she.

Whether she was aware of that or not.

He wanted her. He was sick of pretending that there was nothing going on between them when they both knew that there was. He wanted her in a way that felt different from any other *wanting* he'd felt for any woman in his life before.

He held her gaze for a fraction too long and noted the slow tide of pink that coloured her cheeks.

'I can handle everything,' he assured her. 'And that includes honeypots.'

'Really? But not germs.' She smirked from under her lashes. 'Because, and I hate to point this out, I didn't catch whatever you had.'

Alessandro burst out laughing. He looked at her over Flora's head.

'You make me laugh,' he murmured, leaning into her so that he was whispering into her ear. 'I like that. You go where no woman has ever gone before.'

Alessandro felt the soft tremor that ran through her and half smiled with satisfaction. He'd wanted zero complications.

Sex equated to complications times a thousand.

But he couldn't get her out of his head. Being in the same space as her was a constant tug of war between temptation and willpower.

Self-denial had moved quickly from *compulsory* to *open to debate*.

They were both adults. They wanted one another. Things didn't always have to lead down the aisle. He was sure he could convince her of that because he *felt* her response to him when he got close to her.

She couldn't control it. That was called lust, not love, and why shouldn't she see the wisdom of giving in to it?

Georgie heard those amused, softly spoken words and shivered. She was trying her best but it was agony being in the same space as Alessandro.

She saw the way he sometimes looked at her, as if waiting for her to do the inevitable and succumb, like a cat waiting for a skittering mouse to come to a standstill and admit defeat.

If only she had the right defence mechanisms!

'Really? I go where *no woman has gone before*?' she said when nothing witty sprang to mind. 'I'm afraid I don't believe that.'

She gazed down at Flora's dark, bobbing head but was keenly aware of her father gazing across at *her*.

'Tell me about the guy who broke your heart.'

The question was lobbed at her out of the blue and her eyes opened wide as she looked at him.

He laughed.

'I thought that would get your attention,' he said wryly. 'You've spent the past couple of days pretending I don't exist.'

'You sound like a spoiled kid when you say that.'

'We need to talk.'

'No, we don't. Least of all here! Look. We're at the end of the queue. We'll be on the next batch of rides! Flora! Ready to go on a trip around the Hundred Acre Wood?'

'You can run...' Alessandro's voice was amused as he leant to place a hand in the small of her back, drawing her closer to him while between them Flora positively vibrated with excitement '...but you can't hide. We'll talk later, when we're not surrounded by thousands of people.'

'You can't make me have a conversation I don't want to have,' Georgie hissed back. 'That's not part of my job description.'

'I didn't think there *was* a specific job description,' he mused as people began stepping out of the mobile honeypots, making their way towards the exit, leaving room for the ride to be filled with another tide of eager kids and weary parents, 'but if there *was*, then I'd say we've played fast and loose with it from the minute we got here. So... once we're back at the hotel, no scurrying off or escaping outside like you did yesterday evening. Dinner with me and we can...see where the conversation takes us. Deal?'

'Alessandro...' Georgie looked at him helplessly as Flora began stepping into the honeypot.

Did she want to have a conversation with him? She couldn't think of much else she'd rather do less but how could she refuse?

If she kicked up a fuss about *talking to him on his own*, then who knew where his thoughts would turn, what deductions he would make?

If she was unaffected by him then why would she run away from discussing the stupid little nonsense that had happened between them, which had now grown out of all proportion because she'd made such a big deal of it?

'Okay. I guess so.'

'Splendid! I must say I've missed our cosy little chats.'

'That's something else I don't believe,' Georgie scoffed, letting him help her into her seat and gazing at him as he climbed in after her, rocking the honeypot because he was so big. God, she had to tear her eyes away.

'I'm hurt.'

He was grinning and relaxed as he stretched his arm out behind her on the back of the seat.

'But I'm sure I'll feel much better once we're back on even ground and you're not trying to avoid me.'

Georgie glowered but her cheeks were pink. She barely noticed the ride. She paid next to no attention to their Under the Sea adventure from *The Little Mermaid*. They ate hot dogs for lunch from one of the many stands, milling about with the crowds in the sunshine, like any normal family of three.

Which they weren't.

She would normally have relished the foot-long hot dog but all she could think of was having dinner with Alessandro, not knowing what he would say, not knowing how she would react.

It was a full day.

No dinner for Flora, who had done sterling work with her hot dog and was full.

They took it easy after lunch, strolling through the park, people-watching and then heading to one of the resort beaches, where they enjoyed looking at the boats bobbing in the water while having pineapple whips.

They ended up on the monorail back to the hotel, by which time Flora was dead on her feet.

'But I'm not tired,' she half heartedly protested, stifling a wide yawn.

'Said the very tired little girl, stumbling around on very tired little legs,' Georgie teased, reaching for her hand and volunteering bedtime duties with a sideways look at Alessandro.

He looked even more sexily bronzed after time in the sun. He was wearing a white polo shirt and a pair of cream chinos. He could have stepped straight off the cover of a men's magazine.

He had changed and was waiting for her when, an hour later, she emerged from her rooms, showered and changed and dreading whatever conversation was brewing. Or was *dread* the right word? She wished it were but *excited* felt disturbingly closer to the mark.

The relaxed, amused look on his face didn't help. He handed her a glass of wine and for a few minutes they recapped the day.

'So, spit it out,' Georgie said, cutting to the chase and building some Dutch courage by drinking her wine very quickly and then accepting a top-up.

'Georgie, don't look so apprehensive. I know you want to bury what happened between us—'

'Nothing *did* happen between us!'

'Absolutely nothing happened between us,' Alessandro agreed, relaxing back in the chair and gazing at her mulish expression and lowered eyes.

'So there's nothing to talk about.'

'There's everything to talk about because the *nothing* that happened opened a door to the *something* that should have.'

'No!'

It's not a crime for us to admit that we're attracted to one another.'

'I... I...'

'Are you going to deny it?'

'It *doesn't matter*! It *doesn't matter*, if there's some inexplicable...*you know what I mean.*'

'Can't bring yourself to say it? Shall I help you? *Chemistry? Powerful attraction? Sizzling, suffocating electric charge...?*'

She'd sat on the sofa while he'd taken a chair but now he stood up, slowly and with the sort of economic grace that made him so compelling, and went to sit right next to her.

'Tell me, Georgie,' he said huskily. 'Tell me it doesn't matter when you can reach out and touch me and know that I'll touch you back. Wherever you want me to touch you.'

'Don't.'

She covered her ears with her hands and he very gently removed them and kept them loosely in his. He looked at her seriously.

'Did he break your heart that much that you can't move on, Georgie? Are you going to let him determine the rest of your life?'

'I'm not doing that!'

'Aren't you?'

'You should talk,' she flung at him. 'Aren't you guilty of doing the very same thing?'

'My heart was never broken by my ex-wife,' Alessandro returned kindly. 'My heart was broken long before that, but it didn't set me on a path of pursuing some impossible dream where love conquers all. I realised that the only thing that conquers everything is discipline and self-control.'

'With the exception of Flora,' Georgie said softly and her heart did a little flip as his expression softened.

'She's everything,' Alessandro admitted. 'And, of course, my mother, but when it comes to romance? Love? I don't have the same faith in that as you seem to. I prefer the option of living for today and enjoying what's here without muddying the water by projecting into some time in a distant future and what might or might not work then.'

'I don't project into the future.'

'Of course you do. Isn't that what you're doing now? Writing off this unexpected attraction between us because it doesn't fit into your theory of what should happen next in your life with a man? Because you were hurt once and so the best bet is to batten down the hatches and only allow Mr Right in?'

'That's not what I'm doing...' *Yes, it was, but how could she trust her heart not to be hurt again? She'd spent so long hiding behind an act of being the party girl who didn't care that boys didn't look at her in that way, but she had cared and now this guy...a heartbreaker who didn't even believe in love...!*

'Are you prepared to see your youth disappear in an eternal quest for a guy who might or might not exist? Or worse, for a guy who might end up being a clone of the one who hurt you? There's a reason why so many marriages end in divorce. Nine times out of ten, Mr Right turns out to be Mr Completely and Utterly Wrong.'

'You're so cynical.'

'I'm a realist and I'm not scared to admit that I want to sleep with you. I can't promise love. To be more precise, love is the one thing I *can categorically not promise*. But sex? I'll show you the meaning of fun. Up for the challenge, Georgie, or will you scuttle away in mortal terror? I'll only ask once...'

Georgie had such a vivid picture of Alessandro, naked next to her, his body so deeply burnished next to her pale one, that she wanted to pass out.

'You're tempted...'

Was he right? What was wrong with a bit of fun? She knew the stakes. She wouldn't be hurt...

'I'm really not that kind of girl,' she protested half-heartedly.

In that moment, Alessandro knew that he'd won. She wanted him. The soft yielding in her voice was an aphrodisiac that sent his body into hot overdrive.

'I know you're not,' he said roughly. 'Come to bed with me.' He stood up, glanced towards the adjoining door where Flora was fast asleep. He held out his hand and stifled a groan of anticipated pleasure when she slipped her small hand into his.

'I don't know how long I've been thinking about this... thinking about *you*.' He shut the bedroom door behind them, locked it just in case, moved to close the curtains so that the room was suddenly plunged into shadows and darkness. He switched on the light by the bed and looked at her. 'Don't be nervous.'

'I've seen those pictures of you...catwalk models draped all over you...' But, nerves or not, she'd crept to the bed and sat, drawing her knees up to her chest and wrapping her arms around them to stare at him.

'I've never been this turned on in my life before.'

He began undressing and Georgie looked at him in open fascination.

He'd been thinking about this? If he could get inside her rebellious head, he'd find that she'd been thinking about it for an equally long time. Maybe since he'd first surprised her in his house and she'd looked at him as though she'd never seen a man in her life before.

He was half naked now and her heart was beating madly.

Broad shoulders, sprinkling of hair in all the right places, a bronzed and hard and unapologetically masculine body.

This was a guy with zero feminine streak.

He was watching her, watching him, and as he stepped out of his trousers, it was obvious from the impressive bulge in his boxers that he was as turned on by her as she was by him.

For the first time Georgie knew what it felt like to be truly desired by a man who had eyes only for her and it was liberating.

She knelt on the bed and waged war with her top, finally pulling it off, and then she reached behind to unclasp the something-and-nothing bra she really didn't even have to wear because there was so little to put inside.

The air-conditioning was on and the cold made her nipples stiffen.

'Carry on,' Alessandro murmured, strolling to stand by the side of the bed in just his black boxers, low-slung enough for her to see the line of hair that arrowed down from his belly button. 'Don't let me stop you. I'm already loving what I'm seeing.'

He reached inside the boxers and held himself, stroking and looking at her and, honestly, it was the most erotic thing she'd ever experienced in her whole life.

He hoisted her so that he could tug down the culottes, leaving her in some prim white cotton underwear, which couldn't have been sexier. Georgie was as nervous as a kitten and yet the excitement of this once-in-a-lifetime desire was beating inside her like a drum.

When their eyes met and held, when he lowered his head to trail his tongue against her neck…she wasn't nervous any longer. She felt free.

She leant back with a low moan and wrapped her arms around his neck and pulled him against her so that they toppled back.

She traced the ridge of his spine with her fingers and luxuriated in his muscled shoulders, the hard bulge of his biceps and then the firmness of his narrow waist.

'How are you so *fit*?' she murmured. 'I haven't seen you use the gym once since we've been here. Do you work out?'

'All the time. It's an addiction.'

'Really?'

'No. I never work out. I ski when I can, run when I can and box when I can but I usually can't. Time is money. Touch me…right…*there*… That feels so good…'

Georgie propelled him back and then she devoted herself to touching what she'd wanted to touch for ages.

She showered his neck with kisses, flicked her tongue over his shoulder blades and then over the flat brown nipples, which elicited a groan of pleasure from him.

She revelled in his body. She played with him, teasing his foreskin slowly until he covered her hand with his, tightly, stopping her because he was on the verge of losing it.

'But I'd like to see you lose it,' she whispered on a husky laugh as he flipped her over so that he was now in the driver's seat.

'Why?'

He didn't give her time to answer. Instead, he pinned her hands above her head and reared up to look down at her with an appreciative smile.

'The more I see, the more I like.' He explored her body inch by gradual inch.

He started with her shoulders, which were slender but sinewy from all the sport she played and the outdoor life she lived. When he circled her rosy nipples with his fingers, ending on the stiffened bud at the centre of each, she sucked in a deep breath and closed her eyes.

Her responses were so open, so transparent and so un-disguised and every small utterance ratcheted up his libido until he had to clear his head for seconds at a time or risk rushing into needing to be satisfied immediately.

He licked and nibbled his way down her body, starting with her breasts and devoting attention to them. He could cover one completely in the palm of his hand and he loved the way she moved and squirmed when he did that.

She was so slight that he felt like a giant lying in bed with her. Her stomach was firm and flat and when he held her waist he could feel the slight jut of her hip bones.

'You're like a doll.' He looked up at her and she stared down at him and smiled.

'I used to be so envious of my sisters. They're all boobs and legs and dark hair.'

'Trust me, envy shouldn't be in your repertoire.'

He returned to what he was doing, dipped his tongue into the tiny indent of her belly button and she sighed and sifted his hair through her fingers.

He was desperate to go slow but he'd never been so turned on in his life before.

He took his time with the sweetly prim cotton knickers. He placed his hand over the crotch, felt the wetness against his palm and groaned. Then he slid his hand underneath and stroked her until neither of them could take it any longer, at which point he pulled off the underwear and tossed it over his shoulder.

He almost came at the first sweet taste of the nectar between her legs. He flicked his tongue along the groove sheathing her clitoris and then took his time getting to the throbbing bud.

Her groan was low and guttural when he began to tease it with the tip of his tongue and she began to move against his mouth, pushing herself against him, urging him to do more than just tease, wanting to orgasm because holding off was agony.

He did. He wanted to feel her come against his mouth, wanted to be at the very heart of the moment of absolute yielding and vulnerability.

He had to fumble around for protection. It was in his wallet, which was somewhere in the bedroom. He groaned at the thought of having to break the connection between them, which was hot and intense, and in the end he didn't have to because his wallet was on the table by the bed, although his hands weren't as steady as they usually were when he ripped it open.

He thrust into her, a deep, plunging thrust, and the tightness of her around him was exquisite.

Her body arched and then relaxed as they moved as one, finding a steady rhythm and then syncing as though they had been put on earth to find one another and do just what they were doing now.

Alessandro came with explosive, mind-blowing satisfaction, satisfaction that settled in the pit of his stomach, making him languorous and deeply, pleasurably content.

He swivelled so that they were facing one another, their bodies knitted together, and gently stroked her hair from her face.

'I'm sorry, *cara*...'

'For what?'

'For rushing, but I couldn't help myself.' He slid his hand over her thigh. 'But no rush this time... Now, where was I before I rudely hastened proceedings?'

Georgie sighed with pleasure. Her body had never felt so alive, so complete, and the fact that he hadn't rolled over and called it a day because he had satisfied himself felt like a timeless gift of absolute thoughtfulness.

True to his word, he took his time.

He followed the slow stirrings of her body as it came to life all over again. He teased her nipples with his tongue, which drove her insane. He guided her hand to touch him, told her what felt good, asked *her* what felt good.

He was a lover who considered his woman and she felt as if, in this moment, there were no one else in the world but the two of them and their languorous touching of one another.

His arms were solid with muscle under her fingers. She stroked him and opened her legs so that he could cup between them as he settled to rouse her with tiny nibbles on her neck.

They built each other up and, this time, the tempo between them was in perfect rhythm when they came, bodies fusing into one. Her short nails dug into his back as a shudder ripped through her and she arched against him.

'I enjoyed that,' he murmured huskily.

'Ditto,' Georgie agreed drowsily.

'Would you believe that normally after making love the first thing I want to do is hit the bathroom, get dressed and see what work I have to get through? But look at me now. Talking.'

'Just look at you.' Georgie slid her fingers through his hair and cupped his beautiful face. 'Why would you want to skip the bit where you lie in bed gazing into your lover's eyes and whisper sweet nothings?'

She was teasing but suddenly there was a sharp pang for something she really wanted that felt impossibly out of reach.

She smiled to clear her head. 'No, don't answer that, you're not a *sweet nothings* kind of person.'

'Never have been.'

'I understand.'

'Do you?'

'You grew up to be so independent that sometimes it becomes impossible to do anything but pull away in moments of intimacy.'

Alessandro grinned and raised his eyebrows and kissed the tip of her nose.

This would be over in a matter of days, at the end of which reality would await and he would return to it refreshed, recharged and with a closer and more relaxed relationship with his daughter.

'What pearls of wisdom,' he murmured.

'Passing observation.' Georgie shrugged and nestled against him. 'Feel free to ignore because, like you've said, this is just a bit of fun.'

Alessandro realised that he loathed having his words thrown back at him.

'Never a truer word spoken,' he agreed silkily but, even in the intimacy of what they were sharing, there was a sudden cool remoteness in his voice and Georgie could instantly recognise the sound of someone backing away.

She immediately changed the subject. Just in case the lines were getting blurry, he was subtly reminding her of their existence.

He'd crossed a few himself. Was he also reminding himself of their existence? Or was that optimism on her part that he was sensing something between them that was deeper than simply a physical connection?

He was a lot more experienced than her and primed to protect himself from emotional involvement.

The feathery unease of danger made the hairs on the back of her neck stand on end. He represented everything logic warned her against when it came to her heart.

She'd given him a long speech about just how unsuitable he was, just how safe he could feel with her because she wasn't interested in him as a life partner.

There would be no awkward business about her falling for him because he wasn't on her radar when it came to those types of emotions.

But how much chance did logic stand when her heart decided to go its own way?

Alessandro was powerfully attractive, extremely sexual and stupendously clever and with all those attributes came a level of self-assurance rarely encountered.

What chance did her heart stand against all that?

She buried her head against him to hide her inner confusion from his sharp gaze.

Was she falling in love with him?

How could that be possible? After the debacle with Hans, she had set strict guidelines when it came to falling for a guy.

Surely she couldn't have been thrown so off course after, literally, *five* minutes by a little good looks and charm?

Except, a voice in her head murmured, *this man was so much more than that, wasn't he?*

She took a deep breath and when she angled herself to meet his eyes, she was back in control, at least on the surface, even if underneath the turmoil continued unabated.

'So where do we go from here?' she asked bluntly. 'I mean, here we are, having a bit of fun, and the reason I ask is because last time I looked at the date on my phone, we still have a few days left here.'

Alessandro burst out laughing and looked at her for a few seconds with a slow, hot burn in his eyes that set her nerves tingling.

'You don't beat around the bush, do you? Well, we definitely won't be playing the *let's-pretend-this-never-happened* game.'

'No.' She reddened. 'I don't think it's going to be possible to pretend that this never happened. Don't get me wrong, though. I'm not asking about what happens when we leave here in a few days' time. I'm asking what happens for the remainder of our stay here.'

'What would you like to happen? I know what *I'm* in favour of. I want to keep this going while we're here, Georgie.'

He swept his hand between her thighs.

'Let's enjoy one another before we get back to reality. What do you say…?'

'Only,' Georgie returned, heart flipping over, 'if you can guarantee that you won't do anything stupid like fall in love with me.'

Which made him laugh again.

'You have my word.'

CHAPTER NINE

ROOM SERVICE. PERSONALISED MENUS created just for them and delivered with the pomp and ceremony of a Michelin-starred restaurant.

Alessandro and Georgie quickly realised that they preferred it to going to any one of the amazing restaurants in the hotel and the park even though it would have been no trouble arranging a babysitter.

When money was no object, nothing was too much trouble, but the intimacy of having dinner with no one around was irresistible.

Alessandro had told her that he liked being with a woman who didn't spend hours getting ready to go out and whose enjoyment didn't come from basking in other people's admiration, with whatever food that was on offer playing second fiddle.

Now, Alessandro was sitting on the sofa with the menu on the table in front of him, not that he needed a menu. Whatever he wanted was cooked for him. He watched her as she emerged in a fetching ensemble of grey silk culottes and a matching vest with tiny buttons down the front.

It was loose and fell to the waist and he could see that she wasn't wearing a bra. Her small breasts jutted against the thin silk, her nipples pushing out in two tiny cones.

'You look good.' He stood up to hand her a glass of wine

and then continued standing until she was close enough to breathe her in.

'So do you,' Georgie quipped back.

'There. Compliments out of the way. We both look good.'

'Oh no! Are the compliments done already? I wanted them to keep coming.'

'I figure you're only half joking when you say that. Thinking that you were second best to your sisters because you weren't as academic has taken its toll. I was shocked when you told me about your dyslexia. Shouldn't be but… no, shocked isn't the right description. I was…gutted for you. So what I'm saying is that I can rustle up a couple more compliments if you like.' Alessandro grinned and patted the space right next to him as he sat back down. He wanted to feel her small body curving against his, so that he could dip his hand at will underneath the loose silk top and play with her breasts until he knew what effect he was having between her thighs.

Georgie blushed, sat next to him and rested her head against his shoulder before pulling back to sit and look at him.

'I thought you didn't like the psychobabble stuff. Are you going to start analysing me?' She wished he would. He could spout the psychobabble stuff till the cows came home as far as she was concerned, because it would prove that he cared. Telling him about her dyslexia had felt natural and she'd been thrilled when he'd responded with a look of sympathy and tenderness.

She'd stopped pretending that she didn't have feelings for him and she was willing to see every small concession of affection from him as a declaration of an emotion he didn't know he possessed.

From nowhere, hope had sprung like a weed, stubbornly

pushing past common sense and reason and sending shoots down deep inside her.

For the past three days the sex had been mind-blowing… the holding hands had made her heart beat fast…and the stolen looks with Flora in between them had sent her nervous system into skittering free fall.

Just looking at him now, casually dressed in Prada and Ralph Lauren, all black polo shirt and black jeans, was enough to make her mouth go dry.

'I'm beginning to get a kick out of this psychobabble stuff. Maybe I chose the wrong career.'

Georgie laughed. 'I'm not seeing it,' she told him wryly. 'Anyway, women might get too distracted to spill their hearts out if they were lying on a couch looking at you. Not that I think the lying-on-a-couch thing still happens.'

Alessandro looked at her thoughtfully.

'We should talk.'

The smile on Georgie's face tightened but she kept it pinned there. Her eyes, though, were glassy and she lowered them. A conversation had to be had. Would it be too much to hope that he might want to see where this wonderful thing between them might lead?

'Good idea,' she managed in a normal voice. 'You read my mind.'

'Drink some of your wine and let me just feel you for a bit first.'

He slipped his hand underneath the vest and covered her breast with it, teasing her nipple until she was moaning softly and squirming. When he pushed up the top so that he could suckle the pink, throbbing tip, she slipped down the sofa and relaxed back to enjoy what he was doing.

Georgie's mind went blank, the way it always did the second he started touching her.

She let one arm dangle off the side of the sofa and watched him as he laved her nipple with his mouth. Her legs parted and she waited with mounting pleasure for him to touch her. She knew how his hand felt as it trailed along her body, she knew where it would linger and how that touch would lighten or strengthen depending on where he touched.

Right now, he was touching her just where she wanted to be touched, circling her belly button, dipping into the small indent with feathery softness before continuing a downward spiral to the elasticated waistband of the culottes.

He slipped a finger inside her, rubbed her clitoris. She looked through half-opened eyes at the bulge of his hand under the culottes and that, in itself, was a turn-on.

She sighed, closed her eyes and moved to keep rhythm with his gently exploring fingers, angling her body to maximise her pleasure, and as his rubbing got stronger and firmer, she sucked in her breath and came in a long, convulsing shudder that drained everything out of her on a high of intense, shattering ecstasy.

She struggled back up into an upright position when she eventually returned to Planet Earth to find him smiling at her like the cat that got the cream.

The talk...a conversation that needed to be had...

She thought about the chasm between them, the chasm that they had both chosen to forget about temporarily but which was now rising up from the depths to confront them.

Why let him take the initiative? She was never going to open herself up to being vulnerable in front of a guy again, never look across to see him kissing another woman or else just walking away from her, smiling and waving and knowing he'd stuck the knife in because she'd given herself away.

Inside, she could be as vulnerable as she wanted and give as much airtime to hurt as she wanted but, no...she would be in charge of the narrative.

'It's our penultimate night here tomorrow. I guess that's what you want to talk about?' Her heart was racing, thumping so hard it felt as though it would smash right through her ribcage. 'I might need to actually do some work. I have reports to write and I need to start planning next term's curriculum. Once the ski season starts coming to an end, I have to get into gear for a change of tempo when the outdoor activities change and I think that this is going to be my last season there, anyway.' Voice perfectly normal but, inside, everything in wild turmoil.

'What do you mean?'

'I need to start putting down roots. Proper roots. This has been fun and it's served a purpose, as you know, but...' Her voice tapered off.

Alessandro frowned.

In the pit of his stomach, he felt an unsettling flare of panic. *Putting down roots? Quitting her job at Whistler? How had that been the last thing on his mind? And when she spoke about putting down roots, where exactly were those roots going to be planted?*

The depth of his reaction set alarm bells ringing in his head. Why was that? This was only ever going to be a brief fling. In fact, it wasn't going to be anything at all...it was meant to be no more than an enforced situation that they would both endure before walking away back to the reality they'd left behind.

Shutters slammed down, an automatic self-defence mechanism to protect himself from hurt.

He barely acknowledged that it was there. He just knew to back away from questions to which the answers might not be what he wanted to hear and the question he wanted to ask her was *why would you leave me?*

He detested himself for the vulnerability in himself he

was suddenly exposed to and he didn't know where it had come from.

He'd always known how to keep the vault in which his heart lay under lock and key. Now it felt as though a crack had opened up in the layers of steel.

To acknowledge that crack was one thing, of course. However, to explore where that crack might lead was off the cards.

'Of course,' he said abruptly. He reached to tuck some of her unruly blonde hair behind her ear, keeping his voice controlled and light until his absolute self-control was back in place, although he knew that his hand was just a little bit unsteady. 'What happened between us was never on the cards in the first place. When you talk about putting down roots, what roots are you talking about? Career roots?'

'I suppose so.' Georgie wasn't looking look at him. 'Find a place in London. Find a job that pays enough to afford somewhere not too crime-ridden. I can spend the next few months, until September at least, saving madly so I might be able to muster a deposit and, of course, the money I got for this stint will go a long way to realising my dream. So thank you for that.'

'London...'

'I was never planning on staying in Canada for ever.'

'But while you're here, Georgie, and this is what I wanted to talk to you about...' *She would leave to return to England. Naturally. That wasn't gut-wrenching at all. In fact, it was terrific that she wasn't being clingy! That she was already making plans for moving on with a life in which she didn't want him to play any part at all.*

Wasn't it?

After Sophia, clingy, needy women who wanted more from him than he could ever give were off-limits. He'd always made that clear. In fact, he'd made it clear to Georgie from the start, if he recalled. It was all about protecting himself and his daughter from anyone who might see him as a meal ticket or as devoted husband material, willing to change himself for the greater cause.

He scooped his hand in her hair and angled her so that they were looking directly into one another's eyes.

'I don't want this to end.'

Georgie, ensnared by his dark gaze, felt her heart leap inside her as hope kicked in and with it all those expectations she had kept at bay. Love, marriage, babies, the dog…a retriever, maybe…?

'What do you mean?' She cleared her throat. Inside the flames of hope licked higher and higher.

'There's no reason for us to end this just yet. Hear me out. On more than one level, it makes perfect sense. You and I are supposed to be in a relationship. When this first kicked off, I remember telling you to keep your distance from Flora but that hasn't happened. If you disappear, she'll be upset and understandably so. So were you to stick around for a few more weeks…then what we have could taper off…'

'Taper off…' Georgie repeated in a daze.

'In a natural, organic way. The way two people come together, think it's the real thing, only to discover that they don't have quite as much in common as they originally thought.'

'Yes, I see…yes, those relationships…the ones that never last, hope that fades, dreams that come unstuck…' Tears clogged somewhere deep inside, in her soul.

'Yes. Just so! That way your departure will be a gradual process that Flora won't find too upsetting. Wouldn't you agree?'

'She might be shaken if I were to vanish all of a sudden is what you're saying.' Holding hands one minute, Georgie thought, and then going in separate directions the next minute, with just a backward glance at something that had never, ever stood a chance.

How could she have been so stupid?

'Exactly what I'm saying. I'm glad we're both on the same page. Excellent!'

'What's the other level?' She cleared her throat in an attempt to clear her head, to sound normal when she spoke. Everything inside her was hurting.

'Come again?'

'You said *on more than one level it makes perfect sense.* So what's *the other level* it makes perfect sense on?'

'We still want one another, Georgie. I can feel it in you every time we touch and it's the same for me. We could both pretend that we could walk away from this in a couple of days' time and look back as though nothing's happened, but something as strong as what we have needs to run its course.'

'Why? Isn't that just stupid self-indulgence?'

Alessandro kissed the words away, a long, lazy kiss, and then, when he was about to draw back, he resumed his devastating assault on her senses.

'You speak your mind,' he murmured. 'And I love that. And you make me laugh and I love that as well. Georgie, we get along. That's why it makes so much sense for this to carry on to its natural conclusion.'

'Because we get along? Because I'm honest and don't pander to you like all those other women you've dated in the past probably did? *That's* why this has to continue? Until you get bored of me and my honesty? Or I get bored of you?'

'I enjoy you.'

'But this isn't all about you, Alessandro, is it?'

Georgie had heard enough. The hope that had been shooting off in all sorts of ridiculous directions when he'd opened his monologue by telling her that he didn't want things between them to end had taken a sizeable battering.

She'd leapt to all sorts of conclusions, had misread the situation and she had only herself to blame.

She'd had another Hans moment, even though she'd spent months upon months on a learning curve that would henceforth protect her from making another mistake when it came to guys and misreading their intentions.

So much for learning curves.

That said…she wasn't going to run away with her tail between her legs, mopping up her broken heart with her friends when she got back to the ski resort, and she wasn't going to let him see how much she was hurting.

She was going to be in control of herself, at least with him, and if she wasn't when she was on her own, then no one would witness her devastation.

Wasn't that what inner strength was all about? Being dignified in the face of loss?

'I enjoy being with you as well, if you want complete honesty. And the sex is off the chart but that's not a reason for me to want to carry on with this situation until it fizzles out. I have a life waiting for me after this and plans to make about returning to England. I need to get on with that life and move on from what we have here, which was only ever going to be a blip.'

'A blip?'

'Yes, Alessandro, *a blip*. We both know that, and *you* might think it's great to carry on until you're stuffed and feeling sick but that's not me. I don't see the sense in continuing with this, behaving like a couple of kids in a sweet shop, until we both get sick of the sweets on offer. I know Flora will be upset but that won't last. Kids get over things quickly. She'll be back at school in the blink of an eye and I will become a distant memory for her, just like I'll become a distant memory for you.'

'Why are you making a straightforward situation so damned complicated?'

They had pulled apart, confrontational now rather than conspiratorial.

'I'm just being honest and it was never that straightforward, if we were both to tell the absolute truth. It was crazy to end up in bed together but we did, and I don't regret a minute of it, but that doesn't mean that I want to continue until…it just fizzles out. Look, Alessandro, we're here for a tiny bit of time longer. Why not enjoy it without wanting to prolong something that was never going to stay the distance anyway?'

She'd been through the eye of the hurricane and now…now was time to get to clearer skies. The hurricane would return later…when she was on her own.

'I never thought you were that sensible,' Alessandro said in a driven undertone.

He had pulled back from her and stiffened as the conversation he had foreseen swerved off on an unexpected tangent.

'What did you think I was?'

'More spontaneous.'

'After Hans, the next guy I invite into my life is going to be someone who is serious about a relationship.' She paused. 'You were right about the fun thing, though.'

'The fun thing…'

'I went from a broken heart to, as you said, battening down the hatches, but in between I needed to loosen up and have some fun and I have. Here. With you. Fun fun. Not serious fun.'

He'd been a bit of fun? Fun fun?

What was going on here? Wasn't *he* supposed to be the one talking sense in a polite, warm way as he wrapped things up? And why did this feel so weird and painful?

'So you're turning down my offer to carry on with what we have…' His voice was incredulous. 'Is that what I'm hearing?'

'Correct.'

'You'll return to the ski resort and pick up where you left off.'

'That was the deal, wasn't it? I could continue doing the cleaning at your house? You're not going to renege on that, are you?'

'No! Dammit, Georgie…now we're talking about *bloody cleaning*?'

'Good, because the more I have towards a deposit, the better. You wouldn't believe the prices of shoeboxes in London. Crazy.'

'I could buy you whatever you want. All you have to do is say the word, no strings attached,' he muttered with a hint of challenge in his voice.

'Why would you do that, Alessandro?'

Good question, was what Alessandro was thinking, suddenly bewildered at his own suggestion. Why would he?

'I'm a generous guy,' he said, with just a hint of defensiveness in his voice.

'Yes, you are. I mean, I just have to look around this place to know that you live in a *no-expense-spared* world.'

'I came from nothing. What's the point having everything if you forget how to spend what you have? Well? What's your answer?'

Georgie looked at him narrowly. 'There's no such thing as a gesture like that that comes with *no strings attached*.

You might have good intentions, and one thing I've realised is that your intentions *are* good, despite my first impressions, but—'

'But you think that if I buy you an apartment in Mayfair, I'll be tempted to think that sleeping with me would be on the cards?'

'Wouldn't it?'

'I don't know. Georgie—'

'I can't, Alessandro. I just can't. I'm not like you. But I appreciate the offer and at least you're honest. Actually, even if sleeping with you *wasn't* on the cards, I wouldn't accept your offer. Something else I just couldn't do.' Underneath the controlled voice, Georgie could feel her heart collapsing on itself. 'I couldn't, Alessandro, because it would make me feel…cheap. It would demean everything we've had, make me feel as though I was being paid for services rendered.' She forced a smile but her jaw ached from the effort. She leant into him and curved a trembling hand on his cheek. 'Let's not talk about this any more. Let's just enjoy the time we have left together.'

Three days later Georgie was back at the ski resort. Her nerves were shredded.

But she had her memories. Making love…those last few hours at the park, laughing at Flora zooming higher and higher on a ride she'd been saving for last. Alessandro's laughter as he scooped Flora up into the air and swung her high until she squealed. The way he'd looked across at Georgie with an expression she couldn't read…

They'd parted company with a kiss, a chaste, formal kiss while Flora had looked on, holding Alessandro's hand and wearing an outfit he had bought for her the day before as a souvenir.

'But when will I see you again?' Flora had asked, staring up at her with an anxious frown.

'Soon!' Georgie had said with forced cheer. 'As soon as I get to grips with some work issues!' She'd stooped to Flora's level, smoothed her velvety purple jumper with its bright pink embroidered Disney character and kissed her on the forehead.

But she'd felt terrible.

Now, after a week, she was back into her routine and plastering a smile on her face while she fudged questions about where she'd been.

'Getting away from your horrible germs.' She'd swiped Alison with a tea towel, laughing as they'd cooked dinner together the evening before.

'I know you had a family thing, Georgie, and you don't want to talk about it but, seriously…*no hot guys in Florida*?'

Georgie had quickly changed the subject because immersing herself in a couple of necessary white lies was one thing, expanding on them was another.

She hadn't heard a word from Alessandro. She was due to clean his house on the Sunday and it was going to take lots of deep breathing, willpower and maybe even smelling salts not to wallow in nostalgia. Did she have it in her? She would find out soon enough.

Right now, though…

It was a little after seven in the evening. She was on her own in the house. Alison and Claire were both out and wouldn't be back for ages.

As it stood, though, she was in good company. She had her tabloid newspapers and a selection of gossip mags. Maybe they would take her mind off her messy, painful, tortured thoughts.

Curled up on the sofa with a plate of doughnuts she'd bought earlier, a cup of coffee and with the telly playing in the background, it took her minutes to flick past the obligatory *everything-that-was-wrong-in-the-world* front pages to the gossip selection in the middle of the paper. Mere minutes before she saw the full-blown image dominating the double spread and, with a sickening lurch in her gut, registered the dramatic headline above it.

Alessandro stared down at the photo of himself in the trashy tabloid his PA had kindly put on his desk the evening before with an apologetic note that he might want to have a look.

He got why.

Being snapped occasionally with a woman on his arm came with the territory. He was a billionaire, he was eligible and, without a trace of vanity, he knew that he was good-looking.

And he went to places a lot of people could only dream of going to. Premieres, exclusive fundraisers, boxes at sporting events where it wasn't unusual to spot members of the royal family. Paparazzi were drawn to those venues like bees to honey.

But this…was in a league of its own.

He snatched up the paper, stared at the picture of him and his ex-wife for a few grim seconds and then, yet again, scowled at the glaring headlines announcing with salacious glee that a reunion looked as though it was on the cards.

The picture bolstered the headline.

Sophia was clutching his arm and looking up at him with an adoring smile on her face. He, in turn, was staring down at her, half shielding his eyes from the glare of the still cold winter sun in Manhattan.

They were the perfect loved-up couple. Of course, the truth couldn't have been further from that but…

He walked over to the window of his office, which sat on the top four floors of an iconic skyscraper.

From here, you couldn't even see people down below on

the crowded lunchtime streets. All you could see was what was directly outside the panes of glass and that was the blue of a winter sky and the scudding of white clouds.

Would Georgie have seen that picture? Read the article, which was rife with ridiculous speculation? And if she had...

Alessandro groaned and raked his fingers through his hair.

He'd planned on seeing her. He knew that she would be cleaning his house on the following day, the Sunday, or, as she had laughingly put it, wafting a feather duster over a bunch of surfaces you could see your reflection in.

He'd resigned himself to a conversation that would very likely not go his way, but what happened now?

He grabbed his coat and exited his office at speed. There was no one around because it was nine-thirty on a Saturday evening and anyone with any kind of life to speak of wasn't in an office building.

He would take his private jet to Vancouver and drive to his house. He wouldn't wait for her in the house because he didn't want to startle her. He would wait until she was there and he would ring the doorbell of his own house and wait for her to answer it.

Like someone paying a visit. Crazy, but desperation, he realised, made a person do crazy things.

Desperation and love.

Love. It still left him shaken when he thought about how deeply he had fallen into an emotion he'd thought he could never, *would never*, feel.

Years of building his defences, sealing himself away from anything that could promise hurt and yet... Georgie had walked away from him and he had felt tears in his eyes and a hollowness in his heart that made him want to sit on the pavement and bury his head in his hands.

He'd done nothing. He'd been paralysed by panic and

terror at a place he'd never thought he'd be in. It had been as though the familiar contours of the world had shifted so while everything looked the same, nothing felt the same.

He would think things through. He would let the dust settle. He would come to terms with…the wild, uncontrolled feeling of being vulnerable.

And then he would see her because he had to. But now… with that article out there in the public domain…

It was going to be a very different visit from the one he had originally planned, before Sophia had pulled her last stunt at his expense.

Georgie was wafting the feather duster. Every time she went into a different room in Alessandro's house, she was assaulted by vivid memories of meeting him for the first time, drowning in those dark eyes. She remembered the first feel of his hand on her and that feathery non-kiss that had made her shiver all over.

Then she thought about that headline, thought about him and Sophia getting back together, rebuilding their little family unit, and she wanted to dump the feather duster, grab the rolling pin from the kitchen drawer and run through the house breaking everything that could be broken, screaming out her agony and heartache.

She'd *known* what the deal was when she'd got involved with him. She'd *known* that he was off-limits. She'd *stupidly, nonchalantly, mistakenly assumed* that past hurt would protect her from making another mistake, especially when he'd made it clear that she wasn't to start thinking that what they had was real.

Yet she'd fallen in love with him and now, not only was she dealing with her shattered heart, but she was also having to deal with the cold fact that somehow their brief liaison had propelled him into a change of heart with his ex-wife.

Was it because, for the first time, he had spent undiluted time with his daughter in the company of someone who joined in? Had her presence there, the way she'd bonded with Flora, led him to the belief that he might have ditched his marriage prematurely? That there remained things there that could be salvaged? That he and Sophia could find a way to being the family they should have been when Flora had been born?

Maybe he'd finally realised that he'd made his fortune and he could slow down and, in slowing down, could devote the time and energy needed to be a parent and a husband.

She wanted to take something positive from the experience, wanted to be the bigger person and feel happy that she had been instrumental in him finding the right path and, in so doing, opening up his relationship with Flora so that he could become the best dad she knew he had the potential to be.

Unfortunately, it was a work in progress. At the moment she was going down rabbit holes thinking about him.

She wondered whether she'd done the right thing walking away and then immediately told herself that she had, only to quickly start imagining what life would look like right now if she'd taken him up on his offer.

Rabbit hole.

She swept the feather duster round the sitting room with a flourishing touch by the door and stood back to look at her handiwork, not that much work had been involved. Between their leaving the house and returning to it, the agency had obviously been told to send someone in to do an interim job, and so Georgie had had very little to do on her first day back.

She was heading to the kitchen where she would finish things up when she heard the doorbell and it was such a shock that, for a few seconds, she froze.

She'd never been interrupted doing her cleaning duties before. Ever. Except that one time. But, of course, it couldn't be Alessandro because he wouldn't be ringing his own doorbell.

Which could only mean that it was someone from the agency who'd come to give her her walking papers.

Why not?

Alessandro was on a different path now and the milk of human kindness had probably had time to curdle.

Just thinking about her cleaning his house would be a sorry reminder of a past he wanted to make sure he never bumped into again.

She steeled herself before opening the front door. She pulled it open, braced for bad news and there he was…

Shock tightened every muscle in her body. Her mouth fell open and she stared at him until she could feel the searing heat inside her pour into her cheeks.

She would have slammed the door.

She very nearly did until she remembered that this was actually his house.

And then it hit her. He was a decent guy. Wasn't that part of the reason she'd fallen in love with him? Because beneath the arrogance and the polished exterior and the cool self-assurance, he was *a really good guy*?

He'd come to personally break the news to her because they'd slept together and he'd think that she deserved an explanation.

Oh God. It was going to be a pity fest from him and she couldn't bear the thought of it.

'Georgie.'

'Hi, Alessandro.' Georgie cleared her throat. 'I was just on my way out, actually. I just have the kitchen to get through. Why are you here? I mean, why did you ring the doorbell? Have you forgotten your key?'

'Can I enter my own house?'

Georgie stepped aside but as soon as he was inside, she swung round to look at him and pressed herself against the closed door.

God, he looked stupendous.

Charcoal-grey cashmere coat…black jeans…black jumper…

'I know why you've come,' she said in a burst of *might-as-well-get-it-out-of-the-way* opener.

'Let's sit down.'

His eyes met hers, dark and steady and destabilising.

'Georgie, I came here to talk to you and it's a conversation that can't be had by the front door.'

He reached out his hand and she looked at it incredulously. Did she look so feeble that he thought he needed to give her a hand in case she couldn't unglue herself from the front door?

She drew in a deep breath and handed him the feather duster, which she was still holding.

'Congratulations,' she said coolly. 'That's why you're here, isn't it? I saw the article in the papers.'

'I thought you might have.'

'We don't have to sit down for a heart-to-heart about your reconciliation with your ex-wife, Alessandro. Like we both know, what we had was a passing fling. You don't owe me any explanations.'

'Come on.'

He strode off, looked back over his shoulder and Georgie reluctantly followed him towards the kitchen. He pulled a chair out for her and then sat right next to the chair he'd pulled out.

'Why did you ring the doorbell?'

'Because I didn't want to wait in the house for you to show up.'

'How did you know I'd be here?'

'Sit, Georgie. Please. Would you? I checked with the agency.' He looked at her resentful, distrustful face and had to steel himself against the uphill task staring him in the face.

'I planned on…coming here…seeing you, talking to you before that article came out. I know what you're thinking. I can read it on your face but let me explain.'

God, he'd missed her.

Missed her ready laugh, missed the way she teased him, missed the way her small body curved against his.

She'd left and he'd known. Known that he'd fallen in love with her, that all the wisdom he'd shored up from his disadvantaged childhood and disillusioning marriage had not been enough to stop her from getting to him.

She hadn't even had to try.

'I told you, no explanations needed. I've moved on.'

'Don't say that. Please.'

'Not that there was anything to *move on from*. A bit of fun. That's all there was to it. I'm going to make some coffee. Would you like some? And then I'll finish cleaning here and make a move because I have things to do.'

She stood up abruptly, lowering her eyes and shielding her expression.

He watched her turned back, longed for her…wanted her to turn around, to meet his eyes, and yet was grateful for the reprieve because it gave him a chance to work out what he was going to say.

CHAPTER TEN

'Is that really what you think?' Alessandro asked quietly as she dumped a cup of coffee in front of him and sat back down but on the opposite side of the table. 'That what we had was just a bit of fun?'

He'd warned her about involvement at the start. He'd warned her about a number of things. That warning to make sure she didn't start believing that their phoney relationship was real returned now to mock him because the one thing he hadn't foreseen was *his* involvement. *She*, on the other hand, open and funny and light-hearted, had *not once* done anything to make him think that she'd fallen in love with him.

She'd enjoyed him and then she'd walked away.

Coming here, for him, was the biggest risk he'd ever taken in his life because he was on the back foot and the way ahead was unclear, but love had left him with no choice.

'What I think, Alessandro, is that I don't want to get involved in this conversation. We had what we had and it's over. I don't want to have any post-mortems and I don't want to hear what your plans are for a future with your ex-wife.'

'That article, it's not what you think.'

'Isn't it? Seemed pretty clear-cut to me. Sophia gazing up at you…you gazing down at her…arm in arm after a cosy dinner at a romantic restaurant.'

* * *

Georgie sighed and fiddled with the handle of her cup. Just saying those words out loud felt like a knife twisting in her heart. She was proud, however, that she had taken the bull by the horns and wasn't hiding behind a show of not understanding why he had come.

'I'm glad for you.' It was a struggle to say that and a victory when she succeeded.

'You're glad for me?'

'I know what happened and how it happened. You finally realised just how irreplaceable it is to have family time as a unit. My being there might have been an illusion, but it opened your eyes to what you hadn't seen before.'

'What are you talking about?'

'You know what I'm talking about, Alessandro,' Georgie said impatiently. 'Or you *would* know if you stopped to really think about it.'

He looked bewildered. Guarded but bemused and she didn't want that expression to start making inroads into her common sense.

She didn't want to start analysing it, didn't want to think that there might be more to what she had seen and read, that when he said that it might not be what she thought, he might just be telling the truth.

She was sick of misinterpreting situations and reading men the wrong way.

She was sick *of being naïve.*

Maybe he just hadn't worked out why he and his ex-wife were suddenly getting back together. Or, at least, he hadn't analysed the situation in depth.

Did it matter?

She wished he would just leave but, since it happened to be *his* house, that wasn't really an option.

She could do the next best thing, though, so she began standing up, backing away from the table, eyes riveted to his darkly handsome face.

'Please, Georgie.'

He stood and took a couple of steps towards her and Georgie froze in her tracks.

She was appalled when, somehow, he was towering over her and, *somehow*, he'd reached out and *somehow* her wrist had managed to find itself circled by his fingers.

She snatched her hand away and rubbed her wrist and looked at him with scathing hostility.

'I realise that this is your house, Alessandro, but I'm going to leave now and, much as I like the money this job brings, I won't be coming back to clean for you. I'll let the agency know.'

Her heart was hammering inside her and she couldn't tear her eyes away from his ashen face.

Why was his face ashen?

What did his face have to be *ashen about*?

She was the one whose heart had been broken in two! Her face had a lot to be ashen about!

'I was going to come here to see you even before that ridiculous story broke.'

His voice was low and shaky and Georgie stared at him through narrowed eyes, not trusting herself to give an inch.

She folded her arms and eyed the kitchen door, desperate to flee through it and yet desperate as well to stay right where she was and hear what he had to say.

'To do the decent thing? Fill me in before I found out sooner or later?'

'I was going to come here to...'

The silence gathered around them until Georgie could

feel herself breaking out in perspiration. Her fingers were digging into her arms and she loosened them.

'To what?' she finally asked.

'To ask you to marry me.'

His words floated into her head and she stared at him, open-mouthed and in disbelief. She thought that she might have misheard what he'd said or maybe she'd missed a vital link in his sentence because her nerves were all over the place.

'Sorry?' she eventually stuttered.

'I came here to ask you to marry me, Georgie.' He reached into his pocket, pulled out a little black box and held it towards her.

Georgie stared at it, then quickly looked at him.

'It's a shock. I know that. I can see it all over your face. I know what I said…what I told you about making sure not to get feelings for me…and I know…'

He shoved the box back into his pocket, raked his fingers through his hair and flushed darkly.

'We could have this conversation in the living room,' he said roughly, 'if you'll let me. If you'll hear me out.'

There was a nervousness in the way he hovered and maybe that was what propelled Georgie to nod and follow as he preceded her out into the vast hall and towards the sitting room where, not that long ago, she had bumped into him with his ex-wife and two lawyers in tow.

He'd come to *ask her to marry him*?

That made no sense. They'd parted company with a peck on the cheek. He hadn't, not once, said anything about having feelings for her. The opposite if anything.

Was this about Flora?

'Is this about Flora?' was the first thing she asked when they were in the sitting room and she had sunk into one of the chairs while he remained by the window, perched against the sill, looking every inch the elegant billionaire.

'What do you mean?' He frowned and sighed. 'Georgie, stop theorising and hear me out.'

Georgie barely heard him because she was busy wondering how on earth a marriage proposal could be about his daughter and also *what were those pictures in the newspaper all about*?

Her head wanted to explode.

She glanced up to find that he had strolled towards her and she watched as he dragged one of the chairs across so that he was sitting opposite her, his knees very nearly touching hers.

'When we parted company, I… I thought that my life would return to where it had been before we met. Deep down, I knew that wasn't going to happen but I refused to allow my mind to go off in that direction. Didn't matter. It was stupid to think anything was going to be the same without you around and I knew it, knew it the second I watched you walk away from me. It was like having my heart cut out. Instinct made me want to rush behind you but years of self-control stopped me, made me retreat to think things through…to come to terms with a love that was bigger than me, a love that was never going to go away.' He paused and lowered his head. When he looked up at her, he steepled his fingers under his chin and remained silent for a couple of seconds.

'I spent my life making sure to protect myself against women who wanted too much from me because I accepted that I just couldn't promise the sort of commitment they seemed to want. Sophia and I…? Like I told you,' he said heavily, 'as I've told you so many things about myself in the time we spent together… Sophia and I only married because she fell pregnant. If that hadn't happened, I would never have married her, but I married her and, for a very brief while, I'd hoped that I might find reservoirs of love I didn't know I possessed.'

'But you didn't.'

'But I didn't,' Alessandro admitted on a sigh. 'The opposite. I very quickly realised that I'd never loved Sophia and never would. I accepted that I didn't have it in me to love any woman because I'd grown up far too disillusioned with my own experiences of a childhood blighted by my father's careless abandonment of me and my mother.'

'Yet you were loved, Alessandro. Your mother loved you, set you in the right direction, did everything within her power to make sure you didn't end up destitute or worse. You told me so.'

'I told you a lot of things, didn't I?' He smiled wryly. 'That should have been a signpost to what was happening inside me, if I hadn't been too damn stubborn to realise it. Yes, my mother did a lot for me. Everything, truth be told. But over the years I saw the damage caused by my father walking out on her. She never recovered, never got involved with anyone else. And more than that, I felt the hole my father's vanishing act left in me. Love, in all its complications, left pain in its wake and I decided from a very young age that I wasn't prepared to put myself in the firing line. Maybe if it had been a normal divorce, when I was old enough to understand that sometimes good people make bad life partners...but I was very, very young and the hurt was crystallised in the notion of a man who'd walked out of my life, never looked back, never tried to get in touch, was never curious about the mess he'd left behind.'

'Alessandro, I still don't understand what—'

'When you left to head back to Vancouver, I got in touch

with Sophia, told her that I wanted to meet her. I said that I'd explain everything when we met but there were things I wanted to tell her and I wanted to tell her face to face.'

'You did…'

'She suggested the restaurant and I complied. I felt it was going to be tough enough on her when she heard what I had to say.'

'Alessandro…'

'Don't you believe me?'

'I don't know what to believe.'

'Do you *want* to believe me? That's the question I suppose I should be asking.'

'What do you mean?'

'I came here to tell you that I love you, Georgie. I came here with a ring to ask for your hand in marriage. You weren't interested in the ring and I'm guessing you don't feel the same towards me even though I know that we could work together, that I could be the man you're looking for and I'm willing to prove that to you.'

'I'm in a daze.'

'I'm trying to be as ordered in telling you all this as I can but—'

'You still haven't said what happened with your ex-wife.'

'Let me show you something.'

He reached into his pocket, pulled out his mobile phone and after a couple of seconds he handed it to her.

Georgie glanced down and blinked as she read a thread of messages, brief and to the point.

A single message from Alessandro and it said just what he had told her. That he wanted to meet up, that he had something to tell her and that he wanted to tell her face to face.

Then a flurry of messages from Sophia…wanting more

information, more details…some clue as to what she might expect.

In the absence of any of those questions being answered, she had suggested the place and the time.

A well-known, mega-expensive restaurant in Manhattan. Georgie had vaguely heard of the place, which said something.

She returned the phone to Alessandro and the hope that she had locked away sent tendrils shooting out, curling through her misery and finding a way into her heart.

'When I got to the restaurant,' Alessandro said heavily, 'I should have expected that something was going to happen because Sophia looked elated. She was dressed to kill and was the opposite of the belligerent, bitter woman I would have expected. Fool that I was, I actually breathed a sigh of relief.'

'And then, once you were outside…'

'You guessed it. The paparazzi were out in force. She'd tipped them off that we would be meeting at the restaurant and also hinted that a reconciliation was on the cards. Perhaps she really thought that that was going to be the case, but more likely she put two and two together, maybe gleaned from things Flora might have said, worked out that you and I had a serious connection, one that incorporated Flora, and she decided that she would have one last vicious stab at making my life as difficult as possible. As soon as we left the restaurant, she went into full acting mode and those, Georgie, were the pictures that you saw.'

'I… I…'

'I don't want to put you in an awkward position, Georgie. I needed to explain what happened and I needed to tell you how I felt.' He smiled at her and made to reach out to take her hand but instead drew back at the last minute and linked his fingers loosely between his thighs.

'Don't think I'm forcing myself on you,' he continued gruffly, 'because I'm not.'

'But what on earth did your ex-wife think she would gain by doing what she did?'

Georgie looked at him, perplexed.

Questions were still there in her head but her mind was thrilling to what he'd said.

He loved her? Could she believe it? Why would he lie?

'When you're dealing with someone like Sophia, that's a rational question to which there is no rational answer. It wasn't about what she would gain but what I might lose. At the very least, she would have made my life as difficult as possible and that would have been enough for her. Malice can be an emotion that blinds a person, kills common sense. But you still haven't answered my question. Do you want to believe what I'm telling you? Because if you can bring yourself to believe me, to know that I'm telling you the truth, then I might see some hope that you could give me a chance.'

'I believe you,' Georgie said simply.

She reached out to curve her hand on his cheek and he caught it in his and kissed her palm, raising his eyes to hers while his mouth remained pressed against her skin.

'I was devastated leaving you, Alessandro. I'd fallen in love with you even though I told myself that you were the least suitable person on the planet to fall in love with.'

'Georgie…my darling…'

'My heart stopped when you told me that you didn't want what we had to end, until you added that you just meant that we would continue being lovers until it fizzled out. I knew that I could never have done that. It was so hard making love to you once I knew that we'd be walking away from one another.'

'I wish you'd said. No. It was me. Up to me to have told you how I felt. I'd been the one to lay down all those ground rules. I should have been the one to admit that they'd been broken. By me. I didn't realise at the time how I felt about you. Never put two and two together and worked out that I would only spend half my time confiding if the person I was confiding in was also the person I'd fallen head over heels in love with.'

He shook his head and smiled.

He stood up, pulled her to her feet and, for a few seconds, buried his head in her hair, then he tilted her face and looked down at her.

'I became a different person when I met you. The minute I saw you flash across outside the sitting room, in a world of your own, I got caught up in a place that was alien to me. And I liked it and then I loved it, loved you.' He paused and looked at her seriously. 'We love each other, Georgie, but I'd understand if you still need time to think about marrying me. I've sprung this on you but I'm a man of action and it didn't occur to me to take things a step at a time. I had to see you, had to tell you how I felt and had to ask for your hand in marriage.'

'Maybe I could see that ring of yours…'

Her heart carried on filling up with love, unstoppable, as she watched him reach into his pocket and hand her the small black box she had gaped at earlier with suspicion and disbelief.

She opened it and there it was, the ring she had been dreaming of all her life.

A solitary circular diamond on its thin band of rose gold.

'Do you like it?'

Georgie looked at him and smiled. 'I adore it, Alessandro. It's the most beautiful ring I've ever seen because you're the man who gave it to me.'

He slipped it onto her finger.

'I didn't give a second's thought to the ring I got for my ex-wife,' he confessed. 'I know I should be ashamed about that but sitting here with you… I'm glad I waited because I put my heart and soul into getting the perfect ring for the perfect woman I want to spend the rest of my life with…'

EPILOGUE

GEORGIE'S SISTERS WERE chatting merrily away. They were sitting in front of floor-to-ceiling mirrors next to her. Three of them in a row, two with long dark hair being teased and combed by clever hairdressers, and she with her long, unruly tangle of blonde, which was now beginning to look, she would say, a lot tamer than could reasonably be expected.

Alessandro, she thought to herself with a smile, was going to be in for a shock. At some point she would have to whisper to him that the tamed look was never going to last.

Behind her, she could see her mother in the reflection from the mirror. She was brushing Flora's hair, taking her time while Flora turned the pages of a book and pointed to this and that, waiting for Amity Cross to respond and then giggling because Georgie's mother was putting on a silly voice and making silly faces.

In two hours, Georgie would be walking up the aisle to marry the man of her dreams.

Outside through the huge floor-to-ceiling windows that perfectly duplicated the dimensions of the panes of reflective glass sandwiched between them, Georgie could see the bright blue skies of a perfect July day.

If she stepped towards those windows and looked down, she would see the breathtaking panoramic views of Whistler Mountain and Blackcomb Peak.

The perfect wedding venue.

Not just because of the spectacular scenery or because the exquisite lodge where they would be celebrating was unique in having a vast patio with uncluttered views of the slopes, acres upon acres of them, but because, for her, this place was special.

It was where, on one morning that should have been just like all the other mornings when she had gone to clean Alessandro's house, she had met him.

An accidental meeting that had led, through twists and turns, to this very place where she was now sitting, smiling and chatting with her mum and her sisters and Flora while a hairdresser did clever things with her hair.

Hanging on a hook on the wall was her wedding dress. It was a simple design to suit her boyish figure.

A straight ivory dress that fell to her ankles. It wasn't fitted at all, but managed to emphasise her slenderness, and no plunging neckline because she had no cleavage to speak of.

She had a little posy of tiny flowers for her bouquet and the same flowers would be braided into her blonde hair like a small pink and white and lilac tiara.

'I always knew you'd be a hippy bride,' Katherine, her older sister, had told her, smiling approvingly when she'd seen the dress two days earlier.

Katherine, Emily—sister number two—her parents and a handful of close friends had all been imported over by Alessandro, who had enjoyed meeting all of them and had, predictably, charmed them all.

Finally, there was Flora and now, while exclaiming with delight at the job her hairdresser had done and staring at her nails with their pale pink shellac manicure, Georgie looked at her soon-to-be stepdaughter with love.

Their eyes met in the mirror and Flora smiled shyly and

then disengaged herself from her hair being brushed and skipped to where Georgie was sitting in front of the mirror.

'Are you excited?' she whispered in her shy, sweet voice.

'Are you?'

'Very. This is the first time I've ever been a bridesmaid before. You look beautiful, Georgie.'

'Not as beautiful as you. Did you bring the Disney outfit for later? To change into? You know you can't stay in that apricot dress for the whole time. Not when you've got something purple and pink with crazy cartoon characters on it waiting in your suitcase to be worn.'

Flora giggled.

'I sneaked it in. Daddy told me that would be fine. He said that pink and purple were lovely wedding colours. He said my Disney outfit would look very good on me and all the guests would love it because it'll be a splash of colour.'

'Your daddy the fashion consultant,' Georgie murmured. 'He's a man of many, many talents.'

She smiled, dreamily, chatted dreamily but her beautiful Alessandro filled her head.

The weeks and months had passed and the more she'd got to know him, the more she loved him.

He was tender and adoring and was proving to be a wonderful father, cutting down his hours and throwing himself into the business of being a father and a fiancé.

This time, the smile that warmed her was for her alone because she was thinking of what he had said only the day before, when he had kissed her and told her that he couldn't wait to be her husband.

'I'll never stop trying to prove to you, my darling, that I can be the best husband you could ever have hoped for and the best father not just to my beautiful Flora but to the babies you'll give me sooner rather than later.'

Georgie had chuckled to herself.

She'd said *goodbye* to the pill she'd only been on for the past few months.

Time would tell but who knew what she and Alessandro might be celebrating next?

* * * * *

Did you fall in love with Maid for the Italian*?*
Then you're sure to enjoy these other sparkling stories
by Cathy Williams!

Emergency Engagement
Snowbound Then Pregnant
Her Boss's Proposition
Billionaire's Reunion Bargain
Heir for the Holidays

Available now!

GREEK'S
ROYAL RUNAWAY

TRISH MOREY

MILLS & BOON

To the magical Lord Howe Island, one of the most glorious places in the world. If you haven't been lucky enough to visit yourself, I hope this story gives you a glimpse of the paradise that is Lord Howe.

PROLOGUE

Two hours out of Sydney the small jet banked, jolting Theo Mylonakos' attention from the photographs he was studying. He looked out the window, his gaze snared by the tiny speck of emerald amidst the sea of sparkling sapphire.

Lord Howe Island.

Tropical islands ordinarily held no attraction for him, but this one was different. His eyes narrowed as the plane grew closer, taking in the way the island cradled a coral-fringed bay, the twin mountains at one end looming so high over the peaks at the other, one might wonder why the weight didn't send the island toppling over and spinning to the bottom of the ocean.

And somewhere down there, pretending to be an everyday nobody rather than a member of one of Europe's oldest royal families, his quarry was hiding, Princess Isabella d'Montcroix, no doubt congratulating herself that she'd managed to evade those looking for her for the best part of six weeks.

Her brother, Prince Rafael, had led them to believe that the Princess was simply that—a typical twenty-something princess. Refined. Demure. *Innocent.* And when he looked at the photographs of the pretty hazel-eyed blonde, he'd believed what he'd been told, that she was your everyday princess, living in a privileged bubble filled with parties and balls and designer everything, and most of all, without an ounce of street smarts. Exactly why he'd delegated to his trusted operatives the task of finding her and delivering her home, until all attempts to find her had failed and it was clear he'd have to chase her down himself. Nobody had entertained any idea the Princess had the slightest clue about staying out of sight and eluding those searching for her for so long.

If he had to admit it, he held a grudging admiration for the way she'd done it, never staying in one place long enough to be noticed, jumping sideways and backward in her travels and always one infuriating step ahead, this latest move the most audacious, the most surprising.

But at the same time, she'd outsmarted herself, and the time for admiration, along with the hunt, was over. He had his prey all but in his sights. An island that hosted no more than four hundred guests at one time along with a handful of locals and casual workers.

And as the plane came in to land, the blood in his veins pumped fast and furious.

He had her.

CHAPTER ONE

ISABELLA CYCLED ALONG the palm-lined road leading from the café where she'd just finished her third lunch shift waiting tables, unable to stop a grin from splitting her face. Her third shift in a row, and now she'd been asked to do both lunch and dinner tomorrow!

She couldn't believe it. She, Princess Isabella d'Montcroix, actually had a job and was working. *Really* working at a *real* job, just like a normal person, and she hadn't messed up. Sure, they didn't know she was a princess, and in truth, she'd had to work at it. Memorising table numbers and orders and working out how to stack a table full of plates on one arm and not drop them on the way back to the kitchen while she was being yelled at by Chef to hurry up had almost done her head in—but she'd survived, and now she was being rewarded with more shifts.

Dappled sunlight played through the shadows, brief flashes of light amongst the twilight of the lush rainforest surrounds allowing glimpses of the cerulean lagoon to one side. It had rained this morning, a light shower that coupled with the day's sunshine, had heightened the earthy rainforest scent. Izzy breathed deeply of the heady combination of forest floor with the lagoon's salt air, a smell she would forever associate with the smell of freedom, and she grinned some more. Finally, she could feel the tension of the last few weeks slip away.

Finally, she was starting to believe that she was safe and could stop looking over her shoulder every other minute.

Hopefully for long enough to enjoy it.

But more than that, hopefully long enough to convince her brother to abandon his abhorrent plan to marry her off to one of his cronies.

Because there was no way she was going home until he did.

A van trundled past at the requisite twenty-five-kilometres-per-hour island speed limit, the driver lifting a hand to her as he passed. Jack, she realised, the owner of the café, on his way to meet the afternoon plane to pick up fresh fruit and vegetable supplies. She waved back, her heart skipping a beat as the bike wobbled, before she replaced her hand on the handlebars, steadying both her heart rate and the bike. Riding a bike had been another challenge, but here on the island, it was either that or walk, and she was rapidly conquering this new learned skill too, discovering muscles she'd never realised she had as she turned her bicycle up the road heading up the hill and away from the lagoon, towards the row of cabins let out to the casual workers who serviced the island's resort and hostel labour needs. Backpackers like they assumed she was, just another tourist from Europe working a few weeks or months to replenish travel funds before once more, moving on.

She jumped off when she met the steep path leading to her cabin, pushing her bike past pink and red flowering hibiscus bushes and waving to her neighbours, Sven and Inga relaxing on their small balcony. That was another thing she loved about the island. Everybody waved and said hello, whether you were a casual worker, a tourist or one of the sprinkling of island residents who'd lived on the island for generations.

'Come and join us,' said Inga, holding up her bottle of lager. 'We're celebrating surviving the climb up Mt Gower.'

'You did it?' Izzy asked, parking her bike against her veranda railing and unclipping her helmet. She had hair to colour tonight, part of the disguise she'd assumed to camouflage her blonde hair, but that could wait a little longer. Right now she wanted to hear about her neighbours' climb. The island boasted dozens of bush walks through its kentia palm and banyan tree subtropical rainforest coverage, with the eight-plus-hour return hike up the nearly kilometre-high mountain the number one challenge.

'Congratulations,' she said, pulling up a chair beside them as Inga pulled a beer from a six-pack and handed it to her.

Izzy smiled as she clinked longnecks with her neighbours before taking a sip of the amber liquid straight from the bottle. Another new skill she'd acquired since being in Australia. Her brother would be horrified if he could see her right now, and that made her smile widen. 'So tell me, what was it like?'

'Amazing,' Inge said. 'You have to do it. The views are breathtaking.'

Sven nodded after taking a long swallow. 'It's tough, but worth it. You should definitely do it while you're here.'

'I will,' she said, excited at the prospect and loving the buzz of being able to decide what she wanted to do and then simply go do it without an entire palace deciding on whether or not it was an appropriate occupation for a princess before then planning it down to the tiniest detail, right down to laying out the appropriate outfit she should wear.

It was liberating, this new freedom. Intoxicating. Addictive. 'I am definitely going to do that,' she said, making a promise to herself and sealing the deal with another sip of her beer. 'Cheers.'

Later that evening Isabella applied a fresh layer of chalk to her hair. She'd read that the best way to disguise yourself was not necessarily to add glasses or another disguise, but to take something away. She was taking away the platinum blonde, which was far too Princess Isabella for her liking. And now that every second woman seemed to have brightly coloured hair, nobody looked twice at hers. Job done, she checked out her hair in the mirror, now red and purple with the odd strip of teal. She smiled. Perfect. Nobody would guess she was a princess.

She made herself a mug of tea and stepped out onto her little porch in time to catch the dying rays of the sunset over the tops of the palm trees, painting the sky a brilliant red. She put her mug down and watched a while, in awe as the colours intensified, then shifted and softened. God, it was a gorgeous place to live.

She'd come here seeking sanctuary. A hideaway. But the longer she was here, the more she loved this island. Here, she was accepted for herself, not for her association with the royal Montcroix family of Rubanestein. And as much as she loved her European homeland and knew how privileged she was, it was refreshing to be somewhere where she could be known for herself, not just for being a princess.

Lord Howe Island was the perfect place to hide.

Here on this island, nobody grilled her about her accent because it seemed like every second person she'd met was from somewhere else.

Even better, not one person questioned why she was here, because everybody knew the answer. Because who wouldn't want to be here, on this island paradise?

Izzy smiled to herself as she headed inside to make a fresh mug of tea. Nobody in a million years would pick she was a European princess, and nobody could know, given her passport was safely tucked away in a safety deposit box in Sydney.

Nobody would find her here.

CHAPTER TWO

THE RUNWAY WAS little more than a short strip of tarmac between the neighbouring hills, the terminal no more than a shed, cows grazing on a nearby field. Theo took a moment at the top of the small flight of stairs to take it all in. The small-town vibe was a world away from the sumptuous palace overlooking the Mediterranean coastline that was Princess Isabella's home in the smallest principality in Europe, but maybe that was all part of her twisted logic to come here—because who would think to look for a precious princess in a place where luxury appeared to take a back seat?

But twisted logic it was, because now she was trapped, caught in the web of her own making.

He dragged in a breath as he set off down the stairs. The salty air was flavoured with avgas, but all Theo could smell was success.

Hell, forget smelling it, he was so close, he could taste it.

A group of travellers stood at the gate, waiting for the return flight to Sydney. A few families with children, a group of older people in leisure wear and a sprinkling of couples kitted out in hiking gear.

He scanned their faces. He hadn't come this far to lose her now. But no, there were no princesses that he could see amongst their number.

'You must be Theo?' a broad Australian voice said, a sixty-something man with a weather-beaten face approaching, a sign bearing the name of Theo's accommodation in one hand. 'Tom Parker's my name,' he said, glancing at the leather duffel bag in Theo's hand. 'Any more luggage to collect?'

Theo shook his head; he wasn't planning on staying long. He didn't need it. 'No luggage,' he said.

'Right-o,' said Tom, 'let's get going.' And he led Theo through the tiny terminal to a late-model sedan in the car park just beyond.

'You here on holidays, Mr Mylonakos?' he said, eying Theo's suit and tie as he stashed Theo's carry-on in the boot. 'Lord Howe Island is the perfect spot to wind down.'

'A short one,' Theo said, opening the passenger door and sliding in. 'I'm meeting a friend.'

'Oh. Someone staying with us?' The car engine purred into life.

'I'm not sure.'

The man looked at him sideways.

'It's a surprise,' Theo said. Because it would be, and then he added a little white lie. 'It's her birthday.'

'Ah,' the older man said, smiling now, a twinkle lighting his eyes. 'Well, it shouldn't take long to find her on this island. Only so many places a person can hide.'

Theo allowed himself his first smile of the day. *Exactly what he'd been thinking.*

'What's her name then?'

'Erin,' Theo said, giving the name on the passport she'd swapped with a girl she'd met in Sydney—the name she'd used on the travel documents to Lord Howe Island to try to elude anyone trying to find her. 'Erin Kowalski.'

The older man's brow puckered as he slid in behind the steering wheel. 'Nope, doesn't ring any bells.'

It was a long shot, he knew, but Theo handed him a photograph, of the Princess in a day dress, minus tiara, at a horse race. It was the most casual likeness he had of her, the wind had ruffled the ends of her blonde hair and the photographer had caught the excitement in her eyes as the horses had neared the finish line. It was the least regal photo he'd been able to find, because if the Princess was altering her appearance to fly under the radar, she wouldn't be wearing gowns and jewels now.

'Hmm,' the man said, his brow knotted as he stroked his chin.

Theo's pulse lurched. 'You've seen her?'

'Not so sure about that,' he said, as he handed the photo back. 'She looks a bit like a waitress I saw working in the café, except her hair's a different colour, and I'm pretty sure her name wasn't Erin.' He shrugged, handing the photo back. 'Then again, all these young people look alike these days, don't they?'

Theo thanked him as he took it back, not entirely defeated. He'd check out the café, of course, but he hadn't expected finding her would be that easy, even on an island the size of a postage stamp. Besides, the Princess was hardly waitress material. She'd been surrounded by staff eager to do her every bidding ever since the day she was born. She'd never worked a real job a day in her life. No, more likely he'd find her lounging on a beach making herself comfortable somewhere.

'I hope you don't mind,' Tom said, 'but I thought I'd give you a brief tour of the island before I drop you at the lodge. Help you get your bearings.'

Theo suppressed his irritation. Now that he was here, all Theo wanted to do was to get to work as soon as possible. He wasn't a tourist. He didn't need a tour. He just needed to find the Princess—before someone else did.

The car set off slowly—painfully slowly it seemed, but apparently that was the speed limit here—along the road bordering the runway that bisected the island, the driver still talking, pointing out the bowling club, the hospital, the dive school, while Theo only half listened, more interested in searching the faces of the cyclists they passed going the other way, looking for a familiar feature. Until he heard something that made him prick up his ears and swivel his head.

'Wait, wait. What did you say?' he asked.

'About the waitress the other night, you mean?'

Theo nodded.

'Well, she was getting a right dressing-down from the chef about being too slow and having to lift her game, poor girl. I thought she was about to burst into tears at one stage.'

Theo's ears pricked up. He spun his head back, more interested now. 'What girl?'

'The girl in the café. The one I mentioned before.'

Theo didn't expect to find his runaway princess employed and working. But if she was—and turned out to be a no-good waitress—what were the chances?

'But her name wasn't Erin, this girl in the café?'

'No, that doesn't ring a bell at all, but I can't help thinking she looked a bit like that girl in the picture you showed me.' He shrugged as they turned right up a hill, buildings set either side, a general store and some kind of town hall. 'Then again, it's a few days back now.' He nodded to the side as they passed a café. 'That's where I saw her, whoever she was. But I'd remember it if her name was Erin.

Struck me at the time that it rhymed with something, except I can't remember what it was now.' He chortled. 'Not to worry, it'll come to me, sure as eggs.'

The hairs on the back of Theo's neck prickled and he had to resist the urge to yell at Tom to stop so he could jump from the car and check for himself. Could it be her? But what would a spoiled princess know about waitressing? Up until now, she hadn't stayed in one spot long enough to find work.

But he said nothing. There was no need to alarm Tom that there was more to his story than what he'd made out, especially if there was no guarantee it was her. Equally, there was no need to rush. If it was her, and the Princess was so confident that her little scheme to slip her pursuers had succeeded and that she could afford to stop a while and put down some roots, then she wasn't going anywhere in a hurry.

Meanwhile he'd book for dinner tonight at the café and check it out for himself.

They left the café behind, the road rising towards a turn-off that signalled Ned's Beach, where Tom mentioned that he could feed the fish for a nominal sum. 'Got any idea what activities you'd like to try your hand at while you're here?' Tom asked. 'We've got diving or snorkelling on the coral reef, or there's game fishing out near Ball's Pyramid. Lizzie, our manager, can book you into anything you feel like.'

'I'll think about it,' Theo lied, knowing there'd be no time to play the tourist. His job was to find the Princess and get her home.

'Of course, that's it!' said Tom slapping his knee beside him. 'I don't know why it's taken so long to remember; it rhymes with Lizzie of course.'

'What does?'

'The name of the girl in the café. I knew it would come to me. The chef called her Izzy.'

Izzy?

Isabella.

And Theo wanted to punch his fist in the air with victory.

He had her.

CHAPTER THREE

THE RESTAURANT WAS buzzing when Izzy turned up for the dinner shift.

'Thank god you're here,' one of her colleagues said as she rushed past with her arms full of dirty dishes. 'It's going to be mental.'

'What's going on?' Izzy asked.

'Palmtrees has lost its generator,' the head waiter said, referring to one of the island's fully catered lodges, 'and their fridges are out. They're sending all their guests here.'

Izzy aproned up and started work. She'd been on the island long enough to work out that with their fridges out, it meant an extra hundred or so hungry people out looking for a meal. No wonder it was so busy.

For two hours she worked solidly, darting between tables, the kitchen and the bar, taking orders and fetching meals and drinks. She'd barely clear a table and it would be full again, and the whole process would start over. She was never more grateful for her earlier shifts.

'Can you get table thirty?' the manager called, backing through the kitchen door, her arms full of plates.

'On my way,' she said, picking up a couple of menus and threading her way through the bustling restaurant. She knew where table thirty was. A table for two, tucked right up the back. She smiled as she approached. A dark-haired man, sitting alone.

He looked up, as she neared, his dark eyes scowling, his gaze as combative as the hard lines of his jaw. Unnerving. Clearly not impressed at having to wait for service, but who could blame him? 'I'm so sorry to keep you waiting,' she started, wanting to head off any cause for aggravation. 'We're very busy tonight.' She placed a menu in front of him, and then one at the empty chair opposite.

'I'm eating alone,' he said, his words terse, and Izzy pulled the menu back and hugged it against her chest. Why she felt like she needed protection, she wasn't sure, but there was something in the deep timbre of his voice that sounded like it was being kept on a tight leash. Had he been stood up or had he argued with his partner and decided to eat alone? Was that the reason for his anger? Although he didn't look like any tourist, more like one of the consultants from the mainland who visited the island for a day or two to call upon their clients.

'A drink then, on the house,' she said, attempting another smile, hoping to appease, 'for keeping you waiting so long.'

A muscle twitched in his jaw, but it was his eyes that unnerved her. The way he looked at her, almost like he was looking inside her. And then he leaned sideways in his chair, crossed his long legs and smiled, and Izzy was taken aback by the transformation. It could just have been the play of light as he moved, the light and shadow moving, but it appeared that his jawline had relaxed, the hard line of his mouth softening, his lips suddenly sensual, and dark-lashed eyes creasing at the corners. All of it framed with thick dark hair. A disarmingly good-looking man when he smiled, and Izzy's heart lurched and found herself thinking, what a waste he was alone.

'Tell me,' he said, giving the menu a cursory glance before looking back at her. 'What would you recommend?'

She blinked, feeling off balance with the change in his mood. She reeled off the list of specials, the kingfish, the fillet steak and the lobster medallions, trying and failing not to notice how well his fine knit sweater skimmed his broad chest when he sat back like that.

'What would you order?' he asked, when she had finished.

'The kingfish is very popular. It's a local speciality. But my personal favourite would be the paella.'

He cocked an eyebrow, sitting forward now, like he was genuinely interested. 'Why so?'

She smiled, her mind going back to the tiny fishing villages that dotted the short Mediterranean coastline of Rubanestein, and of the street cafés far below the palace with their braziers alight, topped with vast pans filled with seafood and rice, the warm night air filled with the scent of salt and saffron, the sizzle and smoke of the burners, and the warm-hearted conviviality of the people. 'It reminds me of my home,' she said, feeling an unexpected pang of something approximating homesickness. Not that she had been free to roam the streets of the villages or enjoy the bonhomie of the villagers by herself, always accompanied by her bodyguards and minders. Always. Never free. Not like here. And the homesickness was suddenly snuffed out on a familiar tide of resentment.

'Where is home?'

His words interrupted her thoughts. She'd been miles away. Continents. An entire hemisphere. She shook her head to clear it. 'A little place in Europe,' she said, screwing up her nose. 'You wouldn't have heard of it. Would you like to order now?'

'I'll have the paella,' he said, taking her recommendation, ordering a glass of Tasmanian pinot noir to go with it. He handed her back the menu. 'Thank you for helping me decide,' he said, turning up the warmth in his smile so that it zinged all the way to her toes.

Not just good-looking, she told herself as she weaved her way back through the bustling tables to the kitchen. Seriously good-looking. Even drop-dead gorgeous when he smiled like that.

She returned from the bar with the bottle, pouring the ruby-coloured liquid into his glass, so conscious he was watching her that her skin tingled and her cheeks burned, and it was all she could do to stop the hand holding the bottle from shaking.

'Will that be all?' she asked, her task completed, relieved she hadn't spilled a drop given the intensity of his scrutiny.

'For now,' he said, and there was that zing again.

Millie winked when they crossed paths in the kitchen. 'You took your time out there,' she said, nodding in the direction of table thirty. 'Who's the hunk? Someone you know?'

'No. He just wanted my advice on what to order.'

'Then I think he fancies you,' she said. 'He can't take his eyes off you.'

'Rubbish,' she said, but Millie was already away with her next order, and Izzy similarly loaded her arms up with her next delivery, discounting Millie's comment. But as she worked the tables, she wasn't so sure. Every time she happened to glance over in that direction, her eyes were snagged by his and he would smile, sending warmth rippling down her spine that persisted, even when she'd turned away. She didn't have to look up to know he was still watching her. She could feel his eyes in the tingling of her skin and the fizz of her blood. And she sensed with a woman's intuition that he wasn't just staring at her because he was impatient for his meal to be served.

For a woman who'd never before experienced this zing of attraction, an attraction not based on her title and how that might work for him, but an attraction between a man and a woman, it was as unexpected as it was intoxicating.

'Enjoy your meal,' Izzy said, placing a plate in front of him and the steaming pan in the centre of the table. And yet instead of the fragrant spiced paella, all she seemed to be able to smell was this man, and the warm, clean scent of him. It was unnerving being so aware of a man. Not only because it was an unfamiliar experience, but because it seemed too personal. Too intimate. She backed away as soon as the pan was down, aiming to get away and back to the kitchen as quickly as possible, but not before he could ask, 'What's your name?'

She paused in her retreat, laced the fingers of her hands together in front of her. 'Izzy.'

He leant his head to one side, dark eyes silently appraising. 'You remind me of someone.'

Her stomach lurched, even as she told herself there was no reason to worry. There was no reason to think this man knew who she was. It was the fear she'd been living with for these last six weeks rearing its ugly head once again. The constant fear of being discovered. She pushed loose tendrils of her hair behind her ears, forced a smile to her lips, aiming for casual interest, when she felt a bundle of nerves. 'Do I?'

He shook his head, as if shaking the idea away. 'But no. Her name was something quite different.'

Relief. She smiled and felt herself relax. 'I'm sure we all have a double or two out there somewhere in the world.'

'Yes,' he said, his eyes back on hers, smile back in place. 'That must be it. Very nice to meet you though, Izzy from a little place in Europe I wouldn't have heard of.'

Izzy headed to another table to clear their plates, feeling a little sideswiped by the encounter. Something didn't sit quite right. Something that had turned an exciting stomach-fluttering encounter into something entirely more unnerving. Because the smile that had accompanied his words was empty—words that had included both her name and her home continent, when he'd offered nothing. And even if not specific—if he'd been looking for Princess Isabella it might be enough...

She dropped off the dirty dishes in the kitchen and stole a glance between the bar and the glassware that hung suspended upside down from the rails above it.

He was eating his meal, she noticed, but not like a diner thoroughly taken with the experience, content to concentrate on the food on his plate, or scrolling through his phone as if searching for a whisper of internet, but as if going through the motions when he had another, far more important duty to perform. Like scanning the restaurant and taking notice of every movement. As if searching. Always searching. He turned his head towards the bar and she ducked behind it. Before he saw her? Who could tell? All she knew was that this unsettled feeling in her stomach wasn't going to go away until she could get away.

And she hadn't got this far without taking heed of her gut feelings.

If he didn't know who she was, then her absence wouldn't matter. And if he did—at least it might afford her a head start.

Millie obviously took her interest in her table-for-one for something other than what it was. 'How are you getting on with Mr Dreamboat? Has he asked you about dessert yet?' She followed it with a wicked wink that suggested she hadn't been talking about any sweet on the menu.

Izzy scanned the restaurant. The tables were emptying, the rush over. 'Do you think it would be all right, if I finished my shift now?'

Millie's eyes narrowed suspiciously, her lips curled. 'Are you sure you're not just wanting to sneak off early with Mr Table Number Thirty?'

'No! It's just—' She scrambled for an excuse. 'I'm feeling a little weird.'

'Hey, it's okay, I was kidding. And you do look a bit peaky. Go on, you've already worked longer than rostered.' She leaned closer to whisper in her ear. 'And don't tell anyone I told you this, but Chef is really happy with how quickly you've picked the job up. Any chance you could come back and do another evening shift tomorrow?'

The praise should have bolstered her spirits more than it did. Instead, it was only relief she felt. 'I'll be here,' Izzy promised, crossing fingers behind her back. Because with luck, she would, and this man would be nowhere to be seen. She swiped off her apron and collected her bag, slipping out the back door with a wave and a quiet goodbye to the kitchen staff.

She was probably overreacting, dashing away like this. No doubt she'd feel foolish about it later, but it was better to be cautious. Better to be sure. The interaction with the stranger today had felt both exciting and unsettling. Already she felt relieved to be away from his presence, and out in the clear island air where she could think straight. Her bike was propped up against the building where she'd left it. The wind was gusting, whipping at her hair even as she struggled to pull on her helmet. She'd heard mention of a storm cell possibly tracking close to the island. That might make things interesting for the next few days.

She cycled off, proud of herself for cornering around the side without having to put her feet down. Then she was at the road and the restaurant was behind her, and with every pedal of her feet, she felt the tension leach out of her. The wind rattled through the palm trees lining either side of the road, the fronds dancing on the wind, almost as if chattering to each other, while the ocean waves boomed as they crashed into the lagoon's coral reef. She breathed deeply of the fertile air, laced with salt. She loved this island. It was friendly and so easy to live in and, best of all, she was free, with nobody to tell her what she could and couldn't do and—she shuddered—who she would marry.

Two cyclists going the other way waved to her, a van ambled slowly past delivering a load of diners back to their accommodation, but other than that, the road was empty and dark. Anywhere else in the world, that might feel threatening, or even feel scary. But here she felt safe.

Already, her sudden departure seemed ridiculous. She'd imagined the threat. Blown it up in her mind like the wind gusting off the sea. Soon she'd be back in her cabin and a mysterious dark-eyed man and his unsettling gaze would be nothing more than a distant memory.

The headlights of a car appeared behind, slowly catching up to her, and giving her a wide berth as it passed. She waved but it was too dark to see if anyone waved back—but no matter, as this was her turn. Just up the hill a bit was the driveway to her simple cabin.

She turned into her driveway as another car cruised by—or was it the same one doubling back? There weren't that many cars on the island. She stepped behind a hibiscus tree and waited until it disappeared over the hill. Okay, so she was officially paranoid. They'd probably just missed their turn-off.

With relief she let herself into her accommodation and snapped on the kettle. She really needed a calming cup of chamomile tea. Ten minutes later, she was sitting on her sofa, Andrea Bocelli playing on her speakers, with shoes off and aching feet up and a mug of tea in hands, feeling that all was once again right in Izzy's world.

The knock on the door changed that, a knock on the door that came with no accompanying call from Inga or Sven or anyone who would know to do that. She jumped to her feet, for the first time having cause to question the island's lack of door locks; something that had seemed quaint and old world-y when she'd first been told, something that now felt a whole lot more threatening. All was silent outside, but she could feel a dark presence, malevolent and waiting.

'Who is it?' she called, even though she knew by the chill in her spine and the smothering weight of silence that answered her call. Isabella looked around, needing to think fast. Whoever it was could turn the handle and walk right in. But there was a window in the bedroom behind her. She had no idea where she was going to run—there was no time to formulate a plan. All she knew was that she had to get away. 'Hold on,' she said, infusing a degree of brightness into her voice that she didn't feel, already halfway there. 'I'll be right there.'

She had the window up and the screen off with one leg over the sill and the other close behind, momentum propelling her forward, when she heard a deep voice say, 'Going somewhere, Princess?'

CHAPTER FOUR

IT WAS DARK behind the cabin, all shifting shadows and slapping leaves, but she knew instantly from his voice that it was him—*the man from table thirty*—and she knew she'd been right and that she had to get away. But she had too much momentum to back up. She tumbled headfirst out the window and collided with a wall that shouldn't be there, a wall that encircled her with bands of steel, arresting her fall. 'Oof,' she said, as the air was forced from her lungs. Flight no longer an option, her fight reflex kicked in. 'Let me go!' she said, her heart beating frantically in her chest, her legs kicking, her hands beating at her captor's chest.

'I have to hand it to you, Princess,' he said, totally unmoved by her efforts to free herself. 'You've been very clever. But your little game is over, and now it's time to take you home.'

'You're mad,' she said, still writhing against the wall of his body. The all too hot and hard wall of his body. 'I don't know what you're talking about.'

'So why all that effort to sneak out the window?'

'Because you're stalking me! And now you're making up some crazy story to justify kidnapping me.' She squirmed and tugged, harder this time, but still to no effect, except for the damning friction she created in her efforts. 'Let me go!'

'You must have known that someone would catch up with you eventually. You're lucky that it's me. And now, to quote the classic line from the movies, it would be easier for us both if you came quietly.'

Quietly?

Now there was an idea. There was nothing on this island to confirm her true identity—all her ID was in Erin's name. It was her word against his and who was going to believe a man who wanted to take her from the island against her will? She opened her mouth, only to feel his hand clamp hard over her open mouth, smothering her attempt to scream.

'There's no point fighting the inevitable, Princess. Prince Rafael wants you home safe and sound, and that's where I'm taking you.'

Izzy had always known what being caught meant—an end to her new-found freedom and the beginning of a new hell, a forced marriage to a man she could never love. But it was hearing mention of her hateful brother's name that tipped her over the edge. She writhed and bucked, kicking out at him, trying to find traction even as he held her high and hard against him. But her feet couldn't reach the ground and all she succeeded in doing was landing kicks at his legs. Not that he so much as flinched. Her brother had sent a robot to hunt her down, the man must be made of metal or stone. But curse Rafael and his man-mountain, she wasn't going back. Not if it meant she would serve as a pawn in one of Rafael's selfish schemes.

'Ngh, ngh!' she muttered against his hand, finally finding a crack between his fingers to spit out the words, 'I'll see my brother rot in hell first!'

And the hands wrapped around her eased a fraction, as

a deep voice whispered in her ear. 'Thank you, Princess. You can stop with the pretence now.'

And Isabella knew she'd been had. She went limp in his arms, the fight gone out of her.

'That's more like it,' he said, and swung her into his arms.

'What are you doing?' she protested, as her body slammed against his chest.

'Taking you back through the front door so you can pack your things. Although, if you prefer, I can toss you back through the window the same way you came out?'

He was laughing at her now. And yes, so maybe it wouldn't be the most elegant way to enter the cabin, but she might actually prefer it if he did. It was impossible to think with his arms under her back and legs, impossible to think when she was this close and when his every movement generated friction where their bodies rubbed. And she so needed space to think. Whatever this man thought, she wasn't about to give up her freedom, just because he'd found her. She'd find a way to get away. She couldn't go back. Not to what her brother had planned for her.

'Who are you?' she demanded, turning on her most imperious voice, a voice that had been known to turn grown courtiers into simpering wrecks. 'Why are you manhandling me like this?'

He laughed out loud this time, a gruff laugh that only served to ratchet up her ill humour, as he bounded up the steps to the veranda like she weighed nothing, her body jolting against his firm torso—his *too hard, too hot* torso—with every stride. And the more she tried to squirm away, the more friction she caused. Curse the man, why couldn't he have felt cold, like the stone he looked like he'd been carved from?

'You have the nerve to laugh at me?' she said, if only to pretend she thought nothing of the sizzling heat where their bodies met.

'I don't know who you think you're ordering around, Princess,' he said, 'but it's wasted on me. I'm Theo Mylonakos. The Prince wants you home where you'll be safe, and it's my job to get you there.'

'The Prince wants? *The Prince wants?* And you pander to him like he's the only person who matters. What about what *I* want? Why does what I want count for nothing?'

'You are a princess of Rubanestein,' he said, using his foot to kick the front door closed behind them. 'Your duty lies with your country and its people.'

His words rankled. She didn't have to be lectured about her duty, she'd lived for nothing more than her country and its people for most of her twenty-five years, all through the reign of her father and his premature death, the coronation of her brother and the honeymoon period of his reign—in fact, right up until the time her brother had announced that her premier duty to the principality was to be sold off like she was no more than his personal chattel in order to cover his gambling losses.

'And if I refuse to go?'

He let her go so unexpectedly that her knees buckled beneath her. She would have collapsed to the floor but for the large hands that seized her waist, arresting her fall. Air whooshed from her lungs, not only out of shock, but because there was that burn again, this time at her waist. He had big hands. Long-fingered hands that made such a mockery of the fabric of her T-shirt that it might just as well have been made of silk—gossamer-thin silk that transmitted the heat of his hands to her senses. She could feel the heat from every pad of his fingers, she could feel the press of every single digit of his hand against her flesh.

It was sheer hell. Yet at the same time, it was mesmerising. *Hypnotising.* She knew she should protest at his intrusion, at the personal invasion of her space and her body, but with the sensation spiralling through her flesh, sending sparks to places she'd never felt the touch of sparks—in the tightness of her nipples, in the aching flesh between her thighs, sensation stalled any immediate protest.

She felt his breath fan across her face, and she looked up to see him looking down at her, his face inches away, his eyes dark, his expression stern, like she was some kind of problem to him. And only then did she realise that she must have thrown out her arms in desperation and that her own hands were full, clinging to his firm shoulders.

She tested her knees and found her footing. He was too close, his masculine scent invading her space, and she needed to get away.

But it was he who let go before she did.

She wobbled just a little as she spun away, feeling relief that his hands were gone, at the same time feeling their absence—feeling the lack of his proximity—like a loss. *Madness.* But the heat hadn't gone. It had moved, surging into her cheeks at her own ridiculous thoughts.

She turned back, hoping that he took her reddened cheeks as embarrassment, or better still, outrage. Outrage. *Now there was the preferable option.* And she should feel outraged. She jerked up her chin and puffed out her chest. 'I could order you fed to the palace eels for manhandling me the way you just did.'

'The way I saved you, you mean?'

She snorted. 'Some saviour. Bundling me up like a trussed-up turkey. Dropping me like a stone.'

'I did prevent you from falling to the floor.'

'And I should thank you for that?'

'I don't expect thanks. I'll settle for you packing your things and coming with me.'

'Then you're in for a disappointment. I'm not leaving.'

He took a step closer. 'Sorry to disappoint you, Princess,' he snarled, 'but you don't have a choice.'

His eyes had turned obsidian, the angles of his face turned harsher and more defined, his lips a terse line, and Izzy wondered if she'd imagined the softening in his features she'd thought she'd witnessed at the restaurant. Maybe it had been a trick of the light, because there was not one iota of softness in his features now. His eyes were like stone. His jawline constructed of rigid angles. Hard, unforgiving and immovable. Like the man himself.

He spun on his heel and headed into the bedroom she'd so recently tried to escape from and slammed the window shut. Then he pulled her backpack from the top of the wardrobe and threw it on the bed before stepping back to make way for her. He crossed his arms. 'Now, pack your things. You're staying with me tonight, where I can keep an eye on you. We leave on the first flight.'

'No! I told you, I am not leaving. Even if I agreed to go with you, which I am not, there's no way I could leave tomorrow anyway.'

'Give it up, Princess,' he growled, 'this is getting old already. You've had your fun. Playtime is over, and now it's time to go home.'

She stamped her foot. 'This is not playtime. Don't treat me like a child.'

'Then don't act like one.'

The man was beyond infuriating. 'Look,' she said, pinching her nose and breathing deep, taking a moment to calm herself down. This man was clearly easy to aggravate, so maybe it was time to be a bit more placatory. Hopefully a bit more persuasive. 'So, you've found me—congratulations—you win. But does it matter if it's a day or two later that I arrive home? Because I can't leave tomorrow. I'm working a shift tomorrow evening.'

He shook his head as if dealing with a recalcitrant child, as clearly, he regarded her. 'Forget it. You don't need to work.'

'That's hardly the point. The point is, I have a job and I promised to work tomorrow evening's shift.'

He scoffed. 'You're a waitress. I'm sure they'll manage to cover you.'

It wasn't just the words. It was the disdain that put her back up, his thorough disregard for her work—for *the* work—as if waiting tables was so lowly that it was no kind of job at all. And suddenly she was over with all attempts at peacemaking. She was livid. 'How dare you? How dare you talk about duty and what my duty is when you have no idea what duty entails? I made a commitment to this business, and I intend to see it through. So, if you insist on taking me back to Rubanestein, against my will I might add, then you're going to have to wait until *I'm* ready to go.'

His lip curled. 'Nice speech. So, when are you going to start packing, Princess, or do you expect me to do it for you?'

'So, wait a day! Twenty-four hours. Where's the harm in that?'

'Haven't you heard? There's a cyclone hovering off the coast. I'm not prepared for it to get any closer and risk our chances of getting off this island.'

'Of course I've heard. Everyone's heard. But we're not in the path. It's hardly a problem.'

He said nothing. Just cast his eyes in the direction of her backpack. The man was insufferable.

'In that case,' she said, crossing her arms over her chest, 'you do it.' She was hardly going to help him. She had more important things to do, like work out how she was going to get away. Her teeth played with her lip. She could escape while he was in the other room, of course, the door didn't have a lock, and she'd have a lead of a second or two before he realised. But this man was fit. And he was built. Slamming into his chest had told her that, and that lead of a second or two would evaporate into nothingness the moment he caught on. She needed a better plan. And she had at the very most one night to come up with one.

He looked back at her, his eyebrows raised, his lips curled into a sardonic smile. But he said nothing, simply opened the small wardrobe and peeled from the hangers the few shirts and a sundress she had inside. Turned to a small chest of drawers and pulled open a drawer and scooped out a handful of lace bras and panties and smalls, before he seemed to realise what he was holding and rapidly looked away as he shoved them into the backpack.

The next drawer's contents of jeans and shorts followed her underwear into the pack. 'Is that it?' he said, sounding like he must have missed something.

'Of course not, you'll find the ball gowns and tiaras in the gilded chest under the bed.'

He made a move to glance below the bed before thinking better of it and giving her a glare that could have stripped paint. 'Funny,' he said.

'I thought so,' she said, feeling her lips tweak in spite of the desperate circumstances. 'It sure gave me a smile.'

He growled, a low, deep growl that spoke of his frustration with her. Of his frustration to be done with her. Of his desperation to be rid of her.

'Tomorrow,' he said. 'We fly out tomorrow.'

'No!'

He shook his head. 'You don't have a say in this.'

'Wow. You sound just like my brother. He doesn't think I should have a say in anything either.'

He grunted. 'Maybe he has a point.'

'Or maybe he's just a controlling bastard like you. Congratulations on finding your soulmate. I hope you're both very happy together.'

His eyes turned to slate. His nostrils flared. 'Are you done?'

'Oh, but you provide such rich material. I'm sure I'll find more.'

'Excellent. Then while you're finding things, maybe you can gather up your toiletries in the bathroom and we can get out of here.'

'Why do I need to go anywhere? You know where I'm going to be tomorrow evening—working my shift at the restaurant, no doubt to be glowered at every minute of my shift by your own uncharming visage.'

'Nice try, Princess. Leave you here tonight and discover tomorrow that you've done a runner? It's not going to happen. Now go and get the rest of your things.'

'Where do you think I'm going to run? There's something like two flights out a day and I won't be catching either of them, because, like I told you, I am committed to a shift tomorrow night.'

'So you say. But I can't take that risk. You're coming with me tonight and we're flying out tomorrow. Together.'

Her arms flew wide before slapping back against her thighs. 'What is your problem? I've already been gone for weeks. What difference is twenty-four hours going to make?'

He zipped up the backpack. 'Don't you realise what you're risking, Princess? You leave yourself open to any kind of attack. And in doing so, you expose Rubanestein in the process.'

'And what, pray tell, do you think might happen to me? Do you think there's a chance that I might be kidnapped and taken somewhere against my will?' She snorted. 'Imagine that!'

He growled. 'I'm not kidnapping you. I'm rescuing you from yourself and your foolish actions.'

She put her hands on her hips. 'I am twenty-five years old, and you are insisting on taking me somewhere against my will. I'd call that kidnapping.'

'No, I'm safely returning you to the place where you belong, because if I worked out who you really are, don't you think that anyone else who is no doubt searching for you will?'

Her head snapped up at the thought that others might also be pursuing her. But no. He was trying to frighten her. Of course, he would try to scare her. 'You're bluffing.'

He said nothing. Just stared at her as he stood rock solid in front of her, and his silence slid uncomfortably down her spine, dislodging her rock-solid faith in her argument. 'So tell me, who else is supposedly looking for me?'

'Don't fool yourself into believing that I'm the only one. You've been missing in action so long that, no matter how much the palace has tried to dampen down speculation, your absence has been noted. The fact you missed the Prince's birthday ball three weeks ago only ramped up speculation that you'd run away and were on the loose.'

She made a move to interject and he cut her off with a slash of one hand.

'Don't you see? A runaway princess. Alone. Unprotected. Don't you realise the danger you've put yourself in, not to mention the embarrassment you're causing your country?'

His words stung Isabella's psyche. She hated the thought that her actions might result in embarrassment to Rubanestein, but she knew without a shadow of a doubt that if the true reason for her fleeing was made public, it would cause more damage to her country and the Prince than mere embarrassment. But there was no point trying to explain that to this man-mountain.

Izzy swallowed and spun away. Why did life have to be so complicated? All she'd wanted to do was escape from her brother and his demands and live life on her own terms. And not only was that not acceptable but now there were apparently rogue actors pursuing her?

She took a deep breath as she stared out into the dark. Tried to think. Tried to apply logic to the situation and not let his words frighten her. After all, this was a man who was trying to convince her to go with him and go quietly. Why wouldn't he try everything to make her accede to his every demand? She spun back around. 'But you have me now. You know where I am. I'm supposedly "safe" with you. So where's the risk with waiting one more day? Why should I feel frightened?'

'You should feel frightened, Princess, because, if anyone else catches up with you, I doubt you'll be bargaining for just one extra day.'

Her mouth went dry. If he was trying to frighten her, he was succeeding. 'What does that mean?'

'It means you're lucky I found you first. You're safe with me. I'll get you home.'

'Then maybe I should take my chances with whoever else is after me. Because I'm not safe with anyone who wants to return me to Rubanestein.'

'Stop being ridiculous. Think about your safety if you can't think about your country. I'm taking you back to your home where you'll be safe.'

'That's rubbish. You say I'm in danger here, but if you take me back, you'll be delivering me right back into the lion's den. Why do you think I ran? I'm not some rebellious teenager. Hasn't it occurred to you that I had my reasons for running?'

'I know, you did. You have a conflict with your brother.' He shrugged. 'It's understandable that you would be envious and it's equally understandable that you'd be angry and want to embarrass him.'

'Wait. What? Envious? What are you talking about?'

'Give it up, Princess. You're twelve months older than Rafael and yet, due to Rubanestein's traditional rules of succession, it is he who is on the throne and not you. It must have been a blow to see your younger brother accede to the throne when even the British monarchy, the oldest and most famous royal institution in the world, has modernised its rules so that the crown is passed down the line of succession not according to male-preference primogeniture.'

Izzy blinked, unable to believe what she was hearing. Unable to process it. She half-laughed, half-snorted, a very unladylike-*un-princess-like* snort. 'Is that what my dear brother told you? That I'm envious of him because he's on the throne and not me?'

'Why else would you come up with this little act of rebellion, if not to make some kind of statement?'

'Seriously, do I look like somebody who hungers to be
on the throne? I've known my entire life that, failing a disaster, I would never accede to the throne. I have always
been good with that. Do you really think I ran away because I'm in a snit?' She shook her head. 'You underesti-
mate me, Mr Mylonakos, by a long way.'

He blinked. Slowly. 'Whatever, Prince Rafael is concerned for your safety and wants you escorted safely
home.'

'That's a joke. He's never been concerned for anything
other than his own well-being. He doesn't care for me. He
doesn't care for anyone or anything other than how they
can be of use to him.'

'Then why is he so keen to have you returned home,
if he cares so little for you, his sister, his own flesh and
blood?'

'Because he's racked up millions of Euros in debt and
the Treasurer-General had the intestinal fortitude to prevent Rafael from getting his filthy hands in the Public
Treasury.'

'What does that have to do with you?'

'Everything. He made a deal with one of his cronies.'
She let that sink in for a moment waiting for him to join the
dots. She saw the frown draw his brows together, creasing
his brow. She witnessed the exact moment when realisation dawned on him, his dark eyes incredulous.

'Yes, Mr Mylonakos. He sold me. That's why he's so
desperate to get me back in the palace under his control.
So, he can carry out his plan to marry me off to the creep
who's going to bail him out.'

His tense features relaxed. The corners of his mouth

tweaked up. He shook his head. 'You've had weeks to come up with a story and that's the best you could manage? Don't you think that's just a bit melodramatic?'

'It's the truth!'

'So you say. But your response is straight out of the playbook. Prince Rafael said you'd say something like that.'

'Because it's the truth and he knows it!'

'Sure. Last I heard, Rubanestein was a modern European principality. What you are suggesting is positively medieval.'

She clenched her teeth. 'I see you've met my brother. He and his appalling wedding deal are the reasons I'm not going back.'

He shook his head. 'Princess—'

'Stop calling me princess. My name is Izzy.'

'I can't call you that. You're a princess. Princess Isabella.'

'Then why do you make it sound like an insult?'

Did he? If he did, it was because he was sick of the chase. He was sick of the arguments. Responsibility came with being an adult. He had no patience for people who shirked their responsibilities, preferring the easy life, ungrateful for the hand they'd been dealt.

He had people on his books who wanted to be rescued. Who desperately needed to be rescued. People who were a whole lot more deserving than this spoilt runaway who seemed intent on wasting his time.

Of course, he hadn't expected her to come without a fight, but she could have come up with something a bit more original than her evil brother who wanted to marry her off to settle the gambling debts story that she'd spun.

Nothing in his research had so much as hinted at the Prince having a gambling problem.

'I won't call you Izzy. You are Princess Isabella d'Montcroix of Rubanestein. It's about time you started acting like it. Now, we're leaving. You can wash whatever that is out of your hair when you get to my apartment.'

'Won't I be in even more risk of being recognised if I do wash out the colour? What if someone does recognise me and tries to snatch me away from you for ransom?'

He was beginning to think it was a good idea. 'Maybe I'll let them,' he said. 'It would save me a whole lot of grief.'

She laughed. She actually had the audacity to laugh.

'That wasn't a joke, Princess.'

'If I didn't know better,' she said, 'I'd be starting to think that I'm getting under your skin.'

'Don't flatter yourself, Princess.'

'Stop calling me Princess!'

He smiled around gritted teeth. 'Now who's getting under whose skin?'

CHAPTER FIVE

HER BACKPACK WAS zipped and stowed in his car and with nothing of hers left in her cabin, there was no choice for her but to begrudgingly settle into the passenger seat of his rental car. But she was far from settled. She was still thinking, still trying to buy time, still trying to work out a way to escape her captor, still rattled by the strange effect he had on her setting the nerves alight under her skin.

She shivered, wishing she could forget the impact this man had on her senses, and focus on her more immediate problem. This man had assured her that she was safe with him, but how could she believe him? There was no safety while his goal was to return her to the prison of the Rubanestein palace and to a soulless, loveless future.

She *had* to get away. She just had to work out how.

She thought about all she knew about him—about the mysterious dark-eyed man who'd all but bewitched her in the restaurant with his earnest gaze, and a smile that had transformed him into warmth. A warmth that had disappeared the moment he'd followed her to her cabin and hovered outside her door, a dark and malevolent presence. And that was before snatching her into his arms outside her window and turning her mind to the conflict between the outrage that he had dared to do that, and the unwanted distraction of the heat she felt where their bodies had connected.

That, and his story that he was somehow now her saviour. Surely saviours were supposed to be more recognisable. Like a hero who catches a runaway skier before they plunge headlong into a ravine, or the firefighter who runs into a burning building to save a baby lying in its cot, or the heroine who stops her car at the scene of a car crash to give a victim life-saving CPR.

Like an angel.

The concept of saviour hardly applied to a man who insisted on taking her back to her odious brother, and to the marriage and hellish life he intended to commit her to.

Similarly, the concept hardly applied to a man who might even be acting for someone other than her brother— one of those "rogue actors" he'd implied were also after her. But if he were a rogue actor, he was making a big mistake pretending to be her saviour by promising to take her home.

Big mistake.

The sky was dark, the moon and stars hidden behind the clouds, and it was only the car's headlights that cut a swath through the swaying palms either side to illuminate the road ahead. The slow way forward. The speed limit ensured the car could move at little more than a crawl. She could see from his set features in the glow of the dashboard lights that it was killing him to have to proceed so slowly.

She looked out her window. She could open her door, she mused, roll into the undergrowth on the side of the road, and run. At this speed it shouldn't kill her. And it would have to take him a moment to realise she'd made a dash for freedom, stop the car and come after her. It might not be enough time for her to find a place to hide, but with the rising wind he might not hear her running over the rattle of palm leaves.

Although where she might go then…? Back to her apartment to seek cover with Inga and Sven? But that would be the first place he'd look, and she didn't want to visit her problems onto them. Maybe she could head to the mountains and bury herself deep in the bush?

'Don't even think about it, Princess.'

She looked back. 'Think about what?'

'About running away.'

'Who said I was thinking about running away?'

Did she imagine the tweak of his lips, or was it just the crease in the corners as he pressed them tightly together?

'The doors are locked. You're not going anywhere.'

'I accept.'

'Excuse me?'

'I don't intend going anywhere, either. So glad you finally agree.'

He voiced a word that bore more than a slight resemblance to a curse. 'We've established you're not coming quietly, Princess. But I need you to accept that you are coming.'

'And you, Mr Mylonakos,' she said, abandoning all attempts at being placatory, 'need to accept that I'm not.'

'Princess…'

'No. I will not go with you. I refuse to go with you.'

He sighed. 'Yes, so you said.'

'Then why don't you listen to me?'

'Because you're not safe here. You're not safe anywhere on the planet until you're safely returned to Rubanestein.'

'I'm not safe in Rubanestein! Why can't you get that through your head? Or are you a fan of forced marriages? Is that what this is about?'

'Princess—'

'Princess nothing. What if it was your sister? Would you be happy to marry her off to some creep to settle someone else's gambling debts?'

His eyes were bleak. 'My sister is dead.' His voice was low and thick. Gravel over pain.

Oh. Her jibe about him having a sister was meant to be nothing more than a prompt, a search for empathy if there was any empathy to be found inside the man. She hadn't expected to find tragedy instead.

'I'm so sorry.'

He shook his head, as if trying to shake away her words. 'Don't be. It was a long time ago. It's not your fault.'

'I wasn't apologising. I'm sorry for your loss.'

'Good to know,' he said, perfunctorily, the car pulling into a driveway.

Her eyes opened wide as she realised where she was. 'You're staying here?' She'd only been on the island a few days, but it was long enough to know that Capella Lodge was one of the premier accommodation providers on the island. And one of the most expensive. 'You must have some expense account. How much is my brother paying you?'

He looked skywards as he unclipped his seat belt.

'Nowhere near enough,' she said. 'I get it.'

His head swivelled around, and she could see in his eyes that she'd answered her own question. She shrugged as she slipped her own seat belt from her shoulders. 'You should have asked for more.'

He carried her bag into a suite that was decorated in a calming palette of navy blue and white, broken by cool timber trims and furniture.

'Your bedroom is upstairs,' he said. 'I sleep down here.'

'In case I try to run away?'

'You can try, but what would be the point? There's nowhere to run on this island and there's no way you'll get off it.'

'Isn't that what I already told you?'

'Sure, but if I have to watch you, I'd rather you were here, sleeping upstairs, than at your apartment with me sleeping on your floor waiting for you to jump out the window at any moment.'

She looked around, taking in the décor. It was a world apart from her humble cabin. The suite oozed luxury, the floor-to-ceiling-length windows drinking in the view. In a break in the cloud, a glimmer of moonlight, there was no missing the shadow of the twin mountains looming ominously over them, while the fronds of the kentia palms provided the musical score, chattering and clapping in the breeze. The wind was rising, but that had been expected given the route of the cyclone passing to the north.

'I guess it might be a fraction more comfortable.' She turned to him. 'Now, about my shift tomorrow evening...'

He shook his head. 'Not happening. We're leaving tomorrow.'

'It's just one day,' she pleaded. 'Twenty-four little hours. Where's the harm in that?'

'No chance,' he said. 'With that cyclone brewing off the coast, I'm not risking the airport closing and getting stuck here on the island with no way off.'

'I heard it's changed direction and veered away. Please, let me work this one shift. And then I'll come with you.'

Like hell she'd come with him. When she was no doubt already thinking of a plan to get away and continue her little escapade somewhere else.

She must have read the doubt in his eyes. 'I'm not planning on running away again, if that's what you're worried about. I just don't want to let my friends down. They were good enough to give me a job when I had no experience, and I won't leave them in the lurch, just because you have an overblown sense of responsibility.'

He didn't bother responding. She wasn't going to listen anyway.

'For goodness' sake,' she went on, trying to make him see reason and bend even just a little. 'It's just one more day. Where's the problem with that?'

There was a problem. No, there were two. The first problem was that the Prince had been informed, and Theo would not risk losing the Princess. Not after she'd already embarrassed him and his firm by evading discovery for so long.

The second was more disturbing. There was something about the Princess—something that set alarm bells ringing under his skin. It was bad enough that she was attractive. But he didn't need to know how well she felt in his arms. He knew she was a danger to him—someone he needed to keep his distance from. The sooner he was rid of her, the better.

The Princess was impatient for his reply. 'Check out the weather radar if you don't believe me. The island isn't in the path of the storm.'

He didn't answer. Simply turned away to stash his bag in his room.

'Please,' she said, chasing after him. 'It's important to me. Don't make me let them down.'

He turned back on a sigh. 'It's not up for discussion, Princess. Now, how about you go upstairs and wash out whatever the hell that cacophony of colour is that you've got going on in your hair?'

* * *

Izzy was beyond frustrated. She stepped into the rainforest shower and tilted her head under the cascade of water.
She didn't need shampoo at first, the chalk washed freely
from her hair, turning the floor of the shower stall into a
crazy shifting kaleidoscope.

As the colour bleached away, Izzy felt like she was losing the identity she'd been so enjoying. The free-wheeling
backpacker adventurer she'd been pretending to be was
being washed away, and more and more it felt like she was
being forced back into her previous life. The life of the
Princess Isabella. Bound by protocols. Restricted by rules.

Sold to the highest bidder.

And her captor thought nothing of forcing her back to
the hell-hole she'd escaped. And yet she was no minor
who'd run off in a snit. She was an adult. And if there were
rogue actors out there who were after her for their own
gain, as he'd claimed, maybe it was preferable to risk her
future with them. She'd successfully avoided her pursuers until now, and why shouldn't she keep avoiding them?
There was no safety awaiting her in Rubanestein.

It was clear she was going to have to come up with a
new strategy. Dealing with Theo was like dealing with
a block of granite. The man didn't respond to reason—
he had not one ounce of empathy in his entire body. He
thought she was lying, he thought she was confecting her
reason for running. He had clearly drunk her brother's
Kool-Aid. That, or he was being paid so much that his head
wasn't about to be turned. Whatever the reason, clearly, he
wasn't about to change his mind any time soon.

Which meant she had to up her game.

If she didn't, she'd be on that plane to Sydney tomorrow

and heading back to Rubanestein and a fate and a future she couldn't bear. All she needed was a plan.

From the far edges of her mind random thoughts and possibilities drifted in and out of view, until like jigsaw pieces, some of them fitted together, forming a scheme that she would never before have considered, let alone dared. But these were extraordinary times. Desperate times. And as someone very wise a very long time ago said, desperate times called for desperate measures.

The only question was, was she brave enough to carry out her crazy plan?

CHAPTER SIX

IT WAS A summer trip to the beach, a rare escape from their landlocked village for Theo's hard-working family. The sun shone in a sky of endless blue, the golden sand warm beneath their feet. Together the family built a sandcastle, decorating the walls with shells and digging a moat around it, along with a canal to let in the incoming waves.

Theo's younger sister gave squeals of delight as every wave after wave flowed in, filling the moat surrounding their sandcastle, before draining back into the sea. And when that novelty wore off, Theo and his sister played in the shallows, following schools of tiny fish while their parents took a break under a tent set up on the shore.

It was a perfect summer day.

The change came almost imperceptibly at first. A subtle shift in the weather, the breeze changing direction and turning gusty, stirring gentle waves into whitecaps. Laughter from swimmers turned to whoops, some of delight, some of shock as the waves built.

Theo's father was the first in their family to react. 'Theo, Helena,' he called, rising from his chair, 'it's time to come out.'

Theo agreed. They were still only in the shallows, but a sudden undertow was sucking at his legs. He turned to relay the message to his sister in case she hadn't heard, when he saw a wave break behind her, knocking her off her feet and tumbling her into the wash.

'Helena!' he screamed, bracing himself against the crashing wave before surging through the water to reach his sister. Until just a moment before Helena had been a scant few feet away. But a few feet might well have been light years away. The sea was now a mess of white froth and tumbled sand, his sister nowhere to be seen. The next wave caught him unawares, sending him sprawling.

He felt something brush past his arm—*Helena!*—and he made a desperate lunge for her, but she slipped away, sucked in the backwash. He emerged, gasping from the water, catching a glimpse of his sister being dragged out.

He struck out in his novice freestyle, battling to keep his head above water, struggling to keep her in his sights, desperate to reach her. *Frantic.*

'Helena!' he cried.

But despite his calls and his efforts, he couldn't reach her. He couldn't find her.

He couldn't save her...

'Shh, it's okay.'

He was suddenly aware of the warm press of hands at his shoulders. He was aware of the soothing voice through the pain of his loss. A calming voice that made no sense. It was at odds with his memory—of his father pulling him half-drowned from the sea, laying him on the sand where Theo had retched his stomach out, as much from the seawater he'd swallowed as the knowledge that he'd failed his sister.

'It's okay.' The words permeated the thickness in his mind, yet in an accent that didn't sound like anyone he knew. Not his father who'd plucked him from the sea. A woman, yet not his mother.

Sophia, he thought. It made no sense but it had to be

Sophia. Who else could it be but his wife saying soothing words, blotting out memories of the beach tragedy as she had always done? And the nightmare receded, his jagged breathing eased, as he let himself drift at the comforting stroke of her hands on his arms, at her calming perfume coiling into his senses.

Until something snagged with the sensuality of his dream. A hairline crack in the perfection that jarred.

Because Sophia's perfume had been heady and sensual, rich with the spices of the silk route.

Whereas this scent—this scent was citrus and fresh.

And Sophia?

Sophia was gone.

And what started as a hairline crack grew into a fracture, shattering his dreamlike state and jolting him into wakefulness.

His eyes snapped open. It was dark but he was fully awake. He saw her face—*Isabella's face*—close to his, as she murmured soothing words and heaven turned into hell.

He roared into the darkened room, rearing upright in the bed, pulling the sheet over his body with one hand, seizing one of her wrists with the other. He snapped on the bedside light. She whimpered as she scuttled from the bed as far as she could, as far as she could go with one wrist ensnared. 'You frightened me.'

The colour in her cheeks was high, her hair was mussed from sleep, and had her lips always been that plump and inviting? Her candy-striped pyjama shorts showed off her smooth-skinned legs. Her tiny lace camisole revealed too much the fullness of her breasts, not to mention the pointed peaks of her nipples. He tore his eyes away, half wishing he'd left the light off so he couldn't notice.

'What the hell are you doing?'

'You scared me.'

'Tell me what you were playing at?'

'I didn't mean to wake you.'

'Answer the question!'

'You were having a nightmare. You were calling out. I was worried about you.' She looked down at her wrist, still encircled by his long-fingered hand. 'Are you going to let me go or are you going to hold onto me all night.'

He was in two minds, his thoughts in turmoil. All he knew was that his dream had turned into a living nightmare, and he couldn't get out of bed. He was naked beneath the sheet, memories of Sophia turning him hard. Finding a woman in his bed wearing scant clothing when he was in such a state was next-level hell.

She licked her lips, as if his hesitation was in her favour, her eyes traversing his naked chest as if she was sizing him up. 'Because if you want me to stay…?'

He flung her hand away.

'Don't you realise how dangerous that was coming into my bedroom—where it could have ended up? What it might have cost you?'

'I was worried about you,' she said, a challenge clear in her voice. 'You were calling out.'

He glared at her, hating her for reminding him of the loss of his younger sister. Hating himself more for letting her witness his weakness. And then there was his mad decision to sleep commando. He'd expected the Princess to try to escape—he'd improvised alarms on the doors and windows in case she tried to make a run for it. The last thing he'd expected was for her to ambush him in his own bedroom. He growled at his lack of foresight.

'You acted foolishly, Princess.'

'What else was I supposed to do—leave you to shout the house down?'

'And if I had been less ethical and found you in my bed and taken advantage of you, how would you be feeling now?'

She blinked, her lips curling into a wicked smile. 'Satisfied, I hope.'

'*Vlammeni!*' he said, hitting the heel of one hand against his brow. If the dossier he'd been provided was accurate, the Princess had fled the castle an innocent. He didn't need to know why or how—he didn't much care—all he cared about was bringing her home in the same state. 'You know nothing about what happens between a man and a woman. Your actions were reckless. I expected more of you, Princess.'

She flung back her head, setting the ends of her hair in motion. Platinum-blonde hair now that she'd washed the colour from it. For once it wasn't tied back in a ponytail, allowing the waves to dance around her face, the curled tendrils, still damp, brushing over her chest, over the full breasts that swelled and swayed under her camisole. He swallowed. He really hadn't needed to notice that. He averted his eyes.

'Oh, I know more than you think I do.'

'The hell you do!' He was angry with her. But he was angrier with himself for noticing her hair. Her breasts. And he was angry that she no longer looked like a recalcitrant teenager now that she'd washed the veritable rainbow from her hair, because now she looked like a woman.

All woman.

'What do you think I've been doing these last few weeks? There have been plenty of men willing to educate me. There was this cool surfer guy called Luke from Bondi, who had sun-bleached hair and big blue eyes, and his abs—OMG his abs! You should have seen them. And then there was the Spanish barista, Mateo, from the coffee bar around the corner from Erin's apartment. He was seriously hot. Oh, but then—'

He held out one hand to stop her. So much for getting her home unharmed and unscathed. But if the Princess had made the most of her freedom and was no longer the innocent she'd been painted, he didn't need to know. He didn't want to know. 'But then nothing! I don't want to hear this.'

'I'm just saying I know more—'

It was his turn to cut her off. 'And I said I don't want to hear it. Save it for your girlfriends back home.'

Her chin jutted up and out. 'And just when am I going to have a chance to talk to these so-called friends of mine? Rafael will lock me up like a prisoner the moment you deliver me back into his clutches. Right up until the time he trusses me up like a turkey and sends me off to marry his crony.'

'You're being melodramatic again, Princess.'

'I'm being honest! This will happen! Do you know how hard it was for me to escape the palace? I might as well have been under house arrest. It was a miracle I managed to get away.'

'How did you get away?'

She shrugged. 'I pretended to be one of the cleaners, heading home to the village at the end of the day. All the women were wearing shawls. Nobody at the gate bothers to look at ID on the way out.'

Theo nodded. So security at the palace had been lax. So different from the story that he'd been told of her being spirited out the palace by a gang of enablers. He imagined that someone would have paid for that lapse and that things would be very different now.

'He'll make it impossible for me to so much as breathe once you take me home. Is that what you want for me? To be made a prisoner in my own country before he marries me off to his creepy friend. At least here, I'm free to make my own choices and my own friends.' She shrugged. 'And at least I had the chance to meet a few decent men while I was in Australia.'

He shook his head. He'd heard enough. He had a job to do, and he intended to do it. 'Get back to your room. Get some sleep.' One of them might as well sleep tonight, and he knew damned well it wasn't going to be him.

She tilted her head to one side, her expression turning coquettish as she ran her teeth over her bottom lip. Her full, pink, bottom lip. 'Are you really sure you want me to go?'

'Get out!'

She straightened her shoulders and flicked back her hair and damn if the action didn't make her breasts sway again. 'Then I'll go. But I'll keep an ear out in case you need me again.'

He growled. 'Go!' Wishing she would.

He watched her leave. God, he could have had her and ruined his business in the process. But still he was unable to tear his eyes from the low-slung shorty pyjamas swaying with her hips. She was trying to be provocative; he knew that. She was trying to get under his skin. He pulled on a pair of boxer shorts—he wasn't getting surprised again—lay down and punched his pillow.

The trouble was, she was succeeding.

But tomorrow.

Tomorrow he would be done with her and tomorrow couldn't come soon enough.

So that had been a revelation. Izzy padded slowly up the stairs to her room, her senses still buzzing at what had transpired. She'd been lying in bed for what seemed like hours, trying to build up the courage to sneak down into Theo's room and see if he might welcome her company. But what had seemed a good plan in theory, was proving harder to carry out in real life.

She'd been kidding herself dreaming up her crazy plan. What did she really know about seducing men?

The first time she'd heard Theo cry out, she'd thought she'd imagined it and it must be just another sound generated by the winds, but then it came again, and again. Sounds of distress and panic and insufferable pain, and it had been compassion that had led her feet down the stairs. She'd stood at his open door a few moments to see if he'd calm naturally, but he twisted in his sheets, producing sounds like a wounded animal.

She knew better than to wake someone having a nightmare, but she could soothe him. She drew closer, sitting on the side of the bed, murmuring words of comfort, stroking his fevered skin. Firm skin over corded muscles. Her fingers drank him in, even as she continued to whisper soft words. A sliver of light through the blinds silhouetted his body, highlighting his strong chest and flat belly leading to the tangled sheet below. And she'd wondered—what if she had found the courage to descend the stairs? Could her plan have worked?

Theo was calming, his movements less frantic, his breathing steadier. 'It's okay,' she'd whispered one more time close to his ear, and suddenly all hell had broken loose.

He'd been angry. He hadn't welcomed her with open arms. But he hadn't been unaffected by her either.

And that was encouraging.

Izzy wasn't about to give up her plans to get Theo onside just yet.

CHAPTER SEVEN

THEO SAT AT the dining room table nursing both a thick head and a third mug of black coffee. Caffeine had never been so essential, and if he could find a way to take it intravenously, he would. He'd not allowed himself to more than doze the rest of the night, afraid to fall asleep while on princess watch. He didn't trust her an inch. He didn't trust her assurances that she would come with him. He didn't believe that she wouldn't try to run the first chance she got. The sooner he got her on the plane out of here the better. And then maybe, once they'd got to Sydney and she was on board the private jet that would whisk them back to Rubanestein—maybe then he could get some sleep.

Until then, coffee—and a bucket load of it—would have to suffice.

He heard her light footfall skipping down the stairs before she emerged into the room.

'Good morning,' she said, looking bright-eyed and way too pleased with herself for his liking. She was still wearing the shortie pyjamas, but at least she'd had the good sense this morning to add a robe. Because she was cold? At least he could thank the weather for something. Although she might have thought to tie the robe around her waist instead of leaving it undone and exposing her legs. He looked away.

'Morning,' he answered, rising from the table to pick up the plunger of coffee he'd made ten minutes earlier. Because as far as he was concerned, there was little good about it. He'd already heard the news, that the storm had changed track again, and that there was a chance the airport would be closed today. Which meant at least another twenty-four hours in this woman's presence. AKA, disaster. 'Coffee?'

He was already pouring it when he heard, 'You might be my captor, but you don't have to wait on me.'

'You're not my captive,' he said. 'And no, I don't have to wait on you. I was merely being polite.' He put the cup down in front of her and went to stand with his back against the kitchen benchtop. 'There's bread in the toaster waiting for you. The milk's in the fridge. The sugar's in the dish over there. Help yourself.'

'Thank you, but I take my coffee black.'

He growled under his breath. He didn't like that they had something in common, even if it was as simple as how they took their coffee.

'You don't sound very happy,' she said. 'Didn't you sleep well?'

When he didn't answer, she continued, 'I had the best sleep.'

A burst of rain lashed the windows. The building seemed to rattle on its foundations.

She looked at the windows, to where the palm fronds bent and swayed in the wind and rain. 'Is the storm getting worse?'

'Looks like it. That's why we're getting out of here while we still can.'

She looked at him, all trace of smugness or smarts gone

from her face, and what he was left with was cold hard determination. 'I'm not going back.'

He sighed. 'Princess, face the facts. You are going back.'

'No,' she said, jumping from her chair. 'I will not. Not if it means getting married off to someone my brother chose so he can get his debts paid off.'

'You're a princess. You have duties.'

'I'm a woman, first and foremost. I'm not my brother's chattel to be sold off to whoever can offer him the most. It's wrong. It's barbaric—and if you can't see that, then you're just as much a barbarian and misogynist as he is.'

He was losing his patience. There was no arguing with this woman, no way to make her see sense. 'If I were a barbarian, as you say, things would have ended very differently last night. And you wouldn't be looking quite so smug right now.'

She angled her head, as if weighing up his words. 'Oh, I don't know. I might be looking even more smug.'

He growled again, tossing the dregs of his coffee into the sink, wishing he could rid himself of this troublesome princess just as easily. 'Get dressed,' he said.

'Why? We're not going anywhere. The flight isn't for hours.'

He wanted her out of those shortie pyjamas. No, that was wrong. He wanted her out of those pyjamas, *and* into something thoroughly more all-encompassing. But he was sick of arguing with her. 'Just do it,' he said, and stalked from the room.

God, if it wasn't bad enough that he'd been awake since she'd ambushed him, afraid to fall asleep in case she tried something again. Afraid that next time he might not be strong enough to turn her down. It had been eight years since Sophia had died, and despite plenty of women trying, he'd felt nothing for any of them. But last night that had changed. Last night he'd wanted a woman.

This woman.

The wrong woman, in every way.

And yet still he hungered for her. Found himself almost regretting the fact he'd come to his senses before the unthinkable had happened. The unthinkable—and yet—the very much *wantable*.

What was that about?

Unless his body was finally rebelling about the long drought that had followed Sophia's death? A shame, if that were so, to randomly pick this woman to awaken his desire. She was a rescue. Attraction wasn't an option.

He heard her footfall going up the stairs. At last. He returned to the kitchen and helped himself to more coffee, and just as quickly drained the cup as he paced the suite and watched the rain coming in bursts against the windows. He was going to need all the caffeine he could get before he got on that plane.

He heard the pad of her bare feet coming down the stairs and turned, relieved to know she'd be out of those shortie pyjamas at last. Except… 'What the hell? I thought I told you to get dressed.'

She held out her arms and looked down at herself, as if he were crazy. 'I am dressed.'

Not in his book. She was wearing a bikini, a tiny bikini that left little to the imagination. It was strapless and red, with a little ruffle at the top of the bandeau. If it had ruffles anywhere else, he didn't want to know. And he'd thought her shortie pyjamas were provocative. He closed his eyes and sent up a silent prayer for strength.

'Where do you think you're going in that?'

'I thought I'd take a swim.'

'Outside? Where it's blowing a gale?'

'But it's not cold, Lord Howe Island is a subtropical island so it's not cold, is it? Just a bit windy. And it would be a crime to waste a plunge pool like that, don't you think?'

He didn't think. He couldn't right now. Instead, he rubbed his whiskered jaw with his hand. He needed to shave. He needed more coffee. He needed this woman gone. Out of his sight. Out of his life.

'Go then,' he said, his voice sounding rough and gravelly, unrecognisable even to his own ears. 'Go have your swim.'

She smiled and gave a little curtsy. 'I wasn't actually asking your permission, but thank you anyway.'

He didn't dare look at her as she walked to the door, didn't want to see the sway of her hips or the curves of her body so open to his gaze, didn't want to be reminded of how close he'd been last night. But when the door opened and the storm front gusted in, his eyes found her paused in the open doorframe. For a moment she hesitated, as if she were having second thoughts. But then her shoulders lifted, and she pushed into the swirling air and tugged the door closed behind her.

It was wild outside. The wind swirled around her, tugging at her hair, threatening to blow her sideways at times, but no way was she retreating. Not until she'd wound him in so many knots that he couldn't untie himself. She lowered herself into the plunge pool, exaggerating the sway of her hips as she made her way one slow step at a time. She could feel his eyes on her. She could feel their heat.

And she was determined to stoke it.

What was wrong with the man?

She knew he hadn't been unaffected by her.

And he was all man. So strong. So firm. Even in sleep

his body was hard, his belly taut with muscle. And she hadn't imagined the impact of his heat. One touch and her senses had surged, like she'd plugged herself into a battery pack and felt the energy flare inside her. This man was neither stone nor metal. No robot. This man was made of flesh and blood, the same as her—and yet so very different.

It was almost a shame that he'd woken before she'd had the chance to experience more. But even in her limited experience with men and with this man in particular, she recognised that she'd planted the seeds of desire, and now it was her job to nurture them. If only she could get him onside. If only she could create some kind of rapport between them that wasn't based on his job description and her situation. Then she might have a chance to reason with the man.

What else could she do?

Which was exactly why she was here.

She lay in the pool, her arms beside her on the edge, her legs kicking the surface of the spa as they floated free. The wind buffeted her face, tugging at her hair. She didn't care. The water temperature was perfect, and the wind was the least of her problems. She wondered instead at the words Theo had uttered in his sleep. Wondered what would have happened if he had tumbled her over and finished what she had begun. Her body had been trembling with excitement, she'd felt herself pulsing in places she didn't know could pulse. He was big. And she might be inexperienced sexually, but she knew enough to know that size mattered. Instinctually she knew that size *had* to matter. What must it feel like, to have *that* inside you? To feel that move inside you. Even now the memories of last night had her belly quivering anew, triggering an ache deep between her thighs that she didn't understand or know how to ease. Only that it had something to do with Theo.

She needed more time to explore these new sensations. She wanted more time. But there was no more time. Today she would leave the island, and he would take her back to Rubanestein and into the grasping clutches of her brother Rafael.

If her brother got his way, she'd be married off to Count Lorenzo di Stasio before she'd got off the plane. Love would never come into it. Money ruled her brother's life. Cruelty ruled her so-called fiancé's.

She shuddered. She didn't like any of her brother's so-called friends. She never had. From the time she'd been old enough to notice, they'd watched her with hungry eyes, exchanging secret smiles.

While her father had been alive, she'd been protected. She'd been safe. But her father was gone, and now her brother thought he was master of the universe. Master of her destiny.

To him she was nothing more than a piece of meat, to be sold to the highest bidder. And her not-so-dear brother had done exactly that.

She would not go back.

But if worst came to the worst and this man forced her to do exactly that, she couldn't afford to let her brother win. Not entirely. He might ultimately succeed in marrying her off to the count, but she wouldn't let anyone she didn't want to marry take the one thing she'd protected for so long. She might be up for sale, but she refused to throw in her virginity as a bonus.

So, what choice did she have? Why shouldn't she take matters into her own hands? Why shouldn't her first time be with someone *she* chose? She'd said no to both Luke and Mateo. She'd turned them down because she hadn't given up on the dream that she might marry for love and the man that she married would be her first. Because she'd been saving herself. But time was rapidly running out for her to make a choice of her own.

She knew Theo wasn't unmoved last night. He might have been half asleep, but he had responded to her presence and her touch like he wanted it. Like he welcomed it.

And if she had to decide who to give her virginity to between Theo and the Count de Lorenzo, there was no contest.

Sure, it wouldn't be the way she'd always wanted it to be. She'd always wanted the whole fairy tale. She wanted to fall in love and marry someone who loved her too, the way her mother and father had loved each other. She wanted her first time to be with the man she would spend the rest of her life with.

The wind tugged at her hair, sending ends flicking against her closed eyes. She turned over, resting her head on her crossed arms, catching a glimpse of Theo watching her through the window before he darted out of view.

A frisson shivered down her spine, setting nerves strumming and making her toes curl in the water. Even just a glimpse of him set the space between her thighs tingling. So, maybe her first time wouldn't be with the man she would spend the rest of her life with, but at least it would be with a man who set her senses alight. And clearly, the seeds she had planted were sprouting. She would be the one to choose who her first time would be. And it wouldn't be so bad. She could do a whole lot worse than a man who stirred her senses.

She sighed. Reckless, Theo had called her, and so what that he was right? There was a time for reckless, and with time in short supply, there was no better time for reckless than now.

She just had to work out how and when.

* * *

Theo rubbed the back of his neck with one hand as he strode the length of the apartment. He shouldn't have jumped when she'd caught him watching.

It certainly wasn't that he wanted to watch her. Especially not when she was wearing nothing more than a few square inches of fabric that only served to reveal more than they hid. It was a form of torture she was subjecting him to, and he was in no doubt that was her absolute intention. Her curves—her ample breasts, her tiny waist and the sweet flare to her hips—reminded him so much of both what he'd experienced so briefly while in dreamland last night and what he'd missed and hungered for so long.

In any event, it wasn't like he'd just been watching her, because naturally he'd been anxious about the weather too. The twin mountains of Lidgbird and Gower were now shrouded in a donut of cloud that ominously circled their peaks while the wind thrashed at the palms and the foliage below.

The latest he'd heard the airport was still open and flights today were still expected to go ahead, but he wouldn't relax until they were on the plane and both safely Sydney bound.

But none of that was the real issue.

The real issue was that he wasn't about to risk her running again. He turned back to the window. As difficult as it was, he had no choice but to watch her.

That was all.

It was another twenty minutes before the Princess decided that she'd had enough of flaunting herself in the plunge pool. Finally, she emerged. It was a relief and yet it just proved another set of challenges, because the door blasted open as she entered the room dripping wet. Of course, he thought, teeth gritted, she hadn't bothered taking a towel let alone putting on her robe.

'Go and get yourself showered and packed,' he yelled against the wind, as he battled to close the door. 'As far as we know the flight is still on.'

'But I'm dripping water,' she said, clutching her arms around her waist, her robe trailing uselessly from her hands.

The door snapped closed. 'Then run,' he said, without turning to look at her. He was fed up with her antics.

Thirty minutes later, he was zipping up his duffel bag when above the wild weather, he heard someone beating on the door. 'Who is it?' the Princess said, appearing down the stairs. His gaze flicked over her attire. It was a relief to see her finally wearing something more appropriate— jeans and loafers with a soft knit top.

He held up a hand to shush her. He opened the door a crack. It was Tom Parker outside, bringing the message Theo least wanted to hear. Theo cursed, forcing closed the door after the message had been delivered. He shouldn't have been surprised. The wind had been building all morning, the squalls coming more and more furiously, but still the news was like a body blow. The cyclone had deviated closer to the island. It was expected to track away eventually, but for today, the news was grim. The airport was closed. There would be no flights in or out today.

He turned, his face grave and no doubt betraying his disappointment. 'It seems like you got your way, Princess. The airport is closed. We won't be leaving today.'

It galled him that she looked halfway delighted. 'Oh, that is a shame. I mean, you must be itching to get back to your work. Hunting down international criminal masterminds and all that.'

'I am looking forward to completing this case, yes.'

'So sad, I know how much you were looking forward to be done with me.'

He ground his teeth. 'I can wait a day,' he said, even as his eyes stung from lack of sleep. 'I've waited this long already.'

Her eyes suddenly brightened. 'Then—if we're not leaving, I can work my shift tonight, right?'

Theo pressed thumb and forefinger to the bridge of his nose. He needed sleep desperately. He needed even more not to be bothered with this undeserving princess. But if he could grab a decent meal while keeping an eye on her, the evening might not be a total waste.

'I'll be watching you,' he said. 'Every move you make.'

'Oh,' she said with a smile and a coquettish hitch of one shoulder, 'If you insist. Well, I guess I'd better go get unpacked again.'

'Don't get too excited,' he growled. 'This delay is for a day. Twenty-four hours. Don't bother unpacking everything. I'm sure we'll be on our way tomorrow.'

'We'll see,' she said.

Theo watched her go.

Sure she was happy about their departure being delayed, he got that, but she was almost too happy. Almost flirtatious. What was that about?

Bottom line, after last night's little escapade, he didn't trust her an inch.

'So, what would you like to do today?'

The Princess was standing and leaning her elbows on the kitchen counter, snacking on an apple. Theo didn't like her stance. Mostly because of the way her knit top clung to her curves, accentuating her breasts and then the scoop to her waist, and then that shapely derriere jutting out behind.

Not that he was about to protest the way she was standing and let her know how she affected him. Instead, he said, 'What are you talking about? Haven't you looked outside?'

Her gaze flickered to the windows. 'Sure, it's blowy. But do you really want to waste this bonus time on the island?'

He snorted. 'Bonus time. That's one way to put it.'

'But it is. Do you realise Lord Howe Island is one of Tripadvisor's top ten places to visit in the entire world?'

'And your point is?'

'And you would have had, what?—if this weather event hadn't intervened—just twenty-four hours to experience the island's magic. At least now you have the chance to experience more of what the island has to offer.'

He glanced out the window again. The wind was mad, palm trees lashed from side to side, their fronds buffeting and slapping together in the wind. 'What exactly did you have in mind, Princess? A climb around the cliffs and up to the heights of Mt Gower? A glass-bottom boat tour of the coral reef? Or maybe a scenic flight over the island?'

She put her hands on her hips, slowly shaking her tilted head. 'You are such a fun person, you know that?'

He moved his head from side to side. Slowly. Deliberately. 'I'm not here to have fun. I'm here to do a job, Princess. And I fully intend to carry it out.'

Her smile slid away, her eyes dropped. His words had hit the mark and he'd just reminded her what the end goal was.

Good.

He didn't need the taunting. It wasn't like he didn't know what fun was. He remembered fun. He remembered good times.

Even if none recently.

The fun times, the good times, had ended when Sophia had. When he looked back, he couldn't think of any good times he'd had since then.

Now he didn't look for fun.

Instead, what he'd found in its place was the satisfaction he'd taken from his work. Reuniting kidnapped children with their desperate families. Finding lost and missing and amnesiac adults who appeared to have fallen off the face of the earth without a trace.

He'd been too busy seeking justice to look for fun. Too busy trying to atone for what had happened.

Too busy.

The Princess huffed into the silence. 'Then what are we supposed to do? I'm going to be stuck here in this apartment with you for hours.'

He had no sympathy. He was going to be stuck here in this apartment with her for hours too. Did she really think it was going to be a cakewalk for him?

With one arm he gestured towards a stacked bookshelf. 'Try reading a book,' he said, sitting at the dining table attempting to find a shred of wireless signal to log into his office. He needed to contact Prince Rafael to let him know their return was delayed, and it was frustrating that there was a part of the world that didn't boast superfast Wi-Fi capabilities, and that was where he was now. Whereas Lord Howe Island's isolation had proved advantageous when he'd been tracking down the Princess, it was also proving to be a curse. It was all well and good to sell the island's lack of connectivity as the perfect excuse to chill out and wind down, but when you were trying to work, it was a positive handicap.

Eventually he heard the Princess huff. A glance of his eyes was all it needed to tell him that she was walking towards the bookshelf. Then somehow, he didn't even need to glance to know that she stayed there a minute or two, selecting and rejecting the options—his senses told him that, seemingly becoming hyper aware where this woman was concerned—before apparently finding something that caught her interest, taking it back to the sofa and flopping down on her back to read it.

At last. He let go a breath he hadn't realised he'd been holding. Feeling relief. At least for now. Finally, she'd found something to take her mind off their circumstances. And at least now he could think about something other than a hovering bundle of platinum-blonde nervous tension pacing around the apartment.

All too sexy platinum-blonde nervous tension. He felt that tension vibrate through him, almost like she'd emitted it purely to mess with his nerve endings.

Outside the clouds finally unleashed the promised flood of rain, adding to the cacophony of noise battering the roof and windows. Wild. Primal.

Elemental.

Like the friction building up between them. An attraction unwanted and yet seemingly unavoidable. An attraction coupled with confusion. It made no sense to him.

He looked up to see what was left of the view of the mountains disappear in a cascade of grey. So, the forecasters had been right about the weather worsening? Maybe he should be glad the authorities had closed the airport and their tiny plane wasn't currently trying to struggle its way through this weather.

Then again—he glanced over at the Princess, looking like she was trying to get involved with whatever she was reading. He was relieved she'd stopped pacing. Though that hadn't stopped the gnawing in his gut or the uncomfortable bristling awareness of her. She had one arm behind her head, holding the book with her other hand, and perched up on her chest. Her fine knitted top clung to her curves, showing off the pronounced line where her ribcage ended, before sweeping down to her flat belly to meet her slim fitted jeans. She'd kicked off her shoes and now the nearest leg was bent, showing off the line of her under leg from knee to the sweet curve of her butt where it rested on the sofa.

He dragged his eyes away. He knew he should be relieved she'd finally stopped complaining. But it would be a damned sight easier if the Princess didn't look the way she did. *Theos.* He'd tracked her to the island and found her the first day, only for a simple extraction to be stymied by the weather.

Why couldn't anything be simple?

He turned back to his search to find a wisp of internet to see if his enquiry about drilling down further into the Prince's gambling habits had turned up anything but came up a blank.

Damn it. Maybe it would have been preferable to take their chances with the weather after all.

Not an hour later she sighed theatrically and tossed her book aside. She got up from the sofa and again started pacing the rain-lashed windows back and forth like a caged lion. Then she suddenly stopped, hands on hips, staring out at the palms thrashing in the cyclonic winds and teeming rain.

'I'm bored,' she stated bluntly.

He didn't bother looking up. He knew exactly what she was doing. 'How's the book?'

'Didn't I just tell you? I'm bored. It's boring. Aren't you bored?'

He was frustrated, yes. Annoyed at the delay, certainly. Impatient to get this woman back to Rubanestein and out of his life, hell yes! And then there was that niggling discomfort in his gut that she seemed to somehow trigger just by her mere presence.

But bored didn't factor. Not where this woman was concerned. Not when this woman was proving to be one surprise after another. A princess who'd found work as a waitress and who seemed to enjoy it so much that she was insisting to do one last shift. A princess who'd traded gowns and tiaras for flip-flops.

A princess who'd sneaked into his bedroom last night in an attempt to—what? Seduce him? So he'd be swayed to relent and not to take her home? Whatever other motive could she have had?

She was also a princess who looked too damned good from the rear for his liking. No, that wasn't right. A princess who looked too damned good from any angle and any way you looked at her.

Why the hell did she have to stand there in front of the window that way? It gave him the perfect view of her hourglass figure.

'Maybe,' he said, his voice huskier than he'd intended, 'you picked the wrong book.'

She shook her head, setting her blonde waves dancing. She lifted one hand to her hair and smoothed it back. 'Maybe I'm just not in the mood for reading.'

He raised an eyebrow. 'In that case, I see that one of the bookshelves is overflowing with games. Maybe you could find a deck of cards and amuse yourself that way.'

She suddenly spun around, ignoring the puzzle shelf,

before pulling up a chair opposite him at the table. 'How old are you?'

'What?'

'I said I'm bored. So, since we're stuck here together, maybe we could find out more about each other? So, how old are you?'

He shook his head. 'Princess—'

'Oh, that's not fair. I bet my darling brother has provided you an entire dossier on me. I bet you know everything there is to know about me. Birth date, schools I attended, friends I had, shoe size, probably even my dental records. And yet, here I am, knowing next to nothing about you. Or even if you're one of these rogue actors you're supposedly saving me from. Maybe you might try to persuade me a little that you're who you say you are.'

Theo didn't want to admit that it wasn't just her body, it was the sound of her voice that stirred him. Her voice was melodic and elegant, evidence of her principality's Mediterranean connections with its linkages to both France and Italy. Theo also didn't want to admit that the Princess was spot on. Theo had been given all those details and more. 'It's not usual procedure for a recovery expert to divulge details to a recoveree.'

'I doubt I'm your usual "recoveree". But I'd really appreciate those details. I'd like to know who it is who is abducting me. I'd like to know who that man is.'

'I'm not abducting you. I'm taking you home, before something untoward happens to you.'

'Oh, that's right. You're rescuing me before someone else finds and kidnaps me for whatever nefarious reasons they might have. I forgot.'

Theo closed his laptop and squeezed the bridge of his

nose. 'Downplay it all you like, Princess. Just be thankful I found you first.'

'In that case, tell me, who did find me first?'

'I did.'

'And who are you exactly?'

'You know who I am. My name is Theo Mylonakos.'

'And you're a bounty hunter, right?'

He blinked. Slowly. 'I'm a recovery expert.'

'A bounty hunter, I get it.'

He shook his head. He knew of such agents, who prioritised money before the safety of their clients. He had no regard for them. They cluttered up the field, messing with the tracks, getting in the way.

'You mean you're not getting paid? You're doing this as some act of charity?'

'Do you seriously think I'd be putting up with all this—and with you—for free?'

She snorted. 'So, not a bounty hunter. Just in it for the money. That's so much better.'

'If you say so, Princess.'

She sniffed and looked away, and he wondered if she'd been trying to bait him, looking for a bigger reaction. 'So how much did my charming brother pay you? What's the deal?'

'I'm not going to tell you that.'

'What if I offered to pay you more than he did?'

'It doesn't work that way.'

'How does it work?'

'I find you and return you home. That's how it works, Princess. End of story.'

She sat back in her chair, clearly unsatisfied, but any respite didn't last longer than it took to work out her next line of attack.

'So where do you come from? Where were you born?'

'I'm Greek. From a town called Sparta.'

'Sparta? Isn't that the place where they used to train boys to become tough and battle hard and become the best warrior soldiers in Greece?'

'In ancient times, yes.'

He watched her digest that detail, before she added, 'And you're descended from those people. The tough guys of Greece. Is it that warrior mentality that led you to become a bounty hunter—I mean, *"recovery expert"*?'

'No.' His choice to become a recovery expert had its origins in an entirely different sphere. 'My parents are humble orchardists, like their parents and their parents before them. They still live there.'

She nodded, as if summing up his answers. 'And so how old are you? You never said.'

He sighed. 'Is this entirely necessary?'

'No, but I think it's fair, given you probably know details about me down to my shoe size and whether I squeeze toothpaste from the middle or the end of the tube.'

'I'm thirty-four. And no, I don't know how you squeeze your toothpaste. Nor do I particularly care.'

'Ha, but shoe size, you know!'

He pushed his chair back and stood, unable to sit opposite her any longer. This wasn't about him, but she was like a heat-seeking missile and her interrogation was only serving to ramp up his temperature, rendering him a more susceptible target. He moved to the windows, watching the blurred fronds of the palm trees being pelted by the tempest outside. Curse this weather. A glance at his watch told him that they should be in Sydney by now, boarding his private jet and a mere twelve hours or so away from landing in Rubanestein. Whereas right now he was stuck here on this island, with an ungrateful princess who seemed to want to needle him any chance she got and no guarantees that the weather would be any better tomorrow.

'Feeling better?' she asked.

'Define "better".'

She laughed. And he cursed that even her laugh held that accent that seemed to want to coil its way into—not just his hearing—but through his skin and into his bones.

'So, do you have a wife—or a lover—at home?'

He spun around. 'That sounds odd coming from the woman who didn't seem to care last night that she could invade my bedroom and throw herself at me. And only now you think to ask if I was in a relationship.'

'I didn't throw myself at you. I was worried about you.'

He put a hand to his brow. She had a point. It was he who'd had to resist pulling her into the bed and tumbling her beneath him. But it was she who'd put herself into that situation. It was she who'd made his body react.

'So, is there someone special in your life? Are you married?'

His eyes swept the ceiling. 'I was.'

'You were? Separated or divorced?'

He ground his teeth together. 'I'm—a widower.'

She looked sideswiped. 'Oh. I didn't mean—'

Theo didn't wait to hear what it was she didn't mean. He shoved his chair back and stood. 'Now, if you're done with the questions? Because I sure am.'

CHAPTER EIGHT

ISABELLA WATCHED HIM stride from the room. Until her final question, when Theo had snapped, she'd been enjoying the question-and-answer session. The man had to have a weakness somewhere and she was determined to find it. Anything she could glean, she figured, would flesh out more about her captor and had to help her in her quest to escape.

She knew she hadn't learned enough to save her yet, but she now knew more than she had. Theo was a proud Greek, a protector, a bodyguard—and a widower.

That was news.

She wondered about his late wife. What kind of woman could possibly have tamed this cold and hard man-mountain into a loving husband?

And what had happened to her?

Two things were clear—she'd made him angry by raising the topic. And the other more important thing he'd revealed—he wasn't in a current relationship. Because she'd given him every opportunity—surely he would have said if he was? Surely he'd be wanting to deter her from making another attempt at invading his bedroom and throwing herself at him?

And yet he'd not said anything.

Interesting.

Encouraging.

Because he wasn't immune to her. She knew that, from his reaction last night, and from the stolen glances he was so eager to pretend were all about making sure she wasn't trying to run away. She knew that he wouldn't suddenly dart out of view and pretend he wasn't there if he was simply keeping an eye on her to ensure she didn't try to escape.

And now she had one more night.

This time was a gift. Another opportunity to convince Theo to care enough for her that he would listen to her and believe her and wouldn't return her home.

One more night, that's all she had. She just prayed it was enough.

Talk that night at the café was all about the storm. Flights home cancelled. Climbs of Mt Gower, fishing and coral viewing tours cancelled—and the weather outside might be wild, but even with the cancellations, nobody present was complaining about their forced detention on Lord Howe Island. A delay in leaving was a positive. Even if the weather was rubbish, an excuse to extend a holiday was a win. Because nobody really wanted to go home to work and study. The complaints were happily relegated to the holidaymakers on the mainland with bookings to get to the island who were seeing their holiday shrinking by the day.

Nobody seemed glum about their forced retention on Lord Howe Island—apart from Theo.

He sat at table thirty with a dark look of thunder plastered to his face. 'What will it be tonight?' Izzy asked, when she went to take his order. 'The paella again?'

She was sure she almost heard him growl. 'The kingfish,' he said.

'Good choice,' she said. 'And a drink for you, sir? A glass of wine perhaps?'

'Just table water.'

'Wise choice. So that's it?'

He grunted and she spun away back to the kitchen. Millie stopped her behind the bar after she'd delivered the order to the kitchen. 'How's it going with Mr Dreamboat?'

Izzy snorted. She looked back over her shoulder and caught his glare. 'Mr Scowly-Face you mean. Sorry to disappoint you, but nothing's going on.'

'But he's back here tonight and he can't peel his eyes from you.'

She shrugged. 'He's stuck on the island like we all are, and at a guess I'd say he's not happy about it.'

'Do you know he left last night just after you did?'

So, it had been noticed? 'Really?'

'Do you think he's stalking you?'

She shook her head. Not anymore. Theo had already done that. He'd already found her.

'But maybe better safe than sorry. Maybe we should call the police? Get him to have a word.'

She caught one of the diners at one of her tables gesturing for attention and Izzy, grateful for the change of topic, put her hand to her friend's shoulder. 'Thanks, for worrying about me, but no. There's no need for that. Besides, there's a cyclone causing all kinds of problems on the island. I'm sure the police are busy enough as it is.'

She made her way to the table requesting service. She'd thought about appealing to the police, of course, because she could do with another person in her court and to run interference, but she wasn't convinced the police were going to help her. She was no political prisoner seeking asylum. She was a runaway princess who'd gone missing from her country—and if that wasn't enough to raise a goodly number of questions—she'd escaped to the island using someone else's identity. That was going to provide another uncomfortable line of questioning surrounding identity theft. It might have delayed her departure from the island, but in the end, they would probably have handed her back to Theo, happy to see the back of this troublesome princess.

So no, seeking help from the police was no guaranteed way to protect her and prevent whatever Theo had planned.

She had worked out a fallback plan though. If nothing else that she attempted worked between now and their time of departure, she would make a last-ditch attempt at freedom by making a scene at the airport. Hang the uncomfortable consequences, accusations of kidnapping tended to get the attention of security.

Meanwhile she was going to have to find another way around her current problem.

And she was seriously crossing her fingers that she had...

Outside the restaurant the wind howled, buffeting the windows and doors and sending gusts of wet and wild air through the restaurant every time someone attempted to enter or exit. And then the rain started pelting down again, pounding a tattoo on the roof. At the back of the restaurant Theo was protected from all but the mightiest blasts, but still the spray was a bitter reminder of why he was stuck here, on this dot of an island in the middle of the Tasman Sea.

He was so close to closing this deal. He'd managed to hunt down the Princess. He'd located her when nobody else had been able to. How could such a simple thing as the weather be his undoing? And now, instead of delivering the Princess home, as he had been contracted to do, he was stuck here watching his target wait tables.

Wait tables.

A princess.

If he hadn't seen it with his own eyes, he would think it unthinkable. Unimaginable.

And yet, for all he doubted it possible, for all he could see, she was doing a good job. Whatever issues she'd faced during her first shift were clearly behind her. Tonight, the crowd was less frenetic, the guest house with the generator problems having apparently sorted its issues, but still the Princess was run off her feet with the hungry crowd.

She wasn't being precious. She wasn't holding back. She was fully engaged in her work, and with conversations with her tables. More than a few clients, he'd noticed, had ordered the paella. On her recommendation? The diners wouldn't be disappointed. What he'd tasted last night of his meal had been perfection.

She hadn't lied about how good it was. It was no surprise it had reminded her of home.

And again, he had to admit a kind of grudging respect for her. He'd assumed her plea to work her shift tonight was no more than a ploy for her to delay their departure and allow her more time to attempt to escape.

And while there was still an element of truth to that— she'd made it crystal-clear that she didn't want to be removed from her bolt-hole and delivered home and she was going to use any delaying tactic that she could—it was also clear she was good at her job. She might have had a rocky start, as his driver, Tom had alluded to, but clearly, she'd picked up the skills required of her very quickly. Something he hadn't expected of a pampered princess.

She didn't look like any pampered princess now. She looked like any other hard-working waitress, a notebook in her hand, pen behind her ear at the ready.

Why was she here? Why had she run? Her tale of a brother wanting to marry her off was medieval, if not pre-historic. So, was her brother right, that she was envious that he would take the crown when she wasn't able to? A woman who thought she should be the ruler of Rubanes-tein and yet, here she was, waiting on tables. Hardly the actions of someone who believed she was top of the tree rather than a worker bee. Unless that was part of an act to impress him, to convince him that she was fully invested in her work? He pondered that possibility as he watched her dart between tables, efficiently taking orders, deliver-ing pizzas and paellas, bottles of water and glasses of wine.

No, he decided, that didn't make sense. She appeared too capable in her work here. More than that, she clearly enjoyed it. This was no act.

Which raised even more doubts in his mind about her brother's story. Where the hell was that report he'd re-quested?

But even without that report, he sensed there was some-thing he was missing. What was the real reason for her running?

He watched her gather up plates from a table. Her blonde hair was tied back, but coiled tendrils had escaped to fall about her face as she dipped lower. He caught the moment she glanced over at him. She looked away and straightened the second she saw him watching her, before walking stiffly to the kitchen.

Oh yes, Princess, he thought, *I'm watching you.*

And maybe the only good thing was, it was no hard-ship to.

* * *

The night was growing old. The tables were thinning out, customers donning waterproof coats and jackets before exiting into the wild night air to board guest house buses or hire cars. Nobody was walking or had cycled tonight.

And the weather wasn't improving. From the few meteorological sites he'd been able to access during dinner, the cyclone was circling closer, the winds growing wilder. Some reports expected the winds to blow out overnight, while others expected conditions to persist for another day or two.

He didn't want to think about what that might mean. A twenty-four-hour delay had been bad enough.

The Princess appeared at his table to collect his empty plate. 'Would you like coffee or dessert, sir?'

'You don't have to act with me,' he said, tossing his napkin on the table. 'I'm not your target audience.'

She swiped her hands on her apron and smiled. 'I'm just doing my job.'

He didn't bother to smile back. 'And I'm just doing mine. As soon as this weather moves on, you're going home.'

Her smile brightened as if he hadn't just tried to puncture her mood. 'So, no coffee or dessert then?'

'No,' he growled, annoyed that she hadn't reacted. Okay, so she was probably feeling smug that the weather had delivered a twenty-four-hour delay in their departure, and by all accounts, there was a chance the same might happen again tomorrow, but he wanted her to show some vulnerability.

He wanted her to react. He wanted her to stop fighting the inevitable and accept that she was being taken home whether she liked it or not.

Damn it.

He wanted her to understand that he wasn't some plaything she could use to get her way. She needed to understand that he was no Luke or Mateo that she could use and bend to her will.

Instead, she was too confident. Too sure of herself for someone he'd taken to be young and innocent. Not that she'd turned out to be innocent given her experiences with the likes of Luke from Bondi and Mateo the barista, and certainly not after her late-night intrusion into his own bedroom last night. The Princess had been on the run for weeks. Goodness knows how many encounters she'd had along the way.

Was she imagining that he would be the next notch on her belt? Did she believe that if she managed to seduce him, that he'd change his mind about delivering her home?

Because if she thought that, then she wasn't just crazy. She was certifiable.

There was absolutely no chance of him getting involved with the Princess. She was his charge. His responsibility. Sure, she came all wrapped in a pretty package with her blonde hair and her sweet curves, but even if his body told him he was tempted—which he most certainly was not— she was forbidden to him.

Messing with the Princess would be a huge betrayal of professional trust. He wasn't about to sacrifice either his career or his business for this spoilt princess.

Whatever the Princess had in mind, whatever plan she had come up with to prevent her return to Rubanestein, it wasn't going to happen.

CHAPTER NINE

THE HEAD WAITER appeared in the centre of the restaurant, clapping his hands, getting the few remaining patrons' attention. 'Apologies, everyone, but I need to make an announcement. We've just been advised that the worst of the storm conditions will hit within the next two hours and may become quite dangerous. We want all of our guests and workers to get back to their accommodation safely before then. Consequently the restaurant will be closing a little early tonight. At this stage, if the forecast that the weather is easing during tomorrow is right, we expect to be open tomorrow for both lunch and dinner. Thank you for your patronage tonight. Get home safely and we'll see you next time.' He nodded and returned to his station by the door.

The restaurant rapidly emptied. The Princess appeared, clearing tables, collecting plates and cutlery. He left his seat and joined her, picking up plates from the rest of the tables.

'You're not expected to do that,' she said, frowning.

He shook his head. He wasn't doing it out of the kindness of his heart. He'd heard the tempest build outside. The Princess was his responsibility and all he wanted to do was ensure her safety. 'The sooner this place is cleaned up, the sooner we can get back to the apartment.' Their arms laden, they made their way to the kitchen, where Millie was busy loading the dishwasher. She looked up as they approached, her eyes widening as she saw Theo following Izzy.

He caught the Princess give Millie a brief shake of her head, as if to warn, *don't ask.*

Millie bit her lip, before smiling. 'Thanks, guys,' she said brightly, her voice at odds with the uncertain looks she sent from one to the other as they deposited their dishes on the sink. 'Appreciate it. You two better get away while you still can.'

It was a slow journey back to the apartment, the car crawling along the road in the wild weather, barely managing to achieve the speed limit, let alone exceed it. Even on the road bordering the protected lagoon, the seas were high, salt-laden spray and rain lashing the windscreen, the wipers battling to clear it before the next splatter. Winds buffeted the car, just like the palm trees either side of the road, the gusts pushing it sideways. Fronds torn from the palms crashed heavily onto the pavement around them.

It was wild.

Mad.

Scary.

The head waiter hadn't overstated the situation. If anything, the worst of the storm was impacting earlier. No wonder he'd wanted the patrons returned safely to their accommodations.

Izzy shivered as she looked out at the wild, untamed night. Rain battered the roof of the car, so loud that it rendered speech impossible.

Until now, the island had provided her with sanctuary. Theo had threatened that when he'd found her, but Theo was not the least of her problems.

This storm was different. Instead of the island providing

a sanctuary, for the first time Izzy felt threatened, not just for her future, but for her immediate safety. She could feel her fear in her shallow breathing and escalating heart rate as the storm raged around them—the howling winds, the raging lagoon to their right, the foliage whipping around the car in the wind.

Be careful what you wish for.

The cautionary tale was known worldwide, and it was true. Izzy had wished for their departure to be delayed and it had been, and now it looked very much like the airport wouldn't be reopening tomorrow, once again delaying Theo's attempts to return her to Rubanestein.

She'd got what she'd wished for.

But there was no victory. She felt no success. There was no easing to her nerves.

Nothing would ease her nerves while this storm raged around them.

Right now it was only Theo's driving expertise giving her a degree of comfort. She snatched her eyes off the road ahead to glance over at him, his gaze fixed on the road ahead while the threats kept coming from above and beside. He was frowning, she could tell in the soft light cast from the dashboard display, his jaw tense. Concentrating hard on keeping them safe.

She was grateful for his skill, as he negotiated a path around the debris on the road and out of the way that was being flung down from the treetops. So grateful that she wasn't driving. Even more grateful that she wasn't trying to make it back to the apartment on her bike.

Strange, she hadn't expected to feel grateful to Theo for anything. Theo was part of her problem. Escaping from him before he could take her back to her brother in

Rubanestein was her mission. Maybe the storm and her nerves were getting to her.

Or maybe it was being trapped in a sedan with a man-mountain beside her. A warm man-mountain.

In the apartment she could get away from him. In the restaurant she'd been busy, too busy to spend time next to him. But trapped here in a small hire car, in the midst of a raging storm, he was too close, his masculine scent worming its way into her senses, the brush of his arm against hers as he changed gears in the small sedan ratcheting up the tension.

'The storm's getting worse,' she said, in a lull in the tattoo on the roof of the car. She could hear the tremor in her voice, the shakiness that spoke of her fear.

'Yes,' he simply answered, not averting his eyes as he concentrated fully on the road ahead. 'There's no way the airport will be reopening tomorrow. I expect you'll be happy about that.'

'Right now, I'll just be happy if you get us back safely. Tomorrow can take care of itself.'

There was no time to read his features, as another gust hit them, doing its best to blow the car off the road at the same time the beachside palms bent and thrashed under the onslaught.

Izzy saw it happen. Fast motion that seemed to happen in slow motion. A frond torn from on high that was careening downwards, spinning, toppling directly towards their windscreen.

'Look out!' she cried, covering her eyes in case it smashed into them.

Theo was already on it. He swerved wildly, pulling the car away from the path of the toppling frond. Instead of the windscreen, it slammed with a sickening thud onto the hood and fender before crashing down onto the road. The car bucked as the back tyre lurched over the thick stem, before jolting back onto the road surface. Izzy let go a breath she'd been holding.

'Are you all right?' he asked.

'I don't think I've ever been more scared in my life.'

'Hey,' he said, taking her hand in his, wrapping his long fingers around hers and squeezing her hand reassuringly. 'I'm not going to let anything happen to you.'

Because he was afraid he wouldn't get his reward money?

But the accusation she might once have immediately launched at Theo refused to emerge from Izzy's mouth. There was no way she would aggravate him while her hand was encased in his, his hand lending her strength, his strength feeding into hers.

Madness. Theo holding her hand. They didn't even like each other. But that didn't mean she was about to shrug his hand off hers. Not while her skin tingled at his touch, and not just her hand itself, because warmth seemed to radiate up her arm, filling her body with a feeling unfamiliar to her. There was warmth there. There was tenderness. But there was also a thirst, as if it didn't have to end here.

He only let her hand go to change gears as he pulled into the driveway.

Izzy closed her eyes and leaned back into her seat. She'd never experienced near cyclonic conditions before. Everyone had told her that this brush would be mild. But if this was mild… And then there was Theo's generous gesture, to hold her hand and reassure her that all would be well.

And for the last few minutes of their journey, she'd felt completely safe.

He'd done that. Theo had made her feel safe.

Another deluge of rain unleashed on them.

'Okay?' he said.

She took a deep breath. 'Thank you for getting us back safely.'

He looked over at her then, a frown adding to a look of surprise on his face. A look of surprise that evaporated a moment after she'd witnessed it, so much that she wondered whether she'd imagined it.

'We got here,' he said. 'Are you ready to make a run for it.'

Izzy looked at the rain pounding the car. 'You don't have an umbrella?'

'An umbrella would be next to useless in these conditions. Stay there.' He pushed open his door and rounded the car to her door. He pulled her door open, threw his jacket over her head and shoulders as she emerged from the car, and with his arm around her, set off to race the few metres through the pelting rain to the door.

Everything happened so quickly. They were racing for the front door, getting battered by the heavy wind and rain, when Izzy's foot slipped on the wet surface. She stumbled, only for Theo to catch her, tumbling her into his arms to carry her to the sheltered space by the front door.

A moment later, they were inside, the door slammed behind them against the weather, both of them panting hard as Theo leaned with her against the wall. He let go her legs, letting her find her feet, but he kept hold, his free hand going to her waist, as if to make sure she wouldn't collapse to the floor.

She was still catching her breath after their frantic dash to the door, her arms still wrapped around Theo's neck, when a bubble of laughter escaped Izzy's mouth. At the madness of their desperate dash. At relief at being inside and out of the immediate danger of the storm.

'Wow,' she said, sounding as breathless as she felt, 'you are quite the hero. Driving safely through the storm. Getting us both unscathed to the front door. Thank you.'

Her mistake was turning her face up to his. She'd expected to see her laughter mirrored in his eyes. She'd expected their relief at escaping the storm to be shared.

Instead, when she looked into his features and into his dark, dark eyes staring into hers, she saw no humour. Instead, she saw need. She saw—*hunger.*

And she knew he wasn't still holding her because he was worried she'd topple to the floor. He was holding her because he didn't want to let go.

Her heart lurched. Her breath hitched. She licked her lips.

His eyes dipped, following the movement of her tongue. Time stretched as if made of wire, pulled taut by conflicting forces. Slow motion became slower. How was that even possible, when your blood throbbed faster, harder, your ears ringing with the sound of the blood pumping around your body, blocking out the sound of the rain pelting down outside.

Theo looked down at her, his dark eyes tortured and wild like the tempest outside. He muttered two strained words. 'Princess,' he said gruffly. 'Isabella.'

His lips brushed hers in a pass as tender as a butterfly's kiss yet still enough to make her entire body tremble. Her back arched, her arms winding more tightly around his neck, her lips melding with his, welcoming the contact. Parting softly when he ran his tongue along the line of her mouth. As if tasting her. Inviting his kiss.

Her tremor seemed to trigger something inside him. He made a sound, a low groan that came from the back of his throat, a groan that spoke of uncoiling need, of letting go.

Then his arms suddenly tightened around her, collecting her closer as he deepened the kiss.

And like the storm raging around them, his kiss stormed her senses, sending her thoughts into turmoil, challenging everything she thought she knew about this man. Challenging everything she thought she knew about kissing. His lips were warm and yet surprisingly soft, his mouth was hot, his tongue knew how to do things she'd never imagined. Her senses were full of him, his taste, his heated touch, his breath mingling with hers, his own masculine scent, musky and warm. It was an onslaught to both her body and her senses. Every part of her—every cell it seemed—was attuned to him. Preparing for him. Nipples straining. Her thighs thrumming. It was almost too much but at the same time, she never wanted it to end.

And it was like everything she'd planned. Only better. *Seducing the bodyguard.*

This is what she had wanted. This is what she had planned, hoping to bend Theo to her will.

But planning and execution were two different things.

Execution was threatening to make her forget what her plan actually was...

Right now she didn't care about her plan. All she cared about was the feel of Theo hard up against her, his mouth on hers, his big hands spanning her waist, his long fingers achingly close to the breasts that hungered for his touch, her nipples jutting hard and straining against his chest, the humming between her thighs becoming a symphony.

And she wanted more.

'Theo,' she whispered breathlessly between kisses, her hands framing his whiskered face. The man was a masterclass in contrasting textures. Soft yet firm lips, a whiskered jaw, the hard wall of his chest and abs and the heat of his hands. So much to explore. So much to discover.

If he'd heard her utter his name, he made no acknowledgement. He was under the same magical spell that she was, the outside storm moved inside.

His mouth moved back to hers, his lips meshing with hers, his tongue dancing with hers, and Izzy lost the will to think and gave herself up to sensation.

The sound of his name came as a vague intrusion on his thoughts. But only vague. He had more important things to consider. Like the woman he held in his arms. Her taste was like a drug and now he was addicted. An addict that wanted a fix.

An addict who was seriously in need of a fix.

And he intended to get it.

The crash outside tugged at his senses, senses that were fully diverted elsewhere. But the sound was as unsettling as it was unwelcome. The sound said something was wrong, and no mere desire to ignore it—not even this woman melting into his arms and body—could make it go away.

With an iron will he put his hands on her shoulders, stood back, and took a deep breath.

She stood in front of him, her hazel eyes looking dazed and confused, her pink lips plumped and parted. And with the force of a sledgehammer, it hit him. He'd been kissing the Princess—the woman he was engaged to protect—the woman he'd wanted to make love to.

And red-hot anger—at her for being who she was—but mostly at himself, for forgetting who she was—surged through his veins.

What the hell had he been thinking? He dropped his hands from her shoulders and turned away. That was an easy question to answer. He hadn't been thinking. Not with his brain.

Instead, she'd looked up at him with those innocent hazel eyes, uttering her words of thanks from that lush mouth, and relief that they'd escaped the storm had only served to ignite yet another storm. A storm that had been brewing ever since he'd laid eyes on the Princess. A storm between the two of them.

Gamo!

She was a princess.

She was his responsibility.

He had no place kissing her.

He spun back. She was still looking confused. 'What's wrong,' she said, looking like she was about to slide down the wall behind her. Which only served to remind him of how liquid she'd felt in his arms.

Vlaka!

What wasn't wrong? He hit his forehead with the heel of his hand. He was a fool. But there was no time for that now. 'Didn't you hear it?'

'Hear what?'

'The crash.'

She shook her head, still looking confused. 'What crash?'

He ran his hand through his hair. Pulled open the door and stepped outside into the storm. Where the cause of the crash became obvious. A tall palm tree from the beach had been toppled, blocking the road, its crown landing mere inches from the front door, its remaining fronds splayed and distorted haplessly against the ground.

Thankfully no damage done. Not to the outside of the property. As far as Theo was concerned, the damage had all been wreaked inside. No, it had started before that, when he'd taken her hand in the car to reassure her. She'd been so afraid. She'd felt so fragile. He'd wanted to re-assure her. But he'd felt her hand tremble in his and he wanted to protect her. He was a bodyguard, that was what he did. Protect people. Rescue people.

He hadn't expected to enjoy it so much.

He hadn't expected to wish their journey might be longer.

Gamo! He was a fool.

He phoned Tom Parker while he was outside, to let him know that a palm had fallen and that the road was blocked. In reality, it gave him a further excuse not to go back inside yet, something he didn't want to do until he got his thoughts and his wayward body in order. He needed to stand outside in the blustery winds and lashing rain until the last vestiges of desire-fuelled body heat had been exorcised from his flesh.

He'd kissed the Princess. And not just a passing kiss. He'd made it obvious he'd like to take it further. God, his hands had been all over her, he would have taken it further if a falling palm tree hadn't intervened. It didn't matter that she hadn't tried to stop him. He didn't trust her as far as he could throw her, not after her first night's expedition. After that, he didn't trust her that she might employ her newly found wiles to make him complicit in her attempts to avoid a return to Rubanestein.

Phone call made, Theo took another deep breath, turned, and went inside.

The Princess was nowhere to be seen. He towelled off the worst of the rain, and heard a sound from the kitchen, like mugs landing on a counter. He stopped as she came into sight. She was making coffee, putting a capsule into a machine. She looked over at him, her eyes bright but suspicious. 'Everything all right?'

'A palm tree has fallen across the road. Thankfully no other damage.'

She smiled. 'I wasn't talking about that.'

'Princess,' he said, hauling in a deep breath as the fingers of one hand raked through his hair. 'I'm sorry.'

She frowned. 'What for?'

'For kissing you. I shouldn't have done that. I overstepped the mark. Please forgive me.'

'You didn't enjoy it? I got the impression—'

He snarled. 'It's not about enjoyment. You are my charge. My responsibility.'

'So you did enjoy it?'

'I didn't say that.'

'You didn't not say it either.'

'Stop it,' he said, his fingers now stroking his brow. 'Bottom line, it was a mistake, Princess. It should never have happened. I promise it won't happen again.'

'But how can I be sure it won't?' she said.

'What?'

'I've heard of this before. You seem to assume that I kissed you because I wanted to. But it's a known phenomenon. It's called Stockholm Syndrome, where a captive finds herself enamoured of her captor.'

'I am not your captor.'

'It feels like it. And here we are. Forced together in close proximity.'

'Not my choice. You would already be home if a cyclone hadn't intervened.'

'So now we're forced to weather out the storm together. Is it any wonder that you might become the focus of my attentions?'

'Don't do that,' he said gruffly.

'Don't do what?'

'Try to convince me that something is happening when it's not. Try to make it look like you are attracted to me, whatever your reason, when all you want to do is escape from me.'

'Why can't the two coexist together? Do I have to hate you to want to not be returned to Rubanestein? Why can't I appreciate how sexy you are while still not wanting to be forced back to the hell-hole of what will be my future existence?'

He shook his head, trying to shake away her compliment. He would not be touched by her empty compliments. 'No. Not happening. And you're getting a bit melodramatic again, Princess.'

'Am I? Then how about we put the boot on the other foot, as unlikely as it might be. What if you'd been promised in marriage to a fifty-something-year-old woman against your will, when you'd been always told by your father that you could marry for love, and no matter how far you ran, someone would search the world to drag you back to comply with someone else's wishes? How would you feel?'

He stood stock-still. 'You're saying this man your evil brother has promised you to is in his fifties?'

'Yes, he's in his fifties. But why should age even come into it? Whatever the age, how is it possible that you could wilfully return me to this hell, and to marrying a man that I have been sold to, a man that I can never love? A man that I will never love, knowing the circumstances of our union.'

Her words were tumbling over each other, her colour was high, her eyes beseeching him to believe her.

Theo had to hand it to her. If she were acting, she was giving one hell of a good performance. Theo knew that the Princess would stop at nothing to prevent her return to Rubanestein, and she'd now supplemented the forced marriage story by adding the age detail, in case he wasn't already sympathetic. The Princess was twenty-five years old, and to be promised—if that's what was happening— to someone, a colleague of her brother and not a partner she'd chosen to spend the rest of her life with—that was wrong. And yet, she wasn't a teenager, she was an adult, which raised even more questions.

'When did you think you were going to get married?'

'What?'

'You're twenty-five, and I'm guessing, you have no boy- friend waiting in the wings for your return.'

'And your point is?'

'My point is, it occurs to me that if you'd already been married, your brother—if I am to believe your story— wouldn't be able to marry you off so readily.'

She looked up at him with incredulous eyes. 'You're blaming me not being married for my brother's actions? Are you serious?'

'You have to admit, if you were already married, you wouldn't have a problem. You wouldn't have had to flee.'

'I don't believe it. You are blaming me.'

'No, I'm just saying… No, I'm asking. I'm sorry, Prin- cess, because it's not like you're unattractive, and yet there's been nobody you've been interested in? Nobody you wanted to spend the rest of your life with?' He'd met Sophia in uni- versity, and what started as a friendship had soon turned to love. 'I'm having trouble understanding that.'

She blinked. Long slow blinks that told him she had little regard for his words. 'Thank you, I think. But for the record, there has been plenty of interest—in me. Appar- ently being a member of the royal family—a "not unat- tractive" princess with ready access to palaces and riches attracts plenty of interest. My problem has been deter- mining who is more interested in me, for who I am, rather than my place in the monarchy.' She cocked one side of her mouth. 'As you admitted, you wouldn't understand.'

Ouch.

Theo deserved that. The Princess was wiser and more grounded than he'd ever anticipated. He bowed his head. 'Once again, Princess, I need to apologise.'

'Accepted,' she said brusquely. 'And now, I think I'll turn in. Sleep well.'

She breezed past him and headed up the stairs. He listened to her footfall, heard the slow click of her door closing, and knew there was no sleep waiting for him. Whatever point he'd been trying to make, he'd badly botched. Although it did help him understand why someone as attractive as the Princess hadn't been snatched up already. *Theos.* He'd called her "not unattractive".

It was a wonder she hadn't slapped him across the face.

He glanced at his watch. The Princess was right, it was time to turn in. Time to be done with watching her. Time to be out of her presence. He'd told himself he wasn't attracted to her. He'd tried to convince herself of that. He couldn't afford to be attracted to her.

But truth was, he needed to get away from her, to get out of her presence, before he started to believe her story.

The night was one howling mess. The wind blew, the rain lashed, and the palm tree fronds rattled as they shook and smacked into each other. Theo barely slept, wishing the storm would die down so that the airport would open, no matter how unlikely that seemed with the racket going on outside, and that they could fly out tomorrow. Hoping that he wouldn't be hijacked during the night again. He'd employed the same improvised alarms that he'd employed the night before, his bedroom door was still open in case the

Princess tried to flee out the front door, but tonight he'd secured his door with a tie to ensure it couldn't be pushed open enough to allow someone access—if he even managed to snatch a moment of sleep.

He needed desperately to sleep, but it was too dangerous. He turned over in his bed, punching his pillow into submission.

Given what had happened earlier this evening, if the Princess did find a way into his room again, knowing what he knew and how good she felt, would he even bother to send her away?

Of course, he would.

It was ridiculous even contemplating the question. But the fact he'd even had to ask himself required some serious analysis.

Never before had he felt the pull of attraction for one of his rescues. And not since Sophia had he felt the power of attraction for any woman. No woman could take the place of Sophia. So why did the Princess affect him so?

She was both a rescue and a Princess. Double the reason to deliver her safely home untouched by him. He had a contract to find and return her.

He had a duty to return her.

Attraction didn't come into it.

Her story about her brother selling her off didn't come into it. That wasn't part of his remit. That wasn't something he was contracted to consider. His job was to get her home. End of story.

Except...

Her story still niggled at his conscience. The idea that she'd run away because the Prince planned to marry off his sister in order to settle his gambling debts was fanciful. A fancy she'd then embellished by saying the man she'd been promised to was in his fifties.

Trying to convince him by enhancing the injustice? An attempt to further appeal to his sense of right and wrong by stressing their difference in ages? She'd got him there. The idea that he was returning her home only to be forced to marry a man in his fifties that she wanted no part of— that wouldn't just be a waste.

It would be a crime.

The Princess was young and vibrant and was entitled to be living her life with the man of her choice.

But if she were lying and her story completely fabricated?

On the other hand, her brother's story was equally thin. The Princess didn't look in the least bit worried or envious about not being the one to occupy Rubanestein's throne. If the Princess was so certain she should be the one to sit on the throne, surely she would be bagging her brother's efforts at ruling the principality, pulling him down at every opportunity, pushing her own credibility to perform the role instead. On the contrary, she seemed more interested in just being able to live her life the way she wanted.

Certainly, she'd run for a reason. But right now, uncomfortably, her story was making the more sense.

So where did that leave him? She didn't mean anything to him, not really, other than providing endless irritation one way or another. When she wasn't needling him with her smart tongue, she was driving him to distraction with her lush mouth or her beguiling eyes or her all too bewitching body. She was a pint-sized distraction he didn't need. It would be a relief to see the back of her.

And given he was contracted to return her to Rubanestein, what choice did he have?

CHAPTER TEN

THEO WAS UP before dawn because lying in bed and not sleeping was getting old. A crew came out at first light to clear the road of the fallen palm, Tom delivering the news that the airport would remain closed another day.

It didn't matter that Theo had been half expecting it, given the weather, but the complications of this case were grating on his nerves. Never before had he felt so many conflicting emotions in carrying out a recovery, none of them wanting to be resolved any time soon.

The storm was no longer above and around him. The storm was in his head. A royal storm, named Isabella, occupying his headspace, blotting out reason, testing his patience along with his willpower.

He should never have kissed her. That one thought had played on a loop through his head throughout the night. He should never have touched the Princess. There was no greater truth.

The woman was trouble. She threatened his equilibrium at every turn. She tested his resolve. Worst of all, holding her had felt like someone had turned on a light in his life. Kissing her had felt like hope.

It was so long since he'd felt hope.

* * *

So merely telling himself again and again that he shouldn't have kissed her—*knowing it*—didn't make it any easier to accept it. Didn't make it any easier to regret it.

The woman was trouble all right.

No wonder she was messing with his head.

He was sitting at the dining room table on his second pot of coffee when the Princess appeared in the kitchen looking bright-eyed and well-rested. He sighed. Of course she was.

'Sleep well?' she asked, helping herself to a cup.

It was all he could do not to growl. And not just at the sight of her in her robe, untied of course, and no doubt designed to show off her shortie pyjamas and her perfect legs. What she lacked in height, she made up for in shape-liness, all sweet curves and toned flesh. He turned his eyes away. 'I suspect you know the answer to that.'

'Shame,' she said, covering her mouth with her free hand on a yawn. 'I slept really well.' She moved to the window and stood staring out at the view a while. 'Wow, I can see the tops of Mt Gower and Lidgbird. The weather seems to be clearing.'

'Just not enough.'

'Oh,' she said, taking a sip of her coffee. 'Bad news for you, then. Although I have to confess not being sorry.'

He grunted. 'I didn't think so.'

'So,' she said turning back, 'what are we going to do today?'

'Why do we have to "do" anything?'

'Because we can't spend the entire day inside.'

'I'm perfectly happy spending the day inside.'

'Okay, so there's always the pool, I guess. I could soak in there a while.'

He squeezed his eyes shut. Not the pool. Not the strapless bikini with that little ruffle at the top. Please god, not the tiny bikini again. He was supposed to be reminding himself of all the reasons he needed not to touch her. He was supposed to be keeping his distance. He didn't need a refresher of those sweet curves. But how attractive could the plunge pool actually be after the storm? 'I'm sure the pool will be uninviting—it no doubt needs cleaning after all the debris from the storm landing in it.'

'Hmm.' She seemed to weigh that up as she looked out the window to the deck and the pool outside. 'There is a lot of rubbish in it.'

'There you go,' he said, wanting to sigh in relief.

She turned and pulled out a chair opposite his at the table. 'In that case, I guess we'll just have to chat.'

He pinched the bridge of his nose between thumb and forefinger. 'Or you could get dressed.'

'I will. After breakfast.' She looked around. 'What is for breakfast by the way?'

'I don't know. The maid must be taking a day off. Why don't you look in the pantry and fridge to see what there is to eat?'

'Wow. Somebody got out of bed on the wrong side this morning. Or have you just been taking cranky pills again?'

The smile she added at the end of the sentence was the kicker.

His chair scraped on the floor as he pushed it back, rising to his feet to put more than a table's width between them. 'I'm not cranky,' he said, his turn to look out the windows to the incredible mountain vista that lay beyond. Okay, so it was a lie, but what did she expect, making out that everything was sweetness and light between them when she knew—she damned well knew—that she was goading him, torturing him, with her every appearance, her every word.

She must know that kiss last night was a mistake. She must know the danger she was putting him in—acting in his own interests instead of his client's, and messing with a rescue, a princess no less. He had no place. He had no right.

And yet she seemed so carefree. Almost as if she took delight from tempting him. Had her conquests in Sydney given her confidence and licence to explore her new-found skills while she still had some say?

He was sure her time back in the palace in Rubanestein would be more regulated, more controlled. Even if she tried, she would be known and recognised by the populace. There would be no more casual encounters with someone at the beach or in a café somewhere.

Was this her final fling?

Did she have him lined up as her final fling?

If that's what she'd planned, she was way out of luck, because there was no way he was falling for that. No way he'd give in to her. Sure, she'd felt like light and hope in his arms, but that was an illusion. Something she'd wanted him to feel. Because there could be no light. There was no hope.

Not after Sophia.

Not with anyone.

Especially not with Princess Isabella.

The beguiling scent broke him out of his thoughts. Of onions browning, of capsicum, tomatoes, mushrooms and more. A toaster pinged. He turned to see her adding scrambled eggs to a skillet filled with sauteed vegetables.

She saw him looking at her. 'Hungry?' she asked as she added grated parmesan to the mix.

His stomach growled. Coffee could only go so far. 'You cook?' he asked.

'Of course, I cook. I'm a multitasking princess. Is the concept unfamiliar to you?'

It was out of context. Nothing in the information he'd been provided had pointed to her having a fondness for cooking. It made no sense. When given a dossier on a rescue, everything on the rescue was disclosed. Every like and dislike was listed. Everything that could give insight into where a recovery expert could trace them. Everything.

Who had prepared this dossier? Someone working for her brother? Someone who didn't know her?

'You're frowning,' she said, as she served up three-quarters of the skillet onto a plate for him.

His eyebrows shot north. 'I'm still getting used to the fact you can cook.'

She smiled. 'My father taught me.'

'The Prince?'

'He loved being in the kitchen with my mother. After her influence, he told me that if he hadn't been born a Prince, he would happily have become a chef. Simple food mostly, but good food.' She pointed to his food. 'Sit down. Try it.'

Theo duly sat. Picked up his fork. Sampled a mouthful. And was blown away by the simple yet perfect combination of the ingredients. 'To think I wasted your talents yesterday by serving you a piece of toast.'

Her smile permeated all the way into his bones. 'Don't beat yourself up. It was good toast.'

And even his bones felt happy until he thought about what she was doing. Why was she trying to please him? What was her angle? He couldn't afford to let down his guard now. Tomorrow by all accounts they would fly out of Lord Howe Island. A scant two hours later they would be back in his jet en route to Rubanestein.

He had to keep his guard up. He wasn't about to be way-laid now, not so close to closing this deal.

The frittata was delicious. Another cup of coffee washed it down. Theo was feeling fully satisfied and replete.

And the best thing? The Princess had gone upstairs to shower and change after breakfast.

One more day, he told himself. Twenty-four hours. He'd suffered through worse. The airport was expected to open tomorrow and he'd pulled strings to make sure they were on the first plane out. The end was in sight.

And once he'd delivered her home, he might even be able to forget about this woman's beguiling accent and her fresh citrusy scent and the too-sweet curves of her body. He might even be able to stop thinking about her twenty-four hours of the day.

He could hardly wait.

Isabella looked at her scant wardrobe. She'd brought only basic items with her to Lord Howe Island. Beachwear. Casual clothes. Sundresses. Along with shorts and jeans and T-shirts to get her through any days of work.

She surveyed her meagre collection, wanting something that Theo hadn't seen. That might just tip him over the edge. He was close. She hadn't had much experience with men, but she could see that he was battling his own inner demons. Trying to pretend she didn't affect him when she was clearly driving him crazy. Otherwise, why would he be so awkward around her?

A jumpsuit caught her attention. A jumpsuit she'd found at a Saturday market on the Sydney coast that spoke of summer and would be a forever reminder of her time down under. Cap-sleeved and short legged with a printed fruit salad pattern, watermelon, pineapple, dragon fruit on a white woven cotton background. Now that the weather had moderated, she knew it was the perfect choice for the day ahead.

Theo was drinking yet another cup of coffee when she re-appeared downstairs.

He looked up. Took her in. Immediately looked down again.

'You probably shouldn't drink so much coffee,' she said.

'Thanks for the advice,' he said. 'Next time, wait until I ask for it.'

She snorted. 'I did tell you, you've been taking cranky pills.'

'I'm not cranky.'

'So you say, and yet, you seem so defensive.'

Defence was the best form of offence. But he didn't have to react to her ridiculous claims. He didn't have to prove anything.

She sat down opposite him, her jumpsuit at least hiding more of her than her pyjamas had done.

'So if we're not going out, maybe we could use this opportunity to learn more about each other.'

'Like what?'

'You were married, right?'

'Yes.'

'And you loved her?'

'Of course I did.'

'And she loved you.'

'Princess,' he said, his voice thick. 'Where is this going?'

'But she did, right?'

The words felt like they'd been wrenched from his soul. 'She did.' Not that he'd been able to honour that love, not in the end.

She seemed to contemplate that for a minute. 'What did that feel like—to have someone love you so much?'

'It was—perfection.'

'I love that,' she said. 'That is everything every person wants.'

And Theo knew exactly where this was going before she'd even uttered her next words.

'Because that's what I want. To feel someone to love me so much and me love him that it's perfection.'

'It's a worthy goal,' he said, intentionally keeping his distance.

'My father promised that I could marry for love. I was never going to accede to the throne, so he promised me that I could make my own way. But how am I to find that love, how am I ever to feel that same feeling, if my brother is to marry me off to someone I don't love. Someone I could never love?'

Her voice was rising. 'Princess—again, you're becoming over melodramatic.'

'You don't believe me,' she said. 'You don't believe what my brother has in store for me.'

'There are no indications.' He'd had nothing back on his request for information but given the threadbare Wi-Fi and the weather, that was hardly surprising. Then again, maybe it was because there was nothing to find.

'No indications? What are you waiting for? Of course he's not going to "give you indications". He needs you onside. He needs you to deliver the goods. And that's all I am to him. The goods. The ticket out of his massive debts.'

He said nothing. Given the lack of any evidence, there

was nothing to say. She sipped her coffee and he assumed she was done.

He was wrong.

'My brother has always had a mean streak,' she said, flopping into a chair, rubbing her forehead with one hand. 'It was always tempered when my parents were alive, but even when they weren't around he'd find ways to bully me. I thought once he acceded to the throne, he'd have enough on his plate to worry about and he'd forget about me. But I was wrong.'

Theo looked up. A bully? There had been something in the dossier that had hinted at the Prince's authoritarian personality, and his strong need to control, but this had been painted as unsurprising, given his station and the leadership role expected of him. But could there be something darker behind it?

'Did he ever hurt you? Physically, I mean.'

She sniffed. 'No. Not me. Nothing that would show. But I had a six-month-old puppy called Coco. My parents had given her to me for my twelfth birthday.'

Chills skittered down Theo's spine. 'What happened?'

'I couldn't find her one day. I called and called but she didn't come. And then Rafael appeared, holding Coco. It was wrong. Coco hated Rafael, she growled whenever he was around. But now she was crying. Whimpering. And I could see that one of her legs was just hanging. Limp. She fell down the stairs, Rafael told me, and then he smiled. And I knew—I just knew that he'd done it. My parents believed him—maybe they just wanted to believe him— because my father visited me that night while Coco was being cared for in the veterinary hospital. He hugged me tightly and told me that he was sorry for how the way things were. He told me that things would be different one day. He promised me—' She pulled her legs up onto the chair and wrapped her arms tightly around them.

And Theo's senses were stretched piano-wire tight. He ached to get up and wrap his arms around her and comfort her—but that was because it provided him with the perfect excuse to do so. To do exactly what he wanted to do. But he couldn't reach out. He couldn't afford to make a move.

Her story might be compelling. Heart-rending, even. But convincing? And did it even matter? She was a rescue. He was a bodyguard. She was his mission. No matter what he felt right now, emotions didn't come into it. His job was to get her home, no matter the sob stories along the way.

No matter how hard it might feel.

Nothing was working. Izzy rose from her chair to pace the suite. She didn't know how to break through the walls that Theo had erected around him, walls that seemed to offer a crack, a crevice, a mere promise every now and then to let her in to get a glimpse of the man and let him see her, only to have him plaster over those walls, raise the drawbridge and withdraw into the inner sanctum.

One night. One more night was all she had to convince him not to take her home. She took a deep breath as she looked out the window at the grey skies, the swirling clouds around the tops of the mountains and the swaying palm trees of the rainforest below.

But she wasn't done with trying yet. Maybe she just needed to try a different tack…

'So,' she said, turning, 'you were married.'

He looked up from the messages he was reading on his phone that the trickle of internet had finally allowed through. There was a crisis developing in a recovery happening in Istanbul, a complication with another in Athens, and he was still waiting on information he'd urgently requested about Prince Rafael, but his attention was now one hundred per cent focused on the question this woman had just asked.

Where the hell had that come from? Unless this was another tilt at the fifty-year-old fiancé thing. He half expected her next question to be, *'How old was she?'*

'I think we've established that I was married, Princess.'

'And you've made love with a woman.'

'What's that got to do with anything?'

'You're right. Silly question. You were married and of course you would have made love with your wife, and probably a bunch of women besides.'

'Not while I was married to my wife.' *Not since, for that matter.* 'Now where is this going, Princess?'

She shrugged. 'Only that you're a man. And you look like someone who would know how all the bits might work.'

There was no preventing his eyebrows shooting north. 'I doubt there are many adults alive on this planet who don't know how "all the bits might work". I'm equally sure your education, not to mention your recent experiences, will have filled you in on the necessary details.'

'Well, of course it did, I just wondered what it felt like from the male point of view.'

'Didn't Mateo or Luke or whoever else there was bother to share that information with you?'

Isabella's interest spiked. Theo remembered their names? That *was* interesting.

She shrugged. 'I guess I was too caught up in the moment. I didn't think to ask. So now I'm asking you.'

He bristled on his chair. 'I wish you wouldn't. I'm not comfortable talking about this with you, Princess. It's not appropriate.'

'Not even in general? I'm not asking for specifics. I'm not asking for a blow-by-blow analysis.'

He shook his head. 'Believe me, that's the last thing you're going to get.'

'Right. So, what can you tell me?'

'Nothing,' he said. He slammed his laptop shut. Twenty-four hours had never seemed so long. 'I can't stand another moment of this.'

'So, you agree, we're going out?'

It wasn't his first choice. His first choice would be to lock her in her room where she couldn't constantly needle him with her perfect body and her smart words. But locking her in her room, even if it was possible, was crossing a line he'd never expected to want to cross.

What was it with this woman?

'Well?' she said, looking decidedly more sheepish but not giving up, her hands clasped innocently before her. 'It has to be better than staying here with you getting on my nerves and me getting on yours.'

It was ridiculous. Going out in this wild weather was ridiculous. But maybe she had a point. Staying here with this woman in this apartment for however long the storm was going to last was impossible. He might not be attracted to her—he refused to admit the truth that he was attracted to her—but just being in her proximity was on his mind—and her nerves—one hundred per cent of the time.

'What did you have in mind?'

Ten minutes later they pulled up at the island's visitor centre. The rain had eased although the winds were still high, the palm fronds thrashing above their heads. 'So why are we here?' Theo asked.

'To learn,' she said, 'it's interesting.'

Theo doubted it, but what else did he have to do? And maybe it would give him a break from the constant headache that was trying to exist in close proximity to this woman.

Inside there was a café and store that sold books and all manner of souvenirs. A family sat at a table in the café, eating lunch.

Theo wasn't a tourist. Souvenirs didn't interest him. But he stopped to pick up the odd book and flick through the pages. He looked up and realised he'd lost sight of the Princess. His heart missed a beat. Had the Princess sneaked out the door while he was reading? Had she used this excursion as cover for one more of her attempts to escape? But no—he caught a glance of her through a doorway leading to another room. He put the book down and headed in. It was clearly the museum part of the building, overflowing with naval and aerial artefacts along with evidence and artefacts from the island's whaling past. The history of the island was laid bare in the displays. The island might be tiny, but it had a big history. Formed from the remnants of an ancient volcanic eruption, there were black and white pictures of times gone by where there had been no airport or runway and when seaplanes had serviced the island, taking off and landing on the lagoon. And then there was a case containing bones, a skeleton of something resembling a massive turtle, at least a metre long, but this turtle came with a skull bedecked in a tiara of horns and a permanent grimace. The bones of its long tail were similarly barbed. It looked menacing and fierce.

'It looks grumpy, doesn't it?' she said, appearing next to

him unexpectedly, bringing with her the fresh citrus scent she wore. He edged away. Once he'd realised she hadn't tried to run away, he'd been enjoying another brief moment of space away from her, but that opportunity had clearly come to an end. He didn't want her so close to him. The whole purpose of the outing was about getting some distance from each other, but here she was, edging up next to him and setting the nerve endings in his skin on red alert. Hadn't she told him that he was getting on her nerves? She was showing no signs of it. Instead, she seemed intent on crowding his space. What was her game?

His senses bristled at the proximity. He was hoping that he could make it through the day unscathed, without another attempt by her to seduce him, without another stupid kiss he'd planted on her.

Unscathed?

Theo wondered if it were possible. The longer he spent in this woman's presence, the more he felt scathed—by her mere presence, by her touch.

By her scent, fresh and citrusy, that suited her perfectly.

By her lips. Enticing. Full and pink.

By her eyes. Her impossible cat-like eyes. Hazel. Or were they more amber, with flecks of gold in their depths? Eye colour that seemed to change with the light.

'I told you it was interesting, didn't I?'

She had and as much as he hadn't cared one way or another, the small museum was full of surprising displays and facts. The tiny dot of an island in the middle of the Tasman Sea, halfway between Australia and New Zealand, had a rich and fascinating history.

'It's an ancient horned turtle,' she said, not waiting for him to answer. 'They used to live on the island around forty thousand years ago.'

He nodded. 'I think I'm relieved they don't still live here.'

She laughed. 'Wow, you made a joke. How about that?'

Had he? He'd thought he was merely stating a fact.

'You know what, though?' she said, looking from the skeleton to Theo and back. 'There's a definite resemblance. It reminds me of you.'

He snorted. 'Very funny.'

'No, seriously. He looks cranky and fierce. Just like you.'

Excellent. She was comparing him to a forty-thousand-year-old skeleton. He turned away, as much to escape a scent that was becoming more alluring by the minute, as to get out of range of her verbal barbs. There was a reason for his crankiness, and the Princess was a big part of it.

Wrong, he corrected himself a moment later. The Princess *was* the reason for it.

'Are we done here?' he asked, impatient to move on in case she started comparing him to more of the relics in the museum.

'If you're ready.'

Theo was more than ready.

The Princess directed him up a hill and along a ridge that seemed to run along the spine of the island, before taking a right turn that led them down a beach. It was a small bay on the northern side of the island, with a cluster of rocky islands out to sea and with grassy picnic grounds adjoining the sandy beach, where wave tumbled over wave on their frenetic way to the shore. Nobody was picnicking today. Theirs was the only car in the car park. Clearly, they were the only mad people who wanted to be out in this weather. Everyone else must be hunkered down riding out the storm.

'Okay,' he said, thinking they were on a fool's errand. Getting out of the apartment to avoid getting on each other's nerves might have sounded like a good plan, but it wasn't like they weren't together. As far as he could tell, it didn't matter where they were—they were still going to get on each other's nerves. 'So, we're here. Why?'

She smiled on a shrug and once again he was struck by the change in his perception of her, that once he'd thought she looked like a teenager with all those mad colours in her hair, young and innocent. She wasn't an innocent—he knew that now—and maybe that's why she looked like a woman. And yet still her delight right now was more like that teenager, or maybe, he conceded, someone who had discovered something special. Was it really that special? 'Come and see,' she said.

The wind caught her door, flinging it open. She whooped as she grabbed at it, fighting against the wind to close it.

He sighed. Utter madness. He followed her out onto a path leading to the beach. The wind whipped at his hair, tugging at his shirt. She stopped at a shelter containing a basic vending machine.

'What is that?' he asked, as she exchanged coins for two bags.

'You'll see,' she said. He didn't see anything beyond the loosened tendrils of her hair whipping around her face in the wind. 'I'll show you.'

She led him down towards the water, kicked off her sandals on the sand, and waded into the water. She looked back at him, while he was still wondering what the point of this was. The wind was still wild, clouds building, whitecaps mashing on the sea. The sea was a mess. It would rain later, the forecast predicted. 'What are you waiting for?' she yelled over her shoulder. He could barely hear her over the gusting wind. He was still waiting to discover the point of this mad venture.

She threw out one arm and whooped, or was it a scream? Suddenly, the water around her bare legs frothed and churned and it looked like whatever it was under those turbulent waves was trying to eat the Princess alive.

Did they even have piranha in Australia? Or was it one of those ancient horned turtles that hadn't died out after all?

'Princess!' he called, tossing off his shoes and ploughing into the water, determined to get to her. He hadn't put up with all he had to lose her now. He reached her and swooped her into his arms, but something was missing. *Blood.* There was no blood. Surely if she was being attacked, there would be blood.

And surely, he'd be being attacked right now too. And while something down there bumped and nudged his legs, there was a remarkable absence of teeth.

'What are you doing?' she laughed, grinning madly in his arms.

Good question. What was he doing?

'Put me down,' she said, laughing. 'The fish are missing the tourists.'

Fish?

And the nudging and bumping into his calves suddenly made sense. He put her down and she handed him a small bag. 'Here, take this.' He looked at it. Tried to make sense of the label. Fish food. That's why they were standing in the shallows while the tail end of a cyclone whipped the air around them? They were here to feed fish? She had to be kidding.

But he could feel the slap of warm bodies against his ankles and shins before he could discern them in the choppy water. 'You see,' she said, laughing as she scattered around some of the fish food. 'Look!'

The water whirled and swirled around his knees, whipped up by the wind, but yes, he could make out the fish crowding around his legs. Big fish, small fish, some silvery and sleek, some long and fluid, some brightly co-loured, more fish than he'd ever seen in one place in the wild, but all of them angling for a treat. And with every wave breaking on the shore, it brought still more fish.

'So feed them,' called the Princess.

And through the turbulence of the last two days he re-membered something that Tom Parker had mentioned on his whistle-stop tour of the island—Ned's Beach, where he could feed the fish. He'd paid scant attention at the time—it had made no sense—and yet, here he was now.

It was crazy. This was seriously the most ridiculous thing he'd ever done. The most pointless. But he dipped his hand into the fish food, scattering it all around him. The water erupted in a fevered flapping rush of silver and scales as open mouths fought for the food. Fish buf-feted his shins, their bodies sleek and surprisingly warm, swept back and forth by the tide, swept up in the fight for the food.

It was like nothing he'd ever experienced. It was un-imaginable. It was almost like the fish had been so well trained that they were waiting for bare legs to appear so they could rush into shore and be first for the feed.

He scattered another handful, and then another, enter-tained by the feeding frenzy and reminded of another day, long ago, when he and Sophia had celebrated the end of their university studies by taking a holiday in the United Kingdom. They'd hired a camper-van and criss-crossed the country. They'd stopped at St Ives, in Cornwall, treating themselves to cod and chips from a takeaway near the harbour. Sampling the local cuisine. Playing at being locals. They'd sat by the harbour wall and tried to eat their fish before the diving gulls could fly over their shoulder and pluck their meal from their hands. Competitive and determined, the gulls seemed to work in tag teams, one distracting you, the next taking advantage of an outflung arm bearing treasure.

It was a contest to see who would prevail—the humans or the birds. In the end, it was more of a draw. The gulls had won some points, but the best bit was when Theo and Sophia tossed the rest of their chips skywards and watched as the gulls engaged in a chip war with each other, any hint of cooperation or tag-teaming thrown asunder, the sky over them filled with the raucous flapping creatures.

They'd laughed so much. And when they found the signs afterwards requesting visitors not to feed the gulls, they'd realised their tourist faux pas and laughed even more. It had been one of the best days of their holiday.

Feeding these fish was a similar experience—except apparently here feeding the wildlife was allowed. Even actively encouraged.

The fish danced and darted around his shins, fighting for the food, fighting for supremacy, and it was so mad, so out of his world, that he did something that he couldn't remember. He felt it coming, bubbling up inside him, a feeling so unfamiliar that he didn't at first recognise what it was. Until delight erupted from his mouth in a bubble of laughter.

How she heard over the wind whipping around them, he didn't know. 'Do you see?' the Princess yelled over the wind. 'Isn't it fabulous?'

Theo couldn't deny it. And yet, as he scattered the fish food into the water, it wasn't just fabulous, it felt cathartic.

It was therapy. Laughing at the antics of the fish. Letting go.

It was—*fun*.

A fish nibbled one of his toes, taking a chunk of skin out of it. 'Ouch,' he said, but he was laughing, and when he looked up, he saw her watching him, and he stilled.

Her eyes glittered. 'You see. This island is magic.'

And in spite of himself, Theo was starting to believe it.

CHAPTER ELEVEN

THEO WAS CONFLICTED as he prepared for dinner. Isabella had requested for their last night on the island, that they book a table at the restaurant where she had worked. Still acting, or so she could say goodbye to the crew she'd worked with, the crew that had given her a chance and made her welcome.

He wasn't crazy about the idea. He didn't want the Princess exposed to the public eye any more than she already had been, but he wasn't a monster. And after today's excursions, he had to admit his attitude towards the Princess was changing.

She was much more of a surprise package than he'd been led to believe. Sure, she was young and naive, she was a twenty-five-year-old innocent Princess, and yet she'd proved herself so much more than that. She shown she had street smarts by evading recovery for so long—nobody had expected that.

She was no poseur; she had a natural way about her that belied her royal heritage. And if she hungered for the throne, there was a complete absence of evidence for that. Could she hide a yearning for the throne that well? No. Surely if she was planning some kind of coup against her brother, to take the throne in his place, she'd want to be working inside the institution that was the palace of Rubanestein, and not in some far-flung island half a world away—where internet was thready at best and totally absent at worst.

Hardly the place to plot a coup.

Perhaps most surprisingly, she was fun to be with. Sure, she could be annoying and problematic and too much in his face, like today when she'd sidled too close to him for his liking at the museum, but today had been fun. He'd forgotten about fun. He'd left fun by the wayside when Sophia had gone.

He'd had no place for fun.

But today the Princess had reminded him of the simple pleasure of fun. The simple pleasure of laughter. And that was no small deal.

No. The more Theo reflected on the case, the more he learned about the Princess, the less sense the Prince's reason for wanting Isabella back in Rubanestein made. Was Rafael more worried about her safety out in the big world without security and so over-egged the pudding? That was possible, especially if he were the bullying kind of character the Princess had claimed. A runaway royal lacking security was always going to be fodder for every nefarious group out there. The Prince hadn't needed to add to the story by claiming it was an act of rebellion by the Princess for not acceding to the throne herself.

All he'd had to say was that he was worried for her safety, exposed and alone in the big bad world. Theo would have believed that. Anybody would have believed that. Because the Princess was in danger. She might have been lucky or clever until now, but sooner or later her luck would run out and the other people interested in finding her would.

But none of that explained why she had run.

Her story that her brother had sold his own sister in exchange for the funds to pay his gambling debts was so far-fetched. He knew people were capable of evil deeds, he'd be out of a job if they weren't, but this was a prince, the ruler of his principality—and to sell his own sister, to marry her off to one of his cronies as if she were no more than a piece of his property, was so heinous—was it any wonder he had trouble accepting her claims?

Then again—why had she run? If it wasn't for that, what was it?

He ran his hand through his hair. The Princess—this entire case—and the extended time spent together because of this damned cyclone—were messing with his head. And today's fish feeding excursion was not helping.

It had broken too many barriers. He'd let his game down. He didn't do fun. He didn't want to do fun. Not with anyone. Least of all with her. Of course she would want to sway him. But she was a job. A rescue.

He just had to keep reminding himself of that.

Isabella showered and changed into a sundress for dinner at the café, knowing that time was short and that she was running out of options. Theo had advised her that the airport would reopen tomorrow, and that they would be on the first flight to Sydney. So that left her with just one night to convince Theo that he shouldn't drag her back to Rubanestein.

She took a deep breath. They'd had a good day today visiting the museum and Ned's Beach. They'd had a fun day. Even Theo couldn't deny that. She was hoping that Theo's attitude towards her might be softening, and that he might see her as less problem rescue and more as a woman.

He was starting to feel something for her, she could tell from the way that she caught him looking at her, but as yet there was no indication that he was not intending to carry through his mission.

It was frustrating and there was so little time left. She sensed that he was starting to see her not as a mere rescue, but as a person. A woman. He was softening to her. So, yes, her clumsy attempt that first night when she'd sneaked into his room had ultimately failed. But then, last night he'd been the one to kiss her.

What a kiss.

And today, he'd enjoyed their time at Ned's Beach. Theo couldn't fake that. She'd got the impression that Theo faked nothing. What you saw was what you got.

Isabella checked her reflection as she looked in the mirror. She'd twisted her hair into a messy bun with tendrils coiling around her face, and tonight she'd even added a touch of make-up, circling her eyes with a smoky kohl, adding a hint of blush and a smear of gloss to her lips.

She took another deep fortifying breath.

There was one chance left. *Tonight.*

One night to put Plan A into practice.

Seducing Theo. Getting him to admit that she meant more to him than any other rescue. Getting him to admit that he cared about her enough to not want to simply hand her over to her brother. Surely, if he made love to her, he would rethink his plans?

And if he didn't—well, if he didn't, and he still insisted on delivering her back to her ever-loving brother—she still would have a memory to look back on in the long, loveless years ahead.

One way or another, she needed Plan A to work. Otherwise she'd have to resort to Plan B. She hadn't got this far without having a backup plan.

Plan B was way less fun but could prove just as effective. Make a scene at the airport on their departure. Find security and plead for help. Accuse Theo of kidnapping and trafficking her and maybe worse. Making sure that he was the object of the authorities' attention. Her own ID borrowing would no doubt be an issue when that came out, but if it delayed the legal process, that was good. That worked for her.

But she didn't want to have to resort to Plan B. She didn't want to throw Theo to the wolves. She knew how the media worked. They would tear him apart based on a false accusation.

Ordinarily she hated women who made false accusations. It brought all women down, minimising genuine grievances. But right now, when she was desperate, what other choice did she have?

So, Plan A was it. She just had to pray that it worked.

'It's time,' she heard Theo call from downstairs. She bounded down the stairs and met Theo at the front door. He looked her up and down and for a moment he appeared dumbstruck. And then he said, 'You look amazing.' Had his voice gone down an octave? Whatever, the sound seemed to vibrate into her bones.

'Thank you,' she said, her eyes drinking him in. He was wearing suit pants and a crisp white shirt that clung to his torso in the best possible way. Even better, the shirt was unbuttoned at the neck exposing a triangle of olive skin dusted with black hairs. 'So do you.'

They remained there for moments, seconds, before he seemed to remember that they were supposed to be leaving. He cleared his throat. 'We should go,' he said.

The minutes it took them to drive the slow route to the restaurant no longer felt like a penalty. Instead, it felt delicious. Isabella's senses were on high alert. Today they'd broken the barrier between hunter and hunted. Today they'd found common ground.

Happy ground.

And now, her senses buzzed at his proximity, at his clean masculine scent. She would be happy if this ride never ended. Except there was the anticipation of the after, and the prospect of that was even more delicious. And after today, after witnessing his joy at one of the island's simple pleasures, after witnessing Theo unwinding, there was a chance it might even work.

She sucked in a breath, heavily laden with the heat and scent of Theo. Was he wearing after-shave or was it his own signature scent that wove its way into and beguiled her senses?

And curiosity powered her conversation. 'What's the name of the after-shave you're wearing?' Because if she never met him again, she wanted to be able to buy it and be reminded of his scent and this time in her life.

'I'm not wearing after-shave.'

Damn. So much for buying a bottle. But she found a smile. 'I like it.'

'I said I'm not wearing any.'

'I heard.'

She sensed his head swivel towards her. She just kept smiling and turned her head out her window.

Around them, the palm trees swayed, while the waves crashed into the coral reefs surrounding the lagoon, the background music of the island restored to normal settings now the cyclone was moving away. Isabella had fallen asleep to the island's music night after night. She knew she would never forget this sound.

She turned back to him. 'You're so lucky the cyclone closed the airport.'

'Am I?'

'Of course. How else would you have seen anything of the island. But now, at least you've seen some of the sights.'

He grunted as he pulled into the restaurant's car park. 'I consider myself blessed in that case.'

She smiled to herself. He didn't sound it. It was fun teasing him.

The head waiter showed them to their table—table thirty—at the back of the restaurant.

'What are the chances?' Isabella said as she sat down.

'I requested it,' he told her as he pulled out his chair, 'Just to ensure you couldn't easily be spotted by any walk-ins.'

Isabella screwed up her face. 'Your job seems to suck all the joy out of life. Are you ever able to relax?'

'Yes,' he said. 'Between jobs.'

'I thought you'd relaxed today.'

'There were moments,' he said.

'You were happy,' she insisted. 'I saw it. You can't deny it. It was fun. How long is it since you last had fun like that?'

Theo didn't want to think about it. His mind was on tomorrow. He didn't want to be reminded of that day in St Ives, when he and Sophia had broken the local protocol and flung chips into the sky and set off world war three—or the *gull war*, as they'd named it. He hadn't wanted to be reminded of it. It somehow felt disloyal that he'd had fun with another woman. *This woman.*

He'd never wanted any other woman. But getting involved with this woman would break all the rules. Personal and professional.

'A while,' he simply said.

'That's so sad.'

Her expression looked sad, but the Princess was so upbeat. What was going on? She'd been almost flirty in the car. And yet tomorrow she knew that he would be taking her back to Rubanestein. Surely, she should be fearful. Apprehensive.

Instead, she seemed almost gleeful. What was that about?

Unless this entire adventure of hers had been a fraud, an adventure of her making, and now she was relieved that the game was over, and she was glad to be going home.

For Theo, who'd rescued people who'd wanted to be rescued, who'd wanted to go home, her constant flip-flopping made no sense.

Except, he had to admit to his own flip-flopping. His take on the Princess seemed to change at every turn. She was supposed to be innocent and naive. She'd proved herself to be anything but. She was supposed to be a woman who hungered for the crown, and who'd turned her platinum hair, her crowning glory, into a crown of colours, and shown not one iota of interest in wanting to be the leader of Rubanestein or in inciting some rebellion. On the contrary, she seemed to be happy living half a world away and having nothing to do with her homeland.

Theo tried to pull it all together as Millie delivered menus to their table, trying to pretend she wasn't intrigued at them being together. Her brother's story made little sense. Her story made less. But maybe, just maybe her story was right. What if her story was right? It was bizarre and so far out there that it seemed impossible, but what if she'd been telling the truth all this time?

Millie arrived to take their drink orders. There was more she wanted to say, Theo could tell, seeing the questions so clearly swimming in her eyes, but she said nothing, merely taking their orders. Sparkling water for the table, and a glass of pinot noir for Isabella.

'Do you want to tell me about it,' she asked, 'about that other time you felt so happy?'

'Not really,' he said, turning his attention to the menu. 'Now, what do you like to order?'

'We had a good day today,' she said, looking over the menu.

'Haven't we already discussed this? Why are you bringing that up again?'

'Because we did.'

He could find no way to disagree. 'It was fine.'

'You laughed,' she said. 'You had a good time.'

'It has been known to happen.'

'I bet, not for a long time.'

He said nothing but his silence spoke volumes.

'So,' he said. 'What would you like to order?'

'I think I'm going to have the steak,' Isabella said, closing her menu, 'medium rare. With the garlic roasted chats on the side.'

Theo grunted.

'Something wrong?' she said.

'No,' he said, closing his menu as Millie returned to their table bearing their drinks.

'Are you ready to order now?'

'Two scotch fillets, medium rare, with side of the roasted chats for two. And if you could,' he added, 'we'd appreciate it if you would move us up the order.'

Millie nodded and smiled. 'I can do that,' she said, and promptly disappeared into the kitchen. Isabella surveyed him through her lashes as she took a sip of her wine. Was that the reason for his grump, that she had chosen the exact same meal as him? Was he annoyed that they had even this one more thing in common than the way they took their coffee?

Theo was baffling to her. An insufferable mix of kidnapper and yet self-proclaimed protector—allegedly. Every time the door opened, his head swivelled, checking who was going in or out.

'You're making me nervous.'

'What?'

She waved an arm towards the door. 'All that constant head swivelling. Who are you expecting?'

'I'm protecting your safety. If you don't appreciate that, then I'm sorry.'

'If you're interested in protecting my safety, you wouldn't be delivering me back to Rubanestein like a trussed-up chicken. You'd be helping me get away and stay away. You'd be protecting me from my brother.'

'You keep saying that.'

'Because it's true! And you are going to feel like one stupid jackass when you realise it.'

Theo said nothing. Simply swivelled his neck when the door opened again. Isabella turned to look, too. Theo stared at the entrants, a couple with three children, and turned back, apparently immediately discounting them as a threat.

'Gosh,' she said. 'Do nefarious agents not use children for cover any more? Times have certainly changed in the world of subterfuge.'

'Give it up, Princess. That family was in the museum when we visited today. If they'd wanted to make a move on you, they could easily have followed us to Ned's Beach and snatched you there.'

'Oh.' Isabella vaguely remembered other visitors being in the shop when they'd visited but hadn't taken in the details.

'Yes. "Oh." You see, I do know something about my business.'

Isabella felt the rebuke like a smack. Even though she no doubt deserved it, she regretted her words. She was supposed to be trying to make Theo feel closer to her. To make him warm to her. To make him see that she was more than just another recovery.

Thankfully Millie arrived then, delivering their meals. 'Two steaks, medium rare,' she said, placing the sizzling plates on the table in front of them, 'with a side of garlic roasted chats.' She held her tray vertically in front of her. 'Is there anything else I can get for you? Are you all right for drinks.'

'Thank you,' Theo said. 'Nothing else.'

The steak was perfect. Izzy's knife sliced through the tender steak as if it were butter, the roasted potatoes crispy garlic perfection. She'd ordered thinking she needed to keep her energy for the night ahead. But her appetite had disappeared, and she barely finished half her meal.

It was impossible to eat while she felt her frustration mounting. This was crunch time. Tomorrow hung over her neck like a noose. She had to make one of her plans work. But she had to get him talking. She had to get him warming to her.

Theo was not acting like someone who wanted to talk or warm to her. It was like he'd recognised that he'd let his guard down at Ned's Beach today, and that he'd revealed too much of himself and so was trying to shut himself down. She took a deep breath. What she needed was a different angle. Less combative.

'So, the plan for tomorrow is that we take the flight to Sydney,' she started, twirling her glass of pinot noir, 'and then we board your private jet to Rubanestein?'

'That's the plan,' he confirmed.

'Still the plan?'

'Still the plan, Princess. The plan hasn't changed. The plan has always been set in concrete.'

'I knew that,' she said on a sigh, because Isabella couldn't help but be dismayed. She'd hoped Theo's attitude to her was softening, but despite her arguments and her pleas, he was resolute in returning her to the place she least wanted to be. 'But is there any chance you might possibly relent? Maybe give me more of a chance to prove what's in store for me when you return me home?'

'Why would I do that? You've already had two days to convince me, and you haven't yet.'

She lifted her glass, went to take a sip and put it down again out of frustration. 'I hate that you don't believe me. I think I hate you right now. Excuse me, but I need to go to the bathroom.'

'Don't try to sneak out a window, Princess. We've already done that. It's getting old.'

She stood up and walked away. What chance did she have to win Theo over to her side? How was she going to seduce him? Her Plan A was a confection. A faint hope.

How could she possibly seduce a man who was more like a robot? Unemotional. Wedded to his purpose. Oblivious to reason. His brief glimmer today of a human hidden beneath that shell of concrete completely and utterly snuffed out.

How did anyone, let alone her, seduce a man made of stone?

It was impossible.

Millie caught her arm on her way back. 'What's going on?' she whispered. 'Are you sure you don't need help? I can call the policeman now, if you want.'

Izzy shook her head, running a hand through her hair. 'It's a long and boring story, Millie. You really don't want to hear it.'

'You're wrong there, but I guess if you can't tell me, you

can't tell me. And if it's an easier question, let me know how you're placed for shifts next week.'

'I wish, but it looks like I'll be leaving the island tomorrow if the airport reopens, so tonight looks like it's goodbye. One day I hope to be able to explain it all.' *Although she very much wondered when that might be possible.* Izzy wrapped her fingers around Millie's hand. 'Meanwhile, thank you so much for your friendship. It's been fun working with you.'

Millie frowned. 'Are you sure it's all okay between you and—' she glanced over Izzy's shoulder '—him.'

'It's, uh, complicated. Trust me, and maybe one day I can tell you.'

'I want that,' Millie said. 'I want to know all is good in your world.' The two quickly embraced. 'And know that whenever you come back, you'll always have a job here.'

Izzy felt tears pricking her eyes. 'Thank you. That means the world to me.'

Izzy was almost back to their table when Millie caught up. 'Oh, I almost forgot to tell you.'

'Tell me what?'

'Apparently two guys came in today at lunch when I was off duty. It was weird because they said they were looking for someone called Erin but they showed a photo that looked a bit like you.'

Ice flowed through Izzy's veins, fear stiffening her spine. 'What were they told?'

'That they didn't recognise the photo. But apparently it really looked like you, Izzy. Apparently, now you've washed the colour from your hair, she looked like a dead ringer for you.' Millie frowned. 'Are they looking for you? Are you sure you're not in trouble?'

'What's going on?'

Neither Isabella nor Millie had noticed that Theo had joined them. Millie started, as if afraid to confront Theo directly.

'Someone was asking questions earlier today,' Izzy said. 'Someone looking for a blonde woman who looks just like me.'

'But how did they get here?' Theo asked. 'The airport is closed.'

'Apparently a private launch arrived this morning, mooring at the supply boat dock. People noticed it because it was so crazy to attempt making the crossing from the mainland in that weather. Nobody had seen either of them before. They must have been from the boat.'

'Can you describe them?'

'Only from what I heard. They were broad-shouldered and wearing suits. They didn't look like tourists.'

Theo cursed. 'Get your things,' he told the Princess. 'We have to go.'

'Should I call the police?' Millie asked.

'No. No police.' He dropped a stack of bills on the table. 'That should take care of the bill and a tip for you.' He nodded. 'Thank you. In case anyone asks, we weren't here.'

Millie was still chewing her lip as Izzy squeezed her arm. 'Don't worry. I'll be fine.'

Izzy wished she believed her own words as Theo headed the car for the apartment. He was angry, she could tell, no doubt at the accursed weather for delaying their departure, no doubt at knowing that whoever else was tracking her was getting close.

But his anger in no way matched hers.

'Well played, Theo. You were the one to demand I wash the colour from my hair.'

'What of it?'

'And so people noticed a resemblance. It's only because the waiters were suspicious that they pleaded ignorance. But who else have they—whoever they are—flashed that photo to and who aren't suspicious enough to want to protect my privacy? You did that. You made me instantly recognisable by making me wash the colour from my hair.'

'You don't know that.' But he did know for a fact that he'd flashed the photo of a smiling blonde princess to Tom Parker, and it had stirred his memories, even though her hair had been coloured all the colours of the rainbow.

'You do! You were so incensed that I'd dared colour my hair and sully my Princess roots that you made me wash it out. You were so sure that we'd be on a plane the next day that you didn't think for a moment that maybe it was better to keep my disguise in place until we were on our way?'

He growled, a low and guttural sound emanating from his throat.

'Is that all you've got to say, bounty hunter?'

'Anyone might have recognised you in that photo anyway, colour or no colour.'

'Might have. But you ensured it was a certainty. Thanks for protecting me. I think I was actually doing better by myself.'

She flung her head back against the headrest. Hell. What was she going to do now? Her backup plan to make a scene at the airport was looking increasingly more perilous. If she made a scene, if there were agents on the island looking for her, and one of them was no doubt stationed at the airport watching every departure—it wouldn't just be security who noticed.

Was that preferable to trusting Theo?

CHAPTER TWELVE

THE PRINCESS WAS RIGHT. It was Theo's fault. He'd known people had been on his tail ever since he'd taken over the case, it had only ever been a matter of time before they would discover the identity swap the Princess had made in Sydney that he'd discovered himself. It followed that it would only be a matter of time before they'd follow him here, to Lord Howe Island.

Theo had led them straight to her.

Thank god he'd found the Princess first, but now that the storm had prevented them leaving the island, they were sitting ducks. No wonder she was angry. The only silver lining now was that she might actually believe him, that others were actively searching for her. But he wasn't about to throw that in her face. This wasn't a point scoring exercise. This was serious.

'I'm so sorry,' he told her on their way back to the apartment. 'I'm so sorry I've brought this down on you.'

'You should be,' she said, her teeth troubling her bottom lip. Her options for escape were shrinking. Hope evaporating with it.

Escaping Theo was one thing, having plans to change his mind or elude him, was one thing, but knowing there were others also after her complicated any hopes of escape.

The ride back to the apartment was no way a repeat of

their ride to the restaurant. Now the slow ride was painful. A painful reminder of all the things that remained unresolved between them. Now their drive seemed never-ending as her brain tried to work a solution.

How was she supposed to seduce him when anger fired her blood and filled her veins? What point would there be even trying if he was so determined to bring her back to her former life and a loveless future, whatever she tried? And if she couldn't, how was she ever going to succeed at making a scene at the airport and getting away. The airport had only a handful of flights in or out. It was the first place the agents would have staked out.

What the hell was she going to do?

At long last they arrived at their accommodation and Isabella sprang out of the car the moment he pulled up. 'I hate this,' she said, storming down the hallway. 'You have stolen my freedom from me. You've entrapped me and given me no choice. Are you happy about that?'

'What?' he said, tossing car keys down on a hall table.

'What do you think? Now that there are people somewhere on the island after me, I have no choice but to return to Rubanestein with you.'

'You were always going to be returned to your home, Princess. Either that or be caught by rogue actors. You just didn't accept it. Thank your lucky stars it was me who found you first.'

She tossed her head. 'Thank you? For putting me in this situation? For insisting on dragging me back to Rubanestein when it is the last place I want to go? I don't think so.'

'So what of your other choices?'

She kicked up her chin. 'I had plans.'

He snorted. 'Well, good luck with those, Princess.'

'I was doing fine until you showed up. Maybe you

should just leave me here, to deal with whoever else it is looking for me. Surely my fate couldn't be any worse than being returned to Rubanestein.'

He shook his head. 'Please, Princess, your brother is trying to save you from danger.'

'And what about the danger to me being sent home? My brother doesn't give a damn about me. He believes I'm his chattel—nothing more than a bargaining chip he can auction off to the highest bidder.'

'Stop it. I don't want to hear it. You're a princess. How did you expect your life to unfold?'

'I expected to marry for love!' She furiously paced the length of the living room and then back again. 'Didn't I tell you? Weren't you listening? My father knew that I would never accede to the throne. He knew that. I knew that. So, he promised me that even though I wouldn't take the crown, I would be able to marry for love. I wanted to marry for love and that was his solemn promise to me. What is so wrong with the concept of marrying for love?

'What is wrong with saving myself for the man of my dreams. So how do you think I felt, once I discovered that I was going to be deprived of any of that, that I was going to be married off to some revolting crony of my brother's in order to pay off his gambling debts, and that I didn't have a say in any of it—why are you surprised that I ran? Why are you so surprised that I don't want to go back? Don't you think I had good reason?'

He pinched the bridge of his nose with his fingers. 'And wanting to marry for love is the reason why you threw yourself at every surfer and barista going during your little adventure? Because you wanted to save yourself for your one true love?'

Her jaw jutted. The golden lights in her eyes glowed

hot. 'What else was there to save myself for? What was the alternative? My choice, or my brother's, someone determined to decide for me?'

He ran a hand through his hair. 'This is getting old, Princess. You have to take this seriously. You need to pack. There's no point us trying to find somewhere else to stay tonight. The last place we want to be is on the roads when the top speed limit is twenty-five kilometres an hour when there are people actively searching for you. We'll hunker down here. I promise I won't sleep. Nobody will get to you.'

'But you're here. And you're just as bad as them.'

'Princess—'

'Don't "princess" me! I'm clearly worth nothing in your eyes. No more than one more so-called success story to attach to your CV. Yet another notch on your gun. You disregard everything I say while you drink up every word my silver-tongued brother feeds you as if it's the gospel truth. Do you hate me that much that you could deliver me back into the living hell my brother has in store for me? Do you just plan to hand me back, take your thirty pieces of silver and then wash your hands of me, job done?'

She made a sound of desperation. Half gasp, half sob. Her lips pressed tightly together and she put her fingers over her mouth. But it was too late to hide her raw emotions. He could see the tears springing from her eyes even as she squeezed her eyes shut, her shoulders juddering as she gave in to her feelings.

And Theo was torn between his duty and her distress. Torn between admiration that a naive princess had eluded discovery for so long, and frustration that she refused to accept what her discovery meant. Torn between respect for the fight in this pint-sized princess, and desire. Desire that had been building from the moment Theo had captured her in his arms and felt the heat triggered between them and smelled her citrusy scent.

Because she was wrong about one thing. She wasn't worth nothing in his eyes. She was worth so much more than that. But she was still a princess. He had no right to have feelings for her. He wasn't entitled to feel anything for her. She was a case. She was a rescue.

But she was also a woman. A woman in pain. And her coming undone broke something inside him.

'Princess,' he beseeched, taking a step closer. 'Please?'

Her eyelids scrunched even tighter. Her mouth screwed and twisted under her fingers. There was the briefest shake of her head before she turned away on another sob and fled towards the stairs.

'Princess,' he called, chasing after her. 'Isabella.'

He caught up with her before the stairs, catching her by one arm, the momentum swinging her around. She crashed into him, and immediately raised her fists, pummelling his chest. 'I hate you,' she said, 'I hate you.'

He got that. He understood why. He understood why she needed to take her frustrations out on him.

For a moment he let her beat his chest with her fists. She was so impassioned. So fiery and fierce. 'It's okay, Princess,' he said, holding her by both shoulders now as her fists continued to rain down on him with no sign of relenting. 'Let it out. Let it all out.'

The Princess didn't need encouragement. She continued to take out her rage against him, but her fists were beating slower now, her sobs less frequent, until her head lobbed down against his chest, soaking his shirt with her warm tears as her shoulders continued to shudder under his hands. Now her fingers were curled, clutching the fabric of his shirt, clinging to him.

She wasn't acting. She was broken, deflated, her spirit shattered. The spirit he'd admired, even grudgingly, ever since he'd taken on this case and found the Princess to be more than just a naive twenty-five-year-old royal.

'You're right, Princess. I deserved that. I'm sorry.' He dipped his head down to hers. It was a mere impulse that his lips brushed her hair, kissing her softly on the head. Nothing more. An act of consolation, that was all it was intended to be. Sympathy. Empathy. The tiniest of kisses as he drank in her so familiar citrus scent. And it occurred to him that he would miss that when he'd returned her home.

Damn. He would miss more than that. He would miss this woman, with all the frustrations that came with her. More than that, with all the temptations that came with her.

Her shoulders stilled as slowly she raised her head, lifting her tear-streaked face to his. Her eyes were red-rimmed and puffy from her tears, her cheeks hot where they'd rested against his chest, her lips still pressed tightly together. But in spite of that, she was still one of the two most beautiful women he'd ever met.

And this woman was here.

Now.

It wasn't a conscious decision. It wasn't any kind of decision at all. It was more an imperative. 'Princess,' he said, as his head dipped lower. 'Isabella.'

Her breath hitched. Her eyes widened. Her pink lips parted on a gasp. And it was all the encouragement he needed, any glimmer of doubt that he was doing the wrong thing disappeared in less than a puff of smoke. His hands moved from her shoulders to skim her back and wrap her in his embrace.

His lips met hers. Softly at first, drinking in the sweetness of her mouth, tasting the salt of her tears, making him want more of her. Making him want all of her. He wanted to experience all her flavours, the sweetness and the salt, the spice and the umami.

She took her sweet time, almost as if she didn't trust him, thinking that he might once again realise he'd overstepped a mark and that he would pull away like he had done last night. He didn't break the kiss to assure her that wouldn't happen. He sought to reassure her with his mouth and lips moving over hers, with his hands and arms pressing her closer to him. Maybe it was all of those things, or maybe it was his tongue, plundering the hot depths of her mouth, enticing hers into the dance, because suddenly, like a switch had gone off inside her, she kissed him back with a fervour that matched his own, her hands framing his face, pulling him deeper into a kiss that rocked his soul and that told him one thing—he hadn't been wrong to kiss her last night. The only question in his head as her mouth opened hotly to his was why it had taken him so long to realise?

His hands skimmed down her sundress, relishing the feel of tight, toned skin beneath, cupping her buttocks and squeezing their ripeness. She groaned in his mouth as she arched her back, pressing her breasts and the hardened bullet points into his chest. Breasts that didn't require any bra. Breasts he ached to release from their bodice. Breasts that had driven him crazy ever since he'd seen her in first her pyjamas and then that tiny bikini that had tied him up in knots.

And suddenly he couldn't wait to see them anymore. He

lifted her to his waist. She went with him, wrapping her legs around his torso, the action pulling her skirt up high, baring her legs. He groaned. He only had two hands, and two hands were nowhere near enough when he had this much going on around him. Smooth, slim legs, the sweet curve of a buttock. Everywhere his hands glided was filled with reward. But standing up was not where he wanted her now. He backed her into his bedroom, dropped to his knees by the bed, and folded her gently down onto it.

She looked shocked that he'd let her go, her eyes wild with surprise, desire and need. Until she realised where she'd been laid. A brief smile touched her lips. 'Theo,' she said, in that beguiling accent she had and that held an inherent promise that banished sense from his head and punched a hole in his heart at the same time.

He reefed off his shirt, got to his feet and shucked off shoes and pants. His erection sprang free and he witnessed the Princess's eyes widen, looking hungrily at him.

'I think I'm overdressed,' she said, her voice husky. Shaky. Uncertain.

'I'll take care of that,' he said, slipping off her shoes before sliding his hands up her legs, hooking fingers into her underwear, and tugging it slowly down. There was nothing for it then but for her sundress. He skimmed it up her thighs, then her waist, and slipped it over her breasts. She gasped, as if feeling the rush of cool air against her nipples, but lifted her head so he could fling the garment away.

And then he looked down at her, drinking her in with his eyes. 'Perfection,' he said, taking the time to drink in her petite hourglass figure. His cock bucked in agreement.

She held out her hands. 'Please,' she said, as if uncomfortable with his gaze. 'Please.' Okay, so she was relatively new to this, and maybe her lovers hadn't taken the time to show their full appreciation. But then he wasn't inclined to take his time now, not when she was so eager.

And it had been so long.

He didn't want to think about how long. That time ceased to exist. He just wanted to live in this moment. He wanted to bury himself in her. Here. Now.

Bury himself in Isabella.

Except… *Protection.* He wasn't carrying. He'd given that up years ago. He'd given up thinking he'd ever need it again. But he was sure he'd seen something discreetly positioned in the side table. He reefed open a drawer. *Bingo.* He pulled out a foil packet, tore it open with his teeth and sheathed himself.

Next time they could take their time, he told himself, as he lowered himself over her perfect body. Because he knew with the certainty of a man who had found a second chance at paradise that there would be a next time.

He kissed his way up her legs while she squirmed on the bed, her breath coming in heady gasps and mewls of surprise and delight as his lips made their way north, over her jutting hip bones and the slightest swell of her belly to her ribs. He kissed one tight bud of a nipple and then the other, before he circled it with his tongue, and drew her breast into his mouth. Her spine arched, forcing her breasts higher to meet him—to welcome the attentions of his hot mouth and to turn his attentions to her second breast.

His cock bucked, aching for completion, but it was no hardship filling his mouth with her second breast. Her skin tasted delicious. Of warmth and honey and that increasingly familiar citrus scent that suited her so well. That he would never forget.

And all the time her hands were in his hair, her nails raking his skull as she clung to him as he made his oral onslaught. When he found her mouth, she drank him in like she'd been trapped in the desert and he was the oasis, the water source, the life giver.

Little had he realised that it was she who was the life giver. Little by little, day by day, she was giving him back his life.

Laughter. Joy.

Hope.

Resting over her on one arm, he swept the other down the side of her torso to her hips, where his hand found her mound, his fingers separating her, sliding into the folds between her thighs. He was rewarded by her heat and slickness and the promise of magic.

His erection juddered against her belly at the knowledge. She shuddered and shifted one arm, and the next thing he knew was that she had taken hold of him with one hand, encircling him with her fingers and taking him to the limits of his control.

She groaned, a sound of need that fed and built his own. 'Please,' she cried, urgent and insistent and almost like she was pleading for her life. 'Please!'

He was already primed to go off. Her touch only notched that up. And he knew that there was no more time. There was no more waiting.

Next time, he thought in what was left of his remaining brain cells, next time, they could take their time. Next time they could explore each other's bodies at length, tease each other until they were both begging for release.

Next time.

But next time could wait. This time was now.

He positioned one knee between hers and she opened for him. Opened herself up for him. He found her core, found his place. He still wanted to take it as slow as he could. Wanted to preserve this perfect moment where his mouth was on hers, his arms cradling her head, her arms at his shoulders, clinging on, anxiously waiting.

The breathless moment before. The moment of anticipation where time stood still.

Suddenly he couldn't wait a moment longer. His cock bucked one more time and his hips moved with it, pushing him, driving him into her. Except, in spite of her slickness that met his glans, there was no easy glide, instead he met resistance that made no sense. But then, it had been a while, he was rusty at this. And the resistance just made his thrusts work harder.

Until something gave, there was a sound, and he was inside her, her walls wrapping tightly around him in the most intimate of embraces.

Bliss.

Theo wanted to howl with success. He let himself feel the perfection of being enclosed by tight flesh that wrapped around him, cocooning him, before he was withdrawing, his hips moving to their own score. Not all the way, this connection was too important to lose. Before he plunged into her again. And only then did the sound he'd heard make some kind of sense. A cry, coupled with the resistance he'd felt. He didn't want it to register. He wanted to blot it out, he wanted to deny it, refute it, his body already on a trajectory that he could no longer stop or wanted to, but one that he sensed could ruin his life— and hers—forever.

But it was too late, and right now there were more important things to worry about.

She cried out, calling his name, her muscles tightening around him, urging him on, desperate to hold on to him when he withdrew, welcoming him when he plunged ever deeper. Until he emptied himself in one final juddering thrust. Her cries told him of her own climax as her whole body shuddered around him with her own orgasm.

His bliss was short-lived, as the whole horror of what he'd just done registered. And post-coital bliss turned to self-hate in an insta-second. There was no time for wrapping her in his arms and cuddling her next to him. No time for breathy kisses and warm shared words as their bodies hummed down from their heights. Instead, Theo pulled out of her, sat up on the side of the bed, rubbing his jaw with one hand before he headed for the bathroom, wanting to rid himself of the evidence of his actions as if he could so easily wipe out the truth of it. He returned to the bedroom to pull on his underwear, before turning to look at her.

'Why didn't you tell me?'

The Princess looked still shell-shocked, like she'd been thoroughly made love to as she had, her hair mussed, her features in glorious post-coital disarray, and that didn't help matters at all. That just made him angrier.

'Tell you what?' she asked breathlessly.

'What do you think? That you were a virgin!'

Her eyes flickered between opened and closed. 'Oh, wasn't that in the dossier you were given?'

'Actually, it was. But since then, you've had however many flings with some surfer dude and a barista and who knows however many else. Isn't that what you said?'

She sighed, pulling the covers up over her, but not before he saw a telltale smear of blood on the sheets.

'Did I ever say that I'd slept with any of them?' She raised herself up on one elbow and looked at him disingenuously. 'I might have admitted to being tempted, but I never admitted to having sex with anyone, did I?'

It was worse than Theo had imagined. It was a horror

story but a horror story of his own making. His rescue was a virgin—*had been a virgin*—and he'd been the one entrusted to return her home, but he'd been the one to deflower her. It was a nightmare.

'That was—um, nice,' the Princess said from the bed. 'Is there any chance we might try that again?'

'No! Was this one of your plans, then, Princess? To seduce me and try to convince me not to return you to your homeland?'

She blinked, looking sheepish. And he didn't need her to answer to know that he'd been played. That this had been her plan all along. To seduce him, to bend him to her will. A pity it wasn't going to work.

He pulled the bedcovers from her. 'Get out of my room. Pack your bag. And stop with the tears, because, like it or not, you're going home to Rubanestein tomorrow.'

He didn't wait for her response. He took himself to the bathroom, stepped into the shower. If he couldn't erase every memory of what had just happened, he could at least try to erase every possible scent of her from his body.

Forget thinking that the Princess might be telling him the truth. Forget thinking that she might have a case. She was a manipulator, pulling his strings any way she could. A sob story about her brother bartering her off. A sob story about him abusing her puppy. Forget feeling sorry for her, or that her brother was taking advantage of her. She'd just pulled the worst strings of all.

Her story was rubbish.

As a result, he was more determined than ever to deliver her back to her home. She would be someone else's problem then.

And they were welcome to her.

CHAPTER THIRTEEN

ISABELLA MADE HER WAY back to her bedroom trance-like, her clothes clutched in her arms. Theo had made love to her, worshipping every part of her body, and it had been spectacular. More spectacular than she could have ever imagined. There had been no time for her body to recover, she was still glowing, her senses still hypersensitive, the space between her thighs still humming.

And for once it almost didn't matter that he was still determined to return her to Rubanestein. Not after tonight. Tonight, she'd discovered the wonder of what making love to a man you wanted to make love to was like. This is what she'd always wanted, to know what it was like to make love to a man that meant something to you.

Okay, so this wasn't a man who was going to marry her, but her dream of marrying for love was already in shreds, and if she had to take a second option, she'd settle for making love to Theo. She'd never have come up with Plan A if she hadn't been attracted to him. If she hadn't felt the heat of their connection. If she hadn't felt the magnetism between them.

And whatever happened in the future, she wanted to file that memory away, knowing that this one time she had actually had sex with someone she wanted to. And it had been glorious. And Theo had seemed to be enjoying it too, if she hadn't been mistaken. He'd been so eager for her. So hungry.

Until the moment he'd realised.

A shame. She'd wanted Theo to be on her side. An ally. She'd so hoped he would be on her side. He was a protector. She needed protection.

But there was no more protection for her. Theo was more determined now that he would deliver her back to Rubanestein and would walk away, leaving her to her fate. And maybe he had cause for walking away, but she would never forget him.

She'd railed against him from the very start, fighting against his heavy-handed insistence that he was taking her home against her will. But at the same time, she'd been fighting against an attraction to him that had been so unwanted and unexpected and yet so stealthy that it had managed to worm its way into her senses. Or maybe it was him, his voice, his scent, his body heat that had wormed its way into her senses?

That would do it.

Maybe that's what had done it.

Maybe that's why she felt conflicted, and why she couldn't deny feeling something for him even while she resented him for being so insistent on taking her back to her brother. Because she did feel something for him. She didn't have the wherewithal or the brain power to analyse that right now. Her mind was too heavily engaged in replaying over and over what had happened tonight. The good bit. The first bit, before he realised and sent her packing.

She laid her head on her pillow knowing she wasn't even going to try to sleep, because her memories of being made love to by Theo, of being reminded of his touch, of his hot mouth, of the feeling of being filled by him, were far more compelling.

Who needed sleep when your body had been awakened to the pleasures of the flesh?

The next morning the winds had eased, the cloud cover evaporating. The traces of the cyclone had moved away, the twin peaks of Mt Lidgbird and Gower now clearly visible under an ever increasingly sunny sky.

But while the weather had moderated, the relations between the two occupants in the apartment hadn't. The mood in the kitchen was frosty. Words hadn't been exchanged since last night's lovemaking. Any hope Isabella had that Theo might have relented in the night, and that his thoughts would soften towards her after what they'd shared turned to nothing. Theo almost refused to acknowledge her.

There were no offerings of making coffee or tea or toast from either of them. It was every man and woman for themselves. Bags were duly packed and waiting at the front door.

It was frustration that forced Isabella to speak after Theo pointedly refused to acknowledge her presence. 'How exactly are we supposed to evade whoever is after us? They must know what times the flights come in and out.'

He glanced at her, his eyes cold, as if he'd wished she hadn't spoken. 'Exactly why we're going out on a private flight I've organised. If they're watching the airport for scheduled departures, hopefully we'll catch them off guard and be gone before they notice.' And then he turned away to check whatever news had just burped into his phone.

'Why are you being so cold to me?'

'What?' he said, wanting to focus instead on the update he'd received from one of his agents.

'If I remember correctly, we made love last night. Do you even remember making love to me?'

'What if I do?'

'You weren't cold to me then. Instead, you were hot—'

'Forget it,' he snapped. 'Last night was a mistake, Princess. Last night didn't happen. And I would seriously advise you to wipe it from your memory.'

'Oh, but it did happen, and I'm not convinced I could actually forget. I'm not sure I want to.'

He turned away. 'It was a mistake.'

'It was the most amazing experience of my life.'

'I'm happy for you, Princess.'

'But I wasn't a princess to you last night, was I, Theo. I was Isabella, pure and simple. I was a woman.'

'In reality you were a princess then, and you're a princess now.'

She shook her head. 'Do you want to know why it was the most amazing experience of my life?'

'Not really. I don't think we need to do this. I really don't want to hear it.'

'I think you do. I thought we both enjoyed a connection that had been growing, and that culminated last night in the most amazing experience.'

'Last night was the only "connection" we had. End of story.'

'No. We shared something more impactful than that. I know you did. I felt it. And I doubt I will ever experience sex like that again, making love to someone that I wanted to.'

'It was sex, Princess,' he said dismissively. 'It was a primal need. It was a scratch following an itch. Nothing more. So don't go reading anything romantic into it.'

'You say that, but I'm grateful to you. I'm so glad you

gave me that experience, that you were my first. So that I know how good making love can be. So that I can remember. In all the rubbish days and nights ahead.'

He shook his head. 'I wish you'd stop lying to me. You led me to believe you were an innocent.'

'I never told you that. That's what you'd been told. All I said was that I'd met other men.'

'You lied by omission!'

'I never lied, by omission or by any other means. If you assumed something, that's all down to you. You believed what you wanted to believe. You'd been informed in your dossier on me that I was a virgin. I mentioned meeting Mateo and Luke and how hot they were, and your mind goes there. That was never me. That was you, filling in gaps, the way you wanted to fill them. I told you from the start, I wanted to marry for love.'

He arched an eyebrow at her. 'So what was last night about? If not trying to seduce me around to your cause so I might look more benevolently upon you. So I might be more inclined to take your side and be less willing to return you to Rubanestein?'

She looked down. 'That was my plan. True.'

'You admit it. Bravo.'

'Except,' she added, licking her lips, 'I think there's something we're both missing.'

He sighed. 'And what would that be?'

'Last night was amazing. You can't deny that. Last night wasn't an accident. Last night was mutual. You wanted to make love to me as much as I wanted to make love to you.'

'Princess…'

'No, listen to me. Whatever plan I might have to make you relent and to bend you to my will—and I admit that was my hope—what was your plan? Why did you make love to me?'

Because he couldn't help it. He couldn't prevent himself. Because this pint-sized princess had somehow wormed her way into his senses, and he couldn't resist her any longer.

But he could hardly admit that. 'It was a mistake,' he said, needing to shut this conversation down. 'Why can't you simply accept that?'

Why was he even arguing with her? What was the point? After he'd made some necessary calls making arrangements for the next morning, he'd spent the night trying to work out where he'd made the fatal mistake of crossing not just a line, but an entire eight-lane expressway. He'd beaten himself up about it until his psyche was bruised, his mind bloodied, and yet still, there was a part of him that couldn't forget how good she'd felt in his arms.

And he hated himself all the more for the fact it wasn't clear-cut. That he was conflicted. That he couldn't simply put her out of his mind. That part of him was drawn to her even when he knew she'd played him every way until Sunday.

He wished he could tear that part of him down, rip it away and toss it asunder. He had a job to do. He had to focus. She was a princess. A rescue he had to get home. Nothing more.

She couldn't be more.

It was impossible.

The arrival of Tom Parker's van in the driveway was a relief. Finally, they would be on their way.

Tom loaded the bags into the back of the van. 'Unusual to be leaving this early for the airport,' he said. 'The flight's not until eleven.'

'Private flight,' Theo said. 'Beating the rush of all the people backed up wanting to get off the island,' he added by way of explanations. 'But that's just between us. I'd appreciate it if you didn't pass it on.'

'Got you,' Tom said, conspiratorially tapping the side of his nose with one fingertip, as Isabella emerged from the apartment. Tom smiled a greeting at her. 'I'm just glad you managed to find your friend. I hope you had a happy birthday, Izzy.'

Theo thought back to that first day, when he'd first shown that picture of the Princess to Tom and asked if he'd seen her, leading to him finding her that night at the café.

Theo clapped his hand on the other man's shoulder, 'You helped me no end,' he said, before holding that same hand out to the Princess, throwing her a warning expression at the same time. 'You got a big surprise when I found you, Izzy, didn't you,' he said.

She regarded him warily, her eye twitching at his informality, but still she took Theo's hand. 'A bit of an understatement,' she said, adding a small laugh. 'But thank you, yes, it was most definitely a surprise.'

'I'm glad,' said the beaming Tom. 'The island prides itself for being a magical space. I'm glad the magic worked for you both.'

Theo pressed his lips together as they climbed into the car. There had been moments of something resembling magic, but they had been few and far between, most of his time here marred by frustration borne by both lack of sleep and exasperation. Ultimately any magic the island could bestow had been wasted on them. Okay, so it would be pointless denying that there was an attraction between them, but no amount of island magic could change the facts of their situation. Bodyguard and rescue. Commoner and

Princess. He was a professional first and foremost. He'd always been going to bring the Princess home.

What had happened last night was an aberration. Nothing more.

The airport car park was quiet, too early for scheduled arrivals and departures. The windsock stirred half-heartedly on its pole, the fury of the storm moved on. Theo made sure to check out who was there before he gave the all clear, Tom whisking their baggage from the car and into the tiny terminal even as a small plane could be seen approaching the runway.

'That's us,' Theo said.

The plane landed, taxiing to a stop just outside the terminal. Propellers stopped. Stairs lowered. And within a few minutes their luggage was stowed and they were boarded, Tom farewelled and the plane was already taxiing for take-off.

Then the small plane lifted off and the car and anyone chasing after her were left far behind them.

And Theo sighed, closed his eyes thinking, with a two-hour flight to Sydney, and nowhere for the Princess to run, that maybe, finally, he might be able to get some sleep.

He closed his eyes. Drifting with the small plane's rumbling into that blessed sleep state.

Soon, he thought. Soon—*finally*—he would be rid of her.

CHAPTER FOURTEEN

Turbulence was something Izzy was used to. She'd flown over European mountain ranges, she'd landed in helicopters in high winds over ski fields and into deep valleys, but as Theo's private jet approached Rubanestein airspace, the turbulence in the air was nothing compared to the turbulence going on in her mind.

Their escape from Lord Howe Island had been smooth and effective. Their transfers at Sydney's airport had been slick, through private lanes where they were treated as VIPs, clearing customs and immigration. It wasn't just that she was a princess, Isabella could tell. It was some kind of clout that Theo had. Almost as if he was known and recognised.

She'd considered trying her abandoned Plan B, to make a scene at the island's airport on their departure to alert security. She'd considered trying it in Sydney but abandoned the idea just as quickly. Theo seemed to have some sort of cachet with the authorities. Like he was the one more likely to be trusted.

And then, knowing that there were people after her and so close behind, did she really want to risk being restrained in Australia?

It was the worst of all worlds. What choice did she have?

It wasn't long before they were welcomed onto Theo's

private jet. The plane was luxury personified. A sleek jet with cream-coloured leather seats, panelled timber walls and a lush, carpeted floor, the kind of flooring she'd noticed on her recent travels that you didn't find in the commercial cattle class she'd used to hide her travels.

Beyond the stylish lounge, dining and office seating, she'd been shown a luxurious bedroom and bathroom she was welcome to use.

At any other time, in any circumstance, Isabella would be happy to take such a flight. But her relief at getting away was rapidly giving way to a growing dread. Of being returned to Rubanestein, her brother and his plans for her.

There was no escaping his plans for her.

And the closer the plane got to Rubanestein, the more her dread rose, like bile in her throat.

'We'll be landing in thirty minutes,' the flight attendant told her. 'Is there anything I can get you before we start our descent?'

She shook her head. 'No.'

She knew the instant the plane started its descent. Izzy felt it in her gut, and felt all hope go south with it.

She turned to the man in the seat opposite, the man who had said not a word to her this flight. 'You won't tell my brother, will you?' she pleaded. 'You won't tell him?'

He looked up. 'Tell the Prince what? That we fed the fish at Ned's Beach? Something else?'

'That I tried to seduce you. And then that you made love to me.' Her eyes pleaded with him.

He sighed. 'Do you really think I want to tell the Prince that?'

'No. Maybe not straight away. But it could get out. Another way. In the press or on social media. You know the sort of thing. *"A close source says that while the Princess was in Australia she was uninhibited. Desperate, and begging for sex."* Do you realise how much that might compromise me in the future?'

'Oh Princess. Do you really think me capable of that?'

'For money? If someone offered you enough?'

He shook his head. 'You don't know me at all, do you?'

She thought she did. At least a little. But they'd had such little time together, what did she really know of him? Except for how hot he was and how good he'd felt inside her.

'But you're doing this for money, aren't you? Returning me to Rubanestein for money?'

He slow blinked. 'Yes, I get paid for returning you. But that's not my motivation.'

She considered that for a moment. 'Oh, so you're just the good guy. The saviour. Doing good for good's sake. How noble of you.'

He sighed. 'You're angry with me. Because I'm bringing you home, or for some other reason?'

'You made love to me,' she said.

'I did,' he admitted. 'And I told you it was a mistake. I told you I was sorry about that.'

Her lips pursed. 'But I'm not sorry. I'll never be sorry for that.'

She turned away before he could see the truth in her words, before he could witness the single tear that escaped from each eye. She'd treasure the memory of that night forever, the memory of feeling wanted. Even loved. The way she'd always wanted to be loved.

By a man she'd set out to seduce to make him protect her.

A man who'd turned into someone she believed she

could love, and yet a man who'd betrayed her. She wanted to hate him for delivering her back to her brother's clutches.

She wanted to hate him.

But all she felt was sorrow.

CHAPTER FIFTEEN

THE JET WAS on final approach to Rubanestein's one and only international airport when Theo's phone buzzed. He found the message as their plane taxied to the private aviation area. It was a relief to have a diversion from the Princess's latest outburst. 'There's a banquet at the palace tonight and I've been invited,' Theo told the Princess. 'Apparently the Prince is celebrating your return. It seems you've been missed.'

'Lovely,' she said, her expression deadpan. 'Just what I wanted, to have to endure another few hours in your presence.'

Theo was equally unimpressed. He'd expected to bring the Princess to the palace, collect a cheque, turn around and fly home. But given the pilots and crew had earned a break after their arrival, Theo would be going nowhere. Apparently, the Prince wanted to thank him personally. It was a polite gesture. Very civilised.

What Theo wasn't surprised about was the Princess's response. He'd expected her to be dismissive. She'd become more and more sullen the closer they got to Rubanestein. Because of course, she hadn't got her way. She'd been delivered back to Rubanestein, to her own country. To where her duty lay. But most of all, out of harm's way. What was her problem? She'd had her flings. She'd had her freedom flight. Whatever grievances she had with her younger brother, why couldn't she accept that her life should be one of duty in the country of her birth?

And he didn't feel guilty in the least, because she'd deceived him. If she had told him the truth from the start that she had been a virgin, he would never have touched her. She knew that. Instead, she'd flaunted tales of her times with Luke and Mateo and hinted about others and made him believe that her innocence was no longer an issue.

She'd tricked him, tricked him into betraying his trust. Tricked him into betraying his duty of protection for her.

So he couldn't blame her entirely for that, because she'd always been forbidden to him, virgin or no. He never should have touched her. And not just because she'd been forbidden. But damn, now he didn't think he'd be able to get the taste and feel of her out of his head.

How did one erase one of the most sublime moments of your life? One of the most life-changing? She'd moved like liquid silk in his arms, so responsive to his every touch, so reactive to his seeking mouth and tongue.

Liquid silk.

Hot and fluid. She'd moved like a ballerina in the bed. Graceful and lithe, as she'd wrapped him in her limbs and welcomed him into her body.

And it had been wondrous. Magical. A revelation. Until he'd felt that unexpected resistance.

But by then it was too late and his next lunge swept away any and all hint of resistance. Leading up to that, he'd heard her whimpers of need, he'd heard her jagged breathing, sounds that had fed into his own building need, but when he'd heard her cry out as he'd lunged into her, he'd realised what he'd done.

Fool.

He was supposed to be a rescuer. A protector. A body-guard.

If there was a bodyguard how-to book, Rule Number One would have been, don't fall for your rescue. Don't engage in some kind of reverse Stockholm Syndrome, where you fell for the person that you were rescuing, no matter how attractive and sexually alluring and infuriating they were.

He'd broken the first rule in the book.

And broken it big time.

And the Princess was worried Theo would tell the Prince that he'd deflowered his sister? Not a chance.

The plane came to a halt. The door was opened, the steps lowered just as a cavalcade of dark-windowed SUVs drove alongside, a red carpet rolled out for them to disembark, before whisking them away to the palace, a fairy-tale castle atop the clifftop complete with towers topped with slated turrets and bearing the flags of the principality.

The Princess was shown to her wing of the palace while Theo was shown into a suite of rooms, in which he saw a king-sized bed laid out with a formal outfit he was apparently expected to wear tonight, along with an entire wardrobe from swimmers and gym wear to casual wear, everything he might need for his stay.

It seemed his every need had been anticipated.

It made a kind of sense, he thought, because none of the luggage he had brought contained anything formal enough for a banquet. It was a kind and thoughtful gesture.

He checked the labels. The sizes were spot on. Somebody had clearly done their homework.

He took advantage of the pool with a long swim. With lap after lap he felt the tension easing from his muscles, his body releasing the tension that had been accumulating these last few days. It was relief to be here and have the Princess safely returned to her country. It would be more of a relief when he had departed, closed this case and moved on. This dinner was an inconvenience, a timing issue, nothing more.

He refused to think about what had happened between him and the Princess—a mistake—but for now, it was good to know she was back where she belonged and the sooner he could get away, the better. The sooner these unnerving feelings would disappear. It was proximity making him feel this way. He needed to be away. Divorced from the drama of a runaway royal and whatever angst she was feeling.

He was dressing for dinner when the report he'd been waiting for lobbed into his inbox—the deep dive into Prince Rafael's gambling proclivities, if they indeed existed as the Princess claimed. Quickly he opened it, scanning the contents.

Interesting.

More than interesting.

Damning.

Because apparently the Prince was neither a fan of the horses nor one to frequent the casinos that graced Rubanestein's shores, confirming what Theo already understood. But there was shade, his researcher had found. Something that Theo hadn't known. Something that nobody had known. Details were sketchy, disguised under layers of cybersecurity, but there were indications the Prince may have had a penchant for bitcoin and other cryptocurrencies and had taken to crypto gambling in an effort to try to leverage his gains. A high-risk strategy where the chance of losses and accumulating debt was also high.

Gambling.

Theo thought about all the times the Princess had claimed that her brother had racked up gambling debts. Gambling with cryptocurrency on online unregulated casinos—there was a potential recipe for disaster.

And Theo's spidey senses quivered on high alert.

Because, if the Princess hadn't been lying about the gambling? What else might be true?

Theo was directed to his seat of honour, a seat next to a bejewelled throne where Prince Rafael would sit. On the other side of the empty seat, a wiry man sat down, grinning and bowing his head to Theo, introducing himself as Count Lorenzo di Stasio. Theo nodded and smiled in acknowledgement.

'We are beholden to you for returning our Princess,' he said.

'Thank you,' Theo said. 'But I was just doing my job.'

'And you did it well.'

They were interrupted by the blare of trumpets as Prince Rafael stood at the door, in the uniform of Rubanestein, a gold sash over his chest, and a beautiful woman on his arm. The Prince's consort, Theo guessed, though he'd missed that detail in the dossier. She was dressed in a strapless gown of pink lace, a long scarf of the same fabric wound around her neck, her blonde hair in an updo, curvy tendrils framing her face topped off with a diamond-encrusted tiara.

Everyone at the table stood as the couple came closer. Wait? *Blonde hair?*

He looked closer. Her eyes were smoky with kohl, her lips were painted the same shade as her dress. But it was her. This was the Princess Isabella, in full royal regalia.

He was so used to her dressed in beach wear, casual summery island wear that he almost hadn't recognised her.

And Theo had to acknowledge, she was magnificent.

She hesitated as she regarded the room. Before she took a seat beside the man opposite who took her hand and kissed the back of it while the Prince moved to his place at the head of the table.

She looked up at Theo then, just a momentary glance—a glare—before she swallowed and then looked away.

And Theo's spidey senses went into overdrive.

Everyone sat, and the Prince turned to Theo. 'It is good to meet you at last, Theo Mylonakos. Do you find your accommodations comfortable?' he quietly inquired.

'Exceedingly so, Prince Rafael, I thank you for extending me your hospitality.'

'What else could I do?' he said, his arms raised either side, 'But welcome the man who has brought my errant sister home. You have done our principality a great service.'

Then he turned to the room. 'It is a beautiful day,' he said, his voice booming in the vast banqueting room. 'I have called this banquet in honour of my sister and our Princess Isabella being returned to us and our family reunited. It is a day for celebration. It is a day for celebrating family.

'And I have to thank my firm friend, Theo Mylonakos, for making it possible. This man, above all odds, found our adventure-seeking princess and brought her home.'

Applause met his words, the guests universal in their nods and smiles and the enthusiasm of their applause.

Applause that didn't sit well with him when Theo was in more doubt that he'd done the wrong thing, and he deserved censure rather than applause.

'But right now, there is a feast to be enjoyed. Please,'

the Prince said, benevolently spreading his arms out wide.
'Enjoy.'

A bevy of waiters delivered platters of food to the table.
Fluffy flatbreads and dips, salads and other offerings.
There was spit-roasted lamb, lemon-roasted chicken and
potatoes along with baked fish and eggplants roasted in a
garlic yoghurt sauce. Along with of course, the paella for
which the coast was famous.

Theo sampled it all. To the left there sat the Prince, to
his right there sat the head of the security services who
made polite conversation about Theo's work.

Music interludes smoothed the spaces between the conversation, but all the while he was watching what he said
while keeping an eye on what Isabella was doing.

She barely made a move towards the food. Despite her
make-up, she looked pale, her eyes wary. The man next to
her—the Count—seemed to dominate her, directing her
choices to what he permitted her to eat. He was middle-
aged, Theo guessed. Probably in his fifties. And Theo's
gut churned.

Minute by minute as the meal progressed, the sick feeling—the fear—inside Theo grew. Theo tried to engage
with the Princess a few times, but the Count soon shut
down the conversation. Theo wanted to shut him down.
But he couldn't do that. But still his senses crawled. And
Theo hated it.

The dinner was winding to an end, the Prince calling
for a toast.

Theo imagined that it would be a toast to him, for bringing his sister home. But no. It was a toast to his sister's
upcoming marriage, to the Count Lorenzo di Stasio, a
wedding that would take place tomorrow.

And after he'd dropped that thunderclap, he turned to

Theo, and said, 'Of course, you must be here for the wedding. I insist. The union that you've made possible.'

The Count smiled and bowed while the Princess shrank in her seat, looking more afraid than he'd ever seen her.

The Princess hadn't been lying.

Why that should have smacked into his head with the force it did made no sense. Hadn't he been suspicious of the Prince's flimsy story? Hadn't he been partial to believing hers, of her brother's bullying, of his cruelty? At least until they'd made love and he'd discovered that she'd omitted to tell him that she was still a virgin and he'd wanted to punish her.

'Congratulations,' Theo said through clenched teeth, recovering enough to raise a glass. 'Of course, I'll be here to witness the happy event. To the happy couple.'

Everyone joined in with the toast. Everyone he noticed, apart from Isabella, who skewered him with daggers from her hazel eyes.

And he knew he deserved every one of them. He'd failed to believe her. He'd let her down. And so much of her marriage tomorrow was of his doing. He'd delivered her up to this. Because he was angry with her. Because she'd been a virgin and she'd led him to believe otherwise. Any sympathy for the Princess had evaporated on the spot. He was taking her home. Instead, he'd brought her to the gates of hell of a forced marriage.

Her head was turned towards the table, but her eyes were upturned to his and he saw them glaring at him. Hating him.

And he knew he deserved it.

But what did she expect him to say? How could he object? How could he protest? He was in Rubanestein. Even if he wanted to, he couldn't simply snatch up the Princess and run. They would be caught before they reached the airport, his jet already impounded.

No, he needed another way. His mind scrabbled to find one. He could not leave the Princess to marry this wiry, aged Count, who did not deserve to sit next to her, let alone share her bed.

It came to him as the banquet wound down, desserts served and consumed. It was clear that Prince Rafael was a man motivated by money. It was also clear during the banquet that he was a man fond of his wine.

The banquet at an end, the Prince invited Theo, the Count and the Princess to repair to the salon for port and cigars. The men sprawled in armchairs, while Isabella sat apart, her posture stiffly erect, looking more and more downcast.

Theo accepted the cigar, also accepting a glass of port while the other men employed cigar cutters to remove the cap before lightly toasting the end.

The Prince watched on, as if in no hurry to light his own cigar. 'I have to hand it to you, Theo, we thought your business had failed in your quest to find the Princess. The agents I sent out to follow you admitted that they were no match.'

'You sent out your own agents?'

'Of course, I did. They thought they had you two days ago. It was the closest they'd got. Maybe if the storm had lasted longer on the island, they would have caught up with you? But maybe they served their purpose in hurrying you home.'

Theo swallowed. Those two agents on the island that night were Rafael's agents? Those two agents who'd set tempers flaring between Theo and the Princess, which had dominoed into them making love only to discover the

Princess was a virgin, turning his anger upon her, when she'd never deserved it.

His throat was dry. But it was neither port nor a cigar he needed. It was to spell out the truth.

'Your sister is a lucky woman, Prince Rafael,' Theo said, 'to find such a worthy husband. How did their engagement come about?'

He caught the arrows the Princess fired at him from her eyes.

The Prince snorted. 'Simple,' he said. 'Count Lorenzo offered me the most money to take her off my hands.'

Theo laughed along with the Prince. 'Genius,' he said, raising his glass to him. The Prince, as he'd expected, drained his, clicking his fingers for a refill.

'So, how much is the Count paying you?'

The Prince smirked. The Count laughed and interjected, 'One hundred million dollars. US currency.'

Isabella interjected, clearly aghast. 'You are that much in debt from your gambling?'

'No, silly woman—but I need to be left with some play money after the dust has settled. Surely even you can appreciate that?'

'Women,' Theo said dismissively. 'They have no concept of the price or value of anything.'

'You see that, Theo? You are indeed my brother.' The pair clinked glasses. 'You understand how the world works.'

Theo fully understood how this man worked. 'One hundred million dollars,' Theo said, nodding. 'That's not bad.'

'It's excellent. And you made it happen by bringing her home.'

The Count was laughing. 'I told you we appreciated your assistance.'

Theo could see the Princess fuming. He could almost see the waves of heat rising from her. Right now, he imagined her painting him as much of a bastard as her brother.

Hang in there, he wanted to say, but he could say nothing.

'But one hundred million US dollars?' Theo mused. 'Is it anywhere near enough for such a prize? The Princess is of good child-bearing age, and to her credit, not entirely unattractive.'

The Prince spluttered. 'What do you mean? Is it enough? It's one hundred million US dollars.'

'But what if you could do better?'

The Count jumped to his feet. 'We have a deal!'

The Prince waved his hand at the Count. 'Sit down, sit down. Tell me, Theo, my brother, how could I do better? It's the best offer I've had.'

'What if someone offered you double?'

Isabella's head snapped up. Suddenly she was interested in what was going on.

'Who is this someone?'

Theo let the silence settle. He took a sip of the mellow wine and this time he enjoyed it. 'Me.'

Isabella gasped, standing up. The Count grabbed her arm, pulling her back down. The Count started spluttering. 'We had a deal. We *have* a deal! The wedding is tomorrow. Prince Rafael, you can't change your mind now.'

'Shut up,' the Prince snapped at the Count. Before scratching his chin and turning back to Theo. 'Double, you say? Two hundred million US dollars.'

'Exactly. And I'll waive my recovery fee in addition.'

The Prince sat up. 'Well, that shines an entirely different light on things.'

'I object!' said the Count. 'We made a deal. The wedding is planned for tomorrow.'

'Ah, true,' said the Prince, stroking his chin. 'We had a deal. And it would be wrong to not acknowledge that. So I'm giving you an opportunity. Can you match Theo's offer? No—can you better it? Because there's already a better offer on the table.' He turned to address the Count directly. 'You need to offer more.'

The Count visibly swallowed. 'Prince Rafael, this is so unfair.'

'Can you?'

The Count's voice was getting weaker. 'We had a deal…'

'I see. So you can't. Then I have no choice. Theo Mylonakos, in exchange for two hundred million US dollars, the Princess Isabella is yours.'

CHAPTER SIXTEEN

IT TOOK SOME twenty-four hours before the money transfers had been successfully concluded and they were on the plane and out of Rubanestein airspace. Finally, Theo allowed himself space to breathe.

His nerves had been on a knife-edge ever since that dinner invitation. Ever since finding that report in his inbox, ever since seeing the Princess sat beside an older man that she'd clearly not wanted to have anything to do with, his sickening spidey senses had told him that the Princess had not been lying.

And that Theo had personally delivered her. He might as well have wrapped her up in a sparkly gift box wrapped with a big red bow.

But now the jet and they were safely away. Theo unclicked his safety belt and stood. He needed to walk. He needed to find a way to burn off this nervous energy that had surrounded him for too long.

The Princess he could see was sleeping in her seat. She'd fallen asleep the moment they'd taken off.

God knows what the last few days had been like for her. Afraid of her impending arrival back in Rubanestein. Afraid of the impending nuptials her brother had planned. Afraid the Prince might change his mind again, after he'd agreed to take Theo's money in place of the Count's.

She'd had more at stake than he'd ever had, and he knew how nervous he'd been this last twenty-four hours.

He hated himself for delivering her lock, stock and barrel into a marriage she wanted no part of. A marriage she'd warned him was going to happen if he returned her to Rubanestein. And yet, he hadn't believed her. Even though he'd been swayed, wanting to believe her, she'd then lied to him and that had turned him against her.

He was wrong.

So wrong.

He just hoped that one day, she might forgive him.

An hour later the Princess stirred. Refreshments were served. 'How are you feeling?' he asked.

'Better,' she said, cradling a cup of tea. 'Relieved.' Then she looked up at him. 'I haven't had a chance to properly thank you yet.'

'Don't thank me. I did you no favours. I should have believed you. There were times I wanted to, but it seemed so mad, so unbelievable that your brother would want to do that to you.'

She smiled. 'My not so darling brother. I'm sorry to leave Rubanestein and its people, but I'm not sorry to leave him.' She shuddered. 'And the Count. You know, I actually believed you were going along with the Prince at the banquet. Do you know how much I hated you in that moment?'

'I knew. The look in your eyes made that crystal-clear.'

She shook her head. 'And then you pulled a rabbit out of a hat. Two hundred million US dollars. Where did you even get that kind of money?'

'The rescue business pays well—so long as you can rescue people, that is. I make it a point of rescuing people.'

'You save people.'

'I try to. I made it my job. And when there were too many cases or one person, I expanded my business. Nobody realised how many cases there were. Missing babies. Sons and daughters gone missing. Partners disappeared. Princesses disappearing off the face of the earth.'

She looked up at him. 'Did you have many princesses disappearing off the face of the earth?'

He shook his head. 'Only one, and she proved to be the case to end all cases. She evaded all and every attempt to track her down. We're going to have to rewrite the book about runaway royals after this.'

'You found me,' she said.

'You didn't make it easy.'

She laughed and smiled up at him, 'I'll take that as a compliment. But I'm so glad it was you who found me.' But where did that leave them? Where did they go from here?

'So, what happens now?' she asked, licking her lips. 'I owe you for what you've rescued me from, and you bought me, so do you own me? What do you expect me to do?'

He shook his head. 'Nothing. I don't own you. You're a free agent. I bought you your freedom, not your life, and certainly not your servitude. And after what I did, you owe me nothing. Accept your freedom as my apology. You now have all the freedom you always wanted.'

She nodded. Freedom. It sounded good. It sounded like exactly what she'd been seeking.

Except...

On a deeper level it was also disappointing. She paused, searching for the right words, knowing this moment was make or break. 'What if I don't want to be a free agent?'

'What?'

The Princess licked her lips. 'What if I'd prefer to spend my life with someone else?'

The growl rumbled deep and dark from the back of his throat. 'You're still thinking about Mateo or Luke or whoever else there was?'

She smiled. 'I'm touched you remember their names.'

He shook his head. 'Look, I don't care who it is. I don't want to know. You're free to be with whomever you like.'

'Except I don't know if it's possible. I don't know if this person feels the same way.' She tilted her head. 'Would you agree to take me on, for better, for worse, for richer or poorer, in sickness and in health?'

'Wait. What? Are you proposing to me?'

She swallowed. 'I told you once before that my dream was to marry the man that I loved. Are you the man I'm going to marry? Are you going to make my dream come true?'

'You don't marry someone because of a dream.'

'No. You marry someone because you love them, and you want to spend the rest of your life with them.'

It took Theo but a moment for her words to register. He understood now why he had such a visceral reaction when the Count had pawed the Princess at the banquet. He understood what had been staring him in the face ever since he'd taken her to his bed on Lord Howe Island. He understood what had been building ever since she'd tumbled into his arms from her bedroom window and what had driven him crazy every time she was close. Every time she was near.

He'd fallen in love with someone he should never have fallen in love with.

He'd fallen in love with Isabella, but now he could finally admit it.

He pulled Isabella from her seat and into his arms. 'Princess,' he said, his mouth hovering over hers, 'Isabella, I love you so much.' Their lips met, and Theo felt something powerful crack open inside him, the stone walls that had surrounded his heart since he'd lost Sophia, and now his heart was open. Open to welcome Isabella.

But kisses were not enough. He needed to show her just how much he loved her. Needed to finish off what they had only just started at. He swept up her legs and carried her to the bedroom, closing the door behind him with his foot.

He laid her on the bed so tenderly, like she was made of porcelain, fragile and delicate. He knew she was far from that; she had an inner strength that belied her age and upbringing. She was clever and resourceful. Bold and beautiful. But to him, in this moment, she was the most precious creature in the world.

Looking back, Isabella couldn't quite remember the order of things, who shed their clothes first, whether it had been her to tug off his shirt and pants or whether she'd been too busy in the tangle of arms and limbs and seeking hands tearing her own clothes off. But then they'd both been naked and it was magical. Skin against skin. Lips and hot mouths against skin. Senses overloading. Need spiralling, until Isabella was spiralling with it, losing her mind, losing control.

When he entered her in one long thrust, this time he met no resistance, she felt no shock of pain. Instead, she welcomed him into her depths knowing that this man was the one she'd been waiting for her entire life. Knowing that he was the one. The only one.

He built momentum with each thrust, building the desperation, the madness consuming her, until with one final thrust he sent her over the edge, and she was flying, literally and figuratively into the sky.

He followed, juddering into her, rolling her climax into crested waves of paradise.

Afterwards they lay together panting, their shared breath fanning across the heated skin of their bodies. It was bliss to share this time together while their bodies hummed down from their peaks, a magical time that had been denied them last time.

He leaned over and kissed her on the forehead. 'I love you,' he whispered, smoothing back loose tendrils of her hair.

'Thank you,' she said. 'I love you too.' But his heartfelt words had brought tears to her eyes. She swiped the dampness away.

'You're crying?'

She sniffed. 'Happy tears,' she said. 'Happy because I'm with you.'

He kissed her. 'I think I must be the happiest man in the world to find love not just once, but twice.'

And because Theo had brought the subject up, Isabella felt emboldened to ask, 'How long were you married?'

'Six years.'

'No children?'

He shook his head and sighed, probably not even aware that he was stroking Isabella's hair. 'It didn't happen,' he said gruffly, 'not until it was too late.'

Isabella felt a wall of longing and pain behind the simple words he'd uttered, but she wasn't about to ask what he meant.

'What was she like?' she asked instead.

'Sophia had dark hair and even darker eyes. She was beautiful, inside and out. She was perfect.'

Isabella pressed her lips together. It was ridiculous to feel envious of a dead woman, but it was impossible not to. If Theo felt even a fraction of that emotion for her, she'd be happy. But Sophia had set the bar so impossibly high.

'How did you two meet?'

'At university in Athens. We studied economics and international relations together.'

Isabella nodded. She sensed there was a world more pain behind his tortured eyes and strained words.

She smoothed his brow with one hand, trying to ease whatever pain he was feeling—whatever pain he was remembering—and after a while, he sighed. 'She was the daughter of an international banker. She was kidnapped and held for ransom. The police bungled the recovery. She was killed when they stormed the building where they discovered they were keeping her.'

He sighed. 'The autopsy discovered she was pregnant.' He looked at her then, his eyes tortured, his brow twisted. 'She hadn't had a chance to tell me.'

'Oh my god, I'm so sorry.' She raised herself up on one elbow and looked down at him, her fingernails tracing through his chest hair, and there, in the depths of his dark eyes, she witnessed the extent of his loss. 'And that's why you do what you do?'

He pinched the bridge of his nose. 'That's when it started, but I think the seeds were planted years before when my younger sister drowned. We were at the beach together, caught in the same rip and though I tried, I couldn't reach her. I couldn't save her. I hated that I couldn't save her.

'And then, when Sophia was killed, I made a solemn vow to do my utmost to prevent anyone else suffering the same fate.'

'You can't be blamed for failing your sister.'

'I know.' He took one of her hands in his, and kissed the back of it. 'But it made me realise what loss felt like. Coupled with the loss of Sophia, it made me want to save others from that pain.'

'I get that,' she said.

He shook his head. 'Sophia was amazing. I was the boy from the country. I never knew what she saw in me.'

Isabella was in no doubt. 'I know what she saw,' she said. 'Sophia saw a man of honour. A strong man. A protector. A man who would fight for what was right. She saw that in you, I know. Because that's what I see in you. That's who you are.

'And that's who I know you to be. Because you saved me,' she said, 'from a life of bondage and enslavement in a marriage I never wanted nor could be happy in. I can never thank you enough.'

'No.' He raised himself up to push her down on her back. 'It is I who needs to thank you,' he said. 'I was stuck in a life of endless guilt for failing to save my sister and my wife and trying to make up for it every day since. I was stuck in a life chasing my tail and never catching it. And for forgetting about the simple things in life. Like what it felt like to have fun. You reminded me what fun was. You reminded me what it felt like to laugh. You reminded me what it felt like to love.'

He pressed his lips to hers. 'You saved me,' he said, before he kissed her thoroughly again. 'And I love you forever for it.'

Isabella was breathless by the time they paused for air. But there was one question she still needed to ask. 'By the way,' she said, 'you never answered me.'

'About what?'

'Will you marry me?'

'Do you want my answer in words, or deeds?'

'How long have we got before we land?'

He smiled, looking hungrily down at her. 'Hours and hours.'

She scrunched up her nose, wove her arms around his neck and pulled him down to her. 'I guess there's no harm trying deeds.'

He kissed her lightly on the lips. 'That's the right answer.'

EPILOGUE

LORD HOWE ISLAND'S Ned's Beach had turned on its best weather. The sea shone cobalt blue under the sun, the waves softly rolling, the sea breeze softly tugging at hair and fluttering silken scarves.

The guests were gathered on the lawns that bordered the beach, waiting for the main event, while tourists paddled through the shallows, laughing and delighted at the feeding fish frenzy that ensued every time they scattered another handful of fish food.

Their focus was all upon the fish wars at their feet, until the car arrived with the bride on board and the whoops of those feeding fish quieted, as all eyes turned to the bridal party alighting from the car.

Tom Parker opened Isabella's door, and she stepped from the car, her veil immediately captured by the breeze, fluttering up behind her. She took a moment with her bridesmaid Millie to check each other's dresses and lipstick, before the two gathered their bouquets. Millie exchanged a hug with the bride before setting off towards the assembled guests. Once Millie reached the aisle, Tom Parker held out his arm for her. Isabella took a deep breath, steadying herself, before she inserted her arm through his, and they set off.

Isabella was so happy as she made her way towards

the aisle, she felt like she was sure she must be glowing brighter than the sun. Smiling wasn't an option, it was an imperative. This was the culmination of everything— a life of believing that she would marry a man who she loved, then months and weeks of stress and uncertainty and the fear that her dream would be snatched away from her. Only to find love in the most unlikely of places. In the man who had intended to return her to her hellish future, until he stepped in at the last minute and rescued her.

And now she was marrying him on the island that had provided her with sanctuary, and where that love between them had sparked and grown. Tomorrow she and Theo would climb the heights of Mt Gower, the first day in the rest of their lives together, every day providing new heights.

Tom turned down the aisle, and Isabella saw the man who had claimed her heart standing before the simple altar. Theo. The man she loved. His mother and father looking on, beaming. For a second she paused, her heart skipping a beat. It was almost too much. It was unbelievable.

'All okay?' whispered Tom beside her.

She sniffed as she turned her face to his. 'Never better,' she said, small tears of happiness squeezing unbidden from her eyes. He smiled, giving her arm a reassuring squeeze, and they resumed their slow march down the aisle.

Theo waited at the altar. Never before had he felt so nervous. Sure, he'd done this once before, with Sophia, and that time had been magical. But he'd never expected to find love a second time. Life was never expected to be so kind. But life had served him up a second chance.

With Isabella.

He knew the moment she'd started down the aisle. He

heard the guests' 'oohs' and 'ahs'. He'd told himself he wasn't going to look. He fully intended not to look but he couldn't help himself.

He couldn't wait. He couldn't stop himself from turning.

And at the sight that met his eyes, he was so glad he did. He saw Isabella heading down the aisle towards him. Towards their joint future together.

She was dressed in a gown, form-fitting and sleek, a halter neck exposing her perfect shoulders and arms, smiling at those she passed. She was a vision.

Perfection.

As if knowing he was looking, she looked up at him and as their eyes connected, a bolt of lightning coursed through him.

Moisture welled from his eyes. He had to twist his lips shut in an effort not to give a very un-man-like sob. Because happiness was so large a gift that he had been given. And because he knew, without a shadow of doubt, that this was supposed to happen. Their pairing was fate. Their pairing was destiny. This was the second chance he'd never believed he was entitled to, but which fate had decreed he was.

He watched her make her way towards him. He didn't mind the slow bridal march. He didn't care how long it took. Because before this day was over, he knew that they would be married, and that Isabella would be his wife.

She met him at the altar. 'You're so beautiful,' he said, taking her free hand in both of his, overcome with the emotion of the moment.

'I love you,' she said.

'And I love you. You've given me back the light. You've given me laughter. You've given me love. More than that, you've given me hope. I can never thank you enough for that.'

She squeezed his hands and looked deep into his eyes. 'And you've given me freedom. To live the life I want. To love the man I want to love. You are that man. I love you, Theo. I will love you forever.'

The registrant waiting before them subtly coughed into his smile. 'Perhaps we might get this wedding started...?'

* * * * *

If you fell head over heels for Greek's Royal Runaway, *why not explore these other sensational stories from Trish Morey?*

Bartering Her Innocence
A Price Worth Paying?
Consequence of the Greek's Revenge
Prince's Virgin in Venice
After-Hours Proposal

Available now!

MILLS & BOON®

Coming next month

ENEMIES UNTIL AFTER HOURS
Natalie Anderson

Mia drew on a defensive smile and headed into Sante's office—leaving his door wide open behind her.

Trying to steady her heartbeat. The appalling thing was that increasingly her body responded with chaos to his proximity. It didn't seem to care that he was a heartless jerk who'd betrayed her brother, her body just wanted his near. So, she was ignoring her body. Controlling it.

'You've screwed up my scheduling.' He glared at her. 'Where?'

He jabbed a finger at the screen, and she was forced to round his desk to study it. Big mistake. There was nowhere near enough of a barrier between them and she desperately needed to calm her overexcited response.

'You've blocked out a significant portion of my day tomorrow.'

She leaned closer and he turned his head toward her, meaning his mouth was only inches from hers. It was *searingly* intimate. It would take nothing to lower hers and—

What the hell was she thinking? Why had the idea to kiss him popped into her head? She stared into his brown eyes for three seconds too long.

Continue reading

ENEMIES UNTIL AFTER HOURS
Natalie Anderson

Available next month
millsandboon.co.uk

COMING SOON!

We really hope you enjoyed reading this book.
If you're looking for more romance
be sure to head to the shops when
new books are available on

Thursday 26th February

To see which titles are coming soon, please visit
millsandboon.co.uk/nextmonth

MILLS & BOON

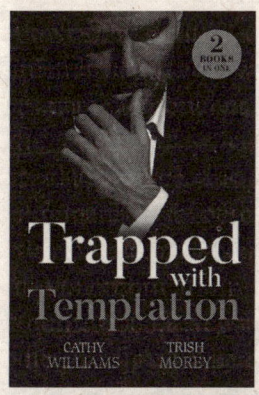

TWO BRAND NEW BOOKS FROM

Love Always

Be prepared to be swept away to incredible worldwide destinations along with our strong, relatable heroines and intensely desirable heroes.

OUT NOW